Heidi

'A summer delight!' **Sarah Morgan**

'Sweet and lovely. I guarantee you will fall in love with Heidi's wonderful world' **Milly Johnson**

'A little slice of joy' *Heat*

'So full of sunshine you almost feel the rays' *Woman's Weekly*

'The queen of feel-good' *Woman & Home*

'A true comfort read and the perfect treat to alleviate all the stress!' **Veronica Henry**

'A story that captures your heart' **Christie Barlow**

'Sparkling and romantic' *My Weekly*

'A delightfully sunny read with added intrigue and secrets' **Bella Osborne**

'A wonderfully uplifting story with a picturesque setting you'll wish you could visit' *Culturefly*

Celebrating Heidi's
20th novel with her readers

'Pack your bags ready for a romantic trip to the Norfolk
coast for the *Best Summer Ever*'
Kirsty Connor

'Hot sunny days and an even hotter hero. Heidi Swain
knows how to put the sizzle into summer reading'
Karen Byrom

'*Best Summer Ever*? Best Heidi Swain book ever!'
Susanne Edge

'A wonderfully comforting read, full of friendships,
romance and new beginnings'
Rea Cobb

'I am always transported into Heidi's world and *Best Summer
Ever* is no different. I can almost taste the strawberries'
Liz Whittingstall

'An absolutely beautiful story'
Cheryl Keith

'Heidi Swain is brilliant and *Best Summer Ever* is her
best book yet! I loved it'
Vikkie W

'Heidi has once again written a 5★ book with a return
to Wynbrook and all the fantastic characters that
live there'
Sue Dawson

'Heidi Swain's books are always a comfort to me'
Hannah Ward

'*Best Summer Ever* is another fabulous book from the
wonderful Heidi Swain'
Jenny

'A lovely, uplifting read from one of my favourite authors.
The perfect read on a summer day'
Karen Kingston

'Love, lives and flowers bloom in Wynbrook'
Sian Watkins

'A beautiful summer read, full of family, friendship and
community'
Sian Sandwith

'The perfect, most romantic and uplifting read'
Linda Hill

'An absolute joy'
Bev Allen

'The perfect feel-good book to warm your heart and banish the blues'
Michelle Ryles

'Heidi Swain gives us pure escapism at its best'
Selina

'Truly the *Best Summer Ever*, I loved it!'
Jill Batchelor

'A marvellously warm and sunny read'
Linda Merryweather

'Whenever you read a new Heidi Swain novel, it's like coming home'
Wendy Robey

'Will warm your heart like sunshine on a summer's day!'
Joanne Baird

'Never mind *Best Summer Ever*, this is the Best Book Ever!'
Kaisha Holloway

'Full of love, laughs and beautiful moments'
Lisa Evans

'A summer of soul searching sees love blooming
in this sizzling read'
Karen Mace

'A gorgeous, summery romance with real heart'
Jo Wood

'A funny, charming and uplifting story'
Noemi Proietti

'A delightfully immersive read'
Michelle Nelder

'The queen of the summer romance is back. *Best Summer
Ever* is packed full of friendship, love and secrets'
Emma Cook

'Delightful, the perfect choice for summer reading'
Diane Clarke

'A Heidi Swain summer read is as essential as sun cream'
Laura White

'As always, Heidi has delivered an amazing story'
Julie Brookes

'A fabulous read with lovely characters and a
beautiful location'
Claire Honhold

'The perfect book for summer – you can feel the
sun on your limbs'
Detta Hannon

'Full of family, friendship and fresh starts'
Miranda Toora

'A blooming ray of sunshine to warm your heart this summer'
Annette Hannah

'Packed with sunshine, new beginnings, hope and sweet
treats, Heidi has delivered another romantic story that is
perfect to escape to this summer!'
Bronagh McAteer

'A simply stunning read by my favourite author'
Kirsty Brickles

'*Best Summer Ever* feels like walking barefoot on the beach'
Annelies Wijnants

'The perfect summer posy of family, friends
and coming home'
Pamela Robertson

Heidi Swain

Best Summer Ever

SIMON &
SCHUSTER

London · New York · Amsterdam/Antwerp · Sydney/Melbourne · Toronto · New Delhi

First published in Great Britain by Simon & Schuster UK Ltd, 2025

Copyright © Heidi-Jo Swain, 2025

The right of Heidi-Jo Swain to be identified as author of this work has been asserted in accordance with the Copyright, Designs and Patents Act, 1988.

1 3 5 7 9 10 8 6 4 2

Simon & Schuster UK Ltd
1st Floor
222 Gray's Inn Road
London WC1X 8HB

Simon & Schuster Australia,
Sydney

Simon & Schuster India,
New Delhi

www.simonandschuster.co.uk
www.simonandschuster.com.au
www.simonandschuster.co.in

The authorised representative in the EEA is Simon & Schuster Netherlands BV, Herculesplein 96, 3584 AA Utrecht, Netherlands. info@simonandschuster.nl

Simon & Schuster strongly believes in freedom of expression and stands against censorship in all its forms. For more information, visit BooksBelong.com.

A CIP catalogue record for this book is available from the British Library

Paperback ISBN: 978-1-3985-3867-2
eBook ISBN: 978-1-3985-3868-9
Audio ISBN: 978-1-3985-3869-6

This book is a work of fiction. Names, characters, places and incidents are either a product of the author's imagination or are used fictitiously. Any resemblance to actual people living or dead, events or locales is entirely coincidental.

Typeset in Bembo Std by Palimpsest Book Production Limited, Falkirk, Stirlingshire

Printed and Bound in the UK using 100% Renewable Electricity
at CPI Group (UK) Ltd

MIX
Paper | Supporting
responsible forestry
FSC
www.fsc.org   FSC® C013604

To my wonderful editor, Clare Hey
Thank you for loving this book as much as I do
and
Sara-Jade Virtue
For setting the wheels in motion a decade ago

Chapter 1

I was a couple of hours into my journey back to Norfolk when it suddenly dawned on me that the universe had recently been trying to give me a heads-up about the appalling behaviour my partner – now ex-partner – had been indulging in and that I could have used it as an excuse to be shot of him weeks ago.

'Oh, Daisy,' I admonished huffily, striking the steering wheel and inadvertently hitting the horn. 'What are you like?'

In my defence though, I had been so focused on looking for a way I could resign from my current job that wouldn't make it look as though I wasn't giving up on the world of work again, that it would have taken a flashing neon sign to make me take notice. The fact that Laurence had practically confessed his infidelity ages before I cottoned on was no comfort now though.

'She's a total ball-buster,' I remembered him saying, when I had asked what his new colleague was like. 'Very focused on getting what she wants.'

His description had been accompanied by a salacious grin he hadn't even tried to suppress, the obvious implication of which should have immediately given the game away. Or at least given me a clue.

'Ball-buster' was an entirely appropriate description, as it turned out. She certainly looked as though she had been busting his balls when I turned up at their office early and unannounced, having finally made up my mind to end things and determined not to wait a second longer to do it.

I had found the pair in a most compromising position. Her skirt hoisted up higher than her hips and him groaning in a way that left me in no doubt what was coming. Pun intended. I had snuck out unseen, rushed back to Laurence's flat and bundled my already haphazardly packed possessions into my car, feeling full of relief that he'd saved me a task I'd been dreading and none of the guilt I had been expecting.

We'd never had much in common and the only people who really thought the relationship might go the distance were my wishful-thinking parents. A former friend from university had introduced me to Laurence when I happened to be waiting on the table that she and some of her friends had booked.

Beth had graduated with a first, but I'd dropped out after my second year and had been floundering ever since, moving from one casual job to another. When she turned up with Laurence and somehow recognised me, I was heartily sick of my drifting and when he handed me the bill with his phone number written on the back, it felt like the ideal opportunity for a potentially fresh start.

Laurence was a proper grown-up with a structured career path and investment plan, and I had hoped some of his ambition would rub off on me and at the start, it had. The initial chemistry between us and the phenomenal sex suggested we were a good match and within six months of getting together, I had moved into his flat and he was helping me get my life in order. It was the first time my parents had looked at me with something akin to pride and I felt my life had turned a corner.

That was almost two years ago and the scales had long since dropped, the rose-tinted specs were definitely off. I was still the same free spirit with no pension plan, who couldn't seem to stick to anything and Laurence was now the most materialistic man I'd ever met and becoming increasingly self-absorbed and even more ruthlessly ambitious as a result. Ergo, we really did have nothing in common and opposites certainly no longer held any attraction whatsoever.

Hence the lack of upset at finding him in flagrante, the hastily scribbled note sketchily describing what I had seen and the mad dash to block his number and leave. I was now heading back to the comfort of my childhood family cottage on the Wynbrook Manor Estate, a couple of miles beyond Wynmouth on the Norfolk coast. The only thing I wasn't sure about was what to tell Mum and Dad.

They had loved Laurence from the moment they met him and I knew they had always thought, like I originally had, that he would be the making of me. That his work ethic would be a steadying influence and, with him by my side, I would finally settle down and stick with something. Not only had Laurence now been culled, I also still had the ability to rinse through jobs faster than the North Sea tide could turn and as a result, I had no money, no prospects, no options . . .

'Home sweet home,' I nonetheless said, as the road sign for the familiar coast flashed by.

Perhaps I could put off Mum and Dad's crushing waves of disappointment about letting Laurence go a little longer, courtesy of some real waves?

In spite of the parental predicament, my heart soared as I drove through the village of Wynmouth and around the Green and its row of brick and flint shops, with the car windows wound down. The air that rushed inside was hot rather than warm and carried with it that most welcome salt-laden smell and taste of home.

My heart happily thumped even harder as I carefully turned into the top of the one-way narrow lane, which had the Smuggler's Inn situated on the left, rows of traditional fisherman's terraced cottages along both sides and a path straight down to the beach directly in front. It then almost leapt completely out of my chest as a guy, with a huge rucksack on his back, appeared from nowhere and stepped out in front of the car. I stamped on the brake and only just tamped down the urge to give him a blast on the horn. That would have done nothing for my discreet return to the county.

He stepped quickly out of the way and bent to peer inside as I drew level.

'Sorry,' he apologised through the open window, both hands raised.

He had sandy blond hair, blue-green eyes and was wearing at least a couple of days' worth of stubble, a light cotton red and blue checked shirt and jeans.

'I got so excited to see the sea,' he added as I tried to pin his accent to the right American state, 'that I forgot myself and stepped straight out.'

I felt a creeping heat spread up my neck. I didn't want to be charmed; I wanted to be huffy, but his apology and hundred-watt smile were both extremely disarming.

'It's OK,' I said. 'No harm done.'

'Well,' he said again, straightening up and looking back up the lane, 'that's all right then.'

I lingered for a moment, then realised one of the beach tractors that hauled the few fishing boats in and out of the sea had turned into the top of the lane behind me, so I had no choice but to carry on. Rucksack guy raised his hand in salute and then strode off towards the beach. I indicated and carefully turned left into the tiny car park that belonged to the Smuggler's Inn. I was sure Sam, the pub owner, wouldn't mind me parking up for a while.

'Please be here,' I begged fervently as I made my way, bare-foot, across the warm sand towards the row of prettily painted and much-loved beach huts.

There were about a dozen in total and one of them, the pink, orange and yellow brightly painted hut, belonged to the Wynbrook Manor Estate, which was where both my parents worked and where the cottage I'd spent my childhood growing up in was located. The estate owner, Algernon Alford, very kindly allowed his staff access to the hut and the key was kept for safe-keeping, unimaginatively, in a small box on a ledge above the door.

'Bingo,' I exclaimed, as my fingers closed tightly around the box.

The sight and smell that rushed to greet me as I opened the door instantly carried me back to childhood on a nostalgic wave of happy memories. Unlike the other estate families, Mum and Dad had never ventured further than the beach during the holidays and consequently, Wynmouth and the row of huts felt as familiar to me as home had once done.

The interior paintwork was a little faded, peeling in places, and the bench seat cushions weren't quite as plump, but it was all achingly familiar, right down to the enamel plates and cups on the shelf in the tiny space carved out as a kitchen.

Having already checked the tide times, I tied up my dark hair, slipped quickly into my swimming costume, then ran down to the sea, dumped my towel a way back from the shoreline and strode in. The temperature was bracing and it took my breath away, but I knew that the trick to coping with the shock was to keep moving, so I began to swim straightaway.

I also knew it was vital to get back to the shore before I started to tire, but I was very nearly tempted to stay in the water longer than I should. My mind had cleared completely as I powered through the sea, my thoughts only returning when I stopped to check how far out I was and saw rucksack guy on the sand, shielding his eyes from the glare of the sun and looking in, what I thought, was my direction, before striding away.

I didn't track where he went after that and carried on until the cold really started to make its presence felt. Only then did I reluctantly head in. I was shaking with cold as I wrapped my towel around me, but the sun was brightly shining and I was almost warm again by the time I'd crossed the sand for the sanctuary of the beach hut to get dressed in.

My temperature soared sharply to somewhere around tropical, however, as, completely naked, I roughly rubbed myself down and the hut door opened, exposing almost all of me to the rest of the world.

'Hey!' I yelped, quickly covering myself up with the length of the towel. 'This is private property!'

'Sorry,' came that American accent again. 'I'm so sorry. I didn't realise anyone was in this one.'

'Well, I am! I'm in this one!' I shouted after his retreating back, as I slammed the door shut and turned the key in the lock.

I wondered, once I was dressed and as I attempted to run my fingers through the tangles in my hair in lieu of a hairbrush, just how much of me he'd seen before he'd turned tail and if his vocabulary ever extended further than making apologies.

'Daisy?' said Sam, the handsome green-eyed owner of the Smuggler's Inn, when I ventured along to the pub. 'What are you doing here?'

'Well, hello to you too,' I laughed, as my eyes became accustomed to the dark interior after the bright July sun, and I perched myself on a stool at the bar.

'Sorry,' he laughed as well, 'it's just that I haven't seen you in years and I didn't know you were coming back. Penny and Nick haven't mentioned that you were going to be in the area.'

Penny and Nick were my two closest friends. We'd been at school together since kindergarten. Unlike me, they'd both stayed local and also unlike me, they'd been far better at keeping in touch. They were also both single and absolutely perfect for one another, but completely clueless about that.

'That's because Penny and Nick don't know,' I told Sam, feeling bad that I hadn't kept my besties in the loop about my life for quite a while.

'A surprise visit,' Sam continued to smile, unaware of my guilt. 'They'll be thrilled. Your mum and dad will be chuffed too.'

My parents were actually the reason I'd decided to call in at the pub. I'd experienced something of a lightbulb moment as I'd walked back along the beach and was here as a result.

'What can I get you?' Sam asked. 'It's on me.'

'Thank you.' I smiled back. 'I'll have lemonade with plenty of ice and lemon, please.'

'Coming right up.'

'And a job, if you've got one going,' I further requested.

'A job?' Sam frowned, packing the glass half full with ice.

'Yes,' I said. 'It's looking like I'm going to be here a while and it would be great to be working while I am.'

This was a masterstroke on my part because as long as Sam could offer me some shifts behind the bar, it meant I wasn't about to turn up at home with nothing to offer. If I could soften the blow of my single status with the promise of some work already lined up to see me through the summer, that would hopefully ease some of the frown lines that would doubtless be etched across Mum and Dad's foreheads when I told them why I was back.

'You're serious?' Sam asked, setting the lemonade down in front of me.

'Yes.' I nodded. 'I'm currently between jobs, so some bar work to cover the summer would be great.'

The pub was always a quiet spot, so learning on the job shouldn't prove too taxing. Pulling pints was a skill I hadn't yet added to my repertoire and the quiet ambience of the Smuggler's would be as ideal a place to learn in as any.

'Well, that's actually perfect,' said Sam, rubbing his hands together. 'Because I'm about to lose both Sophie's cooking skills and Hope serving behind the bar—'

'I'm not up to cooking for the public,' I warned him, before he thrust an apron in my direction. 'And I don't actually have any experience of bar work, but I can wait on tables.'

I thought it was only fair to warn him that if he did offer me a job, he would be taking on a total novice.

'Don't worry about that,' he somewhat surprisingly said, 'that's fine. Tess has been learning Sophie's recipes and will do the food, but that will leave the bar a bit short. Would have left the bar a bit short,' he corrected, looking speculatively at me. 'I don't suppose it would take long to train you up.'

I looked at him, oozing hope.

'Go on then,' he finally said. 'You're on.'

'Really?' I gasped.

'Really.' He nodded. 'Come in on Thursday about six and I'll start getting you up to speed as to what's required.'

'That's fantastic!' I gushed, feeling a heady mix of relief and gratitude. 'Thank you so much. You're a lifesaver.'

'As are you,' he said, puffing out his cheeks as I took a gulp of my lemonade.

I hoped I would be.

'So, where are Sophie and Hope off to?' I asked.

Sophie, Hope's mum, had created the most delicious Caribbean slash Norfolk fusion cuisine, which she served in the pub and in her café on the beach, and Hope, if memory served, had her own bespoke biscuit business now. Tess, Sam's partner, and Hope also had the same dad, and he and Sophie were a couple now after years apart.

'They're going to Jamaica,' Sam said in a quiet voice, even though there was no one else around to hear.

'Lucky them,' I sighed.

'Sadly, it's not a holiday,' Sam explained. 'They have an extremely sick relative out there and from what I can make out, I think they'll be saying goodbye to them almost as soon as they get there.'

'Oh, I see,' I said, feeling guilty to have imagined them sipping cocktails and swimming in cerulean seas that would be far warmer than the water lapping the sand in Wynmouth. 'I'm very sorry to hear that.'

'Me too,' said Sam, as another customer darkened the doorway. 'They're both really cut up about it.'

I sat and finished my lemonade while Sam served the other customer and I took the time to count my blessings. At least no one in my family was unwell and I had parents to come back to in my moment of crisis. And now I had a job too. It might only be temporary and part time, but it was a start and I was grateful to have secured it ahead of going home.

I could feel the ends of my salt-laden hair drying in a tangle down my back and knew that if I didn't wash and condition it soon, it would be completely unmanageable. It was time to go home.

'I'll see you Thursday,' I said to Sam, as I made for the door. 'Do I need to bring anything?'

'Just your national insurance number,' he told me. 'And some comfy shoes.'

'Comfy shoes?' I frowned, wondering why I'd need them when I'd probably spend longer on a bar stool than standing.

'Yes,' he said. 'Vital. Hey, look out.'

I turned around and bumped straight into the broad chest of someone who had walked in just as I was walking out.

'Sorry,' we both said at the same time.

I would have recognised that apology and accompanying accent anywhere now.

'Sorry *again*,' said the guy, taking a step back and hoisting his rucksack higher.

'Sorry again indeed,' I repeated with emphasis.

'It's dark in here,' he carried on. 'I didn't spot you.'

'Well,' I said, stepping around him, 'I saw *you* in the beach hut.'

'If it's any consolation,' he meekly responded, 'I didn't see that much of you.'

I didn't know how to respond to that.

'They're not for sleeping in, you know,' I tersely replied, assuming he was most likely on the lookout for somewhere to stay that he wouldn't have to pay for. 'They're private property.'

I ducked outside before he could do or say anything else he was going to have to make amends for and quickly walked back to my car.

Chapter 2

It was a slow drive out of the village, west towards Wynbrook Manor. Not only because I was feeling apprehensive about how my arrival and subsequent explanation of recent events was going to be received, but also because the verges were wildly overgrown and the road was extremely narrow.

The passing places were riddled with suspension-wrecking potholes and the last thing I wanted was to get tangled up with a caravan on one of the many blind bends. My car was practically on its last legs and a nosedive into one of the dips would doubtless sound the death knell.

Fortunately, luck was with me and I drove through the huge, ornate estate gates and across the cattle grid having met nothing more than a hare, which could easily outpace me. The cattle grid wasn't necessary as there was no livestock on the estate now, but Algy liked to keep it in place to slow drivers down as they entered his domain.

The manor itself wasn't open to the public, but there was a large and lucrative pick-your-own fruit farm, managed along with much of the estate, by my friend Nick. Sometimes the gardens, which my dad was responsible for, were available for

Open Garden days and other charitable events. The fruit farm, Nick's place and my parents' cottage were accessed via the sweeping curve of drive to the left, while the beautiful brick and flint manor and gardens could be found on the right.

I felt a lump form in my throat as I drove along the tree-lined drive. Nothing had changed in the slightest and when the cottage came into view, I had to blink hard to turn back an unexpected tide of tears. It really had been too long since my last visit and even longer since I'd made a solo trip.

'Mum!' I called, as I left everything in the car, unlatched the picket gate and raced along the flower-edged path to the back door, suddenly desperate to see her and Dad. 'Dad!'

There was no reply and the door to the kitchen was locked. I had expected to find them both eating their usual early lunch. Mum was housekeeper at the manor and at midday she and Dad had a hot meal together at home. They maintained that, at their age and given the physical demands of their jobs, they deserved a break during the working day.

They had both been in their late thirties by the time they had me. They'd given up after years of trying to conceive and then about a year later, I unexpectedly landed. They were now bowling towards their mid-sixties, but I'd never broached the subject of them retiring as I knew they were both melded to a life working at Wynbrook forever.

I rifled through my bag for my key and let myself in. As I listened to the ticking of the clock above the row of wooden coat pegs and breathed in the comforting smell of home, a wave of nostalgia flooded over me. The oilcloth-covered table was set for one and there was a note next to it. Apparently, Dad had already eaten and gone back to work and he hoped

Mum wouldn't be too far behind him. There was no time on the note so I couldn't guess about that.

With one ear listening out for Mum's potential arrival, I had a speedy shower, pulled on an old floral tea dress I'd left behind in my bedroom wardrobe, properly combed out my hair and headed on foot back along the drive to the manor. It was then long after midday and I wondered what was delaying Mum's, usually set in stone, lunchbreak.

It didn't take long to work out.

'That's as maybe,' I heard her say crossly, as I reached the open back door to the manor kitchen via the herb-filled courtyard, 'but I'm not going until you've eaten yours, Algy, so you might as well get on with it unless you want me to waste away like you are.'

'I've already told you, my dear,' came Algy's shockingly resigned response, 'I've no appetite.'

'You said the same thing yesterday,' Mum exasperatedly said, 'and the day before that. How do you expect to recover if you won't eat?'

'Perhaps I don't want to recover,' Algy muttered mutinously, and I felt further taken aback.

He was always so full of life; he could easily have been mistaken as being more or less the same age as my parents when in fact he was well over a decade older. I had no idea what it was that he was recovering from, and again, felt that pang of guilt for not having kept properly in touch.

'And in the meantime,' Mum wearily carried on, completely ignoring Algy's hint that he was giving up on life, which suggested it wasn't the first time she'd heard it, 'the place is going to wrack and ruin and filling up with cobwebs and dust because I'm spending all of my time trying to coax you to eat, instead of getting on with the cleaning.'

Tough love! That was Dad's forte, not Mum's, so I knew she really was feeling at her wits' end.

'Well, no one asked you to, Janet Patterson!' came Algy's belligerent rejoinder, which was also completely out of character for him.

'Knock, knock,' I said loudly, as I stepped inside and found the pair of them locked in a stand-off, except Algy was sitting.

'Daisy!' Mum gasped.

Her hands, which had been planted firmly on her hips, flew to her face at the unexpected sight of her daughter in the doorway.

'Daisy, Daisy!' Algy echoed, referring to me as he always had and sounding far happier than he had just seconds before.

I rushed across the huge flagstone-floored kitchen to Mum and pulled her in for a hug that she enthusiastically returned.

'My darling girl,' she said, her hands cradling my face when I eventually let her go. 'What a wonderful surprise. What are you doing here? Is Laurence with you?' she hopefully added, looking over my shoulder.

'I was going to wait for you at the cottage,' I said, hoping to distract her from trying to winkle out the details of my return until she and Dad were together, 'but I kept getting the waft of this most amazing smell and I just knew it was your chicken soup, Mum.'

'Would you like some?' she offered, as eager as ever to feed me as she rushed to the cupboard for a bowl.

'You can have mine,' said Algy, sounding mutinous again as he pushed his bowl, with a slightly shaking hand, across the table towards me. 'Because I don't want it.'

'No thanks,' I said lightly, as I sat opposite him and pushed it back, trying not to let the shock of how much he seemed to have aged show on my face, 'I'd like a bigger bowl than that. I haven't eaten for hours.'

Mum ladled out a generous helping of her chicken and tarragon soup from the vast pot on the always-warm Aga and then cut a great chunk of fresh bread to go along with it.

'Butter?' she offered.

'Yes, please.' I nodded. 'And why don't you have some soup too, Mum?' I suggested. 'Dad had left you a note at the cottage, saying he'd missed you when he had his lunch, so I know you haven't had anything since breakfast.'

Algy looked contrite when I said that.

'I suppose I could,' Mum agreed, quickly setting herself up. 'I *am* hungry.'

The soup was as sublime as I remembered, and Mum and I hadn't eaten much before Algy also picked up his spoon, as I had hoped he would, and began to slurp. Mum gave me a knowing side-eye, which I didn't return in case Algy saw and for a minute or two we all carried on eating in silence.

'So,' I said, reaching for the butter and a knife, when I'd had almost half of my soup, 'what's been occurring here then? I'm afraid I haven't been in touch as often as I should have been just lately.'

'Your father and I assumed that was because your new job was keeping you so busy, Daisy,' Mum said, between mouthfuls. 'How's it going?'

The fact that I'd randomly turned up on a Monday was all the answer she should have needed and I felt annoyed with myself for pulling her thoughts back to me when I'd done such a decent job of diverting her before.

'I took a bit of a tumble while I was out in the garden,' Algy said, kindly and no doubt, knowingly, coming to my rescue, just like I'd tried to come to his. 'No real harm done. Just a bit of a bump on the head but everyone seems to think I need treating with kid gloves as a result.'

'Oh, Algy!' I gasped, playing devil's advocate. 'You had a fall.' He looked at me and shook his head.

'I prefer to call it a *tumble*,' he said snootily, as some of the more familiar light started to twinkle in his blue eyes and he readjusted his paisley-patterned cravat, 'as I'm sure you are well aware because I've just described it as such.' I grinned at that. 'A fall makes me sound decrepit and I'm not that.'

'But you will be if you don't eat your soup up like a good boy,' I teasingly nudged. 'You'll be so weak, you'll need one of those walking frames to get about.'

'Daisy!' Mum admonished, sounding shocked.

'Can you imagine?' Algy groaned.

'Yes,' I winked.

'I've already got a stairlift,' he then tutted, sounding disgusted. 'Had it put in last year.'

'Did you?' I clapped. 'Can I have a go?'

'Daisy!' Mum scolded again.

'Oh, she's all right,' said Algy, defending me, just like he used to when I got into scrapes when I was growing up. 'It's very slow, but you're welcome to play on it if you really want to.'

'Come on then,' I said, clattering my spoon in the bowl. 'Let's go and have a look at it and see what it can do.'

By the time Mum and I walked back to the cottage later that
afternoon, I'd been up and down the stairs three times at a snail's
pace and there was some colour in Algy's previously pale cheeks.

'You've always been able to twist him around your little finger,'
Mum said, linking her arm through mine. 'I haven't been able
to get him to eat a thing and then you show up and he's suddenly
stuffing his face.' We'd also had tea and a huge slice of carrot
cake before we'd left. '*And* he's up to mischief again.'

'What can I say?' I laughed. 'I have a gift.'

'You have many,' said Mum, squeezing me closer. 'I just wish
you could find a job where you can put them to good use. I
take it you haven't driven all the way back to Wynmouth on a
single day off? You haven't been with your new employer more
than five minutes, so you can't have accrued some holiday already
and where exactly is Laurence?'

The barrage of questions made me realise I wouldn't be able
to put my explanation off for much longer.

'I'll tell you and Dad together.' I swallowed. 'Look, here he
comes now.'

As Dad started work so early during the summer months, he
generally finished around four in the afternoon. Well, I say
finished, he still went out in the evening to check gates were
locked, water the containers and baskets, and close up the greenhouses and cold frames.

Living and working on the estate, like on many other estates
up and down the country, was a lifestyle rather than a job. It
was a way of life that blurred the work–life balance but was
happily embraced by those who took the jobs on and looking
around at the beautiful landscape and more immediate surround-
ings at Wynbrook, I could understand why.

'Hello Daisy,' said Dad, stooping to briefly kiss my cheek when I was close enough. He was taller than both Mum and me and broad, too. They were both a little greyer than the last time I saw them, I noticed. 'Are you on your own? I did think you must be when I spotted your car while I was putting the mower away.'

Laurence, not that he wanted to visit all that often, wouldn't have dreamt of making the journey to Norfolk in my car. He much preferred his vehicle which offered sleek, air-conditioned comfort to my old banger with its intermittent cooling system, squishy seats and passenger window that had a tendency to open of its own accord. He'd tried to get me to change my little runabout on many occasions, but I'd always resisted.

'Yes,' I confirmed. 'I'm here alone. But how are you, Dad?' I asked, wanting to at least get us over the threshold before I told my tale – or the pared-down version of it that I wanted my parents to know.

'Having a total nightmare,' Dad groaned, once he'd got his boots off and was washing his hands with a bar of soap at the sink and ruthlessly scrubbing his nails with a wooden nailbrush. 'A fella was supposed to be coming today to take on the main-tenance and running of the cut-flower garden, but he called to say he's had a change of heart.'

'Oh no, Robin,' Mum similarly groaned, as she passed him the hand towel in a well-practised manoeuvre. 'That's someone else letting you down.'

'It is,' he sighed. 'So, I'm still no further forward.'

'The cut-flower garden?' I frowned, sadly knowing I was about to let him down too. 'I didn't know there was one.'

'It was Algy's idea,' Dad explained. 'I tried to nip it in the bud at the start of the year, but he was insistent. One whole half of the walled garden has been given over to it.'

'Does the manor need that many cut flowers?' I asked, focusing on the practicality of the project, rather than my memories of the walled garden.

I knew it was a vast area that Dad was describing.

'They're not for the house,' Mum told me. 'They're supposed to be for sale — a scheme to run alongside the pick-your-own fruit farm. Your dad got everything sown, grown and planted up, but now the season is in full swing, he can't maintain it as well. Not properly anyway, not with so much else to do.'

'Can't Theo help?' I suggested, referring to a Wynmouth resident who was a part-time gardener and part-time potter. 'I thought he worked here with you regularly during the peak time now, Dad.'

'He does as a rule,' said Dad. 'Well, he did. He's just gone on paternity leave again.'

'Him and Wren have got three little ones now,' Mum wistfully added.

I had known there was another baby on the way as my friend Penny had bought Theo and his partner Wren's tiny former fisherman's cottage in Wynmouth ahead of them moving to somewhere bigger before the new arrival came along.

'So that leaves me on my lonesome again,' Dad tutted, 'and getting nothing properly done.'

'Just like me in the house,' Mum forlornly added.

I hoped Algy was on the mend now and he'd soon be back on track, but I couldn't help wondering why he had been so keen to get such a labour-intensive garden project up and running when he knew how difficult it would be to secure seasonal staff.

The full-time roles on the estate were always filled, but the seasonal summer jobs, especially those which required some specific skill, were a different matter entirely.

'Algy was asking after the cat again,' Mum said as she filled the kettle, now Dad had finished washing his hands.

'What cat?' I asked, as distracted as they both were.

'Have you seen it?' Mum asked.

'No,' said Dad. 'I haven't, but in all honesty, I haven't had time to look for the damn thing.'

'I didn't know Algy had a cat.' I tried again.

'He hasn't,' said Mum. 'He spotted some mangy feral specimen and started feeding it at the kitchen door, but it disappeared and he's been fretting over it.'

'Is the food he's been putting out still being eaten?' Dad asked.

'Yes,' Mum confirmed, 'but we don't know by what.'

'Maybe you could set up a wildlife camera?' I suggested.

'Maybe, Daisy,' said Dad, pulling out a chair at the table and offering it to me, 'you could tell us what you're doing at Wynbrook on a Monday afternoon so soon after starting your new job?'

'Well, yes,' I swallowed, feeling the whiplash impact of the sudden change of conversational direction that shone the spotlight firmly back on me, 'perhaps I could.'

We sat at the table and I squeezed my hands together in my lap while I explained that the job I had started just a few weeks ago hadn't worked out. It was absurd that I should feel so flustered about telling them at my age, but given that I was also dumping myself back on them as a result of leaving Laurence too, I supposed it was justifiable that I felt a bit on edge.

'But you said this was the job you'd been holding out for,' Dad said, frowning.

He sounded confused as he repeated exactly what I'd told him and Mum when I'd been offered the role.

'You did say that,' agreed Mum, also tracking back to the conversation.

'Well,' I conceded, 'that's because I did think it was the one, but as it turned out . . . it wasn't.'

Much like Laurence. He wasn't the one either.

'What never ceases to amaze me,' said Dad, looking at me intently, 'is how you keep getting job offers when you hop from one thing to another within months of starting. I just don't know how you manage it.'

'I guess I perform well at interview,' I said, biting back what I would have once been inclined to say.

'But badly when it comes to seeing something through,' sighed Dad, stating what was painfully obvious.

'Look,' I said, refusing to get drawn in to raking over old ground, 'I know you're both disappointed—'

'Only disappointed *for* you, love,' Mum kindly cut in. 'We're not disappointed with you, Daisy. You're plenty old enough to know your own mind. And if it wasn't working out . . .'

Dad said nothing as her words trailed off and I felt a hard lump form in my throat.

'I do know my own mind,' I somehow managed to croak. 'And that's how I knew it wasn't working out with Laurence either. We're not together anymore. We've split up.'

I half expected Dad to say that Laurence had probably got tired of waiting for me to catch him up, but he didn't say anything. They both looked shell-shocked and it was Mum who eventually responded first.

'Surely not,' she choked, sounding devastated. 'You can't mean it.'

'I'm afraid I do,' I told her, though I wasn't afraid about that at all.

'Whatever happened?' Mum asked, as her eyes filled with tears. 'What went wrong?'

She was every bit as upset as I had known she would be and I felt no inclination to tell her about the scene I had been privy to in Laurence's office. Even if he hadn't been playing away, I would have ended things between us, so it wasn't fair to blame him entirely for the break-up, even if it would have been convenient.

'So, that explains all the clobber in your car,' Dad said, before I'd thought up what to say to Mum. 'I'm guessing you're planning on being here for longer than just today.'

'If that's all right,' I quietly said.

'Just tell us,' Dad then crossly asked, 'did you give up on Laurence as well as your latest job?'

'Robin!' gasped Mum, batting his arm. 'That's not fair!'

'It might be,' Dad said back. 'Did you leave him, Daisy? Was it you who ended it?'

'Yes,' I sighed. 'Yes, I left him.'

'There you are then,' huffed Dad, his suspicions confirmed.

'Oh, love,' said Mum, blowing her nose on a tissue she'd pulled out from up her sleeve. 'I'm so sorry. We both are. Can you tell us what went wrong?'

'I'd rather not go into it all now, but it wasn't an out of the blue situation. These things happen, don't they?'

'Well, they certainly seem to have a habit of happening to

you,' Dad said bluntly, standing up and shoving his hands deep in his trouser pockets.

I had known Dad, as well as Mum, was going to be upset, but I hadn't expected him to be mean. His attitude almost made me regret my determination not to share what Laurence had been up to. Had it just been Dad I was talking to, I would have told him at that point, but the distressed look on Mum's face censored the potential flow of words. And actually, given that mine and Dad's relationship was still in a somewhat fragile state, I knew I would have regretted taking a sledgehammer to it and cracking it completely.

'So, can I stay?' I asked, before I had further opportunity to blurt everything out.

Given the current atmosphere I wasn't sure I wanted to, but I didn't have any other options. Sofa surfing with either Penny or Nick and becoming a burden to them was far less appealing than squeezing into my childhood bedroom and single bed. At least I could close the door in a room of my own in Mum and Dad's cottage.

'Of course you can stay,' said Mum, reaching over and giving my hands a squeeze.

'Yes.' Dad nodded. 'You can stay.'

'Sure?' I asked him.

'Yes,' Dad said again.

'And it's not all doom and gloom,' I carried on, latching onto his slightly less belligerent tone. 'I've already got some work lined up. Some shifts in the Smuggler's to see me through the summer. Will it be all right if I'm here that long?'

'Absolutely,' Mum said, nodding. 'The longer, the better. I daresay you're more upset than you're letting on and the best place for you is here while you're getting used to the change. Having a job already sorted is wonderful. I admire you for getting straight on with things.'

'I'm starting on Thursday,' I gratefully told her.

'You have a couple of days to settle in then.' Mum smiled again. 'Just what the heart doctor ordered.'

'Thanks Mum.' I sighed, feeling relieved that the hardest part of the conversation had now happened and that I hadn't spilled the beans on my adulterous ex.

'You're sure you don't want to tell us what caused the rift?' she asked, tempting me again.

'Quite sure,' I firmly said, as much to convince myself as her. 'I'm still processing it all, to be honest.'

Dad shifted towards the door.

'Of course you are,' Mum then said with a heavy sigh, before turning to Dad. 'Isn't it good about the pub, Robin?'

'It is,' said Dad, rattling the change in his pocket. 'Come on then, let's get your stuff unloaded.'

'Don't mind your dad,' Mum said quickly as I went to follow him out. 'I know he came across as a bit gruff, but he's doubtless as upset as I am. It's been a shock. He thought a lot of Laurence.'

'I know he did.' I nodded, willing myself not to succumb to tears.

'He's just got a lot on his plate at the moment,' Mum carried on, trying to justify Dad's largely unsympathetic response to my news.

'So have you Mum,' I pointed out, 'but you're being far kinder.'

'He just worries,' she said. 'He wants to see you do well.'

'Funnily enough,' I told her, swallowing over the lump that was still lodged in my throat, 'so do I.'

Chapter 3

I didn't have a huge amount of stuff to add to the cottage, but it seemed to take up an extraordinary amount of space in my small bedroom, the hall and sitting room.

'It won't be as bad when it's all unpacked,' I desperately said as Mum, Dad and I tried to shift the randomly packed boxes about so they took up less space.

'How on earth did you get it all in your car?' Mum laughed, but Dad didn't raise a smile and I could already sense that the summer had the potential to be a difficult one.

'It was jammed in like sardines,' I said, keeping my tone light. 'Like some sort of complicated Jenga. Thank goodness the boot catch held.'

Mum laughed again, but still Dad said nothing.

'I think I might just pop over to Nick's and say hello,' I said, when we'd finally finished moving things about and making them fit as best as we could.

I didn't think it would do any harm to leave Mum and Dad to talk over my unexpected return to the fold. There must have been things they wanted to privately say about it and with me sleeping in the room next door, and with everything extra they currently both had going on, they were barely going to get the chance.

'Unless I can do anything,' I added, not wanting either of them to think that I wasn't going to pitch in. 'Is there anything I can do here? Dishes or anything? Or shall I unpack now?'

'No, no,' said Mum, with a flap of her hand. 'You go. Nick will be thrilled to see you. I'll just go up and check your bed's got fresh linen on, so it's ready for you tonight.'

'I've already done it,' I told her, grateful that I'd had the foresight to have, perhaps a little presumptuously, taken care of that. 'It's all sorted.'

'Look,' said Dad, roughly rubbing the back of his head, as I went to leave, 'I know I didn't do myself justice when you told us what's happened, Daisy, and I'm sorry.'

Mum immediately looked close to tears again.

'It was just such a shock,' he carried on, 'and I should have thought before I opened my mouth. I am upset that you and Laurence aren't together anymore, but that didn't give me the right to base what's happened about that on your struggles to find a job and accuse you of being responsible for your relationship ending as a result.'

Dad had never been a demonstrative man, even less so since the argument we'd had the summer I left for university, but I rushed to hug him anyway. His words meant everything to me and I hoped the squeeze I gave him expressed that and perhaps took us a step closer towards the relationship we'd once had. He patted me awkwardly as I breathed in the smell coming from his shirt. It was a mixture of his familiar scent, warm compost and fabric softener. Earthy, homely and grounded.

'You can take a few of my beers over to Nick's if you like,' he said when I finally let him go. 'I know he drinks the same bitter as me.'

'Thank you, Dad,' I managed to say croakily, knowing my face was every bit as flushed as his. 'For everything.'

'Go on then,' he said. 'Mum can show you where they are.'

'I really am going to try to not be here for too long,' I then told them both. 'As soon as I can find somewhere to go, I'll move out again. I mean that.'

'Pulling pints isn't going to pay much,' said Dad. 'So rather than waste money on rent, you might as well stay here and put a bit by, if you can.'

'But only until I get my head together.'

'For as long as it takes,' said Dad, in another welcoming show of understanding. 'We might not know exactly what's gone on between you and Laurence, but you're better off with us while you get over it.'

'You're right, Robin,' agreed Mum.

I didn't mar the moment by telling them I was already over it, because unsettlingly, I wasn't as convinced as I had been that I was. While we had unloaded my car, I had picked over the last few months with Laurence and fallen to wondering if he'd been unfaithful to me before. Not that I supposed it mattered now, but the thought was humiliating.

'Right, I'm off to shut the glasshouses up,' Dad said as he headed off.

'And we'll sort those beers.' Mum smiled, looking thrilled to have heard Dad's apology.

As I walked to the edge of the estate and Nick's cottage, I realised the homecoming I'd experienced had been entirely unexpected and I wasn't talking about the reception I'd had from Mum and Dad. When I was away from home, I always imagined life at Wynbrook carrying on exactly as it always had, with my parents doing what they always did at the same time and in the same order, but that had been naïve on my part.

So preoccupied with my own issues, I hadn't realised they'd had their own. And the same went for Algy. I loved him like a grandfather and yet I hadn't been properly in touch with him for months either. As I wandered along, carrying the beers in the jute bag Mum had found, I hoped Nick wasn't experiencing some drama too. I didn't think I could cope with more guilt about being so insensitive and out of touch.

'Anyone home?' I shouted into the hallway when I found the front door open.

There was a car I didn't recognise parked outside the gate and too late I noticed a pair of women's shoes kicked off on the hall runner – I hoped Nick wasn't entertaining.

'Daisy?' came a familiar voice and I realised he did have female company, but not the romantic kind. 'Oh my god!' Penny gasped, as she poked her head out of the kitchen which was at the back of the house. 'What are you doing here?'

'Pen!' I laughed, rushing inside. 'What are *you* doing here? Isn't it a school night?'

'Oh, don't,' she said, letting out a flustered breath. 'There's still a week to go until the summer holidays and I'm already at my wits' end. Come in, come through. Nick's just doing the hunter-gatherer thing and burning some meat on the barbecue. He'll be as pleased to see you as I am.'

She did look worn out, but obviously, I didn't say that.

'And I have beer,' I said, holding up the bag so the bottles clanked together.

'In that case, he'll be thrilled to see you!'

I followed her through the house and out into the back garden.

'Look who I just found casing the joint,' she said, stepping to one side to reveal me standing behind her on the patio.

'Daisy!' Nick gasped, looking every bit as amazed as Penny had. 'I don't believe it!'

'That's pretty much what I said!' Penny laughed.

'Why didn't you let us know you were coming?' Nick beamed, then his smile faltered as he looked back over my shoulder into the house. 'Are you on your own?'

'Oh, yes,' said Penny, as the penny dropped. 'You did come on your own, didn't you?'

'I did,' I told them, realising they were both expecting to see Laurence, because whenever I came back to Wynbrook now, it was always with him. 'I'm very much on my own.'

'Well, that's great.' Nick nodded, the grin reappearing.

He'd never been a fan of my former beau, and I knew Penny wasn't particularly keen either, but she had always been better at hiding it than he had.

'Permanently, as it turns out,' I further said, my voice wavering a little, which was annoying. I took a breath before continuing. 'I've left Laurence,' I then more steadily said.

'That's even better,' Nick laughed, and he threw the meat tongs in the air and only just caught them.

'Nick!' Penny gasped, as she looked worriedly at me.

'What?' He shrugged, as he then clumsily flipped a couple of burgers. 'You never liked him either, Pen.'

I looked at Penny and found she'd turned bright red.

'It's fine,' I told her. 'I knew you didn't.'

The truth was, Laurence hadn't liked her or Nick either. In fact, when I thought about it, he was often the one who put me off video-calling and messaging them. Not that I was making excuses for my tardiness, but it was further food for thought. He was in constant touch with his friends, aka work colleagues, but had never encouraged me to talk to my childhood chums.

'I am sorry though,' Penny sympathetically said. 'You'd been together a while.'

'Probably too long,' I tried to say stoically.

'I hated the way he always treated you like his pet project,' Nick then unexpectedly blurted out. He sounded really rattled. 'As if your flighty ways needed fixing.'

His tone was scathing.

'You can't really blame him for that,' I responded, 'because for a while I wanted to be fixed. When we got together, I thought he was going to sort me out.'

'Idiot,' Nick muttered.

I didn't know if he was referring to me or Laurence.

'You *are* sorted,' Nick then more loudly said. 'You're exactly who you're meant to be, Daisy.'

I wasn't sure how I felt about that. If that was the case, I was destined to be fanciful and unfocused forever!

'Do you want to talk about it?' Penny asked, sounding calmer than Nick. 'The break-up, I mean.'

A part of me really did. I wanted to tell them how I'd walked in on Laurence and his colleague working on the wrong sort of project, how status-obsessed he'd become and how unhappy in the relationship I'd been for quite some time, but I didn't. The part of me that simply wanted to relax and enjoy some beer and burgers with my mates won out.

'There's nothing to talk about, really,' I said. 'We just grew apart, I suppose, and I decided to call time. It's all still a bit . . . raw, though. It's only just happened. I've only been back a few hours.'

'Of course.' Penny nodded.

'What have your mum and dad said about it?' Nick more bluntly asked. 'I bet they're gutted. They always thought the sun shone out of Laurence's—'

'Nick . . .' Penny said.

'They're both pretty upset,' I confirmed, thinking of their reactions.

And that was another reason why I wasn't going to talk about Laurence's extra-curricular activities. Neither of my friends were gossips, but I couldn't risk the truth of what had happened getting back to Mum and Dad. It wasn't loyalty to Laurence that stopped me exposing him as the cheat he was, I simply didn't want to make the situation even more difficult for my parents than it already was.

'I can imagine,' Penny sighed. 'Are you heartbroken about it?'

'I'm really not,' I was pleased to be able to honestly say, because my newer feelings about it all weren't *that* distressing. 'I'm still processing, but my heart is intact.'

I was a little bruised and embarrassed, but that was hopefully going to be the extent of it.

'And what about Laurence?' Nick asked. 'Is he suffering?'

I had to smile at the loaded hope in his tone.

'I don't know.' I shrugged, imagining Laurence eventually finding the note that stated what I'd seen and how it had been the proof I'd needed to confirm that ending things was the right, and only, outcome for us. 'I left him a note at the flat and I've blocked his number.'

'That's how you broke up with him?' Penny gasped.

'Yep.'

'Good for you,' said Nick, smiling.

'You don't think he'll show up here, do you?' Penny asked.

'I hope not!' I blanched. I hadn't considered that. 'No. No, he won't come here.'

Hopefully he'd assume that I'd told Mum and Dad what he'd done and as a result, he'd be too scared to face my father. He might try and call me, or email, but he wouldn't have the courage to just turn up.

'Do you mind if we change the subject?' I asked. 'Dad gave me some bottles of bitter to bring along. Where do you keep your bottle opener, Nick?'

'In the kitchen drawer, next to the sink.'

'Well,' said Penny, giving me a sympathetic look, 'if you do decide you want to talk about it, you know where I am.'

'I do.' I nodded. 'And I appreciate that, Pen, I really do.'

'And you can talk to me too,' Nick called after me. 'Though my response might be a bit different to the one you get from Pen.'

'I've no doubt it would be,' I laughed. 'Thank you, Nick.'

Over drinks, a huge salad Penny had prepared and some charred offerings from Nick, we caught up with each other's lives and I managed to keep the details of Laurence's bad behaviour to myself in spite of the inhibition-busting bitter.

'Tell Daisy what you've got lined up for the summer, Pen,' Nick encouraged as he helped himself to the last chicken skewer and she mixed herself another weak shandy because she had to drive back to Wynmouth.

'Something lined up for the summer?' I frowned. 'You're

going to be in recovery from a mad end to the school term for at least a month, aren't you?'

'I am,' she agreed, 'but I'm trying my hand at something different while I recuperate.'

'Oh?'

'I'm taking over Sophie's beach café while she and Hope are flying out to be with a sick relative in the Caribbean,' she announced. 'I can't wait to start working with moreish sandwich fillings and sublime sweet bakes instead of sulky students!'

'You're never doing that?' I asked, feeling shocked.

Normally Penny deservedly took the whole of the summer school break to rest and reset, but running the café wouldn't allow for that. It was a very popular spot, being the only eatery on the beach. Actually, as far as I knew, it was still the only café in the whole of the village and the summer holidays were obviously its busiest time.

'I am,' she confirmed and sounded thrilled about it. 'And it couldn't have come at a better time. This year has been the toughest since I starting teaching and I'm seriously thinking about leaving education for good.'

'You're not?' It was my turn to gasp then.

'Can you believe it?' said Nick, sounding sad.

We both knew what a fabulous teacher Penny was, so her loss would be a severe blow to the primary school she worked in. And the children she wouldn't get to teach, as well. But that said, we also knew how much Penny enjoyed cooking and baking and how hard she'd found it to decide which career path to follow.

'No,' I responded, thinking of the angst she'd gone through before settling on teaching, 'I can't, but I do know you still love to cook, Penny, and given my track record when it comes to the world of work, I'm hardly in a position to try and talk you into sticking with the teaching, am I?'

'Not really,' Penny said, grinning.

'Well, I think it's a shame,' said Nick, 'but I do love your food and knowing what you've been through this year, Pen, I can understand where you're coming from. Life's too short to work at a job that makes you miserable.'

'Hear, hear!' I agreed, holding up my glass and feeling another pang because I didn't know the details of what she'd recently been through.

'I thought we'd just agreed your opinion doesn't count, Daisy,' Nick then teased. 'You've never stuck at anything long enough to find out if you like it or not.'

'Hey,' I yelped, pretending to be affronted and pelting him with a stray piece of lettuce. 'I know my own mind, thank you very much,' I stated, echoing Mum's words. 'I just can't get it to settle on something, that's all . . .'

My words trailed off as I wondered if, in reality, I was ever going to find something I could do, love and excel at.

'It will one day,' Penny then kindly and convincingly said. 'Something will come along when the time is right, just like this café opportunity has for me.'

'Well,' I said, 'the next thing that's coming along in the very near future is pulling pints in the Smuggler's. Sam has offered me a few shifts behind the bar.'

My mind flitted to the American guy who I had earlier crossed paths with and I wondered if he'd been passing through the village or planning to hang around. I might end up pulling a pint for him. Assuming he had a taste for British beer.

'That's a new one, isn't it?' asked Nick. 'I can't remember you ever working in a pub before.'

'Completely new. Maybe this could be that special something I've been looking for.'

'Really?' Penny asked, sounding sceptical.

'Maybe.' I shrugged, even though I didn't genuinely think it would be. 'Who knows?'

'I do,' said Nick, standing up and stretching his arms above his head, which made his shirt ride up and exposed his midriff. 'I give you a fortnight. Three weeks at best.'

'Biff him for me, would you, Pen?' I requested. 'I'm out of salad to throw at him.'

She didn't biff him and when I turned to look at her, I found she was bright red and suddenly engrossed with stacking the plates together.

'Just phase him out,' she muttered, without looking up. 'That's what I've learnt to do.'

Between the three of us, we tidied everything away and I said I'd better get back to Mum and Dad's before the draw-bridge went up because I'd forgotten to take my key.

'Doesn't matter,' said Nick, as he threw a blanket around Penny's shoulders and we headed back into the garden, 'I've got one for the cottage. You can borrow that if needs be.'

'In that case,' I said, quickly sitting down and stretching out on the recliner he had been heading towards, 'I won't rush off.'

'But I'll have to get going in a minute,' Penny sighed, checking her watch. 'It is, as you pointed out earlier, Daisy, a school night.'

'The first of the week too.'

She let out a groan of frustration.

'How can it only be Monday?' she grimaced. 'It's sports day on Thursday and personally I'm hoping for rain.'

Nick reached for his phone.

'The forecast is still showing sunny and very warm,' he said regretfully. 'Hot almost. Though of course, that's exactly what I need to put some paint on the strawberries. Sorry, Pen.'

'How's the fruit farm doing?' I asked, loving his description of the way the sun ripens the fruit. 'It sounds like Dad's got a lot extra on his plate in the garden this year. Have you got more to do on the farm too?'

'Thankfully not and it's going really well,' Nick told me. 'Even better than usual, I think. The weather has been perfect and considering we're not at peak holiday time yet, it's very busy too. Had it been a bit quieter, I would have been helping your dad out in the garden. I know he's struggling.'

'He's told me Algy got him to set up a cut-flower enterprise,' I said. 'I haven't seen it obviously, but I can imagine it's another full-on thing for Dad to have to deal with during his already stretched time.'

'Um,' said Nick. 'It's not really working out because of the lack of seasonal staff. And with Theo gone now—'

'I'm so pleased for him and Wren,' Penny cut in. She sounded as dreamy as Mum had earlier. 'That's three little ones they've got now and a lovely big place to raise them in, just outside the village.'

Penny had always wanted a family of her own, but so far, her Mr Right hadn't come along. Well, he had, only she hadn't spotted him yet. I wondered, as I was going to be back for the summer, if I should take on the role of Cupid. There might not be any love in my life, but perhaps I could encourage some in hers . . .

'I wouldn't sound so chuffed about that,' Nick laughed. 'They might all end up being little terrors that you have to teach before long.'

That made Penny sit up.

'Don't say that,' she huffed. 'I'm sure they're all as lovely as their parents, and besides, I might have left and be happily baking buns by the time they turn school age.'

Nick didn't look convinced.

'Right,' I cut in, not wanting them to bicker. 'I really had better get back. I've got to get used to sleeping in a single bed again, so it could be a long night.'

'Isn't there a double in the spare room?' Nick pointed out.

'There is,' I confirmed. It was the bed Laurence and I used to sleep in when we were visiting together. 'But I'm not moving in there. I already feel as though I'm imposing, so I'm trying to take up as little space as possible.'

Not that all my stuff dotted about the cottage suggested that. Perhaps I'd put some of it back in my car once Mum and Dad had gone to work tomorrow. That would free up a bit of space and I wasn't going to need to unpack everything.

'I'm sure you're not imposing,' said Penny, who had a penchant for looking on the bright side. 'I bet your mum and dad are thrilled to have you staying with them, even if the circumstances are a bit—'

'Mum doesn't seem to mind,' I interrupted, 'but Dad's not quite so thrilled.'

He might have apologised for what he'd said, but I knew that initial gut reactions were generally the ones that revealed what someone genuinely felt about something.

'He's got so much to contend with at the moment,' Nick

said, a little defensively. 'I wouldn't pay much attention to his current mood, if it's a grumpy one.'

'Mum's got a lot on as well,' I pointed out, just like I had to her. 'Do either of you know what happened to Algy?' I asked. 'He was keen to play it down when I saw him earlier, but I know Mum's worried about him.'

'He buggered over when he was out in the garden, searching for this cat he's been trying to look after,' Nick told me. 'Had your dad not been in the garden doing his evening gate check, Algy would have been stuck outside on the ground all night.'

'Dad to the rescue.' I smiled.

'It shook him up, I think,' Nick further said. 'Your dad, I mean. He's a good bloke and he thinks the world of Algy. I know your dad comes across as a bit crotchety sometimes, Daisy, but his heart's always in the right place.'

'Oh, I know that really,' I generously said, though the argument between us in the past had given me reason to doubt it. 'I'm his daughter, after all. And I daresay I wouldn't be overly enamoured if my grown-up girl landed herself on me unannounced with everything else that's going on.'

I could see now that my timing really couldn't have been worse.

'It'll all shake down in a day or two,' said Penny, drawing a line under the conversation. 'Come on, I'll run you back if you like. You can check out my new motor!'

I made all the right noises about Penny's new car, but my mind was elsewhere. I had thought about doing a little preliminary digging into her reaction to the sight of Nick's midriff on the drive back, but the journey was over almost before it had started and I was still thinking about Dad being the person who had found Algy prostrate in one of the flower beds. Nick was no doubt right in saying that it had given him a fright.

Both Dad and Mum were struggling with things I hadn't known about and I felt doubly determined that while I was staying with them, I would be helpful rather than a thorn in their sides. If I could get to grips with working in the pub, help out around the cottage and keep an eye on Algy, then perhaps there was the potential for this to be the best summer ever, rather than a difficult one.

Chapter 4

My determination to be of use while I was back at Wynbrook didn't get off to the best of starts because I slept so late the following morning. Mum and Dad were long gone by the time I surfaced and went downstairs in search of coffee and something to eat.

I wasn't impressed with myself because the last thing I wanted was my parents, Dad especially, thinking that I'd turned back into the uncommunicative teenager who took never-ending naps, which was pretty much the person I had been during the last few months I had lived at home.

Having groggily made myself a strong coffee and slathered toast in honey from the Wynbrook hives, I sat at the kitchen table and tried to focus on how I could make amends for my late start. I would begin by having a good clear-out and shift the boxes about again to make more space and then I'd take Dad something to have with his late morning brew.

I was happily imagining myself morphing into the dream daughter when my eyes fell upon the pinboard next to the fridge and the fantasy was swiftly forgotten. The evidence that I wasn't actually going to be able to live up to the role was proudly on display, right there, for all the world to see. The unbearable and nauseating nephew, cousin Daniel, clearly still filled the top relative spot and by the looks of it, he'd left no space on the podium for me.

'G'day from down under,' I sarcastically read aloud from the postcard I plucked from its pride of place. 'It's a gloriously sunny day here in Oz and I thought you'd appreciate this card from the botanical gardens, Uncle Robin.'

I flipped the card over and frowned at the image of the perfect-looking garden and statement tree at its centre, which was in full bloom.

'What a suck-up,' I tutted, checking the date on the postmark.

The card had been sent just a couple of weeks before and Daniel was right, it was just the sort of thing Dad would appreciate.

'Well done, Danny,' I huffed, pinning it back up again. 'You little goody-goody.'

Even from thousands of miles away, my wretched younger cousin, the son of Dad's younger sister, had the ability to make me feel inadequate. Living his best life in Australia, with a perfect wife, two flaxen-haired, intelligent children and a photo-genic dog, he was the family thorn in my side. I had always known that Dad compared my lacklustre adult life to Daniel's spectacularly shiny one, even though he never would have admitted it if anyone had asked him.

'No,' I said, as I resolutely turned my back on the pinboard. 'No, no, no, you will not start travelling down that road, Daisy.'

I piled my dishes in the sink, then brushed my teeth and got dressed ahead of turning my attention to my many boxes and bags and clearing some space in my room. I didn't need to feel any worse about myself and my life than I already had the potential to do, so thoughts of delightful Daniel were banished, along with Laurence's deceit. Staying focused and on task would get a parental tick in my 'Best Daughter on the Planet' box and that was what I was determined to achieve.

'What on earth's all this?'

With my mini speaker belting out some inspiring Taylor Swift lyrics, I didn't hear the question the first time it was asked.

'Daisy!' Dad shouted and I spun round.

'What's all this?' Mum shouted too. 'What on earth are you doing?'

I lurched for my speaker and in the process knocked into a teetering pile of magazines I'd kept from my teen years and almost upset my glass of water as I fumbled and failed to steady them. Dad salvaged my drink and then turned his attention back to the state of the sitting room.

'What time is it?' I yelped into the silence, now the music had been banished. Taylor might still be able to make a whole room shimmer, but all I could do was turn it into a disaster zone apparently. 'I was going to bring you a mid-morning snack, Dad.'

'It's lunchtime,' he muttered. 'A little after, actually.'

'Did you not read my note?' Mum asked, sounding exasperated. 'I asked you to set the table and heat up the food I'd left in the fridge so it would be ready for us all to eat together when we got back.'

Ankle-deep in all the bits and pieces collected over a lifetime that I'd carried downstairs, pulled out of boxes and then failed to sort through ahead of opening more, and knowing that upstairs and the kitchen were similarly littered, I couldn't recall seeing a note.

'I'm sorry,' I apologised. 'I got caught up doing this.'

'What exactly is this?' Dad demanded, as he looked about despairingly.

'I wanted to clear some space, so I thought I'd go through everything, have a proper sort-out and in the process, hopefully scale it all down so we could get rid of some of the boxes,' I explained. 'This isn't just stuff I came back with, it's things from when I lived here as well. This is all out of my bedroom.'

'Yes,' Dad said tersely. 'I can see that.'

'And that's what you're doing, is it?' Mum frowned. Her lips were a thin line, so I knew I was on thin ice. 'Sorting out? It looks more like a bombsite or a jumble sale to me.'

I looked at the state of the room again and couldn't disagree with her description. I had just reached the point where it was at its worst, but it would soon come together when I started going through the 'toss', 'keep', 'charity' process.

'I'm going back to the manor,' Mum said crossly before I had a chance to tell her what my plans for the muddle and mayhem were. 'I'll eat with Algy.'

'No, don't,' I said, feeling bad. 'I'll clear a space in the kitchen and heat our meal now. It won't take long.'

'I've not got time to wait for that now,' Mum said impatiently and walked out.

'I'll come with you, love,' said Dad, taking the glass I'd nearly knocked over with him. 'We'll see you later, Daisy. Please make sure you've got this lot sorted by the time we get back, okay? Your mother doesn't need the extra stress. And neither do I.'

I felt even worse then. My aim had been to reduce the stress of having me back under the cottage roof, not increase it.

'I just thought it would be easier to look at everything en masse,' I said to his retreating back. 'And I didn't realise how late it was . . .'

Mum's note was on the worktop, right next to the sink. I had no idea how I'd missed it. I scowled at Daniel's postcard and laid the blame at his feet rather than taking it on myself. If I hadn't been made to feel so inferior when I started my day, I was sure I wouldn't have got in such a muddle and further besmirched my chances of being offspring of the year.

'Well,' said Mum, when she returned just before four and ahead of Dad, 'this all looks much better in here, I must say.'

She sounded relieved and my aching shoulders relaxed a little as a result.

'Let's face it though, Mum,' I smiled, 'it couldn't really have been any worse than when you came back at lunchtime, could it?'

I had worked tirelessly to sort out the mess I'd made and now my car was packed practically to the roof with stuff I no longer wanted. A lot of it had been taken out of my bedroom, but some of it was from the flat. Given his behaviour, it would have served Laurence right if I'd left all of that behind for him to sort out.

I might have been relieved that his infidelity had given me the opportunity to walk away from our relationship and not feel guilty about it, but I was still contradictorily smarting a little over the fact that he'd betrayed me and bedded someone else.

'Probably not,' Mum sighed, sitting tiredly in a chair at the table, while I poured her a cup of tea from the pot. 'But what's the rest of the cottage like?'

I shook my head, pretending to be affronted.

'As clean as a whistle,' I reeled off. 'Neat as a pin, with not a thing out of place now.'

'How have you managed that?' she chuckled.

'By applying myself,' I told her, rolling my shoulders and stretching my stiff neck from side to side.

'Wonders will never cease.' She smiled wryly.

'I've had the biggest clear-out in my bedroom and that's made space for everything I came back with and wanted to keep. I've got half a dozen bags of folded clothes for the charity shop in my car and a massive pile of paper and magazines for recycling. Unless Dad would rather burn it all.'

I couldn't remember the last time I'd worked so hard to sort out a mess I'd made, but it had been a cathartic process and I felt loads lighter for having done it. Or I would when I'd offloaded everything I didn't want to the charity shop, the office wardrobe in particular. Workwear had never really been my bag, but I was sure someone would benefit from the smart suits and shoes that pinched.

'Unless Dad would rather burn what?' asked the man himself as he arrived at the door and used the step to lever off his boots.

'I've got loads of paper to get rid of,' I explained.

'Best recycle it,' he said.

I wondered how much more I could cram into the bin ahead of the next collection. It weighed a ton already and the lid only just closed.

'I really am sorry about earlier,' I apologised. 'I honestly didn't realise how late it was or how much I'd spread myself about.'

'No harm done, I suppose,' Mum said kindly.

'You're only saying that because it looks like she's got on top of it.' Dad grinned, crossing to the sink and lifting out the bowl so he could wash his hands.

'How was Algy today?' I asked Mum, before she could agree with Dad's astute observation.

'Much brighter,' she told me, sounding relieved. 'He ate lunch with us, didn't he, Robin?'

'He did. He tucked it away, too.'

'Definitely the most I've seen him eat in a while,' Mum agreed.

'So, you could say,' I smiled, as I poured tea for Dad as well, 'that it was a good thing that I missed your note and you had to eat lunch with Algy, because that encouraged him to have another meal.'

Dad shook his head at that.

'I'm not sure I'd go that far,' Mum said thoughtfully, 'but I do now wonder if he's feeling a bit isolated in the manor on his lonesome.'

'But he's lived alone for years,' I pointed out, not liking that my cheeky comment had triggered that thought in Mum's head. 'And never been bothered about it before.'

'But he hadn't had a fall then,' Dad said.

'A tumble,' I corrected. 'Algy says a fall makes him sound decrepit.'

'Perhaps it's left him feeling a bit vulnerable,' Dad surmised. 'He certainly looked vulnerable when I found him lying on that path . . .'

He gave an involuntary shudder and I realised Nick had been right. Dad really had felt the impact of finding his friend injured on the ground.

'Perhaps it has,' echoed Mum, biting her lip.

'Well,' I said, 'we'll have to set our minds to trying to come up with a solution for that, won't we?'

'Yes,' said Mum, as she picked up her teacup. 'We will.'

The rest of the day thankfully passed without me upsetting either her or Dad. I made sure I took responsibility for the dinner *and* the dishes and then I turned in extra early. The night before, I had struggled with the mean confines of the single bed and that, combined with sorting through my worldly goods and my childhood bedroom, had left me feeling pretty much done in.

I had tentatively considered taking a tour of the garden the next day and looking in on the new cut-flower garden, but the weather had turned so utterly miserable, I didn't feel like it when I got up. It didn't strike me then what a relief that was or why I felt grateful for the rainy reprieve. I put my desire to put it off down to the weather and still being tired out from the mammoth sort-out I'd had the day before.

I had made a point of being up before Mum and Dad went to work and having checked their arrangements for lunch – they were eating with Algy again and invited me to join them – I then set out to the closest town along the coast to drop off the charity bags I'd accumulated and free up the space in my car again.

With my first shift in the bar happening the next day, I felt the urge to get all of my ducks in a row. If this was going to

be a stress-free and straightforward summer spent helping out
around the cottage, keeping Algy company and working in the
pub, then I wanted to be as ready for it as I possibly could be.
I was determined not to let anyone down, get in the way or
generally be a nuisance of any kind.

I was also keen to keep fully occupied because every moment
I was currently without a task, my mind still frustratingly drifted
back to the visual Laurence and his co-worker had treated me
to and I could live without that. I could live without *all* thoughts
of him, full stop.

I wondered how he had taken the news that he'd been found
out and how his face must have looked when he read the note
I'd left. He hadn't turned up pleading forgiveness or offering
an explanation, so he was either as happy as I was that the
relationship was over or he really was too scared to come to
Wynbrook because he assumed that I'd told Mum and Dad.
Given that I was so relieved to be single again, it was maddening
that thoughts of him were still lingering, but it was early days
and I firmly told myself they would soon pass.

'So,' said Algy when I arrived at the manor kitchen after my
charity shop trip and found him, Mum, Dad and Nick about
to tuck into Shepherd's pie and seasonal veg, 'your mum tells
me you've moved back into the cottage, Daisy, and that you're
single now.'

I felt everyone's eyes on me and wondered if they'd been
speculating and sharing information in my absence. The answer
to that was obvious, I supposed.

'That's right,' I said brightly, while I inwardly cursed
Laurence's lingering. 'I am. I'll just go and freshen up.'

I escaped to the cloakroom, which was next to the boot

room, and strained my ears to listen for further chat. The walls were so thick, it made eavesdropping impossible; however, when I returned, Algy looked flustered.

'I think I rather put my foot in it,' he said, with a grimace.

'No, you didn't,' I told him, offering him a reassuring smile.

'And I wasn't gossiping,' Mum quickly said.

'I know that, Mum,' I said, turning the smile towards her. 'It was perfectly reasonable that you had to explain what I was doing back here.'

'*I* was gossiping a bit,' Nick then joined in.

'Now that I can believe,' I tutted and felt grateful to my friend for relieving the undercurrent of tension that I never wanted to feel in Wynbrook.

'Nick wondered if we knew the reason behind why you'd given Laurence the old heave-ho,' Algy elaborated.

'I can believe that, too.' I said, rolling my eyes.

'But it turns out, no one does,' Algy added, looking expectantly at me, along with everyone else.

'Well,' I sighed, 'we just ran out of steam, you know. The relationship had run its course and—'

'So, he *really* didn't break your heart?' Algy queried, looking concerned. 'Because I'd be more than willing to see him off with a pitchfork, if that was required.'

Dad chuckled at that.

'I'm quite certain Laurence would never break Daisy's heart,' he said confidently.

'No.' I smiled at Algy. 'No broken heart, so no theatrics with a pitchfork required. But never mind my unbroken heart. What's happened to the weather, Nick? You predicted sunshine for today, didn't you?'

'I did,' he grumbled, holding up his plate so Mum could fill it. 'I'm hoping this rain is just a blip in an otherwise sunny forecast.'

'That's the joy of living near the coast,' Algy said sagely. 'A storm can whip up out of nowhere in a heartbeat.'

I knew that, but I had been panicking that a different kind of storm had been about to whip up around the speculation of my break-up.

'Shame the rain came today and not tomorrow,' I said, looking out at the sky, still a dark grey sheet.

'Shame it came at all,' Dad and Nick said together and grinned.

'Why's that, love?' Mum asked me, as she held out a hand for my plate.

'Pen has sports day to marshal tomorrow,' I explained. 'She was hoping it might be rained off.'

We each of us gave a shudder.

'I can't think of anything worse than sports day,' said Algy. 'I hated it.'

It turned out, none of us had been keen.

'I was never any good at running,' I laughed, 'but I didn't mind the swimming gala.'

It had always frustrated me that I could swim faster than I could run.

'Thankfully you had the capacity to run home when you needed to,' Algy said with a smile, making me the centre of attention again. 'Not that I meant . . .'

'Come on,' said Nick, 'never mind about that, let's get this lunch down us before we have to get back to work.'

There was a brief dry spell when it was time to leave and Nick walked with me as far as my car, which I'd driven up in.

'I'm sorry if that was awkward,' he said. 'I didn't mean to put you on the spot about you and Laurence breaking up. I just wanted to make sure you really are okay.'

'I've already told you I am,' I reminded him. 'So why would you think I'm not?'

'Just a feeling,' he said, giving me a one-armed hug. 'And you did say you were feeling raw and had stuff to process, as well as that you were all right.'

I felt grateful for his concern, but also relieved that I hadn't shared with him and Penny what had really been the final nail in my relationship coffin with Laurence. There was no way Nick would have been able to keep Laurence's infidelity to himself. He'd tell Mum and Dad, then want to round up a posse with Algy and his pitchfork and personally chase Laurence out of town. I imagined the pair of them leaping to my defence dressed as cowboys on horseback with lassoes.

'Well,' I said, shaking the amusing image off, 'to be fair, it has only been two days, so I'm bound to still be feeling a bit out of sorts, aren't I?'

'I guess,' Nick conceded, letting me go.

'But really,' I smiled, 'I just want to focus on enjoying the summer. You, me, Pen, on the beach and in the pub.'

'Chance will be a fine thing,' Nick laughed. 'I'm going to be flat out here and Penny's going to be run off her feet in the café. I don't think she's realised how busy it gets . . .'

At least I wasn't going to be swamped in the Smuggler's. There was a fine line between busy and stressed and I felt no urge to cross it.

'I'm sure we'll be able to have some time together,' I rallied.

I wasn't willing to give up on the summer idyll just two days in.

'I'm sure we will,' Nick agreed. 'But in the meantime, and as you'll have more free time than Pen and me, perhaps you should think about indulging in a summer fling.'

I looked at him and blinked.

'Where did that idea spring from?' I laughed.

Nick shrugged.

'Just a thought.' He grinned. 'Don't people say that the best way to get over someone, is to get under someone else?'

'Stop right there,' I laughed. 'Besides, who would I fling with? Not that I would consider it, but everyone around here is already spoken for.'

'It's almost holiday season – plenty of tourists poised to pour in!'

'Wynmouth is hardly a holiday hotspot,' I pointed out. 'And besides, I'm twenty-eight, not eighteen.'

'So?' He shrugged. 'Live a little.'

Then he sauntered off whistling 'Summer Lovin'' from *Grease* and I was left thinking that he should take a dose of his own medicine.

Chapter 5

Having just left one relationship behind, I certainly wasn't about to take up Nick's suggestion and start another, even if he had hinted that it could have the shortest possible shelf life.

However, the next morning I was so amazed and dismayed to discover that neither of my parents were genuinely convinced that I really had left my relationship with Laurence behind, that I was almost tempted to consider having a fling just to properly drive the point home. Over breakfast Mum and Dad infuriatingly asked if the current situation might not be more of a brief hiatus or a temporary break, like the one Ross and Rachel had disastrously taken in *Friends*!

I could have told them that in one sense it was – i.e. the part where Ross slept with someone else – but I kept my lips zipped and ducked out of the cottage the second I could leave without them assuming I had something to hide. I had already shouldered the blame for the break-up, so why couldn't they accept the situation and move on? I had unthinkingly assumed they had, but I'd clearly misread their reactions.

As I was now feeling put out as well as a bit jittery about my first shift in the pub that evening, I thought I'd bite the bullet and tackle something else head-on that I was feeling edgy about. The rain had cleared and it was a stunning sunny day, so I had no excuse not to head into the garden.

I used to love playing in it when I was little and then earning pocket money helping Dad when I was older. The garden had been my sanctuary . . . until it wasn't and then I had completely banished it. I hadn't given it a moment's consideration when I decided to move back to Wynbrook for the summer, but now it was on my mind again and I couldn't escape it.

I was distressed to discover that the packed borders and neat lawns didn't soothe me in the same way they once had and I ended up skirting around the periphery instead. I walked right to the very edge where there was a single-storey wooden building with a tiled roof and pretty, covered veranda. It was known on the estate as The Summerhouse, but it was bigger and far more special than its commonplace name suggested.

'Ouch,' I winced, as I inched my way along the overgrown path towards it and my bare left calf rubbed against an encroaching patch of stinging nettles.

I ignored the pain, knowing that scratching it would make it worse and eventually worked my way through the undergrowth to the veranda. I peered through the windows and was disappointed to find the inside appeared to be as sadly neglected as the outside. The two wooden rocking chairs that usually flanked the door were piled up inside and the rest of the furniture was covered in dust sheets. The windows were so grimy, it was impossible to see if there was still a bed on the mezzanine and I wondered if the electricity was connected.

The Summerhouse had all mod cons. Well, running water and electricity anyway, and had been designed as guest accommodation.

Not that the manor wasn't large enough to accommodate a dozen, but Algy had had the garden sanctuary built for anyone looking for a more private and secluded retreat from the world.

I stepped back and took the whole of it in, carefully avoiding more nettles, and surmised that no one had sought refuge in it for quite a while.

'Yet another area of the garden I haven't been able to properly keep on top of,' I heard Dad say resignedly behind me.

'You can't do everything, Dad,' I reminded him. 'You need more help.'

The words tasted bitter in my throat, given the memories that were now churning away as a result of my looking around.

'Yes,' he said, putting down the loaded wheelbarrow and wiping his overall sleeve across his forehead, which was damp with sweat. 'You're right, but getting help is easier said than done. With so much property given over to the tourist trade here now, there are fewer and fewer locals left living nearby every year.'

'Which in turn depletes the local workforce,' I said, nodding along, ignoring the growing bud of resentment that I couldn't allow to bloom. 'And sucks the life out of the community.'

It was a miracle there was still a school within reasonable distance for Penny to teach in.

'Exactly,' Dad sighed. 'Though the village is holding its own where the community is concerned.'

'Well,' I said, trying to cheer him up, 'I'm local and I'm back.'

'But for how long?' he asked. 'I keep expecting Laurence to turn up and whisk you away again.'

I let out a slow, but not particularly calming breath.

'That isn't going to happen, Dad,' I said firmly. 'You need to accept that. You and Mum both need to accept that. I thought you had. I would hardly have gone to the trouble of packing up all of my things from the flat and clearing out my room in the cottage to accommodate them if this was just some silly spat Laurence and I had had, would I?'

'I suppose not,' Dad sighed. 'And as far as I know, he hasn't been in touch?'

'He hasn't,' I confirmed. 'And he won't be.'

'I just hope you don't end up regretting leaving him,' Dad carried on after a beat had passed.

'I won't.'

'Because men like Laurence don't come along all that often.'

I couldn't help thinking that was something to be grateful for.

'I'm well aware of that,' I said, unclenching my jaw.

'Perhaps you'll feel differently once the dust has settled,' Dad suggested, sounding hopeful and making me tense up again.

I thought again of Nick's summer fling idea. Maybe he was really on to something and I should take it up. A passionate and very public romance would get the message across, to Mum and Dad at least, that I'd moved on. Penny, however, would probably assign it to the rebound box, but that wouldn't matter. If it proved to my parents that I was capable of carrying on with life post-Laurence, that would be a definite win.

'Do you think that might be a possibility, Daisy?' Dad asked, as I rubbed one calf against the other and ignored him. 'Earth to Daisy Daydream,' he then said more loudly, recalling another childhood nickname. 'Do you think once the dust has settled—'

'Absolutely not,' I said vehemently, only just resisting the urge to scratch. 'Now, if you don't mind, Dad, I need to get on. I promised I'd go and see Nick this morning.'

It was a blunt departure, but bluntness would, I hoped, at some point work where treading lightly had failed.

'So, what did you think of the cut-flower garden?' Nick asked, when I found him arranging boxes in the barn that was used as the pick-your-own weighing station and after I had explained what I'd been up to ahead of seeking him out.

'I didn't get that far,' I huffed, even though I'd actually avoided that part of the garden on purpose. 'Dad came along and started banging on about Laurence and how he's convinced that we'll get back together once the *dust has settled*.' I gave the final words air quotes and a sarcastic edge.

Nick looked annoyingly amused.

'It's not funny,' I scowled. 'Him and Mum are doing my head in.'

'And you've only been back, what, a week?'

'Four days,' I corrected. 'Just four days. I snapped at Dad, told him I'd promised I'd come and see you, then legged it down here.'

'Don't rope me into the situation,' Nick said, grinning. 'But as you're here, you might as well make yourself useful.'

'What did you have in mind?'

'I'm about a dozen of the kiddies' baskets short,' he told me. 'Would you mind going to look for them?'

'I suppose I could,' I said, sauntering out. 'Anything's got to be better than risking running into Dad again.'

'Thanks. They could be anywhere.'

Abandoned baskets were a nuisance on the fruit farm and in need of regular rounding up. They were as difficult to keep track of as it was to work out how many kilograms of fruit were lost by the *eat three, pay for one*, fruit-picking brigade.

'You'd better wear this,' said Nick, tossing me a wide-brimmed straw hat from the collection left behind over the years. 'It's hot already.'

I thrust it on my head.

'It is,' I agreed. 'I wonder how Penny's getting on. I messaged her earlier, but didn't get a reply.'

I knew the end of term was always hectic and hoped that we'd see more of each other after the school year ended, but knowing now that she was going to be working in the beach café all hours, I wasn't sure how we were going to manage it. I was catching up nicely with Nick, but I wanted Pen back in my life properly too, so we'd have to find a way.

'She was going in extra early to get the course set up, so you probably missed her.'

'That school will be lost without her if she does decide to leave,' I mused.

'As lost as my baskets,' Nick said pointedly.

'All right, all right,' I said, putting up my hands. 'I'm going.'

Nick was right about the temperature. It had risen noticeably during the brief time we had been chatting and by the time I'd found eight of the missing baskets, it was becoming uncomfortable.

A few people had arrived and were keenly filling the larger punnets and baskets with the juicy red strawberries the farm was known for. I'd eaten a couple myself, but hadn't gone overboard. I had no intention of eating into the fruit farm profits.

'I found eight,' I told Nick, when I arrived back at the barn, just after he'd served a customer.

'That's phenomenal,' he beamed. 'I thought I'd only lost six.'

'You told me it was about a dozen,' I protested, as I fanned myself with the hat before tossing it back to him.

'Yes, well,' he grinned, neatly catching it, 'I thought it would keep you out of mischief for longer.'

'I don't go searching for mischief,' I told him, as I snatched back the hat and plonked it on his head. 'It comes looking for me.'

There was nothing for me to help with in the cottage and holed up in my room, the rest of the day dragged, but it was eventually time to set off for Wynmouth and my shift in the pub. I'd had so many jobs over the years that I didn't usually get jittery when it came to fresh starts, but my tummy felt a bit bubbly as I set off and I knew that it wasn't down to eating an excess of summer fruit because I'd strictly rationed myself.

Even though the Smuggler's was only going to be a part-time summer job, it was extremely important in that it had appeased my parents on my return, and the desire to keep them happy *and* convince them that I was here for good as a single woman, or for the summer at least, doubtless accounted for the rolling tum and sweaty palms.

I parked in the pub car park and wrestled with the passenger window. The wretched thing had a mind of its own and I had no choice but to leave it open. The village was hardly a crime hotspot and the vehicle was far from desirable, so I hoped it would be safe enough.

As always, my eyes took a moment to adjust to the dark interior when I stepped inside the Smuggler's, but the cooling effect of the drop in temperature was immediately felt and most welcome.

'Pen!' I waved, spotting her at the table closest to the bar. 'How did sports day go?'

Her face looked rather rosy, but whether that was the result of being out in the sun for hours or from the stresses of coping with the trials of the day, I couldn't be sure.

'About as well as you'd expect,' she told me. 'But knowing I have the pub on my doorstep now and that I wouldn't have to cook my own dinner this evening was a very consoling thought throughout the day.'

I nodded at that. Given how much she loved to cook, that left me in no doubt as to exactly how exhausted she was.

'I'm sorry I didn't reply to your message,' she apologised.

'That's fine,' I said, with a smile. 'I just wanted you to know that I was thinking of you. I saw Nick this morning and he said you were going in early to help with the setting up.'

It struck me then that she must have replied to Nick, for him to know that. Perhaps the pair of them were finally get their acts together and wouldn't need me to intervene on their behalf after all.

'I did,' Penny said, picking up her glass, 'not that I got any thanks for it. Anyway, as soon as I've finished this beer, I'm heading home for a cool shower and an early night.'

'I can't tempt you to stay and watch me making a hash of trying to work behind the bar?' I quipped, attempting to quell my nerves which had popped back up again.

'On any other day . . .' She grinned and I laughed.

'Right then, Daisy,' said Sam, as he came to clear Penny's plate. 'Shall we make a start? I'm not paying you to stand around chatting, you know.'

'Oh, damn,' I groaned. 'That's what I thought this bartending business was all about.'

'In that case,' Sam grinned, 'you've been grossly misinformed. Would you like to reconsider your options?'

'Best not,' I said, giving Penny a wink as I followed him to the bar.

Just as I had predicted, the pub was quiet, which was just as well as Tess was driving Sophie and Hope to the airport as her dad couldn't do it for some reason and it was just me and Sam keeping the place running.

I cleared a few glasses, served a couple of meals and some simple drinks like coke and lemonade and in-between customers, Sam showed me how to work the till, where the empties went and got me up to speed on prices and the local brews.

'Folk are always keen to know about the microbrewery beers we stock now, so it's handy to know a bit about them,' he told me.

'I'll make a note of the names and read up about them at home.'

Sam was thrilled about that.

'Willingness to take on homework noted and appreciated.' He smiled. 'And I notice the shoes too.'

'Well, you did say comfy,' I said, looking down at my worn and much-loved Converse.

I still wasn't sure why he'd been so specific about footwear.

'So,' he carried on before I could ask, 'let's see how quickly you're going to master the art of pulling a decent pint, shall we?'

'Shouldn't we wait until someone comes in who wants one?' I asked, as I looked around. 'It's a bit wasteful otherwise, isn't it?'

Sam laughed.

'Well,' he chuckled, 'I like your faith in your ability to get it right first time and that you're mindful about waste, but it isn't the easiest skill in the world.'

'Oh,' I said, wiping my palms down my jeans. 'Right. Of course.'

'And now I've made you nervous,' Sam observed. 'I didn't mean to.'

'No, no,' I said, 'it's fine. It's just that you and Tess make it look so easy.'

'Years of practice on my part and Tess has been doing it a while now.'

'In that case,' I said, 'let's give it a go. I'm sure I'll do better and learn faster without an audience.'

Unfortunately, that moment had passed.

'Well, well, well,' came a confident voice as its owner crossed the pub threshold, 'if it isn't the woman I can't stop apologising to.'

I looked up and found the American backpacker standing on the other side of the bar. Without the rucksack, he was almost clean-shaven now and every bit as handsome as before. His accent made me go slightly weak at the knees. Well, it was either that or I was feeling more nervous about pulling my first pint than I initially realised. Perhaps I was nervous about doing it with him watching.

'Hey there,' he said, leaning on the bar and treating me to another of his hundred-watt smiles.

He looked like the ultimate all-American boy and I felt my face flush as a result of his attention.

'Hey,' I said and smiled back. 'Hi.'

Sam looked between the two of us.

'So, you two have already met?' he asked, eyebrows raised.

He'd obviously forgotten about us clashing in the pub doorway at the beginning of the week.

'Not officially.'

'Then allow me,' he offered. 'Daisy, this is Josh.'

'Hi, Josh.'

His name fitted him perfectly.

'Josh, this is Daisy. The brand-new member of the Smuggler's Inn team.'

'Daisy,' Josh repeated, his eyes twinkling. 'You look like a Daisy.'

I wrinkled my nose at that.

'And what exactly does a Daisy look like?' I asked.

'Well,' Josh grinned, 'according to Kathleen Kelly in *You've Got Mail*, they look like the friendliest flower, and you look friendly to me, so—'

'Do you like that film?' I swallowed. It was one of my absolute favourites.

'No,' Josh laughed, 'I *love* it, but it isn't my number one. *Notting Hill* has the top romcom spot as far as I'm concerned.'

'Oh my.' I swallowed again. 'I love that one too.'

'Then maybe we could watch it together sometime,' Josh suggested. 'If that isn't too forward a thing to suggest . . .'

'If it was,' I said, trying to pull my soppy self together, 'you'd have to apologise for it and then we'd be back in the old routine, wouldn't we?' He grinned at that. 'Let's see if we can get through at least one interaction without that happening, shall we?' I ventured.

He puffed out a breath as he considered the idea.

'That would be quite a feat,' he said, looking so deeply into my eyes I thought he could see as far as my soul.

'So,' I gulped as I reluctantly looked away, 'what can we, or should I say I, get you?'

Josh opened his mouth to answer, but Sam cut him off.

'Oh no,' he said, waving his hands. 'Hang on. Before we get into that, I want to know what the old routine is. I'm confused as to why you'd have one as you didn't even know each other's names until a few seconds ago. Why does Josh have to keep apologising to you, Daisy?'

'I thought you weren't paying me to chat?' I reminded him.

'I'm making an exception,' he laughed. 'Tell me.'

Josh and I looked at each other again.

'Well, the first time our paths crossed was when Josh stepped out in front of my car.'

He nodded in agreement.

'Yep,' he confirmed. 'I did do that.'

'Well, that definitely warrants an apology,' Sam commented. 'What else?'

'He bumped into me here,' I said, nodding towards the door. 'Literally bumped into me on Monday when I came and asked you for this job.'

'He did,' Sam nodded, 'I remember that now.'

'But really that was a fifty-fifty situation,' Josh jumped in. 'It's dark in here and my eyes were still adjusting when you sort of backed into me.'

'So, why did you apologise?' I pounced.

'Because I was raised right.' He grinned and my knees caved again.

'Josh is right though,' Sam said, not seeming to notice the electricity that I could feel crackling between Josh and me. 'It is dark in here, so we can't really apportion blame on just one of you for that . . .'

'And then of course,' Josh sighed, holding up his hands, 'I walked in on you when you were naked, didn't I?'

'You did what?' Sam gaped.

'And that's it,' I said, tapping the top of one of the beer pumps. 'Apologies all accounted for. So, come on, show me how to use this thing, Sam.'

'Not until you've given me some context to the naked thing,' he insisted.

'Sorry,' Josh grimaced at me, turning endearingly pink.

'And that makes four,' I said, counting each time off on my fingers, including when he'd burst in on me in the beach hut.

Josh grinned at that.

'I was exploring the beach huts,' he told Sam, while I wished the wooden floor would open up and swallow me whole, 'and Daisy was in one of them getting changed after a swim in the sea.'

'I see,' said Sam.

'Nice technique, by the way,' Josh then said to me. 'Swimming technique,' he quickly added as his coloured deepened. 'You swim well.'

'Thanks.' I nodded, feeling rather warm myself. 'And you should know, the huts aren't for exploring. They're private property.'

'I do know that now,' he said falteringly. 'Sam told me when I mentioned them the other day.'

'But you didn't mention the walking in on me getting changed part?'

'I did not.' He grinned sheepishly.

I turned to Sam to ask if he was satisfied with the context Josh had now furnished him with, but he'd had to move away to serve someone else.

'So,' I said, looking back at Josh, 'were you looking for some-where to stay that day?'

'I wasn't planning on hiding out in the huts if that's what you were thinking,' he said. 'I already had somewhere lined up to go to. I just needed to kill some time until I could collect the key.'

'Where are you staying then?' I asked. 'Is it somewhere local?'

'Yes,' he said with a nod. 'Crow's Nest Cottage. It's just—'

'Next door,' I cut in. 'Sam's place. I know it.'

He had just named one of the tiny brick and flint cottages.

'It's pretty cosy,' he shrugged, 'but I don't mind that.'

'Are you going to be around for long?'

'I've booked for the whole of the summer.'

'Wow.' I grinned. 'As long as that.'

There would be plenty of time for us to watch a film or two together – if he'd been serious about that.

'It's a beautiful spot here.' He smiled back. 'I'm in no rush to leave it.'

'There's not much to do though,' I pointed out.

'Exactly,' he said. 'I'm not looking for a lot to do, just enough to keep me occupied for the next few weeks and there's that in abundance.'

'I'm beginning to feel the same way myself,' I replied, rather brazenly.

We looked at one another again and I wondered if his pupils were so dilated because of the low light level in the pub or because I was what he was thinking might keep him occupied. I was certainly thinking that about him.

Nick's summer fling suggestion was looking more attractive by the minute.

Chapter 6

Sam was mightily amused that Josh had walked in on me while I was getting changed in the beach hut – he did say he wouldn't have been as entertained if Josh hadn't been a stand-up guy who had made a genuine mistake – however, he wasn't quite so merry as he watched me trying and consistently failing to get to grips with the art of pint pulling during the early part of the evening.

'You're not tipping the glass back far enough,' he patiently reminded me as I lined up yet another froth-filled glass on the bar.

'But it'll spill if I keep it at such a tilted angle,' I protested. Sam shook his head.

'No,' he said. 'Watch.' He grabbed a glass and again showed me the required technique he had honed to perfection. 'As the glass fills, you straighten it.'

'Right,' I said. 'Right. I'll do it this time, I promise.'

My next attempt was a vast improvement and it wasn't too much longer after that before I was deemed capable of actually serving up my effort to a paying customer. I was mindful about what I'd wasted, but hoped further practice would make perfect.

'Not bad,' the customer said, holding up the glass and insisting that I kept the change to the note they handed over in exchange.

'I'll make a decent bartender out of her yet,' Sam laughed as I counted out the change and tipped it in the pint glass next to the till labelled for tips.

'I think I'll have a gin, please,' an elderly gentleman, who had just arrived with a Jack Russell terrier on a lead, politely requested, having looked at the pint.

'Evening.' Sam smiled at the man as I quickly reached for the right glass. 'Do you know George, Daisy?'

'I know of George,' I told them both.

'Oh dear,' winked the man himself, as he doffed his battered Panama hat in my direction. 'My reputation precedes me, does it?'

'It does,' I laughed. 'But good things only. I've heard it said by more than one person that you tell electrifying and terrifying tempest-tossed tales.'

I knew George was a Wynmouth local. Having come to visit his sister when she lost her husband a few years ago, he had then never left and his scary story-telling in the pub and beyond had developed quite a following.

'Oh, I like that,' he twinkled at Sam. 'Terrifying tempest-tossed tales. We should put that on the posters.'

'Posters?' I frowned as I carefully measured out his gin.

'The posters advertising the pub events,' Sam explained, looking around. 'This place isn't always so quiet these days, hence my desire to get you trained up before the season gets into full swing.'

'Oh, right,' I said, shifting from one foot to the other. Sam had been right about the need for comfy shoes. I already felt like I'd been on my feet for days rather than hours and even in my well-worn Converse, they were starting to throb. 'What's in the pub diary then?'

'Well, this weekend, we have live music on Saturday night,' Sam said, as another customer came in.

'Perhaps my summer job isn't going to be quite as laid-back as I thought,' I said to George as I set his drink on the bar.

'If you're going to be working in here at weekends,' he smiled, 'it won't be laid-back at all. It will be fun though, and talking of fun . . .'

His gaze came to rest on Josh, who was now sitting reading at a table next to the huge, unlit fire.

'Come on, Skipper,' he said to the dog and winked at me again once he'd paid for his drink. 'Let's go and say hello to the lovely American, shall we?'

He was right in that Josh was lovely. He'd proved quite the distraction throughout the evening, even when he wasn't propping up the bar. I'd already noticed how tanned and toned he was (his chest had felt very firm when I'd backed into it), and now, having settled down and immersed himself in a book, he looked Insta perfect, too.

Nick would have called him a triple threat guy and I let out a sigh as I watched him welcome George to his table, not seeming to mind the intrusion at all. Josh really did appear to be the full package.

'I'll have a pint of bitter, please, and a packet of cheese and onion,' came the next request and I quickly refocused on the job in hand.

'So,' said Sam, as my first shift came to an end and the last of the customers, including George and Skipper, got ready to leave, 'how did you find it?'

'Harder on the feet than I expected,' I admitted and Sam nodded. 'And busier too. I thought it would be dead on a Thursday.'

'Thankfully,' said Sam, 'it's not dead in here on any night of the week now. Tess encouraged me to make lots of changes when she arrived in Wynmouth and even Monday and Tuesday nights have decent footfall now.'

'That goes to show how long it's been since I was a regular then,' I said, shifting from one foot to the other.

And it put a rather different complexion on what I had thought would be a cushy option on the work front, but I had enjoyed my evening. It had kept me from brooding and getting under Mum and Dad's feet and I'd enjoyed chatting with the customers too. And surreptitiously eyeing up Josh, of course.

And talking of Josh.

'Board-game night was a revelation,' he said, grinning, as he joined us at the bar.

'That's a Tuesday night,' Sam clarified for my benefit. 'I won't need you to work that night, but you're welcome to join us, of course. Penny and Nick often come along. They love nothing more than falling out over a game of Scrabble.'

My heart had leapt at the thought of them coming to the pub together, but then sank at the mention of them arguing. Cross words over the Scrabble tiles would not a lasting romance make.

'Thanks for the heads-up. I'll certainly keep it in mind,' I told Sam. 'What's left for me to do tonight?'

'Nothing,' he said, looking around. 'We've kept on top of it all and I'm happy to finish up. Tess won't be too much longer, so you can get off if you like. You did really well tonight, Daisy. I hope you enjoyed it.'

'Thank you.' I blushed. It was a long time since anyone had said something kind about my efforts in the workplace. 'I did.'

'So, you'll be back tomorrow then?'

'I will.'

'It'll be much busier,' he told me.

'Turns out, I like busy,' I was surprised to hear myself say.

'Good,' he laughed, 'because Saturday you'll be rushed off your feet.'

'In that case, I'll probably wear the trainers I used to exercise in then,' I laughed back, as I wriggled my toes. 'See you tomorrow.'

'Night.'

'I'll walk you back to your car if you like,' Josh offered, once we were outside.

'Thanks,' I smiled, 'I'd appreciate that.'

The air felt chilly after the warmth of the pub and I could hear the tide was in by how close the lapping waves sounded to the end of the lane.

'You don't really have to walk with me,' I said when we'd taken a couple of steps and I remembered how close my car was.

The cottage was literally right next to the pub so we were already outside the gate and the car park was just a few yards beyond that.

'I'd like to,' Josh said, looking down at me. 'Unless you'd prefer to come in for a while. For a nightcap, perhaps?'

I could see he'd left a lamp on in the sitting room and the interior of the tiny cottage looked warm, cosy and inviting. The front garden was full of colourful hollyhocks, straight and tall enough to rival those at Wynbrook, and there were poppies too.

'Thank you, but no,' I said rather regretfully. 'I really should get back.'

'Of course,' said Josh, distractedly running a hand through his hair. 'I probably shouldn't have asked. You hardly know me, so—'

'Please don't apologise again,' I cut in.

He grinned at that and I suddenly felt aware that even though we'd only met a couple of times before, and for the briefest of moments on both occasions, it actually felt like I knew him far better than the time we'd spent in each other's company warranted.

'I wasn't asking you in for any nefarious reason,' he then said.

'Well, that's disappointing,' I teased, giving him a nudge. 'I'm even more pleased that I said no, now.'

'I just thought it would be nice to get to know you a little better,' he said, sounding heart-meltingly sincere.

I was delighted that he wanted to and wondered if he already felt as relaxed in my company as I felt in his. Not that being around him wasn't a turn-on. There was a definite spark burning in tandem with the familiarity.

'On any other day I would have accepted your invitation,' I truthfully told him. 'Nefarious or otherwise, but with this being the night of my first shift in the pub, I have a feeling my parents will be waiting up to find out how I've got on and it's way past their bedtime.'

It was the sight of the hollyhocks in the Crow's Nest front garden that had put thoughts of Mum and Dad back in my head.

'You live with them?' Josh asked.

'I do at the moment,' I explained. 'I recently moved back. Just on Monday actually. The day I nearly ran you over. I'm most likely going to be here just for the summer though.'

'Just like me.'

'Just like you.'

'You must get on well with your parents.'

'Um . . .' I said, not wanting to paint too rosy a picture. 'We have our moments. Do you get on with your mum and dad?'

'Um . . .' Josh echoed, with a wry smile. 'We have our moments.'

I grinned at that.

'Do you have far to go?' he asked, with a nod to my car.

We'd made it to the car park now and my tatty vehicle was right where I'd left it. I hoped the interior hadn't got too damp with the window down.

'Just a couple of miles,' I told him. 'They live on a beautiful estate in a tied cottage.'

'That wouldn't be Wynbrook Estate, would it?' Josh asked.

'That's right – Wynbrook Manor. I grew up there. How come you've heard of it?'

'Sam mentioned there's a fruit farm there,' he told me after a moment's hesitation. 'A pick-your-own, I think he called it.'

'That's right, there is. My friend Nick runs it.'

'Sam said the strawberries there are the best in the county.'

'I'm not going to dispute that,' I laughed, remembering the delicious berries I'd earlier sampled. 'You'll have to visit and taste them for yourself.'

'I would love to,' he said, sounding disappointed, 'but I'm without a car here. I didn't fancy hiring one and getting to grips with driving on the wrong side of the road.'

'Given the narrowness of the roads, you'd mostly be driving in the middle,' I pointed out, 'but never mind about your lack of wheels because I'll give you a lift out there one day. That is, if you don't mind slumming it in this old thing.'

I nodded at the car.

'I like your car.' Josh smiled. 'It's very . . . characterful.'

He was doubtless referring to the fact that one of the back doors was a different colour to the rest and the bumper had a dent in it. That hadn't been my doing. The poor car had been assaulted while parked and the assailant had fled the scene without leaving a note.

'That's one way of describing it,' I said, as I began to feel more mindful of the time.

'So, what do your parents do on the estate?' Josh asked. 'I take it they work there if they have a tied cottage?'

'It's getting late, so I'd better tell you another day,' I said. 'It'll be the perfect excuse to carry on our conversation.'

'Do we need an excuse?'

'I suppose not.' I smiled, as I pressed the key fob and wondered why I'd bothered to lock the car when the window was wide open.

Josh took a step closer and my head, heart, tummy and knees all responded in a way I hadn't experienced for a very long time. For one heady moment, I thought he was going to kiss me, but then he leant around me and opened the car door.

'Until next time then,' he said, his breath close to my ear.

'Yes,' I said, slipping into the seat. It did feel a little damp. 'Until next time.'

He waited while I pulled out of the car park, having made a total hash of reversing out of the space, even though there was only one other vehicle parked up and it was miles away from mine. He waved when I reached the bottom of the lane and I flicked my hazards lights on in response. That was a mistake on my part as they then stuck on and I had to drive all the way home with them flashing.

I was surprised to find the cottage in darkness when I arrived home and felt rather aggrieved; had I known Mum and Dad weren't going to wait up for me, I would have accepted Josh's invitation to entertain me.

However, all was not lost because Mum had left a note on the table saying she hoped I'd had a good night and informed me there was a chicken salad sandwich in the fridge if I fancied it. It turned out I did fancy it because her sandwiches were legendary and I was famished. As I retrieved it, I noticed Daniel's postcard had been straightened on the pinboard, which further took the upbeat edge off the end of my evening. I childishly stuck my tongue out at it and headed up to bed, taking the sandwich with me.

'So,' said Mum, peeping around my bedroom door at some ungodly hour the next morning, 'how did it go?'

It had taken me ages to get to sleep. Not because I was mulling over my first few hours as a bartender, but because I couldn't stop thinking about Josh. Both his comfortable familiarity and his potential as summer fling material was appealing: he was only going to be in the area for the season, which suited me just fine, he was very lovely to look at, which was also fine, and he clearly didn't think I was hideous, which was a bonus, and . . .

'Daisy?'

'Sorry,' I said, sitting up and rubbing my eyes.

I remembered too late that I hadn't bothered to wash my mascara off.

'How did you get on?'

'Good,' I said. 'Really good. I'd even got the hang of pulling pints by the end of the shift, so Sam was well pleased. It's not as easy as it looks, you know.'

'I can't say I've ever given the technique much thought.' Mum frowned. 'But that's lovely news. I'm so pleased it went well.'

'Me too.'

'Are you going to get up? Your dad was hoping to see you before he goes to work.'

'I'll be down in a sec,' I told her.

I was surprised to find Dad looking, well, shifty was the only way I could describe his expression when I joined him and Mum in the kitchen after washing my face and pulling on my summer PJs. I felt rather unnerved to find him sporting such an uncharacteristic countenance.

'Mum said your shift went well,' he said, when Mum poked him in the back.

'It did.' I frowned. 'What's going on?'

'Nothing.' He shrugged.

'Your dad's done something foolish,' Mum blurted out at exactly the same time.

Dad closed his eyes and sucked in his bottom lip.

'We're sure it won't come to anything,' Mum carried on, 'but we thought we should, I mean *he* should, tell you, anyway.'

'What have you done, Dad?' I asked apprehensively.

He wrung his hands on the table in front of him while Mum busied herself at the sink.

'Well, over the course of yesterday evening,' he began, sounding as though he was relaying details to the police, 'we had three missed calls to the cottage phone. I picked up twice and it sounded like someone was trying to speak before they hung up and the third time, they just hung up straightaway. There was no way of tracing the number because it hadn't been registered.'

'Right,' I said, drawing the word out.

Mum shook her head and gave Dad a look.

'He assumed—' she started to say but Dad put a hand up to stop her.

'I got it in my head that it was Laurence,' Dad confessed and I let out a groan. 'I thought he was trying to get hold of you, Daisy, and was hanging up when he realised it was me who had answered, not you.'

'It wouldn't have been Laurence, Dad.'

'He knows that now,' Mum did manage to say, 'because Daniel sent a message via WhatsApp a short while after, saying he'd been trying to ring for his usual monthly catch-up, but for some reason he couldn't get the call to connect.'

'So, what's the problem?' I frowned. 'It was Daniel. Mystery solved.'

'The thing is,' Dad swallowed, 'that in the meantime . . . before Daniel's message arrived, I rang Laurence at the flat.'

'You did what?' I burst out.

'I wanted to tell him that we wouldn't mind if he called,' Dad carried on.

'Well, I bloody would!' I snapped.

Mum tutted. She hated any kind of profanity. Even a mild one.

'He didn't answer,' Dad then rushed to say, as if that made all the difference in the world. 'Laurence didn't pick up. There was no reply. And I didn't leave a message.'

'But he now knows that someone has called him from this

number,' I seethed, grinding out the words, 'because it will be logged on the flat phone and he's most likely going to assume that person was me.'

'Yes,' Dad said, nodding. 'I can see how he might end up thinking that.'

'And he's the very last person I want to talk to,' I almost shouted. 'The very last.'

'I could ring again and explain that it was me,' Dad suggested.

'Don't you dare,' I said, trying hard to keep hold of my temper. 'Don't you dare.'

'I'm so sorry,' Dad mumbled.

'And I'm sorry too,' said Mum. 'But that said, if Laurence does call—'

'If Laurence nothing,' I cut in. 'I've reached my limit with you pair now. I can't find another way of telling you that Laurence and I are done. Our relationship is over and if you can't accept that and let me get on with settling back here for the summer and trying to get on with my new job, then I'm . . . then I'll . . . I'll move out. I'll leave.'

'Oh no, Daisy,' Mum sobbed. 'Please don't.'

'Don't do that, love,' pleaded Dad. 'I promise I won't interfere anymore.'

'And I promise I'll make your dad stick to his promise,' Mum added.

'Well, you better,' I said, scraping back my chair. 'Because I've just about reached the end of my rope.'

Had I not been so angry, the role reversal would have been amusing, but I had reached boiling point and there was nothing funny about that, at all.

Chapter 7

I didn't need to be back at the Smuggler's until that evening, but I was too wound up with Dad to want to stay either in the cottage or anywhere on the estate. Not even fruit-basket hunting for Nick would have been capable of distracting me and calming the temper Dad's misguided action had caused to flare. There was only one thing I could think of that would help, so I packed up my car and headed back to the beach hut in Wynmouth.

The sea still felt ice cold, but I welcomed the sting of it on my skin and I swam and swam, way beyond the point that was sensible. That said, by the time I arrived back on the sand and flopped down next to my towel, my lungs were heaving and I was so exhausted there wasn't much space left for my bad mood, so the excessive exercise had obviously helped.

I pulled the towel over my head and silently vowed that all thoughts of Laurence from that moment on, were banished, irrespective of the emotion they carried with them. I would no longer be angry with Dad for telephoning the flat or feel humiliated about Laurence's infidelity. No one other than me knew what he had done and as I hadn't been in love with him

anymore when he did it, the feeling of mortification was hardly
warranted, so I was going to chuck it in the very bottom of
the 'stuff it' bucket and move on.

'Hey, Daisy, are you all right?'

'Josh,' I breathed, as I pulled back the towel and turned my
face to the sun to find him blocking it out.

'You were out there for ages and swimming like fury.' He
frowned. 'Are you okay?'

'Yes,' I said, shifting position so I could pull my towel around
me. 'I'm okay. Well, I am now.'

I suddenly felt more than okay given the timeliness of his
arrival.

'You sure looked like you had something to swim off,' he
astutely observed.

'How very perceptive of you.' I wryly smiled.

'I was going to join you out there, but then thought better
of it.'

I had already taken in that he was wearing shorts and an
open beach shirt. His feet were bare and his tanned legs were
covered in golden hairs, just like his arms. He had a pair of
sandals in one hand and sunglasses pushed up into his hair.

'I appreciate that you didn't,' I said, my breath and heart rate
slowly recovering, in spite of the pulse-raising sight of him.
'Are you going to swim now?'

'That depends,' he said, still looking down at me. 'Do you
feel like company?'

'You know what,' I said, holding out a hand so he could
pull me up. 'I would love company if you have time to spare.'

'I have all the time in the world.'

'In that case, come with me.'

We walked back up the beach to the hut and Josh waited outside while I quickly got dry and changed.

'Are you a tea drinker?' I asked, once I'd pulled on a cotton sundress and knickers and flung my towel and costume over the balustrade to dry in the sun.

'I never used to be,' he grinned, 'but I'm acquiring a taste for it.'

'Good.' I smiled back. 'How do you take it? Your tea, I mean?'

'One sugar,' he laughed, 'and a splash of milk.'

He set up deckchairs while I made the brew and between us, we made short work of the makeshift picnic I'd packed up.

'So,' he said, ripping into a sharing bag of Kettle chips, 'do you wanna talk about whatever it was that got you so riled up that you took to the sea to work off your temper?'

'Absolutely not,' I said, wrinkling my nose. 'But thank you for asking. Anyway, how could you tell that's what I was doing?'

'Oh, I've been there myself,' he said, tipping half of the bag of crisps into a melamine bowl and handing it to me. 'Many times actually, so I recognised the signs. My power swimming has mostly been the result of family drama.'

I put one of the crisps in my mouth and let my tongue absorb the salty hit.

'It was a sort of family drama that kicked my swimming marathon off, too,' I told him, even though I hadn't intended to mention it. 'Well, Dad drama,' I amended.

'Yep,' Josh said, nodding between mouthfuls. 'I can totally relate to that. Most aggro in my life comes from my dad.'

'Mine isn't usually such a pain,' I quickly responded. Josh didn't need to know that Dad and I had had a major fallout in the past or that he had a tendency to let me surreptitiously know what a let-down I was and how my life choices were a disappointment. In truth, I wasn't convinced he always realised he was doing it. 'But I've just ended a relationship and my dad, and my mum actually, thought the world of the guy. They're having a hard time accepting it's over, which led to Dad making a dubious decision and doing something infuriating as a result.'

So much for banishing all thoughts of Laurence! I'd made the vow to forget about him just minutes ago.

'Oh, right,' said Josh, taking a moment to consider what I'd said. 'So, they're more heartbroken about the break-up than you are?'

'I'm not heartbroken at all,' I was quick to answer. 'It was time to end it and I'm relieved to be out of it, even if it has meant I've had to move back in with my parents. Something no twenty-eight-year-old generally wants to have to do.'

'Maybe not,' Josh nodded, looking straight at me, 'but some good has come of it, hasn't it?'

'It has?' I innocently asked, trying to hide my smile, as I twigged what he was getting at. 'Like what?'

'Well,' he said, looking away again as his own lips quirked into a grin, 'let's see. You have access to this beautiful beach to walk on, a hut to lounge in and the sea to swim in for the whole of the summer.'

'That's true.' I nodded, playing along.

'You've just about learned how to pull a pint, which opens up a whole employment sector for you on a global scale should you decide to head overseas in the fall.'

'Also, true,' I agreed, my heart fluttering over how he said fall instead of autumn. On his lips, the word sounded so romantic. 'Anything else?' I blinked.

'Hmm . . .' he said, scratching his head and drawing the sound out, 'I can't think of anything else just at the moment . . .'

'Me neither,' I said with a heavy sigh, as I looked towards the sea and pretended I was as mystified as he was as to what other good thing my timely arrival at home could be associated with. 'If that's all the summer has going for it, it's going to be the worst one ever,' I huffed, biting hard on my lip to stop myself from laughing.

'I feel sorry for you,' he said very seriously and when I looked at him, I could see he was also trying to hold back a laugh. 'I propose a toast to combatting the feeling.' He picked up his mug, which was almost as empty as mine. 'To the worst summer ever and doing whatever it takes to turn it into the best.' He did then laugh as I bashed my mug against his.

'I'm happy to drink to that,' I said, my mind playing out all the possibilities of how we could set about transforming the forthcoming sunny few weeks. 'Here's to the best summer ever.'

Josh was excited to explore the Lilliputian proportions of the beach hut and offered to make the next drink. I stayed put, while he exclaimed over everything in the background and I looked out to the horizon, my eyes dazzled by the sparkling reflection of the sun on the sea.

If Mum and Dad really were now going to properly let the Laurence situation go, then the next couple of months, having uncomplicated fun with Josh, did have the potential to be perfect – and with no ulterior motive.

'Here you go.'

'Thank you,' I said, taking the refilled mug.

'It doesn't look as good as yours,' Josh said, peering into the depths of his own. 'But practice makes perfect, right?'

'So I've been told,' I acquiesced. 'Unfortunately, I seem to have developed this habit of giving up on things before I've been practising them for very long.'

'What sort of things?' Josh asked, as he carefully lowered himself back into his deckchair.

'Well,' I said, 'in all the years I've been working since I left home, I haven't found a job that's the right fit yet. My record for sticking at something is far less than a year.'

'I daresay that's only because you still haven't found the thing you love,' Josh kindly said. 'When the right thing comes along, you'll know it and you won't want to give it up.'

That seemed to be a popular opinion and I hoped it was the right one. I had already loved and lost one thing I thought I could go the distance working at and I wasn't sure I'd find another, no matter how long or hard I searched.

'What about you?' I asked, not wanting to dwell. 'Have you found a career you love? How have you managed to wangle a whole summer away from work?'

Josh puffed out his cheeks and took a deep breath.

'Don't feel obliged to answer that,' I said quickly, when I realised I'd put him on the spot. 'I'm just being nosy.'

Given that I was only sizing him up as a summer fling, I didn't need to know every little thing about him, did I?

'Well, let's just say, I was definitely due some time off and decided to take it all in one go.'

'And somehow, you ended up here,' I said, looking at the beach again, rather than asking what he was taking time off from.

'I ended up here,' he repeated.

'I know I've already mentioned the lack of things to do and see here,' I reminded him, 'and there really are far more thrilling places in the UK to spend your summer than Wynmouth, especially if you haven't got a car.'

'And like I said,' he smoothly responded, holding my gaze, 'this place might be quiet and quaint, but it has its attractions.'

I felt myself turning much warmer than the sun could take the credit for.

'I have strawberries,' I said, jumping up because I didn't want to get swept along too soon. The summer had barely started, after all. 'From Wynbrook.'

I went to grab them, along with the beach hut sugar canister and cream I'd pilfered from the cottage.

'The famous Wynbrook Manor Estate,' Josh said thoughtfully, taking the bowl that I'd doled half of the succulent, ruby-coloured berries into.

'I'm not sure it's famous,' I said, as I sprinkled half a teaspoon of sugar over the top.

'Well,' he smiled, adding a hefty dollop of cream to my bowl and then his, 'tell me about it anyway. I want to hear all about the idyllic childhood you must have had there. I can't imagine what it must have been like to grow up in one place.'

'You didn't?' I frowned.

'I did not. My dad moved us around a whole lot while he was getting himself established in my mom's family business and setting up offices in different states. We were never in the same place for long.'

'That must have been difficult,' I said, trying to imagine it. 'How did you maintain friendships?'

'I didn't.' He shrugged. 'It was impossible to put down roots or feel settled anywhere. Nowhere felt like home and I'm an only child, so it was lonely at times.'

'That sounds terrible.'

I might have had some issues with my parents, but at least I had always had the comfort of somewhere special and permanent to call home.

'Sometimes it was terrible,' Josh confirmed, 'but I got to see a lot of the US while I was growing up.'

'Your accent,' I said with a frown. 'I can't place it.'

'Yeah,' he laughed, 'not even I can pin it to any one place because of the constant moving about during my formative years.'

'That makes sense,' I said, taking the first bite of a strawberry and closing my eyes in pleasure as the intense flavour from childhood flooded my tastebuds.

'Oh my god,' Josh rapturously groaned, making my eyes spring open again, as he also bit into one. 'These are heaven sent.'

'That they are,' I agreed. 'That they are.'

We spent the entire day at the hut. I told Josh all about life on the Wynbrook Estate. How Algy was a wonderful employer and friend to everyone who lived there, what my parents' roles were, and Nick's, and how much of a challenge it was to keep a traditional estate and fruit farm running with dwindling local staff and stiff supermarket competition. I might have been out of the loop when it came to news from home, but that much I did know.

In turn, Josh told me some more about his life in America, but not in any great detail. I didn't mind that though. I didn't need to know the ins and out of his entire life – even if he seemed keen to absorb mine – if he was only going to be a summer fling and a welcome distraction from living back with Mum and Dad.

The most important thing I needed to know was that he wasn't already in a relationship. He told me he had been single for quite some time but didn't elaborate, which suited me. I did wonder if he might have commitment issues as a result of his untethered childhood and lack of friends, but that didn't matter to me either. Josh was easy-going company and fun to be around and that more than satisfied what I was temporarily looking for.

We swam together in the afternoon and I had a hard time keeping pace with him. I put that down to the fact that I'd exhausted myself earlier in the day and not because he was a stronger swimmer than I was.

'Damn,' I said, when we went back to the huts to dry off and I realised how late it was. 'I'll never get back to the cottage for a shower before work now.'

I was surprised by how quickly the day had flashed by. I'd never spent such a contented amount of time in the company of a stranger before and it was further confirmation that Josh and I were already getting along wonderfully well.

'You're welcome to shower at mine,' he offered, shaking his head and spraying me with droplets of freezing sea water as it flew out of his hair.

'Don't!' I yelped, but I was laughing. 'No, it'll be fine. I'll see if Penny's at home. I keep forgetting that she has a cottage in the village now. Come on, let's go.'

It was long after four, so I hoped she would be.

'Damn,' I swore, when she didn't answer her door. 'She must still be at school.'

'Look,' said Josh, who had walked up to her cottage with me. 'I need to head to the shops for some supplies, so why don't you take the key to mine and then leave it under the pot on the step when you're done?'

'Are you sure that would be okay?' I asked, taking the key before he'd replied.

'Absolutely,' he said. 'Go on. I won't see you at the pub tonight, but I'll be in tomorrow.'

I was disappointed to hear that, but there was no time to wallow over his absence with the clock to my next shift ticking.

'All right,' I said. 'Thanks, Josh.'

There was no time to linger in the cottage either, which was every bit as beautiful on the inside as it was picturesque on the outside. There was very little evidence of Josh's occupancy, but I did enjoy using his hair products and shower gel. At least he was going to be with me in spirit throughout the evening.

'I'm here, I'm here, I'm here!' I laughed, when I tripped into the pub, just a few minutes after my starting time and with my hair still damp from the shower.

'Hey, there,' said the woman behind the bar, whom I recognised as Tess. 'You must be Daisy.'

'That's right,' I said, quickly stowing my bag away and trying not to notice that the clock was telling me that I was a quarter of an hour late, rather than just the few minutes I thought I had been. 'I'm sorry I'm late.'

'I'm sorry about that too,' said Sam as he rushed through from the kitchen carrying plates. 'Don't make a habit out of it, okay?'

'I won't.' I swallowed, feeling my face flush. 'I'll clear those tables, shall I?'

'That's what you're here for,' he huffed. 'Tess, why don't you head back to the kitchen now Daisy's turned up?'

'On my way,' she said with a nod.

She gave me an encouraging smile as she went, but I knew I was already on thin ice and that I needed to focus on my hours working in the pub every bit as intently as I had just been absorbed with Josh if I was going to make the best of all that this summer had to offer.

Chapter 8

Friday evening in the pub had been busy, but it was nothing compared to the number of people who crammed themselves in for the live music night on the Saturday. I purposefully turned up an hour earlier than Sam had requested because I was keen to make amends for arriving late the evening before. Had I not been so early, I never would have got parked, so that was something to bear in mind where my timekeeping was concerned.

'I really am sorry about being late yesterday,' I apologised again as soon as I stepped behind the bar.

Sam had barely said a word to me during the entire Friday shift, but with a steady stream of customers to serve, there hadn't really been time to chat. I was probably making too much of his assumed bad mood, but thought it was wise to make amends. The last thing I needed was to pee off the boss just two shifts in.

'Well, you're here well ahead of your time tonight.' He smiled, looking more like his usual relaxed self.

'I'm not expecting you to pay me an extra hour though,' I quickly qualified.

'That's all right then,' he laughed. 'It would be great if you could help Tess get ahead in the kitchen until things get more frantic out here.'

It seemed pretty full-on to me already, so he was obviously expecting a really full house.

'Happy to,' I said, hoping there was an apron large enough to cover the dress I'd decided to wear.

'Oh, wow, Daisy,' Tess said, smiling, when I joined her in the already hot kitchen. 'You look gorgeous. I love that dress. Grab an apron from the back of the door.'

'Thank you,' I said gratefully. 'I was hoping you'd have one that would cover it.'

The black, floaty skater dress, which was covered in different-sized gold stars, was my absolute favourite. I'd had it for ages, but hadn't worn it for a while because Laurence hadn't deemed it formal enough for evenings out. Not that I was thinking about those or him.

'I thought it might be nice to make an effort as it's an event night,' I added, as I adjusted the apron straps to ensure maximum coverage.

That wasn't entirely true. The deciding factor in picking it out had been knowing that Josh was going to be putting in an appearance and that the dress would give me an extra dose of confidence.

I'd taken my time over my hair and make-up too, which had the added bonus of keeping me in my room and out of Mum and Dad's way. We were still skirting around each other a bit after Dad's telephone blunder and I knew they were both still worried that Laurence might call the cottage. The terrified look on Dad's face every time the phone rang was a dead giveaway and I hoped things between us would shake down soon. An atmosphere of underlying tension wouldn't be good for any of us while we were trying to get used to living together again.

'Well,' said Tess, who looked hot and flustered as she worked away in front of the searing stove, 'you've put me to shame.'

That hadn't been my intention and what she was wearing looked lovely too.

'Give me an hour in here with you,' I said, deciding not to comment on her outfit in case she assumed I was only offering her a compliment because she'd given me one, 'and I won't look anything like as uncrumpled. Now, what can I do?'

I was assigned simple salad prep, but didn't get to spend the whole hour in the kitchen as Sam needed me in the bar so he could help finish setting up the inside and outdoor areas where the musicians were going to perform. The first half of the evening was happening outside, with a local band playing and the second half was going to be an indoor open mic event. I wasn't sure Wynmouth had that many musicians of note, so that was going to be interesting as well as entertaining.

'Bear with me, folks,' I said desperately, when I looked up and realised how many people were waiting to be served, while Sam was still busy elsewhere. 'This is literally my third night on the job.'

My nerves frustratingly got the better of me once I'd seen the queue and the next two pints I attempted to pour were all froth.

'You're all right,' said the guy at the head of the queue, while he patiently waited for me to have another go. 'Don't stress. No one's in a rush.'

I appreciated his patience and the next attempt was perfect.

'Thanks,' I said, flashing him a smile as I handed over the glass. 'You're very kind.'

'We all have to learn.' He shrugged. 'Keep the change.'

With my confidence restored, I'd only got two couples waiting when Sam finally made it back.

'Sorry about that,' he had to practically shout to make himself heard. 'It took longer than I expected. You've done well to keep on top of everything, Daisy.'

'I nearly didn't,' I called back, but there was no opportunity to elaborate.

By the time the band had set up and were ready to play in the small garden at the back of the pub, my feet were on fire and I was desperate to swap out the shoes I'd ignored Sam's words of wisdom to wear for my comfy trainers again.

'You were warned,' he chuckled, when he spotted what I was doing.

'I know,' I said, having taken a few seconds to stand barefoot on the cool wooden floor and let my toes unclench. 'And it's a lesson learned. I think the trainers look better with the dress anyway.'

I wished I'd had the gumption to realise that when I'd got dressed back at home.

'Textbook Daisy,' I heard Penny laugh, while I was bent over tying the laces. 'She's always been the same. She always has to do things the hard way.'

'How dare you!' I pouted, pretending to be affronted, as I stood back up.

Penny had a twinkle in her green eyes and a smile on her full lips.

'You're going to dispute that, are you?' she challenged me.

'No,' I huffed, knowing full well all of the occasions she could reel off to prove me wrong.

'I should think not,' she laughed.

'What can I get you?' I asked. 'Are you going to have a drink or have you just come in here to tell tales about me?'

'I'll have a pint of Wherry, please.' She grinned.

'And I'll pull it,' said Sam, stepping in. 'Daisy's having mixed results at the pumps tonight.'

'I thought I was doing all right,' I said, deflating a little. 'I tipped a couple away earlier, but the rest have been okay, haven't they?'

'You're getting there,' was as much as Sam was willing to say and I guessed I wasn't quite up to the professional barkeeping standard just yet. 'Why don't you take a break while the band's playing? It'll probably be the only chance you get.'

'Okay,' I said keenly, filling up a glass with ice and water for myself. 'I'm happy to take a load off for a few minutes. Do you want to listen to the band, Pen?'

'No,' she said, looking me up and down as I came out from behind the bar, 'let's grab a table while it's quiet. I love that dress, by the way. Is it new?'

'No,' I told her, letting out a breath as I flopped on to a chair. 'But those dungarees are, aren't they?'

With her slightly fuller figure they looked perfect on her and the pattern was as bright and cheering as she was.

'You know I can't resist Lucy and Yak,' she said with a grin. 'You were saying about the dress?'

'Oh, I've had it for ages,' I vaguely elaborated, 'but I thought I'd give it an airing tonight.'

'Any particular reason why?' Penny asked with emphasis, while looking at me wide-eyed over the top of her pint. 'Any *person* in particular?'

'What's that supposed to mean?' I demanded, narrowing my own eyes.

'I can't help wondering,' she said, 'if you've made an extra effort for the benefit of our American visitor?'

'Who?' I frowned.

She shook her head in disbelief.

'From what I can make out,' she carried on, 'half the village is totally smitten with him and he's all anyone can talk about at the school pick-up.'

'You're not ringing any bells,' I blagged, pretending that I hadn't even heard of any such American.

She let out a bark of laughter.

'Liar, liar,' she giggled. 'I know for a fact that you're aware of who I'm talking about because you spent the whole day on the beach with him yesterday.'

My mouth fell open in shock.

'Don't look like that,' she tutted. 'He's the hot goss right now, and as a result of your beach frolics, so are you.'

'There was no frolicking,' I tutted back. 'And we weren't on the beach the whole day. We spent some time in the Wynbrook beach hut too.'

'Did you now?'

'And in the sea,' I added, with a smile I couldn't suppress. 'We had a picnic and a chat. That's all. Don't forget I'm literally just days out of a long-term relationship, so you can keep your summer fling speculating to yourself.'

I might have been speculating as well, but I wasn't about to make that common knowledge. Not even to one of my best friends.

'Who said anything about a summer fling?' Penny laughed.

'Nick did,' I batted back. 'And you two seem pretty chatty these days, so I know you'll have had your heads together and discussed it.'

She didn't comment about that.

'You might only be days out of a long-term relationship,' she said instead, 'but it was one that you were glad to see the back of.'

She had a point.

'Anyway,' I countered, 'how can you accuse me of being dressed up for Josh when he isn't even here tonight?'

'Oh, Josh, is it?' Penny said in a teasing tone.

'You know it is,' I nudged. 'Are you smitten with him too?'

'You must be joking,' she spluttered. 'I haven't got time to wash my hair, let alone be smitten with anyone. My work–life balance is totally shot so I've no time for romance.'

I couldn't help thinking that taking over Sophie's beach café for the summer wasn't going to help her address that balance.

'Tell me about the café,' I said, as keen to know the details as I was to change the subject. 'Is it open now Sophie's away? I haven't been along the beach that way.'

The café was situated on the opposite side of the beach to the huts and so far, I hadn't walked along the shore in that direction.

'No,' said Penny, 'it's closed at the moment, but I've been in today to check the fridge and freezer are running as they should be and as there's quite a bit of stock in, I've decided I'm going to open it for a while tomorrow.'

I didn't think that was a good idea.

'Are you sure you can manage it?' I asked cautiously. 'You've still got two days left in school, haven't you?'

'Yes,' she said, 'the term ends on Tuesday, but we're only tidying up, playing games and watching films now. Thankfully nothing too taxing.'

'What about inset training?'

'That's scheduled for September, and I'll get the classroom ready then too. I'll be opening the café properly next Wednesday and then carrying on until Sophie returns. It's always been closed on a Monday and Tuesday, but I might open in the afternoons if the beach is busy. Thankfully, all I've got to do is walk down the lane to decide.'

'Your proximity to the beach will be a bonus,' I agreed, 'but I'm worried that you're going to burn yourself out.'

'You sound like Nick.' Penny smiled, nudging me. 'He's worried about it too, but I can't wait to get started. Sophie has agreed that I can add a couple of my own dishes to the menu.'

She did sound excited and I had no desire to dampen her enthusiasm. Her taking the café on was obviously more than a whim.

'Well,' I smiled, 'I look forward to seeing you behind the counter and sampling what you've come up with. You can count on my business, that's for sure.'

'You'll have to bring Josh along,' she suggested and I rolled my eyes.

'I'm sure Josh can find his own way,' I responded. 'Besides, who knows, I might never bump into him again.'

I knew I would, but I was trying hard to play down how I felt about him. Given that I was only days out of one relationship, I was rather floored that I had already met someone who might make me consider another – even if it was only going to be brief.

'Er,' said Penny, 'I think you might bump into him.'

She gave me another nudge and I looked up just as Josh came bowling through the door with a guitar slung over one shoulder and, with terrifying tale-telling George, and his dog, Skipper, hot on his heels.

'Looks like you've got competition,' Penny said in a singsong voice and with a nod to George. I dug her in the ribs with my elbow. 'Ow,' she protested.

'I'd better get back to work,' I said, standing up and read-justing my dress. 'We must have been longer than the few minutes Sam said I could take.'

I wished I had a mirror to look in, but I wasn't going to ask Penny if she had one in her bag, otherwise I'd never hear the end of it.

'You look lovely,' she said softly and I gave her a grateful smile.

'Good evening, guys,' I said to both Josh and George, 'what can I get you?'

Josh was looking at George as I stepped behind the bar, so he didn't get the benefit of seeing me in my darling dress, but I did note how good he looked in his jeans and a navy shirt. The colour was the perfect foil for his tan and he smelt wonderful too.

'Hey Daisy,' he said, looking rather flustered when he turned to me, 'a word with Sam, if he's not too busy.'

'I've got a minute to talk,' said Sam, appearing with perfect timing. 'Have you pair made up your minds then?'

'We have,' George said decisively.

I didn't get the opportunity to hear what they'd decided about, as the band outside finished their set to rapturous cheers and applause and the bar started to fill up again. I collected as many empty glasses as I could find, while Sam and Tess worked the bar seamlessly between them.

'Nice,' said Penny, giving a surreptitious thumbs-up behind Josh's back when I reached the table closest to hers.

'Who's nice?' asked Nick, who she hadn't realised had crept up behind her.

She leapt as high as the low-beamed ceiling and I laughed. 'Serves you right,' I giggled.

'Daisy!' called Sam, sounding flustered. 'Can you give us a hand?'

I quickly deposited the empty glasses and started serving. I hoped he hadn't thought I'd gone over to Penny to have another chat.

'And last, but by no means least, we have a very special final act for this evening,' Sam announced over the speaker an hour or so later.

Given the calibre of a few of the local acts who had taken a turn at the mic, I thought that *special* might be a bit of a stretch, but then, who was I to judge? I'd never have had the courage to stand up and sing in front of a packed pub, even if I could hold a note. Which I couldn't.

'This is their debut duet,' Sam carried on, 'so please give a warm welcome to . . . George and Josh!'

I spun around and looked at the tiny raised platform where the brave participants had been performing and saw Josh step up, looking green around the gills, and George, appearing as confident and poised as always. He stretched out his fingers in front of the keyboard, while Josh adjusted the strap of his guitar.

'Did you know?' Penny, who was sitting where she'd been all evening, only now with Nick, mouthed at me.

'No,' I mouthed back, shrugging my shoulders.

'Hey,' Josh said shakily into the microphone and I felt my heart swoop. 'How you all doing this evening?'

There was a cheer from one of the women in the audience, which made a few of the other customers laugh and left me in no doubt of Josh's popularity.

'George and I thought we'd play a song you might already know,' he said more confidently. 'We hope you like it. Join in if you know the words.'

I was mesmerised as I watched him take a breath and swallow and when he started to play the opening bars of 'Better Together' by Jack Johnson, it was a struggle not to cry. I couldn't risk looking at Penny again. She knew how much I loved the song, courtesy of a teacher we'd had at primary school who had introduced our class to the *In Between Dreams* album. This particular song was subsequently always played on Leavers' Day and at various assemblies throughout the year and I'd loved it ever since.

Josh's playing was perfect and his voice had a quality similar to Jack's, while George's accompaniment on the keyboard took the performance to an all-time emotional high. The pair of them, one older, one younger, performing so wonderfully together, was enchanting.

The bar was completely silent when they finished, aside from a few sniffs and Josh looked around, a frown forming.

'We thought—' he started to say, but was instantly drowned out by a sudden cacophony of clapping and foot stomping.

'Again!' someone shouted.

'Play it again!' someone else joined in and within seconds, everyone was demanding an encore.

I did cry then. I couldn't stop the tears flowing as Josh grinned and George doffed his trademark hat. Throughout the second rendition everyone joined in, swaying if they were seated, dancing if they were on their feet and we all sang along. The third and final time, Josh barely took his eyes off me and I knew I'd never wanted to be with someone more.

'Oh my god,' cried Pen, once she'd made her way to me, her mascara as smudged as mine when Josh and George were finally able to leave the stage. 'Did he know that was your favourite song?'

'No,' I said, trying to sound more together than I felt. 'We've never talked about music. We've hardly talked about anything at all, really.'

'It's fate,' she insisted, taking my hands and holding them in hers. 'That's what this is. You two are destined to be together.'

'I don't know about that,' I laughed, though I was actually inclined to hope she was right, even if only in the short term, 'but I do know that if I don't start pulling pints soon, we'll be stuck in here all night.'

I made my way to the bar and served as many of the extremely happy crowd as I could. I'd lost sight of Josh, but I could see George's hat bobbing about and everyone wanted to buy the pair of them a drink.

'That,' I said to George, a while later, after he'd finally soaked up all the praise and reached the bar himself, 'was phenomenal.'

'It did go down rather well, didn't it?' he agreed. 'Josh has the most amazing voice.'

'He certainly does,' I sighed dreamily, thinking I could have listened to him all evening. 'Where is he?'

'Outside cooling off.' George grinned. 'He made some excuse about ducking out to take his guitar back to the cottage. I think everyone's reaction rather took him by surprise.'

'I wouldn't mind booking the pair of you as a main act at some point in the future,' said Sam, who had come over to join us.

'In that case,' George laughed as Josh walked back in looking flushed, 'we'd better add a few more songs to our setlist.'

'Oh, I don't know,' said Sam, 'I reckon you could have played that one a dozen times over and everyone would have still wanted to hear it again.'

'What did you think of it, Daisy?' Josh asked, fixing me again with his beguiling eyes. 'Did you like it?'

'I loved it,' I gulped, looking right back at him. With me behind the bar and him in front of it, we were face to face and I had to resist the urge to pull him across it and kiss the lips off him. 'I've always loved it and you played it so beautifully, every time.'

He looked choked when I said that and I couldn't believe he had no idea how talented he was.

'I told you,' said George, giving him a wink. 'And now Sam wants to book us properly.'

Josh looked astounded.

'You do?' he croaked.

'Absolutely,' said Sam. 'The pair of you will pack this place out.'

'What do you say?' George asked Josh.

'I don't know,' he said hesitantly. 'I need to think about it.'

As far as I was concerned there was nothing to think about, but he obviously had his reasons and I didn't want to pry. Well, I did, but not in front of everyone else.

'Crikey,' said Sam, 'look at the time. You'd better head home, Daisy.'

'I don't mind helping you clear up,' I offered.

'No,' he insisted, 'it's fine. You get off.'

'And I'm going too,' said George, looking around for Skipper. 'I need my beauty sleep if I'm going to be performing music as well as telling terrifying tempest-tossed tales.'

I laughed when he said that.

'That's right, isn't it?' he twinkled.

'It was definitely something like that.' I smiled, gathering up my bag with my discarded shoes in it.

'I didn't get the chance to say earlier,' Josh said, as I joined him on the other side of the bar, 'but you look really pretty tonight, Daisy.'

I wondered how much of my make-up was left. Probably not a lot, given my earlier teary moment, so I most likely looked less pretty than I had.

'Thank you,' I nonetheless graciously said.

'I'll walk you back to your car,' he then offered. 'Unless, you'd like me to walk back with you, George?'

'No, no, dear boy,' George said, waving the suggestion away. 'You carry on.'

I had a feeling Josh and I weren't going to make it as far as my car.

Chapter 9

'Would you like to come in?' Josh asked, when we reached the cottage gate.

I didn't have to think about my answer.

'I would,' I said, looking straight at him, 'but only for a quick breather before I have to drive home.'

I held his gaze long enough to communicate that might not be strictly true and that I was only saying it for the benefit of everyone else who had left the pub at the same time as us and were also walking along the lane.

'Perfect,' he said and grinned as he ushered me down the short path to the door. 'The cottage is the ideal place to cool off in before your drive.'

Neither of us said another word as he turned the key in the lock. We crossed the threshold, Josh slammed the door behind us, drew the curtains and then we fell into each other's arms.

'Josh,' I gasped, as his mouth urgently sought out mine.

The feel of his lips on my neck, the heat of his hands as they ran their way over the thin fabric of my dress and the urgency with which I started to tug at his shirt buttons, expressed a mutual intensity of desire that I had never experienced before.

My body took over and I gave in to its craving completely. The first time on the tiny sitting-room sofa and the second, more tenderly upstairs in the brass-framed bed and then again, in the roll-top bath that was barely big enough for two, but we laughingly managed to squeeze into it anyway.

It was hardly surprising that we then fell into the bed and a deep sleep after such monumental exertion. It wasn't quite dawn when I woke, my muscles pleasantly aching, and I found I had absolutely no desire to leave. I hoped Mum and Dad hadn't already noted my absence, but I decided to err on the side of caution, albeit a little belatedly.

I tiptoed down the stairs, smiling at the puddles of abandoned clothes littering my path and sought out my phone. There were no panicky missed calls, so I sent Mum a text explaining that I'd stayed over in the village. With any luck, she'd assume I was with Penny. I then crept back up the stairs, took a moment to admire Josh's beautiful body, then snuggled up close to him and drifted back into a dreamless sleep.

'Good morning, sleepyhead,' were the words that I eventually resurfaced to, and they were accompanied by the delicious aroma of fresh coffee and warm pastries. 'Do you intend to sleep through the entire day?'

I inched myself up higher in the bed and rearranged the pillows behind my head as Josh set the tray down on the kicked-back duvet. He was naked from the waist up – a total treat for a Sunday morning. Assuming it was still morning . . .

'I don't much want to get out of bed,' I told him, with a smile, 'but that doesn't necessarily mean that I want to sleep.'

He looked delighted about that.

'In that case,' he said, 'let's get some carbs and coffee into us and see where the day takes us, shall we?'

'Sounds good to me,' I agreed.

A lot more than half of the day had gone by the time we made it downstairs.

'Everything okay?' Josh asked, as I checked my phone.

I'd had a reply from Mum.

'Yes,' I told him. 'Just my mum checking in.'

'That's nice.'

'Does yours check in with you?'

'No,' he said, 'not all that often, but I'm not great at keeping in touch with her either.'

He didn't seem to want to extend the talk about his family, which was fine because I didn't want to spend the day discussing mine either.

'Have you thought anymore about performing in the pub again?' I asked, to change the subject. 'George seemed keen.'

Josh looked at me and cocked his head.

'And when exactly would I have had time in the last few hours to think about that?' he asked with a wicked grin. 'I've been somewhat occupied since I hung up my guitar last night, haven't I?'

'Oh, yes,' I consented as I crossed the room, draped my arms around his neck and kissed him on the lips. 'So you have.'

There wasn't a muscle in my body that wasn't feeling the impact of the last few hours now, but as Josh kissed me back and I pressed myself even closer to him, I knew I was more than willing to put them through their paces again.

'And you've done wonders for supporting Anglo–American relations in those hours,' I said between kisses.

'Is that right?'

'It is.'

'In that case,' he said, lifting me off my feet in one smooth movement, 'let's keep the momentum going, shall we?'

When Josh later turned on some music in the cottage, I couldn't suppress the desire to track back to the subject of his playing in the pub.

'I still can't believe how surprised you looked by everyone's reaction last night,' I told him. 'Your performance was flawless so it was never going to be received by anything other than rapturous applause.'

Josh didn't appear convinced.

'Why do you look like you still can't believe it happened?' I asked him.

'Because I can't, I suppose,' he simply said, as he joined me on the sofa and I draped my bare feet over his lap.

I was wearing one of his T-shirts and felt relieved I still had time to go home ahead of my next shift in the pub. It wouldn't stem any gossip if I was seen wearing the dress I had on last night, especially as I knew, thanks to my conversation with Penny, how minutely Josh and I were being scrutinised.

'But why not?' I probed.

'Because,' Josh sighed, returning to the topic of family, 'in the past, my love of music and the desire I once had to play professionally didn't go down well with my father. My love of music was sidelined by him as a frivolous pastime, a total waste of time and effort.'

My eyes widened in surprise.

'A waste of time,' I echoed, thinking that was the last way I would have described Josh's obvious talent.

'Yes,' Josh said. 'You see, my father has a hatred of anything creative being taken up professionally. He considers it too much of a risk. He's only interested in making money from high-earning, straightforward careers, guaranteed investments and business opportunities.'

'I see,' I said.

I already knew I wouldn't like Josh's dad and that he was nothing like him. Laurence, however, was cut from a very similar materialistic cloth. Not that I was entertaining thoughts about him, but the similarity with Josh's dad had struck a chord and he'd annoyingly popped into my head.

'When I was growing up,' Josh continued, 'I wanted to be a musician. I was obsessed with learning to play the guitar and practised for hours on end . . .'

'But your father didn't encourage you?'

Josh laughed at that.

'I wouldn't call cutting the strings on your son's beloved guitar as showing encouragement, would you?'

'Please don't tell me he really did that!' I gasped.

'Yes,' Josh said, nodding, and I felt utterly horrified by the image which came with it. 'He did.'

My heart broke for him. No wonder he'd been taken aback by everyone's reaction in the pub if he'd only ever encountered such negativity to his playing before. His father sounded like a total monster. It was hardly any wonder that Josh was so happy to be staying in an entirely different country to him.

'What a total shit,' I couldn't stop myself from saying. 'Sorry.'

Dad and I might have had our differences in the past, but they hadn't run to anything as intense as Josh had experienced.

Or was that the benefit of time elapsed that was making me think that? I decided it was best not to ponder.

'No, you're fine.' Josh smiled. 'He's certainly that.'

'So, what gave you the courage to play last night?'

Given what he'd previously experienced, it was an incredibly brave thing to do.

'George. He pointed out that no one around here knows me, so why not go for it? I couldn't argue with his logic and thought I'd just do it and see what happened.'

'Thank goodness for George.' I grinned.

'It had been so long since I'd played,' Josh carried on. 'Dad had completely knocked the enthusiasm for it out of me, but when I mentioned to George that I travelled with my guitar and was hoping to take some time to find myself while I was here . . .'

His words trailed off and his face flushed.

'Go on,' I said gently.

'I know that sounds lame.' He blushed. 'A total cliché—'

'No,' I cut in vehemently. 'It really doesn't. You know, I'm a bit lost myself, so I get it. I really do. What did George say?'

I was discovering that he was full of wisdom.

'Well, he pointed out that I hadn't travelled all this way with my guitar not to play it and he was right.'

'It must have been a cumbersome piece of luggage to haul about,' I considered.

'It was, but I truly had planned to play it at some point. George, however, and the serendipitous opportunity to perform in the pub, rather sped the process along. He had me practising for hours and last night was the result. I'd shared with George my father's antipathy and he in turn told me he'd battled enough bullies in his life to know that succeeding was the best way to beat them. That man has given me more support in just a few days than my own father has in a lifetime.'

He sounded rather choked about that, which was understandable.

'Well, hooray for George!' I said light-heartedly, wanting to lift Josh's mood again and as my mobile started to ring.

'Hooray indeed,' Josh agreed and handed me my phone from the coffee table.

'It's my friend Penny,' I said, having looked at the screen. 'I better answer. Hey, Pen, what's—'

'Oh, thank god you've picked up!' she interrupted, sounding desperate. 'I need your help, Daisy! Where are you?' She bowled on before I could tell her. 'I'm at the café and I can't serve everyone. Can you come? Nick has got no one helping him at the fruit farm as usual, so he can't leave Wynbrook and I don't know what to do!'

'It's fine,' I said, swinging my legs around and standing up. 'Don't panic. I'm actually really close and I'm on my way.'

'Thank god!' she said, letting out a breath. 'That's great. Please hurry up!'

'What's up?' Josh asked, as I jumped up.

'I really need to help Penny in the beach café,' I told him as I looked down at the T-shirt I was wearing. 'She's completely swamped and it's only her first day. I don't suppose you've got a pair of shorts that might fit me, have you?'

Penny was up to her elbows in panini orders by the time I got to the café. I was still wearing my dress from the night before because Josh had absolutely nothing I could wear or adapt in the limited time I had before she called again and berated me for taking so long to get there.

'You're an absolute lifesaver,' she said, dropping her order pad and squeezing me hard when I finally rushed in. 'Now, go and wash your hands and tie your hair up and I'll tell you what I need you to do.'

She was in full-on teacher mode and I didn't dare contradict her. Thankfully, she was too flustered to notice what I was wearing and I quickly covered the dress up with an embroidered Sunshine Café apron.

'I need you to sort drinks and lollies,' she instructed, 'and I'll do the food. It's card payments only today and the gadget is really easy to use.'

She quickly showed me how to work it, even though I had already got the hang of using the one in the pub, and she then disappeared into the kitchen.

'Is that everything?' I asked the impatient-looking guy at the front of the queue.

'Yes,' he snapped, 'and please hurry up, they're melting.'

There was a board next to the counter with all of the prices listed on it, so my job wasn't rocket science, but it was stressful. More stressful than working in the pub because there was currently a multitude of fractious toddlers and moody teens to cope with in the café.

The next three hours passed in a blur and I felt hot and sweaty as the summer sun beat down on the café roof and through the open windows and door, so goodness knows how hot and bothered Penny had got in the kitchen.

'Right,' she said when there was a lull, marching through

having checked the freezers and finding them completely depleted, 'that's it. I'm closing.'

She quickly switched the sign on the door from open to closed before more customers descended, then firmly shut it, locked it and pulled down the blinds.

'We can't stay open if we've nothing to sell and there's barely a crust or an ice cream in the place now,' she pointed out, to justify her decision even though she didn't need to.

'Where did everyone spring from?' I asked, fanning myself with a menu from one of the indoor tables.

'There were a couple of coach trips from Wynbridge way today, apparently,' she said wearily. 'A run out to the coast to recharge the batteries.'

A few curls had escaped her ponytail and were clinging to her face and her skin was glowing. I couldn't imagine this was the introduction to running the café she had wanted and decided not to comment. However, it turned out that she was far more buoyant than I would have been in her position.

'We did it,' she laughed, holding up a hand for me to high five, the second she'd recovered her good humour. 'If I can survive a manic Sunday rush like that, I can survive anything.'

I had to admire her resilience.

'I know I probably sounded a bit panicked when I called and asked you to help,' she confessed.

'Hardly surprising given the number of customers you had when I got here,' I said, 'and you found a way around the problem, didn't you? You called me.'

'Exactly,' she beamed. 'And when I open again, I'll make sure I have everything prepped in advance. That's what scuppered me today. I think Sophie does all the fruit and veg prep and so on before she opens the door.'

'You're going to have to put in a huge order to be delivered before Wednesday. Assuming you're still planning to start then.'

Personally, I thought she should take a break before opening the café again, but I kept quiet.

'Um,' she said, thinking. 'I'll have to log on to Sophie's ordering system and see what I can get delivered in time, won't I?'

'It might be a bit of a squeeze, time-wise,' I grimaced. 'What with you being at school until the end of Tuesday.'

'Damn,' she tutted. 'I won't be around to take delivery, will I?'

'I could be though,' I offered, not wanting to dampen her enthusiasm if she really was that determined to go straight from school teacher to café manager. 'If you give me a list of what you're expecting, I could be here to tick it off and unpack it, couldn't I?'

'Would you?' she gasped. 'That would be a huge help.'

'Of course,' I said. 'I won't be in the pub then, so it doesn't matter when it comes. Oh my god!' I then gasped. 'The pub! What time is it?'

I wrenched the apron over my head and Penny's mouth fell open.

'Where exactly were you when I called?' she asked, taking in the state of my crumpled dress.

'No time to explain,' I told her, feeling flustered and then hot as memories of the night before in Josh's arms, Josh's bed, Josh's bath, crowded in. 'I need to get home to shower and change. I'm going to be late for work *again*,' I squealed.

'Go to my place,' Penny said calmly, reaching behind the counter for her cottage keys. 'You can get showered there and go through my wardrobe. There's bound to be something in there that'll fit you.'

'Are you sure you don't mind?'

'Of course, I don't,' she laughed. 'One good turn deserves another. Lock up and take the keys with you to the pub and I'll come in for them later. With any luck, it'll be a quiet shift and you'll be able to fill me in on *exactly* what you got up to last night.'

'I'm not sure you're ready for it, Pen,' I coquettishly said, then tried to sashay out, but forgetting the door was locked, walked straight into it.

'Idiot!' Penny laughed, letting me out. 'I'll see you later.'

There was no time to admire the pretty coastal aesthetic of Penny's perfect cottage or linger in her shower.

'I know,' I panted, as I rushed into the pub. 'I know, I know.'

In spite of my best efforts, I was a few minutes late.

'You're all right,' Sam said mildly. 'Josh popped in earlier and said you'd answered a cry for help from Penny down at the café.'

'I did,' I wheezed. 'That's where I've been all afternoon. She was absolutely swamped.'

'In which case I'll let you off, but get behind here now so Tess can head back to the kitchen, because it's about to get busy.'

That was the last thing I wanted to hear. Having had such little sleep, I felt like I hadn't stopped since I'd turned up an hour ahead of my shift the evening before.

'Did Josh say anything else?' I tried to ask casually.

Sam gave me a look.

'He might have done.' He winked.

I felt my tummy roll and not because I hadn't had the chance to eat anything since the earlier pastry.

'And what might that have been?' I swallowed, feeling nauseous.

I hadn't had Josh down as the sort who would kiss and tell and felt disappointed in him. Given that he'd shared such intimate details with me about his dad, I thought he might have considered me more than one-night stand material to gossip about, but Sam's knowing wink suggested otherwise.

'Why don't you ask him yourself?' he said, with a nod to the door.

'Hey,' Josh smiled, ducking his head as he came in. He still looked deliciously dishevelled. 'How did you get on with Penny?'

'Good,' I said, then had to move along the bar to serve someone.

'Have you got a sec?' he asked, once I'd finished.

'Not right now,' I said, even though I wanted to get to the bottom of exactly how much detail he'd given Sam. 'It's getting busy.'

'It'll only take a sec.'

'I can't,' I said, feeling rattled. 'Sorry.'

It was ages before the bar was quiet again and, in that time, I'd seen three women flirt outrageously with Josh. He hadn't done anything to court their attention, but it was obvious that he drew people to him like a moth to a flame and as the evening wore on, I became convinced that he had told Sam everything about his first Norfolk coastal conquest. Me.

'You can take a minute now if you like?' Sam offered, making me jump. 'I think Josh is hanging around just to talk to you.'

'No,' I said, 'it's okay. I don't think he is and besides, he's currently occupied.' One of the women was still talking to him. 'If I stop, I might not get going again. As you know,' I more loudly added, 'I've had a long couple of days with very little sleep.'

Josh came quickly up to the bar when he saw there were no customers waiting and that I was talking to Sam.

'Okay,' said Sam, looking at me with a puzzled expression on his face.

'I was just telling Sam how little sleep I've had,' I said to Josh. 'I wanted to confirm your prowess in the bedroom and back up what you told him earlier.'

Josh looked shocked and Sam bit his lip.

'Absolutely no complaints from me.' I smiled, as I breezily set to stacking some glasses. 'We had a great night together, didn't we?'

'Josh didn't—' Sam began.

'It's fine,' Josh cut in. 'I'm going to head off then. I'll see you later, Sam.'

He strode out of the pub without another word and I felt my face flush red.

'He did tell you that we'd spent the night together, didn't he?' I belatedly asked Sam.

'Nope,' he said, 'he told me that having talked it through with you, he's decided he's going to play with George again. I think, just now, he wanted to tell you before I let it slip.'

Chapter 10

I felt immensely grateful that the shift got busier again after Sam's explanation because it stopped me thinking about the horrible assumption I'd made about Josh and gave me an excuse not to have to talk to Penny. The irony that I would most likely have shared the details of my night of passion with her while at the same time feeling affronted that Josh might have done the same with Sam, but hadn't, wasn't lost on me and I felt awful as a result.

'Here are your keys, Pen,' was almost as much as I got to say to my friend in the end. 'I'm sorry I can't stop to talk.'

'It's fine,' she said, looking deadbeat herself, but still sounding buoyant. 'I'm not hanging around. I haven't been home yet and I need to get to bed.'

'You haven't been at the café all this time?' I gasped, forgetting my own worries for a moment.

'I have,' she said, nodding wearily. 'Nick drove down to the beach and let me talk at him about everything I needed to get done ahead of next week as well as describing some new dishes I'm considering. I'm completely on top of it all now and I've put in orders to arrive throughout the day on Tuesday. Are you sure you can still be at the café to receive them?'

'Absolutely,' I confirmed. 'Just message me when I need to be there and I won't budge from the place until everything arrives and is assigned to the fridge, freezer or a shelf.'

'You're a star,' she said gratefully, handing me her set of café keys which I vowed to guard with my life.

I didn't feel like a star, however, when I was sitting with my parents at breakfast the following morning being interrogated about my extra-curricular weekend activities.

'We assumed you were at Penny's place,' Mum said tersely, having watched me bundle my balled-up dress, which I knew still smelt of Josh's aftershave, into the washing machine.

'I was,' I said, reaching for a slice of toast.

She gave me a look.

'I was there for a while,' I amended.

'We know you didn't spend Saturday night there,' Mum carried on, 'because Penny rang the cottage phone and asked to speak to you on Sunday. I'm guessing she tracked you down via your mobile in the end?'

What a nuisance that Penny had called the cottage phone before trying my mobile. Who rang a landline these days?

'Yes,' I said, avoiding Mum's eye, 'she did. And I spent the entire afternoon helping her out in the Sunshine Café before heading to the pub for my shift straight after.'

I didn't elaborate on where I'd been before that. As a fully grown woman, I didn't think I needed to, even if I had moved back into my childhood bedroom.

'You must be all in,' commented Dad. 'I've never known you to work so hard. I'm surprised you're up, given the circumstances. You should be having a lie-in.'

I was also surprised I was up, and the dark smudges under

my eyes were an indicator as to exactly how exhausted I was. Rather than fall asleep the moment my head had hit the pillow, my brain had started berating me for the disservice I'd done Josh.

I had considered knocking on his door on the way back to my car after my shift, but Crow's Nest Cottage had been in darkness and the curtains were all closed, so I thought it best not to disturb him and consequently drove back to Wynbrook with my guilt weighing heavy around my neck.

'I've turned over a new leaf,' I said to Dad, trying to sound brighter than I felt. 'I thought you'd both be pleased that I'm keeping so busy.'

'We are pleased,' said Mum. 'We think it's wonderful that you're so occupied, but while you're—'

'Please don't tell me you're about to give me the whole *while you're under our roof* speech, Mum,' I rudely interrupted. 'I'm twenty-eight, not eighteen.'

'Start acting like it then,' she said crossly.

I realised how childish my sarcastic tone had sounded.

'I'm sorry. But I did text to say I was staying out.'

'But having assumed you were with Penny, we were worried when she rang asking for you,' Mum pushed on. 'We had no idea where you were. Anything could have happened to you.'

'So why didn't you call me and ask where I was?' I couldn't stop myself pouting.

'Because we were trying to treat you like you're twenty-eight, not eighteen,' Dad sardonically piped up, as he pushed back his chair. 'I need to get to work, and I think it best if we draw a line under this conversation. It's no business of ours where you spent the night, Daisy, but if you're going to use your friend as an alibi—'

'But I didn't!' I hotly objected.

'Cover story then,' Dad angrily said, 'whatever. Then make sure she knows about it first, okay? It'll save a lot of grief in the long run.'

'Right,' I said, even though I hadn't done that either. 'Duly noted.'

Later in the day, I was still seething, so rather than attempt to apologise to Josh, I headed out for a walk around the estate instead. I was still avoiding the garden and was marching along the drive when Algy, practically bent double on the side of it, came into view.

'You're not still looking for that cat, Algy, are you?' I asked, as I got closer.

Having been so caught up with Josh, the pub and latterly the café, I'd completely reneged on my promise to keep an eye on the man I considered my surrogate grandad and hoped this might be a fortuitous opportunity to make amends.

'I am,' Algy said, sounding upset as he pushed back the plants closest to the drive with his walking stick in the hope that the feline might happen to be sheltering there. 'There's no sign of my little girl, Luna, anywhere.'

I wasn't sure the cat's sex had been confirmed or that it actually had a name, but I went along with what Algy said.

'Is she still eating the food you're putting out?' I asked him.

'*Something's* eating the food I'm putting out,' he told me, 'but I've no idea if it's her. Could be a fox for all I know. Could be a fox that's had the cat.'

I stepped closer and linked my arm through his. He seemed to have shrunk in the time I'd been away and it took me a moment to match my pace to his slower one as we moved along the drive to the side of the manor. The stick was a new development too, but I assumed he would only be using it until he was properly and confidently back on his feet.

'I daresay the fox would be more interested in your hens than a stray cat,' I tried to say comfortingly, 'though their place is like a fortress and it can't possibly get in.'

Dad had created a huge fox-proof area for the hens to roam in and I knew he personally shut the coop up every evening, just to be on the safe side.

'I suggested to Mum and Dad that you should set up a camera,' I continued.

'A security camera?' Algy frowned, stopping to look at me.

'No,' I said, 'a wildlife one. You could set it up so it's trained on the food bowl. That way you'd know for certain what's been visiting.'

'That's an inspired idea,' Algy gasped, immediately brightening. 'Why ever didn't they mention it? Where can we get one of those from?'

'We can order one online easily enough,' I told him. 'And I can set it up for you, if you like.'

'Let's do that,' he said, setting off again and quickening his pace a little. 'Let's do that right now.'

Within minutes we were installed in his office, which wasn't as organised and tidy as the last time I'd been in there, and I was searching for a basic camera, which was all we'd need. I could hear the drone of the vacuum coming from somewhere above us and hoped Mum wasn't about to descend. I'd had enough of parents for one morning.

'It'll be here tomorrow,' I said, once the order had been

confirmed. 'You might have to wait until later on for me to set it up though as I've promised to do Penny a favour in the day, but we'll soon know if your cat, your Luna, is still in the vicinity.'

'You're very kind to humour an old man,' Algy said, whisking the email confirmation off the printer. 'I think most of my schemes and fancies are more of a hindrance to everyone now I'm over the hill and can't action them myself.'

'I'm sure they're not,' I said stoically, knowing it must be the cut-flower garden that I still hadn't seen that he was referring to.

'Oh, they are.' He nodded, dropping the sheet of paper on top of a pile of receipts. 'Getting old is no fun, Daisy. My advice is, avoid it if you can.'

I'd never heard him talk like that before and wondered if Mum and Dad might actually be right about him feeling lonely living on his own in the manor. He'd done it for as long as I could remember and had always been happy and content in the past, but perhaps the fall slash tumble had instigated a change of heart.

'Well,' I smiled, not wanting to suggest he might be lonely in case I was wrong, 'I'll try.'

'Good,' he said, then eyed me more closely. 'Though I have to say, you're already rather looking beyond your age today.'

'Hey!' I yelped.

'We can't have you looking as old as me, can we?' he carried on. 'I'm relying on you to regale me with youthful tales of mischievous bad behaviour so I can live vicariously through you this summer.'

'I'll see what I can do.' I smiled. 'I'll keep you posted if I get up to anything.'

'You look like you've already started,' he teased. 'What *have* you been up to? Burning the candle at both ends?'

'Something like that,' I confessed, just as Mum chose that exact moment to stick her head around the door.

'There's fresh coffee in the kitchen,' she said, looking miffed.

'Thank you, Mum,' I struggled to say with a straight face because Algy had pulled a face in response to her sour expression, 'that's great.'

'I see you pulling that face, Algy.' She then tutted and he stood to attention, which made me want to laugh even more. 'What are you two up to?'

'Just a little side project,' he said, nimbly stepping in front of where he'd dropped the email. 'And don't look like that, Janet,' he said as I turned away, 'it won't mean any extra work for anyone. Daisy, Daisy and I have got it completely under control. Haven't we, my love?'

'Totally.' I nodded. 'Absolutely under control.'

'Hm,' said Mum, 'wonders will never cease.'

A persistent drizzle had started to fall while we were filling up on coffee and shortbread in the kitchen and this thankfully scuppered Algy's suggestion to take me to see the cut-flower garden. I was relieved that he was having an unusual fair-weather moment, because I was still feeling reluctant to admire the manor's many horticultural delights and opted instead to hide out in the library.

It had been a regular haunt during school holidays when I was growing up and had provided me with a whole variety of different destinations and subjects to encounter from the comfort of the squishy armchairs, which were arranged either side of a vast fireplace.

'Look what I found the other evening,' said Algy, who had opted to join me, once it became obvious the wet weather was set to continue. 'I bet you haven't picked this up in a while, have you?'

I took the book he handed me without initially realising what it was and then felt my heart skip in recognition. The dust cover was even more tattered than I remembered, but Mary and Ben looked exactly the same. As did the friendly robin.

'*The Secret Garden*,' I whispered, feeling a sudden upsurge of emotion. 'You're right, Algy – I haven't read it in years.'

'This was the tome that in part kicked your love of—'

'It was,' I cut in.

'Take it if you like,' he offered kindly, not at all offended by my interruption. 'Read it again at your leisure.'

'I thought you didn't lend books beyond the library door,' I said softly, carefully putting it down. 'Hasn't that always been your mantra?'

'Well,' he said, looking from me to the book and back again, 'I think I can trust you with it. I know where you live, after all.'

I didn't say anything.

'Don't you want to read it?' he asked. 'You used to love it. I can remember you—'

'Please,' I cut in again. 'Can we not talk about that? It's been hard enough having to move back in with Mum and Dad. If I start thinking about what occurred during the time before I left for university, I'll be heading for the hills before I've even made a start on sorting myself out.'

'Might the garden not help you sort yourself out?' Algy suggested mildly.

'No,' I said rather loudly, making him wince.

'I'm sorry,' he apologised, after a moment had passed. 'I'm so sorry, Daisy. That comment, and the offer of the book, was insensitive. I should have realised . . .'

I felt even worse then. I should have just taken the book and hidden it away, then given it back once enough time had passed for him to believe I'd read it. Re-read it.

'It's all right,' I started to say, wanting to make amends for upsetting my dear friend, who obviously hadn't meant to upset me.

'No, it isn't,' he tutted. 'And I am truly sorry. But, do you ever wonder—'

'No,' I cut in again, suddenly feeling less forgiving. 'Never.' Though, in recent days, I had started to . . .

Chapter 11

The next morning, Penny's last day of the summer term and the day she needed me to take in the Sunshine Café deliveries, dawned sunny and bright with warm sun streaming through the gap in my bedroom curtains.

I kicked off the sheet I had been sleeping under, with a strong desire to make the most of the hours I had before I needed to become a helpful friend. I was also determined to push the painful memories that had been dredged up the day before further to the back of my mind.

I hadn't appreciated Algy's misguided deep dive into the past and considered the best way to forget what it had flagged was to focus entirely on the present. I knew he hadn't meant any harm, but it didn't follow that none had been done.

With it all still bubbling away, I didn't want to talk to Mum or Dad and ducked out early, having left them a note explaining my absence before heading into Wynmouth.

'I know you're in there, Josh!' I called through the cottage letterbox, feeling frustratingly thwarted in my determination to make amends. 'Come on, open up!'

'Actually, he isn't,' said a voice behind me and I yelped as I trapped the ends of my fingers in the letterbox as it snapped shut.

'George . . .'

'Hello, my dear. You're about early, aren't you?'

'Lots to do,' I said briskly. 'Is Josh really not at home?'

'No, he's not,' he confirmed, looking at me questioningly as Skipper tugged on his lead. 'He's in the sea, swimming like he's competing in an Olympic final. My guess is he's got something on his mind.'

I would have guessed that, too.

'Thanks, George,' I said, abandoning the cottage, ignoring the pain in my fingers and striding off down to the beach.

I soon found Josh's towel and clothes, and sat crossed-legged on the sand, waiting for him to emerge as I more clearly formulated what it was that I was going to say.

'Here goes,' I breathed, when he eventually strode out of the sea like Neptune on a good day.

He halted when he saw me, a frown knitting his brows, and I ran my sweaty palms down my shorts. Clearly, the sting of my blunder in the pub hadn't subsided.

'Hey,' I brightly said, when he was close enough to hear, the word catching in my throat.

'Hey,' he responded dully, reaching around me for his towel.

'Did you enjoy your swim?' I asked as I jumped up.

'What do you want, Daisy?' he shot back as he rubbed his hair.

'To apologise, of course.' I swallowed. 'To say how sorry I am for assuming that you had told Sam that we'd spent the night together and for putting you in the same dickhead pigeonhole that I've recently shoved my ex in.'

It was hardly an eloquent apology, but it was the truth. I had assumed that because the last man in my life had treated me with such little respect, the next one might too, and that had been a mistake.

'Anything else?' Josh asked, swiping the towel over his chest and down his arms.

I had no idea if he had accepted what I had said, but he sounded less abrupt. I resolutely kept my eyes focused on his face rather than the beautiful body I would most likely no longer be wrapping mine around.

'Not quite,' I carried on. 'After you left, Sam told me that you'd decided to play in the pub again as a result of having talked to me and I'm really flattered about that. If talking to me has helped you pick up something you've always loved, I'm honoured.'

'I see,' he said with a nod.

Was he softening? I hoped so.

'Even if this is it for us now,' I sighed, 'I'm still pleased we had that talk.'

'So am I,' he agreed, a faint smile playing about his lovely lips.

'You are?' I asked, hope bubbling in my chest.

'I am,' he nodded again, then added, 'and I don't think this is it for us, Daisy.'

'You don't?' I croaked, the hope starting to bloom.

He shook his head.

'I feel a connection to you,' he said huskily. 'I can't explain it, but I feel like I've known you for far longer than I have. There's something . . .'

'Me too,' I rushed to say, inadvertently reaching for his hand, which he didn't snatch away. 'I feel that too.'

'You do?'

'Yes,' I said, stepping closer to him. 'Yes.'

He looked down at me. His long eyelashes were still wet and they framed his eyes even more perfectly than usual.

'Do you forgive me?' I dared to ask.

He took a breath and I thought my heart was going to beat out of my chest.

'I do,' he eventually said and I felt myself wilt, 'but you have to promise that you'll never, ever put me in that dickhead pigeonhole again. Do you promise?'

'I do,' I laughed.

'You're sure?' He frowned. 'I know your ex treated you badly, Daisy, but not every guy is like that. I'm not like that. I could never mess a woman around. That's not the sort of man I am.'

'I know. I've known that since Sunday night.'

The look on his face when he walked out of the pub, the pained expression that had furrowed his brow and clouded his usually bright eyes, had been confirmation of that. Josh wasn't capable of hurting me, of that I was certain.

'Good,' he said. 'That's all right then. I might still have some stuff to sort out.' I guessed he was alluding to his family situation, his father in particular. 'But where relationships are concerned, I'm straight down the line.'

'Okay.' I nodded. 'And so am I. However long this thing between us lasts, I won't think badly of you again.'

'All right,' he said, squeezing my hand. 'And thank you for going some way to confirming my prowess in the bedroom when you were spilling the beans to Sam.' I had to laugh at that. 'Though you could have been a bit more enthusiastic.'

'What do you mean?'

'Well, you said we'd had a *great night* and that you had *no complaints*,' he recited, letting go of my hand to put air quotes around the words.

He'd clearly memorised every syllable.

'And what was wrong with that?' I asked.

'Well, it hardly suggests we set the bed on fire, does it? Or the sofa!'

'Given that it's actually Sam's bed *and* sofa,' I reminded him, 'and it was Sam I was talking to, you should be grateful for that. He wouldn't have been pleased to think of either going up in flames, would he?'

'I suppose not,' Josh laughed, flicking me with the towel, 'but I still would have preferred a better review.'

'Consider it something to work towards.' I grinned, skipping off towards the beach hut. 'Let's see if we can get you up to five stars by the end of the summer, shall we?'

'You're on!' he shouted, scooping up his clothes and chasing after me.

Even though I was willing to start working on Josh's sexy summer ranking immediately – not that he needed it because he already was a five – I was determined that nothing was going to make me late for accepting Penny's deliveries to the café and their subsequent unpacking.

'I'll come and help you, if you like,' Josh offered, once he was dry and dressed and we'd kissed and made up. A lot.

I really wanted him to come with me, but café chores hardly felt like the sort of task anyone would willingly want to under-take while they were on their summer holiday.

'Surely you must have something more exciting to do?' I said.

'Don't you want me to come?' Josh pouted.

'Of course, I do. But it won't be very exciting, watching me signing for a few boxes and then lugging them to the café and unpacking them.'

'It *will* be exciting actually,' he said, 'because it'll be you doing it.'

'And the award for cheesiest line ever goes to . . .'

He silenced my drumroll with a kiss and I quickly retracked my statement.

'Come on then,' I said breathlessly when we finally drew apart, 'let's go.'

Had I not helped Penny on Sunday afternoon, I would have thought she'd ordered far too much stock, but having seen how depleted supplies were and how in demand the lollies and so on had been when the sun was shining down on Wynmouth beach, I didn't question the amounts of everything that she'd ordered, even if it was a struggle to carry some of it from the end of the lane, which was as far as the vans could get, to the café kitchen. However, having Josh to help me sped up the lugging and unpacking process considerably, even if we did keep stopping to kiss while we were doing it.

'So, how are you settling into life back at Wynbrook Manor?' he asked, while we were waiting for the last order of the day.

It was mid-afternoon and Penny had messaged to say that I could help myself to anything I fancied for a late lunch as she was aware that I was going to be there for the long haul. I'd made the amount of food I would normally eat and split it with Josh, so still felt a little hungry. Kissing him seemed to eat up more calories than kissing Laurence. Not that I wanted to be thinking about kissing my ex or comparing his technique to the outstanding one of my current beau.

'Um,' I said, thinking how I could answer diplomatically and then decided I didn't need to be tactful, not with Josh. 'It's harder than I thought it would be.'

'Why's that?'

'Well, for a start I very nearly got the whole "while you're staying under our roof" speech during breakfast yesterday,' I told him.

'Oh, crikey,' he grimaced. 'That's never good.'

I had wondered if that would translate, but it obviously did. 'What else?' he asked.

I thought about Algy's faux pas about the book, but didn't want to get into that.

'Just churned up memories, you know.' I shrugged, playing it down. 'Inevitable, but still uncomfortable.'

'Um.' He nodded, looking thoughtful. 'As you say, inevitable when you're revisiting old territory.'

'You've experienced that too?'

'I have,' he said, leaning forward in his seat and looking deep into my eyes. 'Because, you see, the thing is, Daisy—'

A long blast on a van horn along the lane made us both jump.

'Hold that thought,' I said, jumping up. 'That'll be the last delivery. The driver was supposed to message so I could be up there waiting for it.'

'In that case,' said Josh, also standing, 'let's both get up there before they disappear.'

The last order was by far the largest and Josh and I had just finished transferring it to the café when Penny arrived.

'I didn't hang around once the bell had gone,' she said, giving me a hug. 'I couldn't wait to get out of there.'

'I don't blame you,' I said, squeezing her tightly in response.

'Oh,' she said, letting me go as Josh appeared around the side of the building carrying a pile of flattened cardboard boxes, 'you've had help, I see.'

'I hope that's okay?' I asked.

'Of course.' She smiled.

'In that case,' I said, feeling my face start to colour, 'Penny, this is Josh. Josh, this is my very best friend, Penny.'

'Don't let Nick hear you say that,' Penny laughed and when I looked at her, I could see she was flushed too. 'I've seen you around of course, Josh.'

'Likewise,' he said, smiling, and she turned even redder. 'It's great to meet you at last. Daisy talks about you all the time.'

'Don't believe a word of it,' she said, not really recovering. 'Now come on. Dump that lot in the recycling bin and then you can show me what's turned up.'

I had planned to head back to Wynbrook and surprise Algy by setting up the cat camera, but as Penny finished her stock check and Josh paddled in the incoming tide, he called me.

'The delivery truck's broken down and the parcel with the camera isn't coming until tomorrow now,' he said, sounding a bit fed up. 'I know you'd said you wouldn't be able to set it up straightaway, but I thought I'd let you know it hadn't landed.'

'What a nuisance,' I tutted. 'I'm in Wynmouth at the moment, but was just about to come back and do it for you.'

'Just as well I caught you then,' he said. 'How about I message

you when it arrives tomorrow and you can do it then, if it fits
in with your plans?'

'Sounds good to me,' I agreed.

'You're sure?'

'One hundred per cent.'

He signed off sounding marginally happier, though obviously
still keen to know as soon as possible if it was the cat that was
eating the food he was putting out.

'What's up?' Josh asked, as he walked back up the strip of
sand the tide hadn't yet claimed.

'Nothing,' I told him. 'Just a change of plan. I've got a free
evening now.'

'Oh, have you?' he asked, with relish.

'I have.' I knew my smile was Cheshire Cat-size, but I couldn't
help it. 'I don't have anywhere to be between now and tomorrow.'

'Do you not?' Penny gasped, coming out of the café with
a clipboard in one hand and a pen in the other. She really did
have impeccable timing. 'How fab is that?'

'Well, I think it's very fab.' I smiled at Josh. 'Why do you
though, Pen?'

'Because you can both come to the pub, of course,' she
explained happily. 'I was planning to have an end of term
celebration and having you there, Daisy, will make it perfect.
It's been too long since we got merry together. And Nick will
be there too, of course, because it's board-game night, so you
won't be outnumbered, Josh.'

We couldn't turn her down, even though I was keen to have
an early night with Josh. Another adult sleepover was going to
give him the chance to work towards an extra star for his

review. That would make it six, but the more the merrier as far as I was concerned.

'Sounds perfect.' I smiled. 'I'd love to come. What about you, Josh?'

'Wild horses wouldn't keep me away,' he said, grinning.

'And you can stay over at mine if you like,' Penny offered, with a straight face. 'Oh, well, no . . .' she then fumbled. 'I mean, you'll probably want to stay with . . . or you might head back to Wynbrook . . .'

'I'm kind of hoping Daisy will stay with me,' said Josh, coming to her rescue. 'That is, if she'd like to.'

'She would,' I confirmed. 'She'd like that very much.'

'Don't forget to let your mum and dad know then,' Penny said to me, as she walked back into the café again. 'I rather think I put my foot in it when I called the cottage on Sunday, didn't I?'

'Just a bit,' I agreed. 'I'll ring them now before I get . . . distracted.'

Josh raised his eyebrows at that and bit his lip. He looked so sexy, I was tempted to bite his lip, even with Penny still in viewing range.

'But they won't pick up at this time, will they?' she called out of the door. 'They'll still be at work.'

'Exactly.' I grinned, pulling out my phone. 'I'll just leave them a message on the landline.'

So much for previously wondering who in the world still called them.

'I'll see if Penny needs a hand,' said Josh, leaving me to reel off the message.

I simply said that I was staying overnight with a friend in the village. It was enough to let Mum and Dad know I wouldn't be back but not so detailed that they would work out I was flinging with a Wynmouth summer visitor.

'Right then,' said Penny, when she strode out of the café with Josh behind her. 'Let's lock up and reconvene in the pub at six, shall we?'

'Excellent idea,' I was happy to agree.

'Well, come on then,' Penny urged when I didn't move. 'You've got the keys, Daisy. Or at least I hope you've got the keys.'

'Oh, yes,' I said, reaching into my shorts pocket as she shook her head and rolled her eyes. 'Of course. Here they are.'

'So,' said Josh as we waved Penny off to her end of the village and he unlocked the door to Crow's Nest Cottage, 'what are we going to do to pass the next hour or so?'

'Um,' I said, tapping a finger to my chin in thought, 'well, we could start by getting you in the bath, couldn't we? You swam in the sea this morning so you must still be all salty.'

'That's a very good point,' he said, ushering me in ahead of him. 'How would you feel about washing my back?'

It turned out that I was rather keen to wash Josh's back and as a thank you, he returned the favour, which made us late in turning up at the pub.

'Hurry up!' urged Penny, when we finally arrived. 'We want to get started.'

The place was surprisingly packed. I had thought the Tuesday evening games night popularity had been talked up, but apparently not.

'Why's your hair wet?' she asked me.

I looked at Josh.

'Oh, never mind,' she said, blushing. 'Sit down and draw

your counters and I'll tell Nick what you want to drink. He's at the bar.'

'I'll tell Nick,' I said, 'you stay here. What would you like, Josh?'

'A pint of the usual as you won't be pouring it.' He grinned and I gently cuffed him as I walked away.

It turned out neither Sam nor Tess were potentially going to be pouring it either.

'What can I get you?' asked a tall, sun-bleached blonde woman I hadn't seen before.

Her accent was undeniably Australian and it grated a bit. Was everything in Australia so perfect, I wondered?

'Oh . . .' I mumbled, pointing at Nick who was standing further along the bar. Unlike a few of the other customers, he didn't seem mesmerised by the goddess in front of him. 'Um . . . I'm with someone. I'll get him to add what I want to his order.'

'Right you are,' she beamed, looking rather intently at me before moving away. 'Who's next?'

'Who's that?' I asked Nick, once I'd pushed my way through the throng.

'No idea,' he smiled, 'but she seems to be keeping Sam's till ringing.'

'Doesn't she just,' I commented wryly, feeling rather disconcerted.

Sam hadn't mentioned taking on more staff. From the few seconds I'd been watching her, I could see she was a thousand times more at home behind the bar than I was and I wondered if I was destined to be getting my marching orders at some point during my next shift. Just one more messed-up pint or late arrival and I could be out.

'Have you met Marguerite?' asked Tess, as she came along and lined up Nick's pint and something fizzy for Penny.

'Not officially,' I said. 'Could you add a pint for Josh and another of whatever Penny's having to those drinks please, Tess?'

'Two secs,' she said with a nod.

'I'll pay for them,' I told Nick, reaching into my shorts pocket for my purse.

'You can pay for the next round. I'll get these,' he insisted.

'And come up for the next ones too?' I suggested with a glance towards Marguerite.

'Nah,' he said, shrugging. 'She's not my type.'

'Looks like you're the only one,' I said, with a nod at everyone else. 'What is it about Australia?'

Tess laughed at that.

'Don't let Marguerite hear you say that.' She grinned, adding the extra drinks I'd asked for to Nick's bill. 'She's from New Zealand.'

'Duly noted.' I nodded, giving Marguerite another look. 'And what's she doing behind the bar? Sam hasn't mentioned he was taking on anyone else.'

'Oh, he isn't,' Tess was quick to say, no doubt noticing that I appeared rather unnerved by the pretty stranger's competence with the pumps. 'She's not staff.'

She was doing a very good impression of someone on the payroll.

'Who is she then?' Nick asked, as he tapped his card on the reader.

'She's a friend of Hope's. She's spending the year travelling the globe and catching up with friends while she does it. A few weeks in Wynmouth were apparently added to her summer schedule months ago and before Hope was called to the Caribbean. In all the rush for Hope and Sophie to set off, Marguerite's visit was forgotten about.'

'I see,' I said, wondering how on earth anyone could possibly forget about someone who looked like Marguerite. 'So, is she staying here in the village?'

'No,' said Tess, 'she's got an Air BnB further along the coast, so she said she might as well hang around and help out here for a bit rather than reschedule her plans.'

'Will she be helping out during my shifts too?'

'I'm not sure.' Tess shrugged. 'She's something of a free spirit from what I can make out.'

I'd heard myself described that way in the past, but Marguerite encapsulated the very essence of the expression, while in comparison, I felt like an impostor.

'In that case,' I said, 'I'll be in as usual on Thursday.'

And I would make a point of trying to be early again too.

'Good luck at Scrabble,' Tess said, looking over at our table. 'Make sure you sit between Penny and Nick, won't you?'

'Hey,' Nick objected, as he picked up his and Penny's drinks and I reached for the other two.

'You can't deny you have a reputation for arguing over the tiles,' Tess laughed.

'No,' Nick immediately relented and I rolled my eyes. 'I don't suppose I can.'

I wasn't sure what to expect after that, but the evening unfolded with nary a disagreement. Though that could have been helped by the amount of Prosecco that Penny was getting through.

'Why aren't you keeping up?' she asked me, when I stopped matching her after our third glass.

'Because I have to drive tomorrow,' I pointed out. 'And you don't.'

'You do, however, have to be up early to open the café,' Josh smilingly reminded her and that set her off again, reciting all of the new ideas she had for the menu.

She was going to be true to what Sophie always offered, but there were a few additions of her own that she had developed and was keen to try out.

'Another?' Nick offered, holding up his glass.

He'd just been declared the winner and had resisted the urge to gloat. Josh had almost been triumphant, but a couple of his words had been disallowed because they were US equivalents and as he was currently on UK soil, Penny and Nick had insisted those should be the ones he used instead. Personally, I wasn't anywhere near as invested and wasn't bothered either way. I had been surreptitiously watching Marguerite all evening. She certainly had a way with the customers and hadn't mis-poured a single pint.

'Not for me,' I said, as I zoned back in to what Nick had said.

'Nor for me either, but thanks,' Josh added. 'I was going to suggest we head off, Daisy.'

'I was going to say the same,' I quickly agreed. 'Come on, Pen, we'll walk you home.'

'I don't need anyone to walk me home,' she laughed. She then attempted to tip the Scrabble tiles into the bag and spectacularly missed. 'I'm fine.'

'I'll take her,' offered Nick, as I gathered up the tiles from the floor.

'Will you?' Penny beamed, her former determination that she didn't need a chaperone forgotten. 'I'd like that.'

'I'll even get you in the door,' Nick told her.

'You might have to get her up the stairs,' I added.

I hoped she wasn't going to have a hangover on her first full day in the café. With any luck, she'd have enough adrenaline coursing through her to see off a headache and any nausea. Assuming that's how adrenaline worked.

'Shall I get you up the stairs?' Josh whispered in my ear.

'I can't think of anything I'd like more,' I told him. 'Come on, let's leave these two idiots to it.'

He didn't need asking twice.

'I'll see you tomorrow, Marguerite,' he said casually, as we passed the bar.

'You won't forget?' She smiled at him.

'No chance.' He smiled back.

As I lay awake in the bed next to him a few hours later, I reckoned that not asking him what he wouldn't forget was one of the hardest questions I'd ever not asked.

Chapter 12

Algy messaged around ten the following morning to say that
the camera had been delivered, but I felt reluctant to rush back
to Wynbrook. I also felt incredibly uncomfortable about why
I was so hesitant to leave and it had nothing to do with avoiding
the garden.

Josh and I had spent another wonderful night together. He
was a sensual and sensitive lover, who had left me feeling more
fulfilled than I'd ever been. I could have quite conveniently
put my reluctance to leave the village down to an unwilling-
ness to vacate his bed, but the truth was I was still rather
preoccupied as to why he was going to see Marguerite.

I knew, of course, that it was absolutely none of my business
and that I had no right to ask and I also knew, that if I did
bring it up, Josh most likely wouldn't mind in the slightest.
However, there was also a tiny niggling concern eating away
at the corner of what I knew to be reasonable, that having
thought the worst of him once already in our brief time
together, my asking *could* make him mind and possibly even
think that I was doing it again.

What if I said something about them getting together and

he thought I was asking because I was jealous (I was) or because I didn't trust him (I did. Or at least I was trying my hardest to). I could appreciate now that Laurence's infidelity had really done a number on me. I might have initially thought I'd walked away from our relationship unscathed, but I could acknowledge now that he'd left me with some trust issues, and feeling insecure as a result. I hoped neither sensation would last.

In the end, I decided I couldn't risk directly mentioning Marguerite and worked my way around the situation another way.

'Right,' I said, as I stretched out in the bed and felt sensitive all over as Josh lightly traced a finger from my neck to just below my navel, 'I really had better go.'

I'd already made an attempt to head off once and been . . . waylaid.

'No,' he objected, taking his hand away and sitting up, 'not yet. It's still early.'

'It's not that early,' I said, also sitting up. 'And I promised Algy, didn't I? The camera's been delivered and I promised I'd set it up for him, so I really do have to get back.'

The last thing I wanted was Algy asking Dad to do it. Piling that on top of my father's never-ending summer to-do list would be just the thing to put me back in his bad books, especially given that the camera had been my suggestion.

'I suppose,' Josh agreed, but threw himself down on the bed like a petulant child.

I laughed at his convincing impression of what looked like a very sulky man-boy.

'You could always come with me,' I suggested, reaching to ruffle his hair and holding my breath.

'No can do,' he immediately said, propping himself up on one elbow and flattening the bouffant crest my ruffling had created. 'I've got stuff I need to do.'

His answer was a little too quick for my liking. 'Are you sure? I can promise you as many of those famous Wynbrook strawberries, that you have such a fondness for, as you can eat.'

If he didn't come to the manor for me, I thought the temptation of succulent summer fruit might be enough to tempt him. It wasn't.

'I really can't,' he said, screwing up his nose. 'I promised I'd see someone today and help them with something.'

'Right.' I swallowed, as I bent down the side of the bed to scoop up my abandoned and creased clothes. 'Fair enough.'

'I'm sorry,' he said.

He tried to reach for me, but I moved away.

'I really am sorry,' he repeated.

'Honestly, it's fine.' I smiled, not wanting to come across as stroppy. 'And as that's the case, it turns out that it's just as well that I am going, isn't it?'

'What do you mean?' Josh frowned.

'Well,' I said, 'I know you didn't want me to leave, but as you've already got plans, what would I have done while you were gone? Just hung around here until you came back?'

'Of course not,' he tutted, sitting up. He sounded a bit put out, which was hardly surprising, but not the mood I wanted to send him off to see Marguerite in. 'I was going to ask you to come with me.'

'Oh,' I said, surprised.

'I'm going to the pub to see Marguerite,' he said, making me feel awful. 'She's thinking about heading to Maine in the fall, and I know someone who might be willing to rent her a room in their apartment while she's there.'

'I see,' I faltered, completely wrong-footed. 'Right.'

'I'm going to talk to her about where's best to visit and give her my mate's details.'

'That's,' I croaked, then cleared my throat, 'really kind of you.'

'I am kind.' He grinned. 'Haven't you worked that out yet?'

'I'm getting there.' I nodded.

I would brain Laurence if his horrible behaviour scuppered my ability to be with and trust a genuine good guy like Josh, even if it was only fated to be for as long as the summer.

'What did you think of her, by the way?' Josh then asked, pulling my attention away from the lasting potential impact of Laurence's actions.

'Who?' I frowned.

'Marguerite, of course.'

'Oh,' I said, pulling my T-shirt over my head, 'tall, beautiful, talented. All the things I hate in a woman. That was a joke,' I instantly added, without drawing breath. 'I really didn't mean that. I'm all for supporting women. Even the stunning ones who make the rest of us feel like . . . gargoyles.'

Josh laughed at that.

'I should think so too.' He nodded.

'Should go without saying really, shouldn't it?' I sighed. 'What do you think of her?'

I braced myself internally for impact.

'Who?' he asked, playing me at my own game.

'You know who,' I tutted.

'Oh, she's lovely,' he said. 'She *is* beautiful, and like me, she's really kind too.'

'The whole package then,' I sighed wistfully.

They'd make a perfect couple. Not unlike Josh, Marguerite apparently didn't have any flaws either, but I felt like I was stacking up my own by the bucketful.

'And she has the hots for you,' he said.

'What?' I spluttered.

'She asked me about you last night,' he carried on, as he slid his boxers on and stood up. 'When I went to the bar to get a round in, she asked me if we were properly together or just friends.'

'She did not.' I blushed.

'Yes, she did. She wanted to know if you were single. And gay. She's gay and single and hoped you might be too.'

'I don't believe you.'

'Are you flattered?'

'I would be if I thought it was true,' I told him. 'But why would a woman like Marguerite look twice at someone like me?'

'Because,' he said, reaching for me and pulling me back down onto the bed, 'you're lovely and kind and beautiful too.'

I wriggled out from under him.

'I don't think I can believe that,' I told him. 'I'm not always kind.'

'Given that your last boyfriend treated you like crap, I think you're allowed to slip up in the relationship kindness stakes once in a while.'

'Do you really?' I asked.

'Yeah,' he said softly. 'I do. I really do.'

'So,' I carried on, bravely or foolishly testing the water, 'you wouldn't think badly of me if I told you that I had felt jealous that you were going back to the pub without me today and that I'm only now feeling all right about it because Marguerite has said that she fancies me, not you?'

Wasn't that terrible? Where was my sisterly solidarity? Why had I even entertained the idea that Marguerite – who I had known nothing about – might jump on my summer fling? And why had I again done Josh wrong by considering the notion that he might reciprocate if she did? I was an awful, awful person.

'No,' Josh said, 'I wouldn't actually.'

'Really?' I gasped.

'Really,' he said earnestly. 'I know it was only yesterday when you said that you'd never think badly of me again—'

'Oh god,' I groaned, putting my hands either side of my head, 'it was yesterday, wasn't it? Just yesterday. Only twenty-four hours ago and I've failed already.'

'It was only yesterday,' Josh said, pulling my hands away, 'but past hurts, especially the kind I'm guessing you've most likely been subjected to, take longer than that to heal, don't they?'

'I suppose so,' I said, as I wondered what I'd done to deserve having him turn up in my life, right when I needed someone like him.

'And you didn't know that someone looking like Marguerite was going to roll up and test your faith in me so soon, did you?'

'Hey,' I huffed, and he grinned, 'you don't have to keep referring to how she looks.'

'I know,' he said, 'I'm only winding you up. It's human nature that you were bound to feel something though, wasn't it? And if I'd have realised that sooner, I would have told you last night why I was going back to see her today and saved you a sleep-less night.'

'I didn't not sleep only because I was thinking about you and Marguerite,' I reminded him.

'Have I got another star?' he wheedled.

'You have.'

'That's all right then,' he said, pulling me right into his arms. 'And just for the record, if a handsome guy had turned up out of the blue and shown an interest in you, Daisy, I would have felt jealous too.'

'You would?' I asked, looking up at him.

'I definitely would.'

'In that case,' I sighed, 'you might want to change your mind about coming to the manor today after all, because Algernon Alford is a total fox.'

It wasn't until I'd driven halfway back to Wynbrook that I realised I could have gone with Josh to the pub and then we could have made the trip to see Algy together. I did consider turning back, but there wasn't anywhere safe to do a three-point turn on the narrow road and therefore carried on.

'So, what do you think?' Algy asked, once I'd unboxed everything and set it all out on the kitchen table in the manor.

'It looks simple enough,' I said, checking the instructions again before I set about putting the camera together and turning it on. 'I don't think it will take me long to get it up and running.'

'And remind me again how we can check the footage,' Algy asked.

'There's a screen on the camera we can watch it on or we

could set it up through your PC if we want a more detailed look,' I explained again.

'We could do that if something really exciting turns up, couldn't we?' Algy said, his eyes shining.

'Like your cat, for example.'

'Yes, like my Luna, for example.'

I wasn't sure that was the only thing he was now hoping might appear.

'What else are you expecting to see?' I frowned.

'Well, the cat's at the top of my list, obviously.'

'Obviously.'

'But after that, something completely out of the ordinary,' he told me. 'Black shuck or that panther that certain locals reckon still prowls about the roads around the estate at night would be just the thing.'

'The panther they only ever happen to see on a walk back home from the pub after a skinful,' I said sardonically.

'Well,' Algy sniffed, 'you never know.'

I rolled my eyes at that.

'Whatever pops up, it will be good to see it before . . .'

His words trailed off and I looked up at him.

'Before what, Algy?' I frowned, concerned that some of the colour had just drained from his face and the brief spark in his eyes had gone again.

He opened his mouth to tell me, but my mobile started to ring and he snapped it shut.

'Penny,' I said, answering the call. 'How are you getting on? I did message you earlier, but I wasn't expecting a reply, let alone a call. Is everything okay?'

'It's brilliant,' she gushed, sounding on a total high and thankfully not hungover at all. 'There's been a steady stream of customers so far and they've all loved everything I've made for them. I really think I can do this, Daisy.'

'That's brilliant.' I smiled. 'I'm so pleased.'

I didn't point out that the school holidays had literally only just started or that it was before lunch on a Wednesday, hardly prime beach-visiting time, so the customer numbers were bound to be manageable.

'I'll see you tomorrow in the pub, yeah?' she then asked.

'As long as you're not too tired by then,' I replied.

'It's quiz night,' she reminded me. 'I'm not missing that, no matter how knackered I feel.'

'What about Nick?' I asked.

'What about him?' she squeaked.

'Will he be at the quiz?'

'Oh, probably,' she said, sounding more like herself. 'He usually is.'

'How did you get on—'

'I have to go,' she cut in, before I could ask if Nick had seen her as far as her front door or made sure she was tightly tucked up in bed before he left her the evening before. 'Some more customers have just walked in.'

There was no opportunity to wish her luck either because she'd gone.

'Did I hear you say that was Penny?' Algy asked. 'How's she getting on? Nick has told me all about her taking over the café for the summer. She must be bonkers, having only just finished the school year. Not to mention, worn out.'

'I agree,' I said, putting my phone away again. 'But so far, so good. She's loving it.'

'I daresay it's a darn sight less stressful than teaching that class she had this year,' Algy commented, 'and I know how much she loves her cooking and baking.'

'Were they that bad?' I asked, wondering how Algy knew about her mischievous students.

'Yes,' he said, 'they were. They came up here on a school trip and ran us all ragged.'

'Oh, dear,' I sympathised, not wanting to picture the scene. I didn't ask if the trip had happened inside the manor or out in the grounds. Either way, one of my parents would have been pulling their hair out. 'Now, let's get this camera sorted before that panther makes its daily visit, shall we?'

Having fallen to thinking about the stress that Penny's most recent class had left in their wake, I completely forgot that her phone call had cut Algy off and he'd been about to tell me something.

'Is that it?' He said with a frown just a few minutes later as I stood up in the courtyard and stretched out my back.

'Yep.' I nodded. 'The camera's running and it's pointing right at the food bowl. If anything comes within feet of it, the motion sensor will be triggered and it will start recording.'

'So, all we have to do now is wait.'

Algy made no attempt to move, but stared intently at the bowl he'd just replenished.

'I don't think anything is likely to come along with the two of us hovering over it, do you?' I pointed out. 'Least of all a timid panther.'

'That's a very good point,' Algy agreed. 'Come on.'

He slowly wandered further away from the bowl.

'Where are you going?' I asked, following him. 'It's almost lunchtime.'

'I thought we'd take a quick turn around the garden.' I stopped walking. 'I really want to show you my cut-flower project. I'd like your opinion on it, Daisy, and I can't believe you've been back all this time and still not seen it.'

When I first arrived back at Wynbrook, I had intended to see it, but with so many memories being stirred up since then, the ones about how my connection to the garden had been diminished and eventually snuffed out now most prominent amongst them, it was the last place I wanted to visit. Especially the walled garden.

'I'd rather not,' I blurted out and Algy looked hurt.

'Is it because I was clumsy about the book?' he asked. He sounded mortified. 'I know you didn't take it, but I didn't offer it to upset you.'

'Of course, you didn't. I know that.'

'In that case,' he carried on, sounding rather bossy, 'I think you should come into the garden.'

'I've already been in the garden,' I told him, taking a step back. 'Part of it, anyway. And I don't want to go back in again.'

'But I'm sure if you give it a chance, it will make you feel—'

'Please don't push this, Algy,' I pleaded. 'Let's go back to the kitchen. Mum's bound to have lunch ready.'

'You go back then,' he said, turning away from me. 'I'll be in again in a little while.'

I watched him walk through the garden gate and along the shingle path. I felt distressed about not following him, but I couldn't force my feet to take a step towards him.

I hadn't thought properly about the garden for years and my former feelings for it hadn't even entered my head when I had made the decision to move back to Wynbrook for the summer. However, Algy seemed hell-bent on making me think about them now, even though, under the circumstances, they, and the memories of my monumental row with Dad, were the last thing I needed to become preoccupied with. I did love Algy dearly, but sometimes he could be a total nuisance.

Chapter 13

The following morning, I was still feeling rather riled with Algy for bringing the garden up again and as a result, my parents were perhaps undeservedly out of favour too, but there was no avoiding them as we were all living under the same roof.

During breakfast, I was smiling over a rather sexy message Josh had sent my mobile, when I looked up and caught both Mum and Dad staring at me over the top of their matching plates of boiled eggs and precisely cut soldiers.

'What's up?' I frowned, as I put the phone down on the table, screen side down for modesty's sake. 'What have I done now?'

'Who said you've done anything,' Mum tutted. 'No one's said a word.'

'I'm sorry I was on my phone,' I apologised rather sulkily, remembering too late that devices were banished during mealtimes.

I picked my phone up again and lent over to put it on the dresser, hating the fact that moving back into the cottage had turned me into a terrible teenager, especially given that my later teen years had been far from happy. Cue more thoughts about the garden.

Though, I supposed in many ways, my current situation, working at a summer job and indulging in a fling and sunny days on the beach, was actually a teen dream holiday, wasn't it? My return to the fold had enabled me to literally turn back time and rewind an entire decade. If only I could conveniently jump about further in my past and avoid ever meeting Laurence, either at university or after, that would have been perfect . . .

'Well,' I sighed, 'I can tell there's something.'

I'd rather bicker with Mum and Dad over my breakfast than think about my ex or the opportunity I'd been goaded into giving up ahead of applying to university.

'We were just wondering . . .' Mum finally began, but the sentence fizzled out practically as soon as she had started forming it.

'We heard a rumour,' said Dad, picking up the baton Mum had dropped.

'A rumour?' I grimaced. 'What, like local village gossip, you mean? Because I thought we didn't listen to that.'

'Oh, for pity's sake,' Mum said loudly, making me jump. 'Just tell us, Daisy.'

'Tell you what?'

'Are you seeing someone? Have you taken up with some tourist in the village?'

I wanted to laugh at her archaic way of putting it, but could sense that it wouldn't be in any way helpful in smoothing over what was clearly a sensitive subject. For them, at least.

'And don't be pedantic about it,' insisted Dad.

'In that case, yes, I'm seeing someone,' I said succinctly. 'I have definitely taken up with a tourist in the village.'

Dad's shoulders sagged.

'Are you sure that's a good idea?' Mum frowned.

The evidence now on my phone, and stored up in my memory bank of my bedroom antics over the last few days, thought it was a wonderful idea.

'What do you mean?' I asked innocently.

'We just don't want you to get hurt,' said Dad. 'More hurt than you already must be,' he further added.

He sounded so genuinely concerned that, had I not again been feeling the sting of what his words, actions and manipulation had put paid to when I left school, then I might have felt enough compassion to reassure him, but as it was, I stuck to the facts.

'I appreciate that,' I told him, 'but that's not going to happen. The American tourist I'm . . . dating, is going to be in Wynmouth just for the summer. He's single, as am I, and we're . . . keeping each other company until such time as he has to leave or I do. Whichever comes first. There's no ambiguity. We both know what we're doing.'

'I see,' Dad said.

'Spending time with him isn't interfering with my work,' I carried on, 'and I don't think you need to know more than that. I'm not a child.'

Mum still hadn't said a word, but I could tell that my idea about how I should be spending the summer differed vastly from hers. I daresay she and Dad were also both thinking that the fact that I was already seeing someone else really was the death knell for mine and Laurence's relationship. Zero chance of rekindling now. Hooray!

'So, if you message to tell us that you're having a night away,' Dad nonetheless further probed, 'you'll be with this American, not Penny.'

'I'll most likely be with him, yes,' I confirmed. 'Though sometimes I might be with Penny, who, by the way, thinks the guy is absolutely lovely. And Nick likes him too.'

That stopped Dad in his tracks. He thought highly of Nick's opinions.

'So,' Mum finally said, breaking her silence, 'they've both met him, have they?'

'Yes,' I said, 'we were all at board-game night together in the pub and he helped me out at the café, lugging all the orders Penny had delivered on Tuesday, while she was still finishing up the term at school.'

'That was nice of him,' Mum said tentatively.

'He *is* nice, Mum,' I said, wanting her to know that even though Josh was only going to be a temporary fixture, he was a wonderful one. 'Really nice.'

'Oh, well,' said Dad, sounding resigned. 'I suppose that's that then.'

I didn't ask him to clarify what he meant by that because I knew. If I gave Dad the slightest opportunity, he'd bring the conversation around to include Laurence. I'd only just stopped holding my breath that it might be him responding to Dad's call every time I heard the cottage phone ring, which happened a surprising number of times, in the brief hours I was at home, and I didn't want to poke the hornet's nest further.

'I'd best get off,' Dad sighed. 'Every day I feel like I'm getting further behind.'

It was on the tip of my tongue to blurt out that ultimately, he only had himself to blame for that but again, acting in favour of family harmony, I kept my lips zipped.

'Yes,' said Mum, taking a final bite of her toast, 'me too.'

She began to pile the plates together.

'Leave all of that,' I told her. 'I'm not going into the village until later so I can do it.'

'Are you sure?'

'Absolutely,' I said, immediately getting on with it.

I had promised to help out around the house when I first arrived back at Wynbrook, so it was the least I could do.

'Are we likely to get to meet this tourist then?' Mum asked. She didn't use Josh's name because I hadn't supplied it. Given the efficiency of the village gossip I was sure both she and Dad most likely knew it anyway. 'He could come for supper one evening.'

'Well,' I said, unable to picture the scene, but feeling both surprised and grateful that she'd suggested it, 'we'll see. We're only just getting to know each other, but I can tell you, he absolutely loves Wynbrook strawberries.'

'Does he?' said Dad, sounding thrilled as he pulled on his work boots.

Any compliment to the estate earned a big tick as far as he was concerned.

'You'll have to show him the beach hut,' he then suggested, which was as much of a seal of approval as anyone was ever likely to get.

I didn't tell him that I already had or how relieved I was that their idea of me rekindling my romance with Laurence was now finally dead in the water.

★

'Were your ears burning this morning?' I asked Josh as we spread a blanket out on the sand in front of the beach hut later that day.

'No,' he said. 'Not as I recall.'

'That's all right then,' I laughed. 'I wasn't sure if you'd know what that meant.'

'Oh, I do.' He nodded. 'I'm familiar with the expression. And why would they be?'

'Because you were the hot topic at breakfast,' I told him, flipping open the top of my factor fifty sunscreen and covering my arms in a thick layer.

'With your parents?' he asked, wide-eyed.

'Yep.' I nodded, rubbing the cream in.

'What did you tell them?' he asked.

There was something about his tone that made me look at him. He appeared aghast.

'Don't look so worried,' I nudged. 'I gave them the bare minimum. You know, country of origin, potential longevity of relationship. Oh, and that you're a ten in bed.'

He laughed at that and looked relieved.

'They're not expecting you to put a ring on my finger,' I teased, passing him the bottle, 'if that's what you were worried about.'

He rolled his eyes.

'Idiot,' he tutted.

'But while we're on the topic,' I asked interestedly, 'what are your views on marriage?'

'I would need to know the size of your dowry before I got into a conversation about that,' he teased me back.

'Fair enough,' I said, turning over. 'Will you do my back, please? It's hot already, isn't it?'

'Scorching,' he said, making me turn even hotter once his hands got to work.

We walked up to the Sunshine Café for lunch and found Penny feeling hot too. All of the outside tables were full and there looked to be uncleared crockery and cutlery from previous customers littering most of them.

'Oh, crikey,' said Josh, when he opened the door to let me in ahead of him. 'I think we're going to have a bit of a wait.'

The inside tables were also full and there was a snaking queue of customers that we joined the back of. I looked around the side of the person in front of me and could see Penny moving about the kitchen at breakneck speed. She was wearing an expression of calm and control, but I knew her well enough to recognise that wasn't how she was really feeling.

'I'm going to go and clear those outside tables,' Josh told me, before I had the chance to tell him I was going to offer to help too. 'Why don't you join Penny behind the counter?'

'Great minds.' I smiled, twisting round to kiss him. 'We can help her through the lunchtime rush, can't we?'

'Absolutely,' he said with a grin.

I felt my heart flutter as I watched him walk out and begin gathering up the trays and dishes.

'Need a hand?' I asked, as I ducked under the counter.

'Oh, Daisy.' Penny smiled. 'No, it's okay. I think I've just about got a handle on it now.'

I dreaded to think what the situation had been like before if she thought the current one was under control.

'Sure?' I frowned.

'Well,' she said, as she slid a packed tray over the counter to an exasperated-looking customer who had clearly been waiting a while, 'maybe you could just clear some tables. It shouldn't take a minute.'

'Josh is already doing that,' I told her and her face flushed.

'I need to grow an extra pair of arms,' she said, her voice wavering.

'You do,' I smiled, 'and while you're working on that, how about I take orders and make drinks and you focus on sorting the food?'

With another family now waiting, there was no time for her to turn my offer down and we set to work, clearing the queue as quickly as we could. It took a while and by the end of it I felt exhausted.

'You can't carry on like this, Pen,' I said, once there was a break in customers long enough for us to have a conversation. 'You'll be frazzled by the bank holiday.'

Josh was washing dishes in the kitchen because there was no time to wait for the dishwasher to go through a cycle and Penny had quickly set to, prepping more salad and whipping up a dressing in anticipation of the next wave of hungry sun worshippers.

'It's fine,' she said airily, 'I'm still finding my feet. I just need to work out what's achievable. There are a couple of things I added to the menu that are proving too time-consuming to prep, so I'm taking them off.'

I thought it was going to take more than a slight tweaking of the menu to keep control of the footfall, especially if the sun continued to shine.

'Honestly,' she said, when I didn't say anything, 'I can do it.' I wasn't questioning that she could do it. I just didn't think it was achievable for her to do it on her own. 'I really appreciate you and Josh helping, but I would have got there if you hadn't shown up.'

'I know you would,' I said, not wanting to rain on her parade.

I knew how excited she was to have the opportunity to run the café and share her passion for delicious food right at the time when she was considering her future.

'Now,' she said, as Josh appeared, all suds and dishpan hands, 'what can I get you guys for lunch? Late lunch. On the house as payment for helping out.'

Josh opened his mouth to name a dish, but I shook my head.

'Thanks, but we're good,' I told Penny. 'We only came in to ask if you were still up for quiz night in the pub. I'm working, so I won't be able to take part, but Josh's keen. Aren't you?'

He looked hungry, rather than willing to pit his intellect against the Wynmouth great and good.

'Ever so,' he said sardonically and right on cue, his tummy gave the loudest rumble. 'That's excitement, not hunger,' he clarified, knowing everyone in the vicinity of the village must have heard it.

'Like I said yesterday,' Penny repeated, clearly not believing Josh, 'I'll be there. And now I suggest you go back to the cottage to eat, as Daisy won't let me feed you.'

I was about to say I was only trying to save her some time, but a couple of customers arrived and Penny turned her attention to them.

'I'll see you later,' she said. 'And thank you. Both of you.'

Josh and I walked back to the village and straight to the shop to fill a bag with snacks, which we then greedily devoured on the sofa in the cottage.

'Jeez,' said Josh, once he'd made short work of a huge sausage roll that was made on a farm just outside the village, 'I needed that.'

'I know you did,' I said, sitting back. 'Your stomach let everyone within a five-mile radius know how hungry you were when we were in the café.'

'Being surrounded by all that food Penny is selling didn't help,' he tutted, defending his rumbling tum. 'She's clearly a great cook, but she really isn't going to be able to manage on her own, is she?'

'No.' I frowned, as I pursed my lips. 'No, I don't think she is. And I'm worried that attempting to will take the edge off what she's trying to achieve by running it.'

'Which is?'

I checked the time on my phone. It was later than I thought.

'If you run me a bath, I'll tell you while I'm in it.' I smiled winningly, batting my lashes.

'Why do you want a bath?'

'Because I'm due for my shift at the pub soon and I feel sticky as hell covered in all that sunscreen.'

'Fair enough.' Josh grinned. 'Bubbles or no bubbles?'

'Bubbles,' I laughed. 'Always bubbles.'

Having explained to Josh why Penny was running the café, and then shared a bubble bath with him and then the bed, I had to dash next door to the pub to make my shift on time.

'You've just made it,' said Sam, with a nod to the clock above the bar.

'I know,' I said, stowing my bag away and hoping my hair wasn't too tousled. 'I know.'

I looked around as I caught my breath.

'Not that you would have missed me, had I been late,' I pointed out, as Marguerite came in from the garden carrying a tray full of empty glasses. 'Marguerite seems to have everything under control.'

She flashed me a smile as she joined me behind the bar and started to empty the tray.

'Here she is,' she announced theatrically, her eyes suddenly fixed on my face, 'the one woman in this village that I liked the look of and who was already spoken for.'

'And straight,' Sam pointed out. 'At least, I think she is.'

I had wondered if Marguerite might mention something about what she'd said to Josh about liking me, but I hadn't for a moment thought she'd make such a vocal declaration in front of a rapidly filling pub. Or rope my boss into the conversation either. I felt myself colour from my roots to my feet.

'I can't imagine you've seen every woman in the vicinity, Marguerite,' I told her, deciding to go with it. 'And yes, Sam, I am straight. But that doesn't mean the interest isn't flattering.'

Marguerite laughed at that and Sam shook his head.

'And knowing that I'm working in such close proximity to you, will keep Josh on his toes,' she winked, then added, 'I didn't mean that to sound stalkerish.'

It was my turn to laugh then.

'But you shouldn't be working,' Sam said to her.

'I like to keep busy,' she insisted. 'And I'm actually enjoying myself. This place is quaint. I really like it. Everyone knows everyone.'

'And everyone knows everyone's business,' I pointed out,

thinking of the conversation I'd endured over breakfast with
Mum and Dad.

'I think it's nice that you all look out for each other,'
Marguerite said, stepping forward to serve the customer I hadn't
noticed was waiting.

'That's one way of putting it,' Sam chuckled, thankfully not
spotting my ineptitude. 'I'm going to see if Tess needs a hand
in the kitchen.'

Having Marguerite to work alongside made the busy evening
far more entertaining and less stressful than it might have been.
I still wasn't a dab hand when it came to remembering and
totting up large orders, but she didn't think twice or miss a beat.

'It's literally years of experience,' she said kindly, when I
commented on her speedy skills. 'I daresay you're brilliant at
loads of things I've never tried.'

I didn't contradict her comment because she was being kind,
but thus far in my life, I didn't think I'd had the opportunity to
excel at anything and I was now beginning to wonder if I ever
would. Thankfully, Josh walked in at that moment and distracted
me from the sudden downward spiral my thoughts had taken.

'Hey gorgeous,' he said and grinned, leaning over the bar.

'Hey,' Marguerite and I both said together, then burst out
laughing.

A few weeks of fun, I reminded myself, that's what I was
supposed to be having. My best summer ever.

'Are you joining Nick for the quiz?' I asked Josh. 'There's
no sign of Penny yet, so he could do with the company.'

'I suppose I could,' Josh said, with a lazy smile.

When he looked like that, I had no desire to let him move
further away and I wished I'd stalled him.

'He's mad for you, you know,' Marguerite nudged me.

'Oh,' I said, playing it cool, but feeling thrilled. 'I don't know about that.'

'Well,' she said, 'I do.'

I was beginning to feel increasingly mad for him too, but I wasn't about to confess that.

'It's just a summer fling,' I said. 'We're just having fun until the fall,' I added, using a phoney accent that didn't cut it at all.

'You sure about that?'

I looked over to where Josh was sitting and found that even though he was chatting with Nick, he was looking at me. My heart practically somersaulted in my chest.

'Absolutely,' I said, having first cleared my throat. 'Absolutely sure.'

'You can join Nick and Josh for the quiz, if you like,' Sam said to me, making me jump.

I hadn't realised he was there and hoped he hadn't heard what Marguerite had said. Not that Sam was likely to gossip, but word had a way of getting around in Wynmouth.

'No,' I resisted, 'I'm working tonight. It's fine.'

'No one will want a drink while Tess is asking the questions,' he countered.

'And I'll serve them if they do,' Marguerite further said.

I got the impression that she could run the bar, ask the questions *and* cook the food, and all without missing a beat. It wasn't that she was trying to take over or make me feel redundant. Marguerite was too kind for that and I could tell she was an open book, so there was no ulterior motive either. She was simply in her element.

'Well,' I said, 'if you're sure . . .'

My feet were aching after the earlier stint in the café so the option to take a load off was appreciated. I wondered how Penny was feeling and more to the point, where was she? She had been pretty insistent, both times, when I had asked her about it, that she'd be at the quiz but so far, no sign.

'We are sure,' said Sam.

I pulled myself a slightly frothy half-pint and then a better pint for Josh because he hadn't ordered a drink when he came in, and then paid and carried them over to where he and Nick were sitting.

'I wish I knew where Penny had got to,' I said, as I set the glasses down.

'Thank you,' said Josh, when I indicated that the pint was his.

'I know where she is,' said Nick. 'Sorry, I should have said.'

'Yes,' I scolded him, 'you should. I've been worrying. I hope she's not still down at the café.'

'No, she's not. She's sparked out in her armchair at the cottage.'

'How do you know that?' I asked, as I stopped midway to taking a drink.

'I wandered along to her place before coming here,' he told me. 'And I could see her asleep through the window. Obviously I didn't knock for her after that. I don't know how she's going to get through the next few weeks if she's already this exhausted right at the start of the season.'

'Me neither,' said Josh, sounding kindly concerned. 'We were in the café earlier, weren't we, Daisy? And it was rammed.'

'We were,' I said, looking over to where Marguerite was chatting and laughing with a couple of customers while pulling pints at the same time. I couldn't do that. The glasses I filled always required my entire attention. 'But don't worry about it. I have a plan.'

'You do?' Nick asked.

'Well,' I conceded, 'the beginning of one. Just leave it with me.'

Chapter 14

Mindful that I was increasingly in danger of being accused of using Mum and Dad's place as a glorified hotel and needing peace and quiet in which to further develop the idea I'd come up with after losing spectacularly at the pub quiz, I decided to drive home that night rather than stay with Josh in Wynmouth.

He was a bit sulky about it, but only in a play-acting kind of way, and I wondered if Marguerite's earlier supposition that he was mad for me might actually be true. I didn't currently have the bandwidth to think too deeply about it, or what my own feelings for him might be morphing into, so focused instead on what most needed my immediate attention.

When the cottage phone rang early the next morning, it turned out to be Algy.

'There, look,' he said a short while later when I had joined him at the manor and we were watching the cat-cam footage on his computer screen. 'That's her. That's little Luna.'

Filling the screen for just a few seconds was a small, scrawny black cat, wolfing down the food that Algy had put out at an alarming rate.

'I wonder what scared her off,' he tutted, peering even closer as the feral feline looked in one direction, then bolted out of view in the other.

'Maybe it was the panther,' I suggested while stifling a yawn.

I hadn't slept particularly well, but I had almost made up my mind about my plan and as far as I was concerned, that was hours awake in bed well spent. Though perhaps not as well spent as they would have been if I had been awake with Josh . . .

'Hardly,' tutted Algy.

'And you're absolutely sure that's her?' I asked him.

He gave me a withering look.

'Of course, I'm sure,' he said gruffly. 'I'd recognise her anywhere. Though she's much thinner than I remember.'

'Well,' I said, 'at least you know she's still here and getting some of the food you're putting out. Even if she isn't exactly looking like a picture of health, you know she's still alive.'

Algy nodded at that.

'My concern now though,' he sighed, 'is that she possibly isn't getting as much of the food as I thought she was. My guess is that whatever scared her off could have snaffled the rest and that potentially means she's barely getting more than a few frantic bites each time she comes to eat.'

Annoyingly, the batteries in the camera, which obviously hadn't been fully charged, had gone flat right at the wrong moment and that meant it hadn't recorded whatever had come along next, but we knew something had because Luna had pelted off.

'I was going to suggest we try and set something up to catch her,' I told Algy as I set the batteries to charge, 'but having seen her in action, she seems so flighty and nervous, I don't think she'd fall for whatever we came up with.'

'I think you're right there,' Algy said forlornly. 'First, we need to focus on a way of getting more food to her. Just to her.'

'Any idea how to do that?'

'None,' he sighed heavily. 'It might help if we knew where she kept disappearing to . . .'

'Well,' I said, 'let's set the camera back up with fresh batteries and think further about that once more footage has come in. I'm sure we'll think up something between us.'

'Perhaps a walk around the garden might get the ideas flowing,' Algy then suggested.

'Nice try,' I said, standing up. 'But no dice.'

'You can't put it off forever, you know.'

'Thankfully,' I said, 'I'm not going to be here forever.'

Algy looked hurt, but it hadn't been my intention to upset him; I just wanted him to talk about something else. Anything other than the garden.

'Are you really in such a rush to leave Wynbrook again?' he asked sadly, but he didn't give me time to answer. 'Because I wish you weren't. It's so wonderful having you back here, Daisy. You know I think of you, and your parents of course, as family, but you especially. You're the granddaughter I never had. It's really put some pep back in my step knowing there's some young blood here and about the place.'

The hardest lump had formed in my throat as Algy spoke. I knew he had family of his own, a son if memory served, but he had been estranged from him for a very long time. I had only been small when the fallout had occurred and the sad situation had never been resolved and was only ever rarely talked about and always when Algy was out of earshot.

I didn't think it was my place to broach it, but I did wonder if that, combined with his tumble and the possible loneliness my parents had speculated over, might be responsible for some of the melancholy he had been feeling before my return, or was potentially still feeling if his current words were anything to go by.

'There's always Nick,' I pointed out, unable to commit to saying I'd stay for longer than the next few weeks. An assurance that I'd stay would doubtless lift Algy's spirits, but then I'd crush them if an opportunity to leave Wynbrook presented itself sooner. 'He's the same age as me.'

'He's always busy running the fruit farm,' Algy pointed out. 'And doing a wonderful job of it,' he hastily added. 'But that means I barely see him.'

I knew for myself how busy Nick was, especially at this time of year, so couldn't dispute that or suggest that Nick could spend time up at the manor in the evenings. He was generally too worn out to sparkle socially.

'It feels to me like everything is grinding to a halt,' Algy then said morosely. 'We're all getting older and I haven't got around to instigating half of the plans I had for the place.'

I knew the cut-flower garden was one of those plans and had I not had such upsetting memories associated with that part of the garden, I would have seized on that and asked him to show me and share his vision.

'The cut-flower garden, for example,' he said, staring into space, while he neatly followed my thoughts. His expression told me that he wasn't now trying to manipulate me into visiting, he was simply letting his mind freely flow, 'is full of blooms. Fragrant sweet peas and Sweet Williams, cosmos, stocks, cornflowers and Alchemilla mollis, to name just a few . . .'

I unconsciously inhaled the biggest breath, easily imagining both the heady scents and the simple but stunning raffia hand-tied bunches such beautiful flowers could create.

'But there's no one to oversee it and now it's getting choked with weeds, too,' Algy continued in a different tone, and the picture in my mind turned into something far less attractive. 'And everything will soon run to—'

'Seed,' I interrupted. 'I know how often those flowers need cutting to keep more coming throughout the season.'

They needed daily, sometimes twice-daily, cutting and had the garden been opened to the public as Algy had originally planned, they would have had it.

'Exactly,' he said sadly, then carried on in a louder voice, 'but I didn't get you here to bang on about that, Daisy. I do know, and I do understand how you really feel about the garden. It wasn't my intention to bring it up again.'

'I know that,' I said gently, knowing that he was telling the truth. 'I can sense that, but I'm sorry that you're feeling so sad about it all.'

'Inevitable, I suppose,' he shrugged, 'when you're shuffling towards the end of the twig and there's no one to come along and keep feathering the nest you've left behind.'

'Trust you to express it like that,' I said, with a small smile. I leant over and kissed his soft cheek, feeling choked.

'Come on then,' he rallied, 'let's get this camera back up. I daresay you've got a million things to do today, haven't you?'

'Just one,' I told him, 'but it's really important, otherwise I would have stayed.'

Thankfully, Algy was sounding a little brighter by the time I left him. Whether that was genuine or put on for my benefit,

I couldn't be sure. Obviously, I hoped it was the former and that our time together was doing him some good, rather than making him hanker for what he'd once had family-wise and then been denied. Had I not had other fish to fry, I genuinely would have stayed with him longer, but I was desperate to check in on Penny and then see Josh ahead of my next shift in the pub.

'All quiet on the western front?' I smiled, when I arrived at the café and found everything under control and a couple of empty tables.

'I told you I could manage,' said Penny, who was wiping down the countertop.

'And that's nothing to do with the weather today, is it?'

The sky had turned grey and there was a rather mean wind whipping in from the sea, so the beach was all but deserted. I was grateful for the cardigan I'd grabbed ahead of leaving Wynbrook, but my bare legs were goose-pimpled all over.

'It might have some bearing.' She frowned, looking out at the cloud-covered view. 'But like I said yesterday, it's a learning curve and I'm still finding my feet.'

'Have you tweaked the menu now?'

'Yes,' she said, letting out a breath. She was clearly disappointed about that, but I hoped that if my plan worked, she'd soon be able to put more of her own dishes back on the chalkboard again. 'So,' she smiled stoically, 'what can I get you? Or are you just passing through?'

'Passing through to where?' I asked, making a show of looking around. 'My options are somewhat limited in Wynmouth.'

'Don't tell me you're missing city life,' Penny said laughingly, 'because I won't believe that for a second.'

I gave her suggestion a moment's thought.

'No,' I agreed. 'You're right, I'm not, and especially not at this time of year.'

I had often dreamt of escaping to the Wynmouth seaside and swimming in the open sea when I was stuck in the stuffy apartment in the summer, trawling through the employment agency websites looking for yet another job. Penny knew I was a country girl at heart and it was that that she had alluded to.

'And of course, I meant passing through as in on your way to see Josh,' Penny then said as she set about making me a latte, knowing that's what I would be most in the mood for. 'Or have you just come from Crow's Nest?'

'If you'd made it to the pub quiz,' I said, fishing a little, 'you'd know that I went back to Wynbrook last night.'

'I had planned to,' she said, turning back to me, 'but I had the day's receipts to sort through and a couple of orders to make and the time just ran away from me once I'd got home.'

Clearly she wasn't going to mention that she'd been so tired after the influx of customers that she'd crashed out in her armchair as soon as she'd sat down, and I wasn't going to bring it up. I could tell she was still trying to put a brave face on things and Nick might not have told her that he'd seen her through her cottage window, flaked out and dead to the world.

'Well,' I said instead, 'we could have done with you. Sam let me join Josh and Nick, but we were all useless. We barely got anything right.'

'The pub questions aren't that hard,' she teased and I almost regretted letting her off. 'So, why did you head home? Trouble in paradise?'

'Far from it.' I grinned. 'I needed a night off.'

'Daisy,' she said and blushed.

'What?' I laughed. 'It's true. That and I didn't want another lecture from Mum and Dad.'

'Trouble at Wynbrook?' she grimaced.

'You could say that,' I sighed. 'I'm grateful I've got a roof over my head, but I'm not enjoying staying in the cottage. It might not have been so bad if I'd never been away, but I'm used to my independence and space now. I feel like my every move is being watched, especially now Mum and Dad know I'm seeing someone.'

'I can see how that would make things tricky,' Penny said sympathetically. 'And in case you were wondering, my sofa is still at your disposal.'

'Thank you,' I said, taking a sip of the latte, which was perfect for the chilly day. 'I'll definitely keep it in mind.'

Having watched Penny negotiate a surprising rush of customers, given the weather, and having refused my offer to help with any of them because she was worried I'd be worn out ahead of my shift in the pub, I felt further convinced that my plan was a good one. However, before I started to put it into place, I called in to see Josh.

'Hey Daisy,' he said, smiling, when he answered the door. 'I wasn't sure I was going to see you today.'

He quickly crossed the room to where he'd left his laptop open on the sofa and closed it with a snap, before plumping the cushions to make room for me.

'How's your day been so far?' I asked him, feeling grateful to be out of the Wynmouth wind as I sat on the sofa.

'Lonely.' He grinned. 'I missed you last night. How about you?'

'If you're asking if I missed you,' I smiled up at him, 'then the answer is yes.'

'Good.' He grinned, flopping down next to me, which caused me to tilt towards him. 'And today?' he asked, wrapping an arm around me as I snuggled closer.

I didn't want to tell him about the plan I had now properly decided upon, which was all about helping Penny, in case he didn't think it would work and tried to talk me out of it.

'I've been helping Algy with his search for this little feral cat he's taken a liking to,' I said instead.

'And did you find it?' Josh asked, kissing the top of my head.

'Sadly not,' I told him, 'but the camera picked it up for a few seconds, so we at least know it's still alive and in the area . . .'

I had thought that would really cheer Algy up, but thinking back over our conversation, I realised it had only briefly boosted his spirits, and he was still feeling sad.

'And was Mr Alford pleased about that?' Josh asked.

'Mr Alford.' I smiled. 'It feels funny to hear Algy called that.'

'Well,' said Josh, tickling my ribs and making me wriggle, 'I can hardly call him, Algy, can I?'

I didn't remember ever mentioning Algy's surname, but then I wasn't the only person in Wynmouth Josh talked to, was I?

'If you had taken me up on the offer I'd made for you to come and meet him,' I wheedled, 'then you'd know that's *exactly* what you could call him. Everyone does. And in answer to your question, it did please him to know the cat was still around, but not as much as I had hoped . . .'

'Oh, and why was that, do you think?'

I took a moment to consider how to answer. It wasn't my place to talk about the melancholy that seemed to be holding

That was what I was
of his low mood,
the future of

Algy in its grip

beginning to

now that he

Wynbro
'Th
wh   er upset
the

d Tess,

eling frustrated that wherever
o be noticed and commented

gone for   at telling me how close

oking troubled.

u you know where you're going after you've tired of here?'

'I don't think I could ever tire of here,' he sighed, 'but no. I'm still undecided.'

'You must be bored witless,' I teased. 'You've not left the village since you arrived and there's only so many hours you can spend on the beach and in the pub.'

'Well, thankfully,' he said, inching even closer to me, 'I've found myself the most amazing distraction to stop me getting bored.'

'Oh, have you now?' I giggled.

'Yes,' he said, quickly standing up and pulling me to my feet in one swift movement. 'Come on, distraction. Let's see how you can amuse me today.'

'How is it possible that you're late for your shift, Daisy,' Sam said with exasperation when I breathlessly rushed into the pub,

'when I know for a fact that you
cottage?'

'I'm sorry,' I grimaced. 'How d:
was?'

'George was in this afternoon
in,' Sam told me, as I smoothed d
bag under the bar.

'That's village life for you,' s:
kitchen for once.

'And village gossip,' I added, f
I was, my every move seemed
on.

'George was under the impression t
to the pub you were would put my mind at rest about
turning up on time,' Sam added, defending his friend.

'Did you think I might be late then?' I asked.

'Let's just say,' Sam said sardonically, 'it did cross my mind
and as Marguerite isn't coming in this evening, I really need
you on top form.'

It wasn't my intention to mess up, but for some reason that
evening, I couldn't seem to get anything right. I muddled orders,
spilt soup and even smashed a glass ahead of upsetting an entire
bowl of ice.

'Like I said earlier,' Sam huffed, as I started scooping up the
ice and mopping the floor so it wasn't such a lethal trip hazard,
'top form.'

My ineptitude did, however, make the conversation that I
needed to have with my boss somewhat easier.

'Have you got a minute?' I asked, as the last customer left
and Sam bolted the door.

'I was going to ask you the same thing,' he said, looking thoroughly fed up.

'In that case, would it be all right if I spoke first? It would be nice to say my bit before you fire me.'

Sam didn't appear surprised by what I had said and I guessed that either a sacking or an official warning had been heading my way. If he agreed to what I had in mind, it was going to be a novelty for me to leave a position under my own terms. Even if that was only by the skin of my teeth.

'Go on then,' he said, offering me a seat at the table closest to the bar, 'let's hear it.'

I got the distinct impression that he thought I was about to plead for my position on his team and his surprised reaction when I didn't, confirmed that.

'If it's all right with you,' I began, 'and judging by my performance this evening, I have a feeling it will be, I'd like to stop working here, with immediate effect.'

'Oh,' he said, his eyes widening, 'right.'

'Marguerite mentioned that she's keen to stay around here for quite a while and I think she'd love it if you offered her my hours behind the bar. With her taking my place, you wouldn't be left in the lurch over the summer season because let's face it, she's the consummate pub professional and, more often than not, I'm a hindrance rather than a help.'

Sam smiled at that.

'You can dispute that if you like.' I smiled back.

'I don't think I can,' he laughed.

'So, you're happy to let me go?'

He actually looked thrilled, not just happy.

'Yes,' he said, sounding relieved, 'I'm happy to let you go.'

'I'm sorry it hasn't worked out. I didn't think it would take me so long to get the hang of it and I hadn't realised the place would always be so busy.'

'Well,' said Sam, 'you gave it a shot and you were getting there, most of the time. Your time-keeping needs some work though.'

'I blame Josh,' I said, passing the buck and then taking it back again. 'No, I don't. I do need to be more diligent about turning up on time.'

'So,' Sam asked, 'what's next? Is there somewhere new on the horizon or are you taking a break?'

'There's somewhere new,' I told him. 'It's only going to be part-time again, but it would have been hard trying to juggle working here and there.'

'And where is there?'

'As soon as I've told my new boss,' I said laughingly, 'I'll come in and tell you.'

Chapter 15

Knowing it was the first weekend of the school summer holidays and having checked the weather forecast, which was set to be sunny and hot, it didn't take me a second to work out that Wynmouth, and especially the beach, was going to be busy that Saturday. Consequently, I was up with the lark and waiting at the café even before Penny had appeared.

I heard her before I spotted her, rushing along the path and muttering under her breath. She didn't sound particularly happy and I hoped my presence and the offer I was about to make was going to make her day, rather than ruin it.

'Good morning!' I said, jumping up the second she came in sight and relieving her of a large cardboard box she was struggling to manhandle, while rifling through her pockets for the café keys. 'I'll hold this while you get the door open, shall I?'

'Daisy!' she gasped, obviously surprised to see me. 'What are you doing here?'

'Let us into the café first,' I said, because the box was really heavy, 'and then I'll tell you.'

Once we were inside and the door was again closed and

locked, Penny relieved me of the box and having stowed it in the kitchen, began turning on various lights and gadgets.

'I won't be ready to serve breakfasts for a little while yet,' she told me, sounding flustered. 'There's lots to do before I'm officially open for the day.'

'I guessed there would be,' I told her, 'and I haven't actually come for breakfast. Though that avocado, lemon and lardon thing you were on about the other day does sound good . . .'

'That's one of the things I've taken off the menu,' Penny said with disappointment, while my mouth continued to water. 'So, why are you here?' she asked.

'To offer my services,' I declared and I gave her a salute as I refocused.

'As what?' She frowned.

'Your official assistant,' I told her. 'I've jacked my job in at the pub to help you here in the café instead.'

'You've done what?' she gasped, her mouth falling open in shock.

'I'm going to do all of the things that you were struggling with and which meant you were having to compromise on the menu I know you spent so long putting together. Like that avocado dish,' I winked. 'The one I've now got a serious hankering for.'

I knew I had said to Sam that I had struggled with the busyness in the pub, and that the café was equally as packed, especially when the sun was shining, but at least there were no pints for me to get my head around pulling here. I could far more easily manage what was required of me in the café environment than behind the bar, now I knew everything that the role entailed.

'Oh, Daisy,' Penny said, looking tearful rather than elated, 'that's so kind of you, but you really shouldn't have done that.'

I shook my head at her reaction.

'I knew you'd say that,' I laughed, as I unlocked the door again so I could carry out the colourful bistro tables, chairs and sun brollies that were stored inside overnight. 'That's why I didn't tell you before I did it.'

'But the thing is—'

'If you're going to say you can't pay me,' I said airily, 'then I'll put out a tips jar or something.'

The financial aspect was the one thing I hadn't thought through. My shifts in the bar didn't bring in much, but without them I was going to be living on thin air.

'I can pay you,' she started to say, 'but it's only the minimum wage, and only until—'

'That's fine,' I said, waving her words away again as I picked up a couple more chairs. 'That'll be enough to keep me in beer and chips for the next few weeks, won't it?'

I didn't wait for her to answer, but began earning my keep by immediately setting up the seating area and refilling the various water bowls that were dotted around the outside of the café for thirsty dogs.

'Hadn't you better get on?' I called through the open door when I realised Penny was watching me. 'Let's see if we can get ahead before the rush, shall we?'

We did get ahead, but only just, and there was no chance of me sitting down and tucking into any sort of breakfast because the café had a steady stream of customers throughout the day. Even with the two of us on duty, it was a push to keep the queue from snaking out of the door and the only food I ingested was eaten on the go in snatched mouthfuls.

Josh had briefly put in an appearance, but then left again when I told him I was sorry, but I didn't have time to chat and that I'd fill him in about my change of job at the end of the day. I was looking forward to heading to the pub on a Saturday night and staying on the customers' side of the bar. I'd had the foresight to bring a change of outfit with me and, if all went to plan, I'd spend the night with him in the cottage, which would mean an easy commute in the morning. Perhaps even an early swim . . .

'I think you've charged me for three of these, instead of two,' came a slightly irate voice.

I looked at the red-faced man holding up two ice lollies.

'I'm so sorry,' I apologised, with a bright smile. 'You're right. Let me clear the transaction and I'll do it again.'

'I don't know how you do it, working in here,' said the woman who was standing next to the man. 'I don't know how you keep up with it all. Has it been like this all day?'

'Yep,' I said, holding out the card reader that now showed the right amount. 'We've been packed out since early this morning.'

I could see that the beach was still crowded, so there was no respite in sight yet. My feet had ached after an evening working in the pub, but it was nothing compared to a full day in the café. I was going to need to wear shoes with even more support if I wanted to stay upright for the next few weeks.

'You'll sleep well tonight,' the woman commented as she and the man headed back outside into the searing sun.

'That's the last of the crab gone,' said Penny, as she dashed out from the kitchen and put a thick line through that particular dish on the chalkboard, which was screwed to the wall next to the counter. 'And there are only enough prawns left for three more servings.'

'A busy day for seafood then,' I said. 'What will you serve tomorrow?'

'There'll be more crab delivered just after dawn tomorrow,' she told me. 'Perhaps you'd like to be here to sign for it?'

'I can be.' I swallowed, not wanting to think of another day as busy as the one we were currently living through. 'I can do that.'

'I was only joking.' Penny smiled. 'You should have seen your face.'

'Oh, ha, ha.' I grinned. 'Honestly though, Pen, this is mad. Will you really be able to cope when you get back to school having had no time off at all?'

'I'm hoping,' she said, as another family came bowling through the door, 'that the adrenaline won't give out until the autumn half-term, and in the meantime—'

'Four Magnums, please,' demanded one of the children.

'Coming right up,' I responded.

I hoped Penny was right about the adrenaline keeping her going and I hoped I also had the stamina to keep up with what was required. Working in the café suddenly made my shorter shifts in the pub look like a walk in the park, even though my skills, for what they were worth, were better suited to the café. The constant footfall throughout the day had kept me on my toes and the gaff with the ice lolly overcharging aside, I'd just about held my own. On day one. There were still weeks of summer to go and my earlier conviction that I'd made the right decision was already being tested!

'Lock the door quick,' said Penny at the end of what felt like the longest day ever, 'and I'll draw the blinds.'

It was way after the café's official closing time and there were still people on the beach, but the boss had said she'd had enough and I was more than happy to lock up as requested.

'Oh my god,' I groaned, as I collapsed into a chair. 'I can't believe we did that. You never could have managed on your own, Pen. No offence, but it would have been impossible for you to do everything.'

'No offence taken,' she said, wilting into the chair opposite mine. 'You're right. I'd already worked out what it might be like on a weekend after you and Josh helped me out the other day, so . . .' She then stopped and took a very deep breath. 'With that in mind—'

'I'm beginning to think you're going to need two pairs of extra hands, rather than just mine,' I cut in before she'd finished her sentence. 'At least that way you could factor in some proper breaks.'

Penny didn't say anything further and I quickly looked at her to make sure she hadn't fallen asleep already. She hadn't.

'Sorry, I interrupted. What were you going to say?'

'Well,' she said, shifting in her chair and looking upset. 'The thing is . . . and I did try to tell you this earlier . . .'

'Tell me what?'

'That I *have* taken on an extra pair of hands. Two extra pairs of hands, in fact.'

'What?'

'After that crazy day last week, I had a video call with Sophie and she suggested I take on a couple of teenagers for the season,' Penny explained. 'In her rush to leave, she'd forgotten to mention that's what she usually did and it wasn't until I called her and admitted that I was struggling to manage everything, that she brought up taking on summer staff.'

'Oh,' I said, feeling taken aback. 'I see.'

'I should have realised she didn't fly solo through the summer,' Penny carried on. 'So, I took her suggestion to heart and got on with finding some help.'

'So,' I said, trying to sound breezy, 'you don't actually need me to work with you here, after all.'

She shook her head.

'If you'd told me what you were planning to do,' she said, looking upset, 'then I would have explained that I'd already got the situation in hand and suggested you keep your job in the pub.'

'Damn,' I said, putting my head in my hands. 'I'm so sorry, Pen.'

'What are you apologising for?' she tutted. 'I'm the one—'

'You're the one with the friend who impetuously rushed in and wanted to save the day but hadn't given a thought to the fact that you might have already saved it for yourself,' I again cut in.

My actions had been well intentioned, but rash and impulsive too. I had wanted to make the summer easier for my friend and make the experience of running the café what she so desperately wanted it to be. But I could see now that it would have made far more sense to have told her what I was planning, rather than try and make it a surprise.

'And I love that friend for wanting to do that,' Penny said sincerely. 'And I honestly couldn't have managed without you today. I'm sorry I didn't find a way of telling you earlier.'

'It's fine,' I said, wondering how long I would be able to keep the blunder from my parents. I'd have to find another job fast, assuming Penny's tag team were starting soon. Hopefully I'd have a couple of weeks grace to find something. 'So, when do your new members of staff join the ranks?' I dared to ask.

'Next Wednesday,' Penny told me. That was just four days away. 'It's the Smith twins. They're in Spain on holiday until Tuesday, then they'll be here the day after.'

I knew the twins she was talking about and their family. The Smiths were local, affluent and extremely successful, thanks to their inherited work ethic. The enthusiastic boy and exuberant girl would be perfect for helping Penny out. They embodied the ultimate beach aesthetic and with youth on their side, they'd be far more energetic than I was at the end of the busy day.

'You couldn't have taken on anyone better,' I commented kindly.

'They're hard workers, I'll give them that.'

'Oh god,' I laughed, trying to see the funny side. 'I've just quit my other job for two days' work, haven't I? Today and tomorrow!'

'You can come in Monday and Tuesday too.' Penny smiled. 'I'm opening from ten until three, just to see if it's worth my while, so that'll put you up to four days' work.'

'It won't be worth your while if no one turns up and you have to pay me,' I pointed out.

'I won't pay you then,' she teased.

'Hey,' I pouted. 'Seriously though, what a mess. I'm officially useless where the world of work is concerned, aren't I?'

Penny didn't answer that, but then she didn't need to. The question was definitely rhetorical.

'You could always ask Sam—' she began instead.

'No,' I cut in. 'I couldn't. He's got Marguerite now. It's fine. I'll think of something else. How about we call it a day and reconvene in the pub around eight? I might have come up with a plan by then.'

Realistically, I knew there was no chance of that.

'Sounds like a good idea.' Penny nodded, then groaned as she stood up and stretched out her back. 'I'll buy you a pint so you can drown your sorrows.'

'And I'll get Nick to fork out for the next one.'

'I don't think he's coming tonight,' she told me, trying and failing to sound upbeat.

'Not coming to the pub on a Saturday?' I gasped.

'Not this Saturday.' Penny shrugged. 'Someone told me he'd got a date.'

I was desperate to delve deeper, but Penny wasn't the person to ask. When I'd arrived back at Wynbrook, I had been committed to making it my mission to push my two best pals together, but other events had overtaken it and I still hadn't got my original matchmaking plan out of the blocks. That said though, considering how my plan to save Penny's summer had just gone, perhaps I would be best leaving her love life well alone . . .

'So, let me get this straight,' Josh frowned into his pint later that evening and after Penny had gone home, 'you jacked in your job here for another job without asking the person you wanted to take you on if they would?'

We'd already been through it once, but Josh was having trouble processing the details of what I'd misguidedly, but kind-heartedly, done.

'Yep.' I nodded. 'That's it. I quit the pub for the café, but in the meantime, Penny had already found staff to work for her.'

'So, now you're totally out of a job.'

'I sure am.'

'What are you going to do?' he asked.

'No idea.' I shrugged, then drained my glass.

It was my second strong pint on an almost empty stomach, so I definitely wouldn't be driving home. I wondered if the alcohol was playing its part in making me feel less stressed than I probably should have been, because I was rather chilled.

'And what do your parents think about you leaving the pub?' Josh questioned.

'They don't know,' I grimaced, wishing he hadn't brought them into the conversation as my former chill started to warm up. 'I haven't told them.'

'*You* might not have told them,' said Tess, who had overhead the very end of our conversation as she came to clear the table next to ours, 'but it doesn't necessarily follow that they don't know.'

'What?' I gulped, feeling my relaxed attitude melt into a soggy puddle.

'They came in here for lunch,' Tess told me.

'They came in here for lunch,' I echoed.

My parents never came into the pub. I couldn't remember the last time they'd crossed the threshold. I wondered what had tempted them inside on the very last day I could have wanted them to darken the Smuggler's doors.

'They came in for lunch,' Tess said again, 'and your dad asked Sam what time you'd be starting today and Sam said . . .' she faltered, then carried on, 'Sam said, you wouldn't be starting at all, because you'd . . . quit.'

I threw Sam a harsh look and he pulled an apologetic face.

'I didn't think,' he said, looking shamefaced. 'It was busy in here and I just blurted it out before I realised that if he was asking when you'd be in, then he didn't know that you wouldn't be.'

'Well,' I said, as I plunged my hands into my hair, 'he certainly knows now.'

'Sorry,' Sam apologised. 'If I'd known at the time, I would have said they'd find you working in the café instead.'

I'd told Sam where I had switched working to when Josh and I arrived that evening, though not for how long, so he hadn't known I'd found something else when he'd talked to Dad at lunchtime.

'Let's not have that conversation,' I said, holding up a hand. 'I can stay at yours tonight, can't I?' I asked Josh as I clutched his arm, even though we'd already discussed it earlier.

'Absolutely,' he laughed, then lowered his voice, so no one else could hear. 'Given your reaction to Sam's confession, I'm guessing your parents aren't going to be pleased about you quitting your job here?'

'No,' I sighed, 'they won't be and I can't even tell them it's okay because I'm going to be working in the café for the rest of the summer now, can I?'

'Well,' Josh suggested, 'you could just be a bit vague. I mean, you're going to be working there until the middle of next week, aren't you? So, technically you could buy yourself a few days' grace by just telling them you're working with Penny now. You don't *have* to supply them with an end date and in the meantime, you can keep looking for something else.'

I bit my lip and considered what he'd just said.

'That might work,' I eventually agreed. 'That might actually work. Though I'm not sure that I like this sneaky side of you, Josh.' I smiled. 'Even if it has potentially got me temporarily out of a tight spot.'

'It's not sneaky,' he said, pretending to be aghast. 'I'm the king of spin. If I can make something positive out of a difficult situation then I'm going to utilise the heck out of it.'

'In that case,' I said, leaning into him, 'please, utilise away.'

Chapter 16

That night, as I drifted off into a thoroughly satisfying sleep, I was feeling far more content than I had been when Sam had confessed that he'd told Mum and Dad that I was no longer in his employ.

However, I didn't feel anywhere near as happy when I woke just before dawn and had to leave the cosiness of the bed to pad to the bathroom in search of painkillers to soothe my annoyingly thumping head and found that my feet still ached from the hours spent working in the café. The forecast was set for another wonderfully sunny day and I knew I would enjoy working with Penny all the more if I was wearing more supportive shoes. Unfortunately, however, those were all back at Wynbrook.

There was no point in asking Pen to lend me a pair because we wore different sizes, so I scribbled Josh a note, then let myself out of the cottage and drove quickly back to Mum and Dad's. My parents were both early risers, irrespective of whether or not they were heading to work and I knew I had a tight turnaround if I wanted to creep in, grab what I needed and dash out again before they were up.

'Daisy,' said Dad, as I fumbled to unlock the cottage door just as he opened it from the inside.

He was wearing his standard summer work gear, even though it was Sunday and still ridiculously early *and* he was also sporting a deep frown.

'Dad!' I gasped, my free hand flying to my chest. 'You made me jump.'

'Is everything all right?' he asked. 'Surely you aren't just getting in.'

'In and out, actually,' I told him as Mum appeared in the doorway from the hall, wrapped in a cotton dressing gown. 'I've just come back to collect something I'm going to need today.'

'Well,' he said gruffly, 'if you can spare us a minute, and I rather think you can, then you'd better sit down. Your mum and I need to talk to you.'

His tone brooked no refusal and I knew I was trapped.

'Yes,' said Mum, as she filled the kettle and further compounded the ensnared feeling. 'Do sit down, Daisy. This won't take long.'

The following few minutes seemed to last at least an hour and words such as *irresponsible* and *disappointing* littered the one-sided conversation, as did phrases such as *we had a feeling it wouldn't last* and *you can't just swan about for the next few months*. If the intention was to make me feel like I was a naughty child rather than an adult, then it was pretty much mission accomplished and I found myself wishing I'd never driven over the cattlegrid and on to the Wynbrook Estate those couple of weeks ago.

I let a silence fall once Mum and Dad had finally run out of steam. The kettle had long since come to the boil, and I felt that I was about to, as well.

'So, is that everything then?' I eventually asked, making the greatest effort to keep my tone neutral. 'Because I only came back to pick up a pair of shoes. The ones I wore yesterday when I started my new job helping Penny in the café weren't up to all those hours on my feet, so I thought I'd switch them for something different today. I have a feeling it's going to be busy again.'

When Josh had suggested that I put a positive spin on the few days' work I had secured with Penny, I wasn't sure it was the right thing to do. However, having just been verbally assaulted and made to feel like the let-down daughter I obviously was, I had reached for his suggestion and wrung the life out of it. The expression on both my parents' faces assuaged any guilt I might have felt about employing the deception and I felt rather smug.

'Penny was struggling with the summer footfall in the café,' I continued, by way of a more detailed explanation, 'and as I know how much these few weeks working there mean to her, I thought I'd give her a hand. It's hard work and long days, so I couldn't manage working in the pub too. Sam had someone else on hand to take my place so I thought I'd be better off helping my friend. The harder work is worth taking on in this instance, isn't it?'

I left the question hanging and went to retrieve the pair of shoes I needed and another back-up pair, just in case. I also stuffed some clean clothes and toiletries into a bag so I wouldn't have to come back to the cottage until the end of Tuesday at the earliest. Assuming Josh was willing to accommodate me for that long. If he wasn't or couldn't, then I was certain Penny's sofa would.

'We didn't know,' Mum said, when I went back downstairs again. 'We didn't know you were working in the café.'

'Of course you didn't,' I smiled, 'I hadn't had the chance to tell you and Sam didn't mention it because he didn't know when you had lunch in the pub either. What did you have, by the way? The crab dishes are always popular.'

I didn't wait for them to answer because they both still looked so surprised, they probably couldn't have formulated a response if their lives depended on it.

'Right then,' I said. 'I'd better get off. I won't be back tonight or tomorrow, but I'll keep in touch with Algy about the cat camera. Bye!'

I purposefully left the back door open and practically skipped down the path to my car. It felt good to have the upper hand for once, even if that hand hadn't been honestly dealt.

Just as I had known it would be, Sunday was bonkers busy, even more bonkers busy than Saturday had been. I had thought I was going to hate working through another hectic day, but actually the constant queue and unrelenting requests for cold drinks, lollies and ice creams left me no opportunity to dwell on what I'd said to Mum and Dad.

I'd barely pulled into a parking space in the village after our conversation before the guilt had kicked in about misleading them. I knew they'd said some pretty hurtful things to me, but it didn't follow that I then had to be deceitful as a result, did it? I could have chosen a more righteous path, but I'd walked along the easy one instead, even though ultimately it had given me scant satisfaction.

'Yay!' said Penny, as she punched the air in triumph after she'd switched the open sign to closed early Sunday evening and firmly turned the key in the lock. 'We did it!'

'That we did,' I agreed, as I slumped onto a chair and slid my shoes off. 'I'm not quite sure how, but we made it.'

'And we're going to do it all again tomorrow,' she beamed. 'Though not for quite so long.'

'You're mad,' I said, as someone knocked loudly on the door and I wondered why on earth she was opening the café on days when it would usually be closed, even if it was only going to be for a few hours. Her new dream job was nothing like mine. Not that I had yet worked out what mine was, of course. 'Totally cuckoo, Pen. Do you know that?'

'Yep!' she laughed, still looking deliriously happy as she went to open the door again.

'Don't let them in,' I admonished. 'We've only just closed!'

She ignored me and opened the door and I was pleased she had because it was Josh and Nick – Nick was carrying a basket and blankets and Josh had a huge cool bag and his guitar slung over his shoulder.

'Our saviours,' I praised, realising that yet again, I hadn't eaten properly for almost the entire day.

'We thought you might be hungry,' Nick said. 'Even though you're working in a café.'

'Nick thought you might be hungry,' said Josh, unwilling to accept the credit for the food Nick had found the time to prepare, even though he'd been working too. 'I thought you might be in the mood for some music.'

I was thrilled that he was keen to carry on playing his guitar now he'd had the benefit of George's encouragement and the success of performing in the pub.

'Yes, to both,' said Penny, looking thrilled. 'Thanks guys.'

'And I thought you might also fancy a swim,' Josh said to me.

'So I snuck into the beach hut and picked up the costume and towel you left there a few days ago, Daisy.'

'That,' I said, holding out my hand for the costume so I could get changed in the café loos, 'was an inspired idea.'

Josh kissed me lightly on the lips and even though I was exhausted, I felt my libido spring into life.

'And I thought that you, Penny,' said Nick, his voice trembling a little for some reason as he reached into the basket he had put down and pulled something out, 'might like this . . .'

He handed Penny a brown paper-wrapped parcel. It was tied with a blue velvet ribbon. She looked from the parcel to him and back again.

'I hope it's the right one.' He swallowed. 'I think it is. I went to pick it up after work last night.'

'I thought you had a date last night,' I said, releasing Josh and then realising that I might have just ruined what had the potential to be a romantic moment.

Some matchmaker I was . . .

'I did.' Nick grinned. 'Well, not a date date. I did meet someone, but only to get this.' He nodded at the parcel Penny was holding. 'I've had a real job tracking it down and then there were some very specific details to check before I committed to buying it.'

Penny gasped and her eyes widened as she quickly tugged at the ribbon and then pulled away the paper.

'Oh, Nick,' she sobbed, and began to properly cry.

In her hands was a blue hardback book. She pulled in a ragged breath and composed herself a little before opening it.

'This is it,' she sobbed again. 'This is the one.'

Josh looked questioningly at me, but I had no idea what the significance of the book was or even what it was about.

'And there was this too,' Nick said, sounding as choked as Penny as he pulled another book out of the basket, unwrapped this time.

All of the colour drained from Penny's face as she took it and I honestly thought she might pass out.

'It can't be,' she murmured, putting the hardback down on a table and turning her attention to its dog-eared companion. I could see that one was so packed full of loose bits of paper it could barely be closed. 'How is this even possible?'

She looked at Nick and Nick looked at her and then suddenly she stepped forward and kissed him on the lips. She kissed him hard and long, to be precise, and Nick willingly reciprocated and I felt so happy I thought my heart was going to burst right out of my chest. Who knew a couple of tatty-looking books could have such an emotional impact?

Josh started to quietly edge towards the door and I grabbed the blankets and silently followed him. We slipped out of the café and didn't speak until we were down on the sand, for fear of the pair hearing us and ending the kiss I had so longed for them to share.

'What,' whispered Josh, even though we were easily far enough away for them not to catch our conversation, 'was that all about?'

'I have absolutely no idea,' I smiled up at him and only then realised that my eyes were full of tears, 'but that kiss has been years in the making. I had honestly begun to think it was never going to happen.'

'Well, I could see they were made for each other the first time I met them,' Josh grinned, 'but I didn't think it was my place to mention it.'

'I used to feel that way too,' I confessed, 'but I have to admit, it had been my intention to speak up and somehow try to get them together this summer.'

'But those two books seem to have done the work for you.' Josh smiled.

'Apparently so.' I smiled back.

'And they're really nothing to do with you?'

'No,' I said, shaking my head, 'they're not. They're all Nick and they obviously mean something very special to Penny given her reaction to receiving them.'

We giggled about that.

'So,' said Josh, 'do you fancy a swim?'

'I do,' I told him. 'But I need to get changed somewhere first and have something to eat. I haven't had a proper bite since breakfast.'

'Nick has got most of the food in the basket,' Josh groaned. 'You do suppose they'll come out at some point, don't you?'

'Well, let's put it this way,' I said as my tummy rumbled loudly, 'if they don't, then I'll be going back in.'

We didn't have to wait many minutes for our friends to appear and in the meantime, I managed to wriggle into my swimming costume hidden under one of the blankets. I couldn't stop grinning as I watched Penny and Nick walk over to where Josh and I were sitting. They were holding hands and looking happier than I'd ever seen them.

'I don't know what to ask first,' I laughed, looking at the pair of them.

'I think you should start with the significance of the books,' suggested Josh. 'Given your reaction, I'm guessing they're something rather special, Penny.'

'They certainly are,' she beamed. 'And that's why I've left them in the café for now. Absolutely no sand allowed, even though I'm desperate to look through them.'

'So, tell us then,' I said, patting a space next to me on the blanket, 'what are they?'

While we gorged ourselves on the delicious picnic Nick had prepared, Penny explained why she'd been so overwhelmed by what she'd just been given.

'I've been trying to find that particular copy of *Mrs Beeton's Family Cookery* for a couple of years,' she explained. 'It belonged to my great-grandmother and has a very special dedication in the front. I've been searching high and low for it since it was lost during a house clearance organised by my mum. Unfortunately, the book wasn't missed for a while, and in that time, it disappeared without trace.'

'And Penny told you about this?' I asked Nick.

I'd never had him down as a romantic before, but knowing how much Penny loved to cook and what that book must have meant to her, there was no other word to describe his actions.

'Yes,' he said, looking at Penny with unadulterated love. 'She told me a while ago that she was looking for it and I secretly joined in the search too.'

'Oh, Nick,' I said, feeling teary again.

'And what was the other book?' Josh asked, smiling at my reaction to the romantic gesture. 'The tatty one with the pages falling out.'

'That,' said Penny, sounding even more emotional, 'is a hand-written recipe book that has been passed down my family line for generations. It disappeared with the Mrs Beeton and I had

absolutely no hope that it had survived. I hadn't even considered trying to find it.'

'But I had.' Nick smiled.

'And you found it.' Penny smiled back, leaning over to kiss
him again. 'Incredibly, the two were still together.'

Out of every item in the world that had ever come into
Penny's orbit, I knew that book must have meant the most. She'd
never mentioned the Mrs Beeton to me, but I could remember
her talking about the family recipe book and the dishes her nan
and then her mum had made out of it. She'd be able to make
them now too.

As delighted as I was that she now had the books back, I was
also feeling sad that she hadn't talked to me about her search. It
was another reminder of how we'd grown apart during the last
couple of years. I knew that Laurence had done nothing to
encourage me to nurture my childhood friendships, but I couldn't
blame him for us losing touch because I had been the one who
had ultimately allowed it to happen.

Thankfully Josh began to strum softly on his guitar at that
moment and my mind was saved from taking a more maudlin
turn.

'Come on, Penny,' said Nick, pulling her to her feet, 'I've
waited a long time to do this.'

I sat as close to Josh as I could get while he played and my
friends slowly danced around us. My homecoming might not
have been without its hiccups, but the things that really mattered
were playing out perfectly.

Penny was of little use the next day and it was just as well the
café was opening later in the morning as she didn't show her

face until just before ten. I had been waiting at least half an hour for her to show, but I didn't mind because Josh had walked down to the beach with me and we had chatted while we waited for her to turn up.

Given the increasingly intense depth of my relationship with him and the meaningful conversations we had enjoyed as a result, it seemed utterly impossible that I'd only known him for two weeks, two weeks exactly, to be precise.

'Do you realise it's two weeks today since you threw yourself in front of my car?' I nudged him before Penny arrived.

'I can't believe that,' he gasped, but not disputing the fact that he had been the one responsible for the near-disastrous way our paths had first crossed. 'Just two weeks. Are you sure?'

'Absolutely.' I nodded, nuzzling into his tanned neck. 'Feels more like two years, doesn't it?'

He pulled away and looked at me.

'I agree,' he said more seriously than I would have expected, 'it does feel like we've known each other far longer, but is that a good thing or a bad thing? It feels like a good thing for me, but—'

'Oh, it's a good thing,' I interrupted, before he got himself into a tizz and started wondering if I was getting bored with having him around. 'A very good thing.'

'That's all right then,' he said, kissing me. 'I'd hate to think you were considering moving on.'

That was the last thing I was thinking about. Well, where he was concerned anyway.

'The only bad thing is that I still haven't introduced you to Algy,' I pondered. 'And I would love you to meet him.'

I had a feeling they'd really like each other, but I couldn't see how I would be able to instigate an introduction without my parents getting wind of the fact that my current beau had been to Wynbrook and not been introduced to them.

I didn't want Josh to have to endure meeting either of them now, even though Dad had been impressed that he was a Wynbrook strawberry fan. My parents had done nothing to hide their disappointment about my job situation so they doubtless wouldn't hold off from expressing whatever opinion they had really formed about my current relationship.

I just knew that my summer fling was being as frowned upon as everything else now and that's what Josh was, wasn't he? A summer fling . . .

'Sorry, I'm late!' called Penny as she appeared on the path.

Her hair was all over the place and her cheeks were flushed as a result of more than sun exposure.

'You don't sound sorry,' I teased and Josh gave me a nudge.

'You're right,' she beamed, when she reached us. 'I'm not sorry at all.'

'I take it you and Nick had an entertaining evening?' I cajolingly asked.

'Honestly, Daisy,' Penny tutted. 'A lady never talks about her . . . exploits.'

'I told you about mine,' I reminded her and grinned at Josh who raised his eyebrows.

'Yes,' giggled Penny, 'but you're not a lady.'

I was about to defend myself when my phone started to ring.

'It's Algy,' I said, standing up. 'I better answer. It might be cat business.'

'Saved by the bell.' Penny winked at Josh, who also laughed.

*

As it turned out, there was no cat business that day or the day after (Algy had just wanted to chat), and I was able to focus solely on working in the café and spending time with Josh, Penny and Nick in the evenings. Both days were halcyon and I refused to think about what I was going to do when the bubble burst. I hadn't been able to find another job in the vicinity to apply for and heading home and facing the music looked like the only probable option.

'You could always move in with me for the rest of the summer,' Josh kindly offered as the time to close the café on Tuesday came around unexpectedly fast.

There had been enough customers to justify Penny opening on both days, but she'd also had time to sit and pore over the beloved books Nick had so winningly tracked down. She was absolutely in her element and I could already tell that returning to school in September was going to be a hard ask.

'I'd more than happily keep you,' Josh seductively added.

'That,' I said, kissing the end of his nose, 'sounds very much like an indecent proposal.' Josh grinned, but didn't refute what I'd said. 'And whatever your motives, I couldn't possibly accept.'

'I had a feeling you'd say that.'

He sounded rather disappointed.

'Your motives were nefarious, weren't they?' I then gasped.

'Totally.'

'Damn,' I groaned. 'Is it too late to change my mind?'

'Yep,' he said, as Penny locked the café door and pulled down the blind. 'That ship has now pulled up its anchor and set sail.'

'In that case,' I sighed, 'I suppose I'd better go home and face the music, hadn't I?'

Chapter 17

I suppose I could have put off heading back to Wynbrook for another night, but there was always the danger that I would be tempted to find a different excuse to put the inevitable off after that and the longer I transgressed, the worse my familial relationships would be.

Also, I knew I wasn't going to be full of sparkling conversation that evening and I didn't want to potentially ruin Josh's night. Or Penny and Nick's. Not that they seemed capable of looking beyond their loved-up bubble. I absolutely adored that though. It had certainly been a long time coming.

Nonetheless, and in spite of my happiness for my dearest friends, it was with a heavy heart that I drove up to the cottage and the sight of Mum and Dad still looking sour when I walked into the kitchen did nothing to help lighten its weight in my chest.

'Hello,' I said, as I put my overnight bag down and in the process avoided looking at either of them.

'You're back then,' commented Dad.

'Yes,' I responded, 'I'm back.'

'Are you staying tonight?' Mum asked, as she busied herself at the sink, also not looking at me.

'I am,' I answered.

I wondered if this stilted sort of exchange was as good as it was now going to get until I made up my mind about moving on again.

'I suppose you'll be having a lie-in tomorrow,' Dad said gruffly. 'What with no job to have to rush off to.'

My heart felt even more leaden when he said that.

'Why didn't you tell us Penny had taken on the Smith twins?' Mum frowned, as she dried her hands and gave Dad a look. I wondered if she had planned a more subtle run-up to this awkward conversation. 'When we spoke on Sunday, you made out that you were going to be working for her for the whole of the summer.'

'Because when I finished working in the pub,' I told them both, 'I thought I was going to be. I had no idea then that Penny had already made other arrangements to see her through her time running the café for Sophie.'

'But you did know when you came home to pick up your shoes and things, didn't you?' Dad surmised and I nodded. 'So, why did you lie?'

I could feel my frustration starting to bubble again and the excess of it spilt over into my next words.

'If you take just a minute to think about how you and Mum talked to me during that brief visit, Dad,' I said bluntly, 'then you'll be able to guess why. You made me feel two inches tall and talked to me exactly like you used to. Only this time, you were putting in your two pennies worth as well, Mum.'

In the past, Mum had mostly kept out of the rows I'd had with Dad. She had taken on the role of peacekeeper, but she hadn't been particularly proficient at it and last Sunday, she had abandoned it altogether.

'We're just—' she started to say.

'Worried,' I snapped. 'I know. Don't you think I'm worried too? I've very little to show for my life thus far and having the pair of you constantly reminding me of the fact isn't making me feel any better about it.'

'We just want you to—' Mum tried again.

'Get my act together,' I reeled off. 'Toe the line. Settle down. Succeed . . . You know, I think I'll drive back to Wynmouth, after all.'

I scooped my bag back up again.

'No, don't,' said Dad, in a tone that didn't exactly match his words. 'Don't do that.'

'Please stay,' Mum added more kindly.

She looked keener to have me than he did and I stared at her for a long moment. I wondered if she was aware how betrayed I'd felt that she'd joined nagging forces with Dad.

'All right,' I sighed, crossing the room in three strides. 'I'll have an early night then.'

'Don't you want any dinner?' Mum called after me.

'No, thanks.'

I resisted the urge to stomp up the stairs and blinked back the tears I was determined not to shed. However, when I opened my bedroom door, it was impossible to stop a few of them from falling. My breath caught in my throat as I became seduced by the sight in front of me and enveloped in the scent.

Every inch of space on the chest of drawers, shelves and windowsills was filled with jam jars, vases and jugs packed full of the sort of blooms that could only have come from Algy's cut-flower garden. There was a William Morris notecard on my pillow and written on the back of it in Algy's flamboyant handwriting were the words:

If you won't come to the garden, Daisy, then I'll bring the garden to you!
   With love, A x

'Oh, Algy,' I sniffed, tenderly stroking the petals of a sweet pea on my bedside table, before bending to further draw in its beautiful scent. 'Will you ever stop trying?'

I didn't expect to nod off, but that night I had one of the best sleeps I'd had in a long time. I started the day not wanting to put it down to the fact that my bedroom was filled with flowers, but the pleasure that the sight and smell of them gave me within just a few seconds of opening my eyes, soon made me change my mind.

'Where's Dad?' I asked Mum, when I couldn't put off going down for a cup of tea any longer. 'Watering already?'

'No,' said Mum, as she added another cup and saucer to the table. 'He's away for the day.'

'Away?'

Dad rarely left the estate in the summer months and never on a weekday.

'He's visiting a couple of machinery showrooms to try and strike a deal for a new ride-on,' Mum explained. 'The old one is totally on its last legs and he's told Algy he can't put off buying another one until the autumn.'

I was relieved Dad wasn't at home. I didn't much want to

start the day listening to loaded comments about him being surprised to see me up so early when I had nowhere to go and nothing to do.

'Has Algy gone with him?' I asked Mum as I poured us both tea.

'No,' she said, as she splashed milk into her cup. 'He has a follow-up appointment at the hospital later this morning, as a result of his tumble. I'm taking him to that and then we're going on to pick up some new shirts from that outfitter he favours in Holt.'

'That's a bit of a trek for a few shirts, isn't it? Can't he order them online?'

'You know, Algy.' Mum smiled. 'He prefers a more personal service.'

I looked at her as she sat down. She still looked tired and I hoped the strain of having me back for the summer wasn't exacerbating her exhaustion, but I had a strong suspicion that it might be.

'And did he,' I asked, because I found I couldn't not mention them, 'personally deliver all of the flowers currently filling my bedroom?'

I knew that had Dad been at home, I wouldn't have broached the topic, but as talking to Mum on her own hadn't so far felt strained, I was willing to briefly discuss it.

'Algy cut them,' Mum said, finally producing a smile, 'but I arranged them all and carried them up to your room for him.'

I looked at her in surprise. I wondered if Dad knew the room currently looked like a florist shop and if Mum had agreed to arranging them because she had felt bad about siding with him.

'You know,' Mum said quietly, while fiddling with her teaspoon and staring into her cup, 'with your dad at the machinery place and Algy and I at the hospital and then in Holt, you're going to be practically the only person on the entire estate today.'

'Nick will be about on the fruit farm,' I pointed out.

'You know what I'm getting at, Daisy,' she countered, her eyes darting a quick look up at me. 'You know exactly what I'm saying.'

I could have feigned ignorance, but the truth was, I did know what Mum was saying, and Algy's car, which she was driving – he'd favoured them taking out the ancient blue Bentley that day – had barely turned out of the top of the drive, before I acted on it.

I felt a heady mix of emotions as I plucked up the courage to look inside the potting shed, which was located on the edge of the garden next to the machinery sheds and smaller glass-houses and cold frames. The smell of it felt as familiar as the flowers in my bedroom. Compost, warm wood and an under-tone of linseed oil, which Dad applied to the tools every winter, took me back to a time when I had been so happy and so sure in my mind as to where my future lay.

The depth of feeling increased tenfold as, at long last, I made my way right into the garden. Whereas before, I had skirted around the periphery to the summerhouse, that morning I went all over. I traced my hands lightly along the top of the low box hedges in the knot garden. I admired the roses in the predictably named rose garden and watched the sun reflecting off the scales of the goldfish as they darted under the lily pads in the clear water of the various ponds that were dotted about the place and surrounded by pots filled with different varieties of hosta and showy blue and white agapanthus.

Everything looked to be in perfect order. That is, everything looked to be in perfect order until I reached the vast walled garden. The fruit and vegetables were all clearly looked after, but the rows and rows of flowers on the half that had been given over to Algy's passion project were choked with weeds in places, required staking and were all in need of tidying up and deadheading.

This was the part of the garden I had been most reluctant to see and that was because it had been the setting for the final, mammoth showdown I'd had with Dad ahead of relenting and going off to university.

In my head, I could still hear our raised voices rebounding off the old walls, our tempers flaring as we flung cruel words and harsh accusations at one another.

It had been our last interaction for quite some time and even though the memory of it was still all too easy to recall, my desire to make good what was now growing here shockingly and surprisingly stamped out any tendency to dwell on the past. The present and the future was what truly mattered, not the injustice of what had gone before.

With the sun not yet overhead, I clipped the secateurs, my secateurs, which I was delighted to find in their familiar place in the potting shed, to the belt of my shorts, put my water bottle in the shade, readjusted my sunhat and set to work.

'Right,' I murmured to myself as I made a start, 'let's see what we can do here, shall we?'

I had planned to be back in the cottage by early afternoon,

so my presence in the garden would definitely not have been noticed, but I soon lost all track of time. As I worked methodically along the rows, cutting back, tying in, weeding, staking and watering where necessary, time seemed to stand still. I was utterly immersed and I felt completely at peace. I was both relaxed by and enchanted with the project Algy had instigated and which Dad had tried his best to maintain until the demands of the summer mowing regime took over.

As I worked my way along the rows of plants, I imagined how the blooms could be cut, tied and sold. The area was huge and would potentially draw a decent income. It might not be established enough for members of the public to come in and cut what they wanted willy nilly, but I could have easily managed the cropping and, for this season, cut the flowers on their behalf. Then, if the idea really took off, the rows could be extended elsewhere in the garden and the season lengthened, by growing different varieties of flowers to sell the following year.

I noticed Algy hadn't included dahlias or chrysanthemums, but in my mind's eye, I could easily imagine incorporating both for later cutting. And planting spring bulbs such as tulips and daffodils could mean that the garden came into its own even earlier, catching the Easter market. I could see myself doing it all, right down to the apron I would wear and the brown paper and raffia I would wrap the bouquets in . . .

'Daisy?'

My name had been spoken softly, but I jerked upright, almost jarring my back in the process.

'Algy,' I stammered, my formerly relaxed heart thumping hard, 'what time is it?'

'Never mind the time, my darling,' he said with a choked smile, 'look what you've done!'

I took a moment to carefully stretch, then joined him on the path. When I turned to look at the flower garden it appeared vastly different to the state I had earlier found it in and given the ache in my arms and back, and the rumble in my belly, I guessed I had been working on it for far longer than I had originally intended.

'It's transformed,' Algy breathed, his tone full of wonder. 'It looks *exactly* how I had hoped it would when I got your father to set it up in the spring. You're a miracle worker, Daisy.'

'Well,' I said, wishing he hadn't caught me in the act and berating myself for letting my imagination run away with me when it came to seeing myself running the enterprise, 'I don't know about that, but I hope that you'll consider my efforts today as a thank you for filling my bedroom with flowers yesterday. They cheered me up no end.'

'You needed cheering up?' Algy asked, turning his attention from the now-tidy flowers to my face.

'A little,' I conceded.

'But you're dating the hottest tourist in town from what I've heard,' he nudged. 'What have you got to be unhappy about?'

'Oh,' I shrugged, as I brushed my earth-encrusted legs down and refused to feel further nettled about village gossip as it was an integral part of life in a small community, 'all of the usual. Not knowing what my place in the world is. Not having a job. Being a disappointment to my parents, not knowing what I'm supposed to be doing with my life . . .' my grumbling trailed off. 'You're so blessed you know, Algy,' I then said in a brighter voice. 'You love Wynbrook and Wynbrook clearly loves you.'

'It loves you too, you know,' he said softly. 'It always has and there was a time when I envisaged you picking up where your father would one day leave off. You do know that, don't you?'

I did know that because, like Algy, I had once envisaged it too, but it was a long-quashed dream now. Finally quashed on the very spot we now stood.

'Yes, well,' I said bluntly as I hastily tamped the memory down. 'Dad had other ideas, didn't he? He wanted me to make more of myself than he had and vetoed my plans to go to horticultural college when I got better than expected exam results.'

I still didn't know how I'd managed to achieve that, but one thing I did now realise, thanks to a sudden and dazzling light-bulb moment, was that I hadn't been happy since I'd reeled off my GCSE results and Dad had become hell-bent on convincing me to take the academic path rather than the flowery one I'd had my heart set on.

'He told me that gardening was something I could come back to as a hobby if I still had a hankering for it in later life,' I added bitterly, as Algy listened. 'As far as Dad was concerned, it was uni or bust.'

It had been bust ever since I'd dropped out and with Dad's disappointment weighing its heaviest then, I hadn't dared suggest picking up my secateurs when I came home for a while with my tail between my legs. Eventually I'd left again, let the dream go entirely and hadn't given it another thought until this trip back to the estate.

I had always known that Dad had pushed me along a different

path because his father, who had been the gardener at Wynbrook before him, had forced him to take the role on and he had, when he was younger, resented it, but it didn't follow that the green-fingered path would be the wrong one for me, did it? Just because Dad hadn't once wanted to walk it, it didn't mean that I shouldn't have been allowed to.

'You know, your dad never spoke up about not wanting to work on the estate,' Algy said rather defensively, his thoughts mirroring mine. 'I would have supported him if he had and so would my father.'

'I know that, Algy,' I said, feeling bad for making him feel guilty. 'I think he was too scared to defy his father, but he's happy with his lot now.'

'But you're not, my dear, are you?'

'No,' I said, 'I'm not, and especially now I find myself squeezed into the cottage with him and Mum and feeling exactly like I did when I was a powerless teenager. I can't bear it, Algy.'

I forced down the desire to cry. I had found so much peace when I had been working among the flowers in the garden, but mention of the reality of my current situation had sent my blood pressure soaring and my mood plummeting again. I should never have come back to Wynbrook this summer. My return, aside from fun with Josh, and Penny and Nick's blooming relationship, hadn't gone well, even though I had tried to make out my romance and friends were enough. Too much that had been lost in my past had been stirred up again.

'Well,' said Algy, flummoxing me by sounding absolutely delighted that I was so upset, 'I happen to think that's a wonderful thing.'

'What?' I spluttered.

'I think it's good that you feel like that,' he reiterated. 'I'm pleased you feel like you did at eighteen.'

'Why?' I demanded.

'Because you knew what you wanted back then, didn't you?' he said with a wink, 'and I'm offering you the chance to turn back time and take it.'

I looked at him and blinked.

'I'm offering you a job, my darling,' he beamed. 'I want you to maintain and manage this cut-flower venture for me. You can open it the same hours as Nick does the fruit farm and ask him for advice about how to run it if you need to. It's not all that different to the fruit farm, is it? Just a slightly different commodity to crop.'

He made the offer sound so simple and straightforward, but it was anything but.

'And can you imagine what Dad would have to say about that?' I pointed out sardonically. 'Because I can.'

'I'm not worried about what your father would say,' Algy countered. 'I'm only interested in what you have to say, Daisy. What do you think? Do you want the job?'

In that moment, there was nothing in the entire world that I wanted more. I had spent so much of my time that day while working among the blooms, bees and butterflies, fantasising about how it would feel to be the person in charge, what plans I could make, how I could expand the project and extend the cutting season, but that's all it was – a fantasy.

'I would love the job,' I said eagerly, and Algy looked delighted. 'But—'

'No, buts,' he said immediately.

'But,' I carried on, 'the thought of working here all day and then having to go back to the cottage every evening to sit with Dad's disappointment . . .' I shuddered at the thought. The scene was all too easy to imagine. 'I couldn't do it, Algy. I couldn't bear it.'

'I don't think he'd feel that way for long, if at all,' Algy said, 'when he sees what a wonderful job you've done. What a natural talent you still have—'

'I can't,' I cut in. 'I can't manage this project and live in the cottage.'

Algy looked at me for a long moment.

'Well, in that case,' he said, striding off as quickly as moving with his stick would allow, 'we'd better find somewhere else for you to rest your head, hadn't we?'

'You can't be serious?' I gasped, when Algy finally came to a stop. 'You're suggesting I can stay here?'

'I know it needs a bit of work,' he said, sounding less certain as he beat back the patch of nettles encroaching on the path with his stick, 'but it's not that bad.'

'I don't mean that it's in a state, Algy,' I laughed. 'I just can't believe you're offering it to me to live in.'

'Had I known how much you were struggling in the cottage,' he said, as he pulled out of his pocket the bunch of estate keys he always had about him, 'I would have suggested it days ago.'

'But the summerhouse, Algy,' I sighed, looking at it in awe. 'Might you not need it for guests?'

'I'm not expecting anyone,' he said and shrugged, tossing me the bunch of keys. 'The place hasn't been lived in for a while, so sprucing it up a bit will doubtless be required. See if you can find the right key on that lot, would you?'

I soon located the key and the wooden double doors, having warped a little, creaked in protest as I opened them.

'In you go then,' said Algy, ushering me inside ahead of him.

I edged my way around the veranda rocking chairs and took the interior and mezzanine in. It did look to be in a bit of a sorry state, but nothing that a deep clean and good airing wouldn't remedy.

'It's not too bad, is it?' Algy said as he looked around. 'Bit of a whiff, though.'

There was a rather pungent smell coming from somewhere, but some fresh air would soon see that off.

'Electrics still connected,' Algy said, flicking a light on and off again. 'You'll probably need to run the water for a bit to make sure it's clear.'

I couldn't really believe this was happening. First, Algy had offered me a job. The kind of job I had once hankered for but hadn't reconsidered in all the time I had been trying to squeeze myself into an indoor office-based shape, and now he was offering me a place to stay too.

'How much would you want for rent, Algy?' I asked, as I dared to delve into the dream a little deeper.

'I wouldn't want you to pay rent,' he laughed. 'You'd be doing me a favour, getting the place back up to speed and passing for habitable again. It will need to look half decent, when I do get around to . . .'

'When you get around to what?' I frowned.

'And obviously, I'd pay you a wage for working in the garden,' he carried on, ignoring my question and—because I was so excited, I quickly forgot I'd asked it. 'I wasn't expecting you to volunteer.'

'Oh, Algy,' I squeaked.

Was this really happening?

'The cut-flower garden probably wouldn't amount to a full-time position just yet,' he said, 'but you could help your dad with other things in the garden, couldn't you? That would make up your pay packet easily enough.'

And there was the Dad-shaped spanner popping up again . . .

'Stop fretting about your father,' Algy said firmly, when he spotted my doubtful expression. 'He'll come round.'

I so hoped he was right because what Algy was offering me was exactly what I still wanted. It had just taken me years to realise it . . .

Chapter 18

Once I had caught my breath long enough to accept Algy's generous offer, he then suggested he should come back to the cottage to talk to Mum and Dad with me, but I declined his kind suggestion and opted to tell them alone what he had just miraculously done for me.

I had no clue how the situation was going to be received, but as I returned the tools I had used to the potting shed, leaving them exactly as I had found them, I reminded myself that I wasn't a teenager anymore and that I no longer had to blindly follow Dad's plan for me, and again abandon the dream I was finally backtracking to embrace.

Because this time I was actually going to embrace it, wasn't I? The forcefully determined answer that filled every atom of my body and mind when I asked myself this question was a resounding, yes!

'Oh, Daisy!' Mum laughed, when I happily skipped into the kitchen. 'You made me jump. What on earth have you been up to? You look like you've carried half the garden in with you . . .' Her words trailed off as she realised that I must have taken her earlier half-spoken idea to heart. 'You're all aglow. What have you been up to?' she asked, slightly nervously.

'Aglow,' I laughed. 'Do you have to talk like you've just walked off the set of *Poldark*, Mum?'

She had been obsessed with the new version of the show when it was first shown on television, but had always favoured dutiful Dwight Enys over unpredictable Ross Poldark.

'Well,' she smiled, 'you *are* glowing.'

'Sunburn, mostly likely,' I said, as I picked sticky cleavers off my shorts and pulled off my hat. 'I didn't expect to be out for so long.'

I was still so hot, my hair was practically plastered to my head. I knew I must have looked scruffy and soil-encrusted, but I didn't care. It was an aesthetic I had always loved when I was growing up and now I had finally found my way back to wearing it.

'And what have you been out doing?' Mum asked, even though, given the state of me, it must have been obvious.

'Making up for lost time.' I grinned and she smiled back. 'How did Algy get on at the hospital?' I then asked her, having just realised that I had been so entranced by my time in the garden and his subsequent offer that I had completely forgotten he had been for his check-up. 'I saw him earlier, but we fell to talking about other things . . .'

'He was given a clean bill of health,' Mum said happily. 'Now,' she added, 'get yourself tidied up and you can tell me exactly what making up for lost time entailed *and* what these other things are that you and Algy talked about.'

'All right,' I said, as I reached for the nail brush, 'but I'll make some sandwiches first if that's all right? I completely missed lunch.'

Mum made me up a plate while I washed my hands and then tied back my hair. I glanced at the clock as I joined her at the table. With the afternoon practically gone, I was certain Dad wouldn't be too much longer, so if I wanted to sound her out ahead of talking to him, I needed to hurry up.

'And you enjoyed that, I take it?' she ventured, once I had explained, between mouthfuls, how I had transformed the cut-flower patch in the time she and Algy had been off-site at the hospital and then visiting Holt.

'I loved it, Mum,' I told her, my eyes shining. 'I haven't worked at a single thing since I left home that has given me the same level of pleasure or satisfaction. I know now that I should have put my foot down when Dad talked me out of pursuing my horticultural career. I shouldn't have let him bully me into changing my mind.'

'Oh, Daisy,' said Mum, sounding distressed. 'That's a very harsh word, my love. I don't think he bullied you, did he?'

'Coerced then,' I amended, knowing that was an accurate but no less severe description for what he had done. 'Press-ganged.'

Mum looked even more upset.

'He only had your best interests at heart, you know,' she said croakily. 'Or what he considered to be your best interests,' she then surprised me by insightfully adding. 'He just didn't want you to get stuck and not see anything of the world. He didn't want you to have the same narrow world view as he used to think his father had inflicted on him. And you know, I only went along with what he wanted for you because your exam results suggested you really were capable of achieving so much more.'

'Well,' I said, knowing there was nothing to be gained from

quizzing Mum over what she had once thought *so much more* entailed or indeed raking over any of that stony old ground again. It was time I planted a fresh new crop and harvested the rewards. 'Never mind my ancient exam results,' I said. 'The important thing is, I've finally worked my way back to what it is I really love and this time, nothing or no one is going to put me off pursuing it.'

Mum looked delighted about that and I felt almost giddy as a result of her reaction. Everything was suddenly falling fantastically into place; all the years of trying to squeeze myself into a different mould had come to an end and I knew, without any doubt, where I belonged in the world and what the part that I had to play in it was.

'I'm delighted to hear it,' Mum said sincerely, giving my hand a squeeze. 'Because you do look happy.'

I felt it too, even though I still had to face Dad.

'I feel happy, Mum,' I told her, with a smile so wide I could feel it stretching as far as my ears.

'So, what will you do now?' she asked. 'Ask Algy if you can volunteer here for the summer? What did he make of what you've achieved today? I'm guessing it was in the garden that you saw him.'

'It was.' I was then even more excited to tell her the whole story. 'He came into the walled garden while I was still working in it.' I wondered then if he had been looking for little Luna. She seemed to have gone to ground since her fleeting appearance on the cat-cam. 'And he was over the moon with what I'd done. Had he not turned up when he did,' I laughed, 'I'd probably still be there now because I was so engrossed!'

'So, what exactly did he say?' Mum asked.

She had obviously guessed I had more to share.

'He said,' I announced, drawing in the biggest breath, 'that he'd like to offer me the job of running the cut-flower business. Actually, properly managing it.'

I loved that he had enough faith in me to allow me to take over something which clearly, for some reason, meant so much to him. It was a huge boost to my confidence.

'He never did!' Mum exclaimed, suddenly looking all aglow herself.

Her tone was full of surprise rather than shock and I was grateful for that. Shock might have implied that she didn't think I was up to it, but thankfully there was no hint of that.

'He did,' I beamed. 'And, he's offered me the summerhouse to move into, so I can get out from under your feet here. And Dad's, of course.'

'Well, I never!' Mum gasped. 'And what on earth did you say to all of that?'

'I said yes, of course,' I almost shouted. 'To both offers!'

'Oh, how wonderful!' Mum clapped. 'So, you're finally going to be working in the garden properly! The very thing you always loved and you're going to be practically living in the garden as well. Not that you've really been under our feet because you've hardly been here since you met . . .' She didn't pursue that train of thought. 'But I know things here have felt . . . strained,' she continued. 'You'll enjoy having your own space.'

'I certainly will,' I agreed.

I also hoped I would be able to entice Josh to visit the estate now I had my own private place on it and I couldn't deny I was looking forward to sleeping in a double bed on home turf again, too.

'But is the summerhouse even habitable?' Mum asked. 'It's been closed up for such a long time.'

'It does need a bit of a sort out,' I acknowledged. 'But nothing I can't manage.'

'I can wash the curtains in the big machine at the manor,' Mum said pensively as her thoughts instinctively turned to the domestic practicalities. 'We'll never get them in our machine here.'

She sounded keen to help so I had every intention of letting her as I felt certain that if we worked together, Dad would feel less inclined to object to Algy's idea. At least, I hoped he would.

'Would it be all right if I carried on doing the rest of my laundry here?' I asked, my attention also turning to the domestic arrangements. 'There's no machine in the summerhouse.'

'Of course, you can,' Mum said. 'And you can keep your car here too.'

'I thought I might move that up to the manor,' I told her. 'That will be closer for me than here.'

And also my comings and goings wouldn't be so easily noticed.

'Yes,' Mum said, biting her lip as she mentally paced the route out, 'you're right, that will be closer. That would make more sense then. So, when's all this happening?'

'When's all what happening?'

Neither of us had heard Dad arrive home and I felt my face flush when I looked up and saw him standing in the doorway. He already looked harassed and I hoped my news would be a soothing salve as opposed to an irritating inconvenience.

'Oh, Robin,' said Mum, as she stood up. 'Daisy has the most wonderful news. You're going to be so pleased when you hear what it is.'

He looked suspicious rather than inclined to be happy.

'Oh?' he said, coming in properly.

'Go on,' said Mum, as she looked encouragingly at me. 'Tell him.'

Her enthusiasm for my new venture seemed to have convinced her that Dad was going to be keen too.

'Well,' I began and then the words got stuck. 'I'm moving into the summerhouse,' I finally blurted out. 'Algy has said I can stay there, which will stop us getting under each other's feet here.'

'Oh, right,' said Dad, his brow etched with an even deeper frown. 'It's been shut up for a while. I think it'll take a bit of bringing around.'

'I've already been inside,' I told him. 'And it's not that bad. Nothing I can't manage.'

'Fair enough,' he said with a nod.

'And?' Mum urged. 'Tell him the rest, Daisy. Tell your dad what else Algy has said.'

Dad looked enquiringly at me.

'He's also offered me a job,' I told him apprehensively. 'He's asked me to take over the cut-flower garden. Maintaining it and managing the sale of the flowers . . .'

'And all as a result of the work she's done there today,' Mum carried on as my words petered out again. 'Think of the time that's going to save you, Robin. And think how thrilled Algy will be to get something out of it before the season ends.'

Dad looked at me. The frown had gone, but his expression was perplexingly unreadable.

'You've been working in the walled garden,' he said quietly, his tone incredulous.

'And I've had a wonderful time in there, Dad,' I started to meaningfully but shakily say, but then I felt a surge of bravery and my words came out stronger. 'The best day I've had in a very long time, in fact. And with the cut-flower project as my new work venture, I feel like I've finally found my—'

'Excuse me,' Dad cut in, as he turned back to the door. 'I just need to—'

And with that, he walked out.

'I'll go after him,' said Mum in a panic, as her happy bubble suddenly burst. 'I'll talk some sense into him. Or Algy will.'

'No,' I said loudly. 'No, Mum – no one's going after him. He's not a child that needs placating or consoling. Just leave him.'

'But he needs to understand—'

'I agree,' I cut in. 'He does, because I'm not going to change my mind about taking the job on and Dad will just have to get on with getting his head around it by himself. Chasing after him and trying to force the issue won't help. I daresay he's thinking about all the times he's been let down already this year, isn't he? And reckoning I'll do the same . . .'

'What do you mean?' Mum frowned.

'Think of all the people who have been employed to help him in the garden, then either haven't turned up at all or started, then changed their minds and left,' I reminded her. 'He's doubtless thinking of my work track record and that I'll be another name to add to the list in a fortnight's time. Only it will be worse this time because I'm family.'

Mum looked aghast and I was pretty upset myself, but it turned out that wasn't what Dad was thinking and just a few minutes later we were privy to his true feelings.

'Daisy!' he called up the stairs. 'Can you come back down, please?'

I braced myself for the fallout. I found Mum at the table with tears in her eyes and when I saw what it was that she was looking at, I felt myself well up too.

'I thought you might like to use this,' Dad said, his voice catching. 'It was in the potting shed.' He cleared his throat. 'Your secateurs had been on the bench in there too, but they're not now, so I don't know where they are.'

I realised I still had them, so unclipped them from my shorts and set them on the table next to the worn, wooden trug he had given me when I was little and which was still filled with rosettes from the years we had entered the Wynbrook fruit and veg in local shows. A ball of string, small trowel and an onion hoe were also nestled there.

'I used the secateurs in the walled garden today,' I whispered in explanation, my words also catching.

Dad didn't say anything.

'You kept this,' I said softly, touching the trug handle. 'Why?'

It took a moment for him to answer.

'I didn't understand why I hung onto it for a long time,' he sniffed, as a tear rolled down his ruddy cheek. I had never seen my dad cry before. 'But I eventually came to realise that I knew, deep down, that one day you'd come back for it.'

My gaze shifted from the trug back to his face.

'And I also realised, just now when you told me that you were taking the cutting garden on,' he continued, 'that the reason why you've never been able to settle at anything was because I misguidedly took away from you the thing you were meant for. I denied you your destiny because it had been a calling that had never shouted out to me.'

'Oh, Robin,' Mum sobbed, properly crying now.

'I never felt the desire to be a gardener,' Dad carried on. 'Not when practically everyone I'd grown up with was leaving here and moving on. The thought of taking on the job my dad did, and his father before him, was anathema to me. I felt so stuck.'

'But you did it,' I softly said.

'I wouldn't have dared do any different,' he said, reaching for my hand. 'And I came to accept it eventually but as a result, I felt the need to push you away from here so you could achieve something more. I forced my former desire to leave onto you in the hope that you wouldn't feel duty-bound to stay, irrespective of the fact that was what you actually wanted to do and that, for you, the garden was, more.'

'Oh, Dad.'

'And it wasn't until you came back this summer and were so adamant that Laurence was no longer the man for you, that I started to question other things and delve deeper into what I'd done. It was then that I began to realise how deeply those choices I'd thrust onto you had impacted your life. And not in a good way. I'm truly sorry it's taken me so long to grasp what I've done, Daisy. Can you forgive me?'

'But if you felt that way, why didn't you invite me to work in the garden with you the moment you realised?' I asked. 'Why didn't you suggest I help you, when you've been struggling with no staff?'

'Because he wanted you to come back to it for yourself, didn't you, Robin?' said Mum, catching on to what had been in Dad's mind before I did. 'You were scared to push her again, even if you were more certain that this time it would be in the right direction.'

'That's it.' Dad nodded. 'That's exactly it. I didn't want to influence you again, Daisy.'

'I see,' I sighed.

I was astonished. What an unexpected turn of events this was. There I'd been, thinking that I was going to have to talk and talk to try to make Dad understand, when in fact, he'd already worked it out for himself and was just waiting for me to catch up.

'So, do you?' he asked me again. 'Do you forgive me?'

I thought back over the decade I'd wasted, flitting from one disastrous job to another as well as the time I'd spent with duplicitous Laurence and would never get back. It wasn't all bad though. That time and those experiences had confirmed beyond all doubt what it was that I *didn't* want and now I could wholeheartedly and unreservedly embrace what I *did*.

Of course, there was a part of me that wished I could have reached this point sooner, but that wasn't how life worked, was it? Things happened precisely when they were ordained to, which meant that I had returned to Wynbrook exactly when I had been meant to and I was now taking up Algy's offer when it had been destined to be made.

'Yes, Dad,' I said, and he pulled me in for an unusual but hugely appreciated hug. 'I forgive you.'

I could hear Mum shedding yet more tears, but I knew they were still happy ones.

'Thank you, Daisy,' Dad said with feeling, when he finally let me go. 'Thank you, so much.'

'Don't thank me yet,' I laughed. 'You haven't seen the quality of the work I've put in today, have you?'

'I have no doubt it will be exemplary.' He smiled, looking much more like the dad I remembered from my early child-hood. 'It's in your blood, after all, and your natural talent always shone through.'

'That's true,' I agreed, feeling confident enough to acknow-ledge that I had very green fingers, 'but straight after supper, let's go and look at what I've done anyway, shall we?'

Dad was keen to go along with that and I picked up and placed my secateurs in the trug, feeling that one of my biggest ever life decisions had finally, and most importantly, been happily made.

Chapter 19

'So, what do you think would grow better in here then, Daisy?' Dad asked me late that evening as our meandering tour of the garden finally came towards its end.

He had been delighted with what I had achieved in the walled garden and was now showing me some other beds, which had been created beyond it but not with the same success. It wasn't only lack of attention the plants were struggling with. They'd been planted in the wrong place and Dad must have realised that, but I was flattered he wanted my opinion.

'Given the aspect,' I said, turning around to work out when the beds most likely caught the sun, 'I don't think this is a bright enough spot for flowers to properly flourish. It might be more successful if it's given over to foliage. It's a pretty shady spot and there's plenty that would thrive here that I could then make use of in the bunches and bouquets.'

Dad rubbed his chin and nodded.

'I think that might be the ideal solution,' he said and I felt thrilled.

It was wonderful to be working with him, rather than against him. We'd always got along well when I helped out during the school holidays; it had only been when I said I wanted the partnership to continue full-time after I had sat my exams that our relationship had changed, and not for the better.

'*Alchemilla mollis* would be well suited here and maybe even some eucalyptus.' Dad gave me a look. 'As a cut and come again,' I said, grinning, knowing it would need brisk cropping to keep it in check. 'I won't let it run rampant.'

Dad chuckled at that.

'You still know your stuff, don't you?'

'I think so.' I smiled, feeling pleased about everything I had been able to remember.

I had messaged Josh to say something had come up, something wonderful, and that I wasn't going to be heading back to Wynmouth that evening or the next day either. We'd pencilled in plans to spend the night and day together as I was a free agent on the work front, but obviously that had changed now. Josh had immediately messaged back, excitedly asking what the something wonderful was, but I had been adamant that I would tell him in person and I had just the occasion in mind to do it too.

It was after Josh and I had finished messaging and I was scrolling through Instagram while waiting for Dad to change into his work gear ahead of our tour, that I realised my love of gardening and my passion for beautiful blooms had never left me or even waned.

I might not have had a hands-on relationship with horti-culture since leaving Wynbrook, but my knowledge remained and my Insta feed was full of nature, flowers, florists, allotments and before-and-after garden makeover projects. Those images, reels and accounts had been my go-to and a much-loved soul soother during the years I hadn't been getting my hands in the soil.

It was telling that my passion for plants had never left me and in turn, my acknowledgement of that made me wonder what it had been that Dad had wanted to pursue when he finished school and if he still had an interest in it.

'Here you go then, Daisy,' he said, once he'd locked the potting shed and as he handed me a bunch of keys. 'You'd better have your own set. Once you're opening the garden up to the public, we'll need to keep all the sheds locked when we're not in them.'

I clasped the bunch tightly and felt like he'd given me the keys to his castle. I was excited, but I felt the weight of responsibility too. The garden had never been accessible to the public in the way that Algy's venture now opened it up and I was mindful of that.

'I'm honoured.' I grinned as my excitement outstripped any apprehension.

'That you are,' Dad said, smiling back. 'Not even Algy has a complete set.'

'Has he not?' I laughed.

'No chance,' said Dad. 'I'm not having him causing chaos where I've established order. He has a habit of not putting things back where they should be.'

'Does he still garden then?'

'Not often,' Dad told me. 'And not at all since his accident.'

I hoped I would be able to rectify that with some gentle encouragement. As long as I returned the tools Algy used to their allotted hooks and shelves, all would be well.

'In that case, I might see if I can tempt him to help me in the flower garden once I've got the proper measure of it,' I ventured, feeling immensely overjoyed that the ghosts of the arguments of the past had now been thoroughly exorcised and I could wholeheartedly embrace the beautiful walled space again. 'Given that it was his idea in the first place, he should have the chance to play a part in it, shouldn't he?'

'He should,' Dad agreed, 'but rather you than me. You'll have to supervise him very closely.'

'Oh, I intend to,' I said earnestly. 'You don't happen to know why he was so keen to set the venture up, do you?'

Dad shrugged.

'I think he just took a liking to the idea,' he said. 'He most likely saw some diversification scheme on TV and decided to try and apply it here. You know what he's like when he takes a fancy to something. Come hell or high water, it has to happen.'

I had a feeling there was more to it than that and would be giving it further consideration as I got to grips with the job and the finer details of what it was going to entail in order to get it fully up and running.

'While we're on the subject, what was it that took your fancy all those years ago, Dad? What did you want to leave Wynbrook to do when all of your friends were spreading their wings?'

He took a moment before answering.

'I don't want you thinking I've always been unhappy here, Daisy,' he said firmly. 'Things changed once I met your mum and I settled into the job. I'm as melded to this place now as Algernon Alford himself.'

'I know that, Dad,' I said soothingly, 'but it wasn't your first post-school choice, was it? If you could turn the clock back, still meet Mum, but make your own career decisions free of what your dad made you do, what's the path you would have taken?'

Dad had winced when I had mentioned his father and his actions, and I knew he was comparing how he had reacted to what I had wanted for myself when I was in my teens with what his dad had thrust upon him.

'What would you have done, Dad?' I asked again, before he started brooding and became distracted from the wonderfully bonding walk we were currently enjoying.

'Well,' he said slowly, as he thrust his hands in his overall pockets, 'I don't know how my path would have panned out of course, but I would have liked to have started walking it by studying history.'

'History?'

I never would have guessed that.

'Yes, it was my favourite subject at school and I always had a hankering to study more. I would have loved to go to university and then on to who knows where . . .'

As his words trailed off, I began to formulate a plan. If I could find a way to do it, I might not be the only person embracing what my heart had long desired this summer.

I was so excited, I barely slept a wink that night and Mum and Dad were up extra early too.

'Are you likely to see Nick today, Dad?' I asked, when I joined the pair of them for the fortifying breakfast Mum was cooking at the stove.

'I doubt it,' said Dad. 'The fruit farm is getting busy, and he has to be in the vicinity of it all day at this time of year. Why? Do you need him to give us a hand in the summer-house?'

I was interested to note that my moving day had become a family event now. Mum was itching to get the curtains and any other removable fabrics washed and Dad had offered to help manoeuvre any furniture I wanted shifting. The pair were playing to their strengths and I knew that by the end of the day, I would be feeling immensely grateful that they had been willing to get stuck in and see me settled.

'No,' I told Dad. 'The opposite, actually. I haven't told him or Penny about my change of abode or the new job yet and I'm hoping to keep it a surprise. I've invited them both here this evening and will walk them down to the summerhouse when they get here.'

'Penny especially will be so excited,' said Mum. 'I'm sure she must be feeling guilty about you giving up your job in the pub to work in the café for just four days.'

'I daresay you're right,' I agreed. 'So, Mum's the word, okay?'

'I won't say anything,' said Dad.

'Me neither,' said Mum. 'And I'll tell Algy to keep it under his hat too.'

'Thanks, Mum.' I nodded. 'I'd appreciate that. I was hoping to talk to him today, but I don't think there'll be time.'

In the early hours, I had started making notes covering how I thought it would be best to launch the cut-flower enterprise so late in the growing season. I was extremely excited about the prospect of creating an Insta account and thought that selling some sample bunches and arrangements of flowers at the fruit farm shop might encourage folk to come to the garden and buy more. I would have to talk to Dad about the public access aspect too. There might be areas he wanted to fence off. And what about the estate's public liability insurance? Did that cover the garden?

There was so much to think about, but just for that day, my focus was on the summerhouse, making it comfortable and clean and feeling like home. That said, I did give plenty of attention to the huge plate of breakfast Mum was dishing up first.

'I think that was your phone, Daisy,' said Mum, giving it a nod as I got stuck into the crispy bacon and perfectly poached egg.

'I'll check it when I've finished eating,' I said, knowing it would be Josh.

I had invited him to join Penny, Nick and me that evening and I'd been thrilled when he said yes. Penny was going to pick him up, as she lived literally just a few doors away from where he was staying and I was looking forward to finding out what Josh, as well as my friends, thought about my change in circumstances. I might even be able to tempt my summer delight to stay the night and, as a result, repay some of the hospitality he'd shown me during the last few weeks.

I hadn't mentioned to Mum and Dad that I'd invited him because after the excitement of moving day the last thing I was going to want was a big *meet the parents* moment. I was pinning my hopes on sneaking Josh down to the summerhouse and putting that off for another day.

'Well,' said Dad, once we'd opened all of the summerhouse windows and doors and he had pushed a wheelbarrow full of curtains and cushion and chair covers up to the manor for

Mum to work her magic on, 'it could be a lot worse given the amount of time the place has been shut up, but I'd still like to know what that whiff is.'

'Um,' I said, looking about, but finding I was still none the wiser as to what the rather pungent smell might be, 'me too. I was hoping it would have started to fade a bit now we've got the air flowing through.'

I had initially wondered if it might have been the fridge, but that had been left turned off and with the door slightly ajar so was fine. Whatever it was had certainly ramped up since Algy and I had briefly looked in before.

'What's this now?' Dad frowned, looking along the path which he'd kindly and ruthlessly cut back so that the formerly encroaching nettles weren't quite so deadly.

I looked outside and was surprised to find two men shuffling along the narrow path with what looked very much like a brand-new mattress between them.

'Where do you want it?' the one at the front gasped when he reached the summerhouse veranda.

'Oh,' I said, looking at Dad who shrugged. 'I'm not sure . . .'

'Please tell me you do want it,' the man tutted. 'It was a long way, carrying it from the van and Mr Alford said there's one here that needs taking away too. Assuming we've got the right place, that is.'

'It's a moving in gift from Algy.' Dad smiled. 'The bedroom's this way.'

The two men followed him inside and I looked up at the mezzanine, wondering how they were going to perform the tricky swap.

'Looks like you've had company,' said the other, slightly

shorter, man who had been sent up the stairs to retrieve the old mattress. 'Unless you've been sleeping on this . . .'

His face flushed red and I headed up the stairs.

'No,' I said, looking at the mucky state of the mattress. 'No one's been sleeping here and I hadn't realised the bed was like this.'

'I'm not sure we should take it,' he said, scratching the back of his head. 'I'm not sure we should put it in the van given the state it's in.'

'Have you been paid to?' Dad asked gruffly.

'Well, yes—'

'In that case,' I suggested with a nod to the new mattress, 'wrap it in the plastic that's covering that one before you load it up. Most of this mess will likely fall off as you carry it back through the garden anyway.'

They got the job done with much grumbling and there was more complaining when I insisted they waited to put the new mattress in place while I quickly washed, then vacuumed the frame and floor under the bed courtesy of the rechargeable hoover Mum had said I could have because it was the perfect size for the summerhouse.

'Thanks for waiting,' said Dad as they finally got ready to leave and he gave them each a note I couldn't see the value of. 'There was no point putting a new mattress on a mucky frame, was there?'

They were all smiles after that and had barely left before Algy arrived.

'All set for tonight then,' he said, grinning, as he looked up at the pristine new bed.

'I am,' I gushed. 'Thank you so much, Algy. You're very kind.'

'I thought the other one might be past its best and probably a bit damp.'

'Filthy is what it was,' said Dad.

'Filthy?' Algy frowned.

'Yes,' I said, reaching for his hand as I suddenly realised something else I'd noticed about it, 'and covered in black cat hair too.'

His eyes widened and he squeezed my fingers.

'I think we might have found where your feline friend has been hanging out.'

'Oh, yes,' said Dad, 'of course. I hadn't joined the dots.'

There had been no sign of little Luna so far, but that was hardly surprising given the current toing and froing. However, the evidence on the grubby mattress was incontrovertible, even though neither Dad nor I had initially twigged. This was where she had been hiding. I wondered how long it would take for her to put in an appearance, assuming my moving in hadn't scared her off completely.

'That's wonderful!' beamed Algy, echoing my thoughts. 'I wonder how long it'll be before she turns up?'

'I don't think we'll see her for a while,' I told him, erring on the side of caution. 'Not until the activity settles down around here anyway.'

'Of course,' he said, letting my hand go and putting a finger to his lips. 'I'll go and order a bed for her and a few bits so when she comes back, she'll know she's home.'

'So, you're going to be sharing the place with a cat then.' Dad smiled ruefully as Algy tottered away.

'Looks like it.' I nodded. 'Well, if she comes back, I will be.'

'You might not want her to, given that she's such a smelly

specimen,' Dad winked. 'If that mattress was anything to go by, she's going to need de-fleaing and a ruddy good grooming.'

'Hmm, I wonder how she feels about baths . . .'

By the end of the afternoon, I was grubby, tired and hungry, but deliriously happy and looking forward to a scrub up, myself. The summerhouse had been thoroughly cleaned from top to bottom, including the washing of everything in the kitchen cupboards, and the bed was freshly made. The heat of the day might have had me ailing, but it had ensured the curtains and sofa and chair covers had dried quickly and the pretty floral fabrics were looking fresh, much brighter and smelling great as a result of Mum's ministrations.

There was still work to do to add some finishing touches, but for the time being, and while I got the cut-flower business launched, the place was more than comfortable and cosily adequate. Dad had transferred my things from the cottage and with a few of my personal possessions dotted about, my clothes unpacked and a huge jug of flowers gracing the small dining table, I was already feeling very much at home.

As much as I loved the inside, I adored even more the brick-floored covered veranda that wrapped all of the way around the outside. There was room there for a small table and chairs and the rocking chairs, with their slightly squashed cushions, were back in situ along with a few containers of plants Dad had carried round from the greenhouse.

'How's that?' he said, as he stood back to admire the effect.

'Perfect,' I said, giving him a hug. 'The white agapanthus are huge this year and so bright. They look wonderful against the lush green backdrop of the foliage plants.'

'Might be a worthwhile addition to your cut-flower planning,' he commented, kissing the top of my head. 'Hey now, what's wrong with you?'

This was directed at Mum because she'd started to dab her eyes when she joined us on the veranda. Dad let go of me and went to her.

'I'm just so happy,' she sniffed, as he rubbed her back.

'You look it,' Dad teased and she batted him with her hand-kerchief.

'I am,' she insisted. 'It's a dream come true hearing the two of you talking about garden-related things.'

Dad looked at me and smiled and I knew Mum was right, it *was* a dream come true. I might have set it aside for a while, but I was very happy to be living it now.

'I'll tell you what else is a dream come true, shall I?' laughed Dad, giving Mum a full kiss on the lips.

She looked taken aback by the show of affection, but delight-fully so.

'What?' she sighed dreamily and I felt relieved that I was no longer living under their roof if a spark in their relationship had been rekindled as a result of my job news.

'The fact that god awful smell didn't turn out to be coming from the currently absent cat!' he laughed.

'Amen to that,' I joined in. 'We still haven't smelt the cat, obviously, but I reckon those half-eaten mice she'd left in the little cupboard under the stairs were the real source.'

Mum made a gagging sound and I shoved away the memory of Dad carrying the poor decaying things out of the summerhouse on the end of a shovel, before I got to work with the Dettol.

'Assuming the cat put them there,' Dad said.

'Anyway,' I said, not wanting to talk about it anymore, 'the smell has finally gone and if the cat does come back, then I'll be checking she isn't carrying anything before I let her in. Assuming she wants to come in.'

I truly hoped my presence in the summerhouse wasn't going to put her off.

'Good plan,' Mum keenly agreed. 'And now you'd better get cleaned up, Daisy, because Nick will soon be finished for the day and Penny will be on her way from Wynmouth.'

I quickly had a slice of cake, a cup of tea and a shower back at the cottage and had resigned myself to introducing Josh to Mum and Dad because I couldn't think of a way I could sneak him around the outside of the cottage without either one of them spotting him.

I dithered on the cottage doorstep, waiting for Penny's car to come into sight, hoping Josh wasn't going to feel like he'd been ambushed, but in the end my fretting turned out to be unnecessary because he wasn't in the passenger seat.

'Hey Daisy!' Penny grinned as she climbed out of the car and then reached back into it for a huge cool bag that was sitting where I'd expected Josh to be. 'I hope you haven't eaten because I've brought some substantial snacks.'

'Hey yourself.' I smiled, taking the bag from her. It weighed a ton. 'I've had cake, but I could still do with properly filling up. Where's Josh?' I then whispered. 'Have you stashed him in the boot?'

That would have been an extreme act of subterfuge!

'He's not coming, I'm afraid,' Penny said and handed me a crumpled piece of paper. 'I found this pinned to the cottage door when I went to collect him.'

Nick arrived at that moment and while the pair kissed a very long hello, I read what Josh had written.

Really sorry to bail.

George has been a bit under the weather and hasn't felt able to rehearse until tonight. As we're playing in the pub on Saturday – eek – I didn't want to turn him down.

Maybe see you all tomorrow?

J x

I was disappointed that again he'd missed an opportunity to visit Wynbrook, especially as I had such exciting news, but I knew he was nervous about playing in the pub and having not had the chance to rehearse with George would have only compounded that feeling. So, under the circumstances, I was willing to let him off.

'No Josh?' Nick frowned, when he and Penny finally drew apart. 'Don't tell me your summer fling is already flung, Daisy?'

'No,' I tutted. 'Josh just had a better offer tonight, but he's going to be gutted he missed out because I have news.'

I wondered if he had tried to ring my mobile or sent a text before writing the note. I didn't get much of a signal in the summerhouse and obviously there was no phone line or wi-fi connected. I'd have to go for a walk around the garden if I wanted to get in touch with him.

'News?' Nick frowned.

'Oh,' gasped Mum, sounding all aflutter and definitely looking all aglow as she appeared in the cottage doorway, 'it's you, Nick.'

Her eyes darted between my two friends.

'I could have sworn I just saw you two . . .'

'Kissing,' I laughed, finishing her sentence for her. 'You did, Mum. Penny and Nick are a couple now.'

'Well, about time!' she declared loudly. 'Robin!' she shouted back into the cottage. 'Did you know about this?'

'About what?' Dad frowned as he came out to join us.

'Penny and Nick are a couple now,' Mum said happily.

'Well, I never!' Dad gasped. 'Better late than never, I suppose.'

Penny shook her head.

'Are we really the only ones in the whole of north Norfolk who didn't know we were made for each other, Nick?'

'Yes!' Mum, Dad and I all said together and everyone laughed.

'Right,' I said, because I couldn't wait a second longer. 'Come on, you two.'

'Where are we going?' Penny asked, as I started to walk away from the cottage. 'Do we really need to lug this lot with us?'

'You'll see,' I told her. 'And yes, we do. See you later,' I winked at Mum and Dad, who beamed back.

Penny and I carried the cool bag between us and Nick carried a box clanking with bottles and with some punnets of very ripe soft fruit balanced on top.

'The summerhouse,' he commented as we drew nearer. 'It's locked, isn't it?'

'Not at the moment,' I said, opening the door. 'Come on in.'

'Won't Algy mind?' Penny asked.

'I doubt it,' I said, flicking a switch that turned on the warm white strands of lights that ran around the underside of the veranda roof and the outside of all of the windows.

I had been looking forward to turning them on all day and,

as the summerhouse was surrounded by trees and shrubs, the light level was already low enough for them to make the scene even more idyllic.

'What's going on?' Nick frowned, looking about him as we put down the bag and box. 'This looks like a completely different place.'

It smelt like a completely different place too, but I didn't mention that.

'Is Algy expecting visitors?' Penny asked.

'Only me!' I burst out, unable to contain the revelation a moment longer. 'He's invited me to move in *and* he's offered me a job!'

My friends looked flabbergasted and I felt so happy to have something so positive and exciting to share with them. It certainly made a change.

'From tomorrow,' I proudly announced, 'I'm going to be managing and maintaining the cut-flower garden and living here while I do it!'

Penny and Nick whooped and cheered at my sudden good fortune and the celebration went on long into the evening. The only thing missing to make the night complete was Josh, but I tried not to mind too much and, when I finally waved my friends off and made my way up the stairs to my big, comfy new bed, I fell asleep contented, knowing my life had finally turned a very happy corner.

Chapter 20

The first thing I noticed when I woke the next morning was how light it was thanks to the summerhouse having multiple windows; the second was that I could hear a light patter of rain on the roof and the third was that I had been so caught up talking to Penny and Nick about my plans the evening before, I'd completely forgotten to either look at my phone or go for a walk to call and check in with Josh.

I had made Penny and Nick promise not to tell a soul about my change in fortune as I didn't want Josh finding out from anyone other than myself. I was still buzzing with excitement about it all and wanted to be the one to tell him, but telling my summer lover was going to have to wait a little while longer yet as I had so much to do.

'Knock, knock,' I announced cheerfully at the manor kitchen door.

'Daisy, Daisy!' beamed Algy, from where he was sitting at the table reading a newspaper. 'Come in, come in. Have you had breakfast?'

'Not yet,' I said, slipping off my wellies and thinking I could soon get used to my days starting like this. 'I haven't had a chance to do a shop yet.'

My bank account was currently rather depleted so I would be living off staples until I was paid by Algy at the end of the month and Penny for my four days in the café. It was the first of August today, so I had a while to wait, but I knew Mum wouldn't let me go hungry.

'In that case,' Algy insisted, 'come and help yourself to some cereal and toast and when your mum arrives, you can give her a list of what you need to fill the summerhouse kitchen cupboards.'

'Oh, I can't do that—'

'Of course you can,' Algy interrupted, brooking no refusal. 'You've weeks to wait until pay day, so I insist. My weekly order will go up to the village later today so you're just in time. And, in the meantime,' he added, with a nod to the dresser, 'there's a little cash in that envelope with your name on, to tide you over. And before you object, I'll take it out of your first pay cheque.'

'That's so kind, Algy,' I said, feeling choked. 'And so thoughtful of you, especially given that you've already done so much for me.'

'I'd say it's a fair exchange.' He smiled. 'I'm expecting you to make my dream come true. For a while anyway . . .'

I wasn't sure if I'd just heard him right but didn't have time to ask him to repeat what he'd said as Mum bustled in, clucking like a mother hen and looking damp around the edges.

'Daisy.' She smiled, shaking the worst off her umbrella on the doorstep before walking in. 'How did you sleep?'

'Oh, yes,' said Algy. 'How was that mattress? Any good? And was there any sign of the cat?'

'It was perfect,' I told him. 'I had a wonderful night's sleep.

There was no sign of Luna though. I reckon she's probably spying on me from the undergrowth while she susses me out.'

I had a feeling some of my sweet slumber might have been down to the fact that I was blissfully happy. That said though, given my current level of excitement, it was a miracle that I had calmed down enough to nod off at all.

'So was your decent sleep down to the new bed or being worn out?' Mum asked, once Algy had agreed with my thoughts about what the cat was up to. 'It was late when I heard Penny head for home.'

I knew Penny hadn't gone home to Wynmouth, so she must have moved her car round to Nick's cottage after the pair had left the summerhouse. She was thrilled with how the twins were working out in the café and together with her now being coupled up with Nick, her life was suddenly perfect too.

'Probably a bit of both.' I nodded and my tummy rumbled.

'Breakfast,' Algy commanded. 'Then groceries and then work.'

'I'm rather looking forward to work.' I grinned.

That wasn't a statement I made every day!

'So, that's settled then,' proclaimed Algy later that morning. 'We'll set you up with a desk in here.' We were in his office, having gone through things like the insurance. 'And you can use this as your business base when you need to access the internet and check emails and so on.'

'That will be really handy,' I told him. 'I'm going to set up social media accounts for the cutting garden today and I'm planning to officially open to the public from Monday if that suits you, Algy?'

Algy looked pensive.

'Unless you had a different day in mind?' I asked.

'I think it would be more lucrative to tie the opening hours in with the fruit farm,' he suggested and I felt a bit of an idiot for not thinking of that myself.

'Of course it would,' I tutted.

'How about you open Wednesday through to Sunday from ten until three?'

'But that's only, what . . . twenty-five hours a week, Algy. Are you sure that's long enough?'

'I think so.' He nodded. 'You're going to have maintenance to do on top of that and all that social media malarkey and I did say you could help your dad out in other areas of the garden if he needed you, if you remember.'

'Yes, you're right. I daresay the rest of the time will soon get eaten up, won't it?'

'Exactly. Now, as you're so convinced the venture needs an online presence—'

'And flyers to hand out around the village,' I reminded him.

'And those too,' he said, with a twinkle in his eyes, 'I think we need to come up with a name, don't you?'

By the end of the day, Wynbrook Blooms had been launched online and I arrived in the village, eager to see Josh, and with a pile of flyers clutched in my hand.

'Daisy!' he beamed, when he opened the cottage door and found me standing there. 'I was beginning to think you'd been a figment of my imagination.'

'It hasn't been that long,' I laughed, though in the brief time we'd been apart, a lot had happened and I seemed to have forgotten just how gorgeous he was. 'But we definitely need to make up for lost time.'

My libido was certainly making its presence felt and I was eager to intimately reacquaint myself with him again as soon as possible.

'Let's go to the pub and catch up then,' he suggested, stepping out of the cottage.

'Not yet,' I said, pulling him back inside. 'I want to talk to you first . . . amongst other things . . . and I don't think a packed pub would be the ideal place for any of it.'

He followed me back inside and I noticed the coffee table was full of books.

'Is that Wynbrook?' I frowned, recognising the black and white photograph which featured the back of the manor.

'I've been genning up on the local area,' Josh said, as he quickly closed the books and piled them together, before scooping them up. 'I thought it might be nice to get to know something of the history of the place.'

'Well,' I said pointedly, as he put the books away, 'if you do ever take up my offer to visit the estate, you can talk to Algy himself about that, can't you?'

'I'm sorry I couldn't make it last night,' he apologised, pulling me into his arms. 'Did I miss anything good?'

'Just a bit,' I said, wriggling free and refusing to succumb to his kisses until I'd told him my thrilling news. 'What do you make of this?'

I handed him a flyer and took a step away to better gauge his reaction.

'Wynbrook Blooms,' he read aloud. 'I love the image.'

I'd set up some jars of various sizes, crammed them full

of the most prolific flowers the garden currently had and photographed them in the prettiest corner of the walled garden with bowls of strawberries and raspberries for extra decoration.

The image was cottagecore perfection and beneath it I'd listed prices for the size of each bunch and the garden opening times. I'd also bigged up the setting, the locally grown element and the fact that at Wynbrook, you could now pick up fruit *and* flowers. It was a dream combo as far as I was concerned and Nick had loved it when I had briefly stopped at the fruit farm and showed him too.

'All my own work,' I said to Josh proudly. 'And talking of work . . .'

Gratifyingly, Josh hung on my every word as I explained about my new home, the new job and how gardening had long been a passion of mine, but one I'd abandoned as a result of my father's interference in my future when I was an impressionable teen.

'Your father sounds about as stubborn as mine,' Josh pointed out when I'd finished telling him everything, but I couldn't allow that.

Now Dad and I had cleared the air and I had a better understanding of why he'd blocked my desire to dig for a living all those years ago, I didn't think badly of him at all.

'In that case,' said Josh, taking the flyers I was still holding and putting them on the table as he sat next to me after I'd explained, 'it sounds to me as if your life is suddenly coming up roses, Daisy.'

'It certainly is,' I was more than happy to agree as I laughed at the pun. 'Dream job, my own space, sexy summer fling . . .'

'If I'm the fling you're referring to,' he said, seductively caressing my arm, 'then I hope you'll still have time for me.'

'I'm going to do my best to squeeze you in,' I told him, as my breath hitched while he slowly shifted to caress my neck.

'I'm delighted to hear that,' he smiled, looking deep into my eyes, 'and while I've got you here, I'd love to make the most of the moment, if now would be a good time to . . . squeeze me in.'

By the time we left the cottage again, most of the shops were shut. I was able to leave a bundle of flyers in the village store and made a note that the shop's owner had asked if Wynbrook Blooms would be able to supply small bunches of flowers for them to sell.

I hadn't said yes as I didn't want to deter visitors from visiting the garden, but I knew Nick kept the store in summer fruit, so I promised I would think about it. It might end up being a contract to pursue the following year as for now, I needed to make sure I had enough flowers to satisfy demand this summer. Assuming there was going to be some, of course.

'If you leave a load of flyers with me,' Josh kindly offered as we walked back to the pub, 'I'll go around and drop them in the shops for you tomorrow, if you like.'

'You would?'

'Of course,' he said. 'And I'll take some to the café for Penny too. I want to see this venture succeed every bit as much as you do.'

He turned bright red when he said that.

'You do?'

'Of course, I do. I think you need something good to happen in your life, Daisy.'

'Apart from you, you mean.'

'Yes,' he laughed, 'aside from me, and I think this new job sounds like just the thing.'

'Well, that's handy,' I said, standing on tiptoe to kiss him, 'because I think it sounds like just the thing too.'

As tempted as I had been to spend the night with Josh, I drove back to Wynbrook after sharing my news in the pub. I was amused to notice that Marguerite still had the locals eating out of her hand and Sam was delighted about that. When the time had come, Josh had been reluctant to let me leave, but as he wasn't willing to come to Wynbrook, I said a lingering goodbye and headed off.

Walking through the garden to the summerhouse in the late evening light had been bliss, full of fluttering moths and floral fragrances and another sweet sleep followed and after that, a perfect day working in the garden.

'What do you think to these?' Dad asked, showing me a seed and bulb catalogue early Saturday evening.

We had spent the entire day together working in various parts of the garden and I had then joined him and Mum for supper and a marathon seed and bulb planning session which involved poring over catalogues, writing lists and filling out order forms online. Bliss!

'For the cutting garden or the borders?' I asked. 'I think they would be too expensive for my project. I'd have to charge a premium for every stem I cut, wouldn't I?'

'I was thinking of the herbaceous borders,' Dad explained as the cottage phone started to ring. 'In that developing gap at the far end.'

'In that case,' I said, as Mum held the phone out to me, 'I think they're perfect.'

'It's for you,' Mum said and for one heart-stopping second, I thought it was Laurence, but it wasn't, it was Nick.

'Daisy!' he shouted, sounding flustered. 'I've been ringing your mobile for ages. Where the hell are you?'

'Oh my god!' I gasped, jumping up and cursing that I'd earlier put my phone on silent and then forgotten to unmute it. 'I'm coming! I'm on my way!'

'They're about to start,' he tutted. 'You're going to miss them.'

'No, I'm not,' I said resolutely. 'I'll make it.'

'How?'

'You can help,' I commanded. 'Do something. Create a diversion.'

I had completely forgotten that Josh and George were taking to the stage that evening and after a mad dash, I raced into the pub still wearing my grubby gardening gear and with my lungs on fire as I'd had to abandon my car in the village because I couldn't park closer and running had been the only option.

'There,' I wheezed, as I bumped into the back of Nick and bent over to nurse the painful stitch in my side, 'I told you I'd make it.'

'Oh, Daisy!' Penny cried, looking unexpectedly thrilled to see me. 'You'll never guess!'

'Tell her later,' said Nick. 'They're about to start.'

Josh's eyes met mine as he took to the stage and I gave him an encouraging thumbs-up. I was so pleased he'd spotted me. It made the manic drive, pounding heart and out of character sprint to reach him totally worth it.

'Good evening, Wynmouth,' he said huskily into the micro-phone and the room erupted.

I could tell he was playing up his accent, but to wonderful effect.

'George and I are delighted to be with you this evening.'

George gave the assembled crowd a wave and then the pair started playing. Every person present was enthralled. They started with the Jack Johnson tune they'd played before and then covered a Paper Kites song, some Oh Hellos and finished with 'Trouble', by Ray LaMontagne.

Josh didn't take his eyes off me throughout the entire song and it wasn't until the last chord had been played that I noticed Nick and Penny were dancing in the middle of the crowd and everyone was applauding them as well as the marvellous musicians.

'What's going on?' I shouted towards the dancing duo.

'We're engaged!' Penny called back ecstatically and the roof was raised again. 'Nick has asked me to marry him!'

'So,' I said, when I finally had a moment to talk to Nick on his own, 'you created a diversion then.'

'Sure did.' He grinned. 'I had the entire evening planned out. We were going to listen to the music here and then I was going to walk Penny down to the beach, our path lit by the moonlight and then propose with the waves gently lapping the shore.'

'That sounds very romantic,' I said, biting my lip.

'Oh, it would have been,' he nodded, 'but our best friend needed help getting out of a scrape and as I had the ring in my pocket and really didn't think I could manage to wait a second longer anyway, I thought, why not?'

'You're mad,' I said, throwing my arms around him. 'God, I'm so happy for you!'

I wished I'd been there when he went down on one knee, but appreciated the extra minutes his timing had afforded me.

'Me too,' he sniffed; his eyes full of happy tears. 'And proposing in the pub got us a free toast *and* meant I didn't succumb to throwing up because I was really starting to get pent up about asking her.'

'Hey,' Penny, who was very tipsy by now, said to me as she wobbled over. 'Unhand my fiancé.'

I let him go and squeezed her instead.

'You guys,' I said, shaking my head. 'You're engaged!'

'We know!' they shouted together and then everyone around us cheered again.

Much later, Josh and I took the walk along the beach that Nick had planned for him and Penny. I hadn't been drinking because I was going to drive back to Wynbrook, but the emotions Josh's soulful playing had evoked, coupled with my friends' exciting announcement and my sudden change in fortune, made me feel as though I'd had at least three strong cocktails.

'So,' said Josh, as we strolled along the shore, just out of reach of the lapping sea, 'did you forget that George and I were going to be playing tonight?'

'No,' I said, perhaps a little too loudly. 'It didn't *completely* slip my mind. I just forgot for a little while because I was distracted.'

'By what?'

'Seed and bulb catalogues,' I confessed happily.

'Seed and bulb catalogues!' Josh said disbelievingly as he picked me up and spun me around.

I shrieked in protest as he made out he was going to drop me in the sea.

'They're my guilty pleasure,' I laughed, throwing my head back and taking in the constellations, when he stepped back from the tide.

Josh kissed my neck then put me down.

'You don't sound guilty though,' he pouted.

'I know.' I shrugged. 'I'm not really. Sitting and looking through them with Dad was surreal but wonderful.'

'I'm so pleased the pair of you are finally on friendlier terms after everything.'

'Me too,' I sighed and because I wanted everyone to feel as content as I did, added, 'Is there any hope for you and your dad, do you think?'

'Absolutely none.'

There was nothing I could say to that and we carried on walking. After a few steps had passed, I asked, 'Would you have been upset if I had forgotten about tonight and hadn't shown up?'

Josh stopped and I turned to face him.

'Given that we're supposed to be casual,' he said, 'just a fun summer fling, I *shouldn't* have been particularly upset if you didn't make it, but . . .'

'But?'

'But if you hadn't come, I would have been devastated.'

'You would?' I swallowed.

That was a pretty intense feeling for a relationship that wasn't supposed to be heading anywhere other than towards its end, as the summer petered out over the next few weeks.

'I would,' he confirmed. 'And I can't help wondering what that suggests about how I feel about you, Daisy.'

Given that my heart had leapt at the thought of him being so upset about my potential no show, I was starting to wonder what that said about my feelings for him too.

'Hey!' I heard someone shout and laugh, and I knew there was going to be no time to explore those feelings that evening. 'What are you two doing down here?' It was Nick and Penny. 'This was supposed to be our romantic spot, remember?'

'It's a big enough beach,' said Penny, who sounded blissfully happy as she hiccupped. 'We can share!'

Chapter 21

Had I been in any doubt about how my feelings for Josh were developing, they were presented to me in crystal-clear clarity as a result of my reaction to our final conversation before I headed home that evening.

I had asked him if he would like to join me at Wynbrook for Sunday lunch with my parents and Algy, and yes, I knew that had the possibility of being a rather full-on first meeting, but he turned me down anyway, not because of the potential intensity but because he had already made other plans.

'Marguerite has hired a car,' he told me, 'and she's asked me to go with her and look at this place she's thinking of renting if she decides to stay on.'

'Oh,' I said lightly. 'Right.'

'She said to ask you if you would like to come along too but I assumed you'd be getting ready to launch the business next week—'

'So you said no on my behalf?' I cut in, perhaps a little too sharply.

'No,' said Josh, stringing the word out, 'I just said I thought

it was unlikely that you'd say yes because you're so busy, but
that I'd ask you anyway.'

'I see.'

'So, do you want to come?'

'I can't,' I said. 'You're right, I do need to get more work
done.'

'So you *are* too busy to come then,' he said, sounding amused.

'Yes,' I conceded again. 'I am.'

I hated the fact that I didn't like the thought of him and
Marguerite spending the day together, especially when I knew
I had absolutely nothing to feel jealous or suspicious about. I
also knew that I couldn't blame my uncharitable emotion on
Laurence's behaviour. This was all me. Jealousy wasn't a pleasant
reaction to experience, but it did give me a very definite
heads-up about how I had started to feel about Josh.

As a result of my snippiness, we parted on rather less emotion-
ally intense territory than I had thought we'd been heading
towards when we were on the beach.

'He's leaving soon,' I reminded myself, as I glanced at him
in the rear-view mirror as I drove out of the village. 'You've
just escaped one relationship with your heart intact, Daisy, so
don't now risk getting it completely broken by someone who's
supposed to be nothing more than fun in the sun. Especially
now you're in love with your new job . . .'

It hadn't been my intention to put some distance between me
and Josh that week, but with everything I had to do ahead of
opening Wynbrook Blooms on Wednesday, that was how the
situation panned out.

'Wow, Daisy,' said Nick, when I dropped some jars of flowers at the fruit farm early Wednesday morning. 'These look stunning.'

'And they smell as good as they look,' I said, shoving one under his nose.

'They do,' he agreed.

'By the way, thanks for marking up the chalkboard.'

There were clear directions on the board outside the barn about where to find the walled garden and between us, Dad and I had hung up wooden arrows pointing the way from the fruit to the flowers, so hopefully customers would soon catch on.

'My pleasure.' Nick smiled. 'You know, Penny will doubtless be wanting you to supply the flowers for the wedding.'

'Have you already set a date?' I asked, wide-eyed.

'Not quite,' he told me, 'but we're thinking late next May or early to mid-June.'

I was thrilled they weren't wasting any time in tying the knot and also pleased they'd picked a time when I could guarantee them flowers from Wynbrook.

'Oh, Nick.'

'I know,' he said. 'I can't believe it. I love her so much, you know . . .'

'I know you do,' I said, rubbing his arm.

'And,' he then mischievously added, 'I think there's someone who has deeper feelings for you than they might be letting on . . .'

'Oh?' I squeaked.

'You're all Josh talks about—' he started to say, but I cut him off.

'Summer fling, remember?' I said firmly. 'Now, I must quickly tell Algy that I caught sight of the cat this morning.'

I rushed off before Nick could say anything further.

'That certainly sounds like her,' Algy said happily, once I had described the fleeting glimpse I'd had of the tiny black cat sitting on one of the rocking chairs when I left the summer-house that morning.

Algy had joined me and Dad in the walled garden to mark the moment the courtyard clock struck ten and Wynbrook Blooms officially launched. He'd called the local press, but no one had turned up and there were no customers clamouring to form a queue either.

'Not quite the fanfare I was hoping for . . .' I started to say, but then a couple looked cautiously around the gate and Algy beckoned them in and an entire family, grandparents and children included, also arrived.

'You were saying,' Dad said and smiled as I stepped up to tell the visitors all about the beautiful Wynbrook Blooms venture and ask if there were any flowers they would like to buy.

At the end of Friday afternoon, I closed the garden and walked up to the manor to let Algy know how the first three days of trading had gone.

'So,' he said morosely when he caught sight of me, 'screaming success or unmitigated disaster?'

I looked at him and frowned. Mum had said his mood had taken a nosedive again over the last couple of days, but I hadn't seen him to observe it firsthand. Until now.

'Oh, don't mind me,' he huffed. 'I'm just in a bit of a fug.'

'It sounds like more than a bit,' I observed. 'What's up?'

'Never mind,' he made the effort to say more brightly. 'So, what's the verdict?'

He obviously wasn't in the mood to share whatever it was that had put him in such a stroppy place, so I told him about the flowers instead, as had been my original plan.

'I think it's a bit early to say whether it will be a runaway success,' I told him, as I recalled everything that had occurred so far. 'But the good news is, there's been a steady and increasing footfall each day.'

'Right,' Algy said with a nod.

'And I can already tell there are going to be a few flowers we're going to need a lot more of next year,' I continued.

'Next year,' Algy echoed, sounding wistful.

'We could sell double the amount of sweet peas. Probably more like triple, actually,' I told him enthusiastically. 'For the project to really succeed, I reckon we're going to need to double the space given over to growing the flowers that you've got so far. Is there any other area on the estate, but relatively close to the garden, that you might consider turning over to it?'

I stopped to draw breath and realised he didn't seem to be listening.

'Algy? Are you all right?'

'Yes,' he said irritably. 'I was just taking a moment to absorb what you were saying.'

'I'm sorry,' I apologised, feeling hot. He'd never snapped at me before. 'I'm just so excited, I—'

'So do you really think there's some merit in the idea and that it could become a successful project?' he interrupted.

'I certainly do, especially with me at the helm,' I said, smiling. 'I'm loving it, Algy. It's exactly what my heart desires. I'm so happy—'

'Okay,' he cut in again, before I got completely carried away. 'Let's see what the weekend brings then, shall we?'

He wandered off and I was left feeling bewildered. It was a completely out of character and blunt dismissal, causing my heart to feel unsettlingly heavy.

'Earth to Daisy,' said Josh, in a robotic voice as he waved a hand in front of my face. 'Do you read me?'

'Oh god,' I said, plunging my hands into my hair. 'I'm sorry. I've been so keen to see you all day and now we're finally together, I've turned into a total zombie.'

It was Friday evening and we were sitting in the pub with a drink, waiting to eat.

'I take it you've had a busy week.' He smiled. 'Marguerite said the walled garden is stunning.'

I had been thrilled when Marguerite had turned up to buy some flowers to put into the pub vases and she told me about her trip out with Josh. She had ended the retelling with the words: 'Boys have their uses and they're all right if you like that kind of thing, but as you know, Daisy, I don't.'

I had known that, of course, and it made my pang of jealousy about her and Josh spending time together feel all the more unreasonable.

'Such a busy week,' I said to Josh, stifling a yawn. 'And Marguerite's right – the garden is beautiful. I'm hoping you'll see it for yourself soon.' Josh nodded at that. 'And I'm loving the work, but I'd forgotten how tiring gardening can be, even if sometimes the work only entails snipping blooms to make beautiful bunches and posies.'

The job sounded idyllic, and the Insta account I'd set up,

which was gaining followers, made it look extremely attractive, but it was still challenging. I hadn't factored in talking to the increasing number of visitors when I'd taken the role on and it was taking some getting used to.

'Your boss must be thrilled about how well it's going.' Josh smiled. 'From what you've said, you've already had quite a lot of customers coming through and made loads of sales.'

'Um,' I said, wondering how best to answer about Algy. 'If he is thrilled, he's keeping his excitement pretty well hidden.'

'What do you mean?'

I didn't want to talk out of turn, but I needed to confide in someone, and both Penny and Nick had been unsurprisingly unavailable of late. They were either working or together, which was absolutely fine. More than fine, given that I had been desperate for so long for them to get together. And of course, I didn't want to further worry Mum and Dad, who I knew were already wondering what was up with Algy.

'I'm not really sure,' I said tentatively. 'I can't put my finger on what's going on with him, but something is. And Mum and Dad have picked up on it too.'

'You look worried.' Josh frowned.

'I am worried,' I confessed. 'I don't know what's behind Algy's fluctuating moods, but I've never known him to have them before. For as long as I can remember, he's always been the best fun. I know there's some family sadness in his past, but—'

'Hold that thought,' said Josh, gathering up our empty glasses. 'I'm going to get us another drink and then you can tell me all about it before we eat.'

'I'm not sure if I should . . .'

'Well, it sounds to me like you really need to get it off your chest, Daisy.'

I looked up at his kind face and thought, what harm could come from sharing? I might even find the unburdening cathartic . . .

'All right,' I caved. 'Just a half for me though, because I need to drive back.'

'Oh no, not tonight,' Josh insisted. 'Please stay with me, Daisy. It feels like ages since I woke up with you.'

How could I resist a request like that, especially as he'd already forgiven my unreasonable waspishness from the weekend before? I didn't have to be back at Wynbrook much before ten when I opened the garden and waking up with Josh was always wonderful. Every bit as wonderful as waking up in the summerhouse. I longed for the day when I could put the two together.

'All right,' I willingly relented and Josh looked thrilled.

By the time we made it through the door of Crow's Nest Cottage and up the stairs to the bedroom, I felt like I'd had the longest talking therapy session. I'd chattered on for what felt like hours about growing up at Wynbrook, the details I knew about Algy's family rift, my hopes for the new floral enterprise and of course, my current concerns for the man I loved like a grandad and was striving to make happy.

'You're a good listener,' I told Josh as I leant against the doorframe and flicked through the mental Rolodex of everything I'd told him.

He'd sat and quietly listened and barely said a word at all, and I hoped I got the chance to return the favour for him soon as it had felt wonderful to share, vent, reminisce.

'I'll tell you what else I'm good at, shall I?' He smiled seductively, before flinging himself on the bed.

'I'd much rather you showed me!' I giggled.

I quickly leapt onto the duvet and sat astride him. I pinned his hands above his head and prepared myself to receive a wholly satisfying explanation.

Chapter 22

For someone who never drank much, I didn't feel anywhere near as hungover as I perhaps deserved to the next day, and that was a huge relief because Saturday was hectic and Sunday was the busiest day for Wynbrook Blooms so far. I had guessed that the weekends would be the most lucrative and with a cooling breeze coming off the sea and a fair bit of cloud cover, locals and tourists alike had abandoned the beach and flocked to the estate to buy both fruit and flowers.

I felt extremely stiff when I woke on Monday morning – a combination of the physical demands of my dream job and the bedroom gymnastics Josh and I had indulged in for much of Friday night – and I was pleased that I could now have a couple of days' respite. From the most intense gardening jobs, at least. I was planning to see Josh again as soon as possible.

'Well, hello you,' I said quietly, as I went to eat breakfast on the veranda and little Luna, who usually bolted at the merest glimpse of me, stayed stretched out on her favoured rocking chair, pretending to be asleep. 'How lovely of you to let me join you.'

She didn't stay put for long because Dad then came ambling up the path with an envelope tucked under his arm.

'Good morning!' he called out and the cat shot off. 'Is that the cat?'

'It *was* the cat, yes.' I smiled as I stood up stiffly.

Dad chuckled as I groaned.

'Last week was a reminder of what hard work feels like, eh?'

I gave him a look.

'I wasn't being sarcastic,' he insisted.

'I know that,' I told him. I could hardly tell him that it wasn't all garden-related aches and pains I was suffering from, could I? 'What have you got there? More seed catalogues or the latest braggy letter from Oz?'

'Neither.' Dad smiled. 'Funnily enough, we haven't heard back from Daniel since your mum emailed to say what a joy it is to have you back and how you're now transforming the fortunes of the estate.'

I laughed at Mum's description. Evidently, my cousin wasn't the only one who liked to occasionally give the lily an extra gilding.

'So, what is that then?' I asked, still looking at the missive.

'Something I have a feeling you might have been responsible for, Daisy.'

I twigged, and when he pulled the paperwork out of the envelope and I spotted the letterhead, my suspicions were confirmed.

'Turns out it might not be too late for me to follow my dream, after all,' Dad said, sounding thrilled. 'Having read this, I can see there's a way for me to follow your lead.'

'I had a feeling the Open University would be a good fit,' I said happily. 'Are you going to apply?'

I held up two pairs of crossed fingers.

'I already have,' he then surprised me by saying. 'I've got to do an access course first and then I can make a start on the degree.'

'Oh, Dad,' I choked out, as my phone began to ring loudly. 'That's wonderful. I'm so happy for you.'

'Well,' he said, 'it's down to you, love. I never would have given it a thought if you hadn't sent off for the info. Do you need to answer that?'

'No,' I said, giving the phone a cursory glance where it was resting on the table next to my cereal bowl. 'I don't recognise the number.'

'I'm astounded that the call has connected.'

'Actually, so am I,' I said, also feeling startled when I realised what he meant. 'That's the first spot of signal the phone has picked up on since I moved in.'

'You'll have to make a note of the exact location for future reference.'

I wrinkled my nose at the suggestion. The limited access was suiting me just fine.

'You know,' I said, 'I don't think I will. I rather like the radio silence. I'm using the internet up at the manor for the Wynbrook Blooms social media accounts of course, but so far, not much else.'

'Well,' said Dad. 'I'll leave you to get on. I just wanted to thank you for nudging me in the right direction. Have you got anything specific planned for today?'

'I need to talk to Algy again,' I sighed. For the first time ever, it wasn't a prospect I was looking forward to. 'He was in a rum mood last week.'

'That he was,' Dad agreed, letting out a breath. 'Your mum

and I both said the same, as you know. I'll go and find him later as you're going in this morning. He's bound to be pleased about the cat.'

'I hope he will be,' I said, picking up my empty bowl and phone. 'It would be nice if we could find something he was pleased about.'

Unfortunately, as a result of the message that had been left on my phone, I wasn't feeling in a particularly cheerful mood myself as I got ready to walk up to the manor.

'I don't believe it,' I gasped, as I listened to the message, left a terse text response and then immediately deleted the evidence and blocked the number, which belonged to my ex.

Had I known Laurence had changed his mobile number for some reason, I would never have listened to what he had to say, but without that knowledge, I had found myself subjected to his voice and words I very definitely did not want to hear.

Apparently, he'd been working away for a few weeks and therefore hadn't realised that I had called the flat from the cottage phone until he returned and found the number logged. Thanks, Dad! He also cockily said he hoped I might be reconsidering my rash action of walking out and that I would now be pleased to hear from him. He seemed to be labouring under the misapprehension that giving me some space would have made me pine for what we'd had and that I would now be ready to forgive, forget and go back. What. An. Idiot.

My response to his stupidity had been to inform him that it was Dad who had called, not me, and that I had happily moved on with my life.

'Come on, Daisy,' I told myself, in my best sergeant-major tone. 'You've dealt with it now. Let it go.'

To shift my mindset, as I showered and dressed in a floral tea dress and sandals rather than the usual shorts, T-shirt and safety boots that my new role dictated, I recalled the many ways I had moved on since my return to Wynbrook. My fling with Josh, my new home, my dream job, my happiness for my engaged friends, my repaired relationship with Dad . . . they were all wonderful things to celebrate.

And if, I pondered as I walked up to the manor with a spring in my step and my ponytail swinging, I could find a way to combine Josh with Wynbrook, then that really would be the flake in my cone.

'But why is he so reluctant to visit here?' I said aloud. 'Why won't he come?'

He was certainly curious about the estate – his listening ear when I had rambled on in the pub about my childhood and beyond, *and* the books he'd been studying in the cottage were proof enough of that – but for some reason he was remarkably reluctant to step over the cattle grid. Was there actually a reason for that or was I making too much of it?

I came out of my reverie as I heard Algy's voice drift out of the conservatory and I changed direction towards it. Unfortunately, I was about to overhear what should have been a private conversation, although thankfully Algy sounded much happier than he had when he'd been talking to me a few days ago.

'After all these years,' I heard him say in a voice heavy with emotion, and I stopped dead in my tracks. 'I can't tell you what a joy it is to see you again and to actually have you here, at Wynbrook. Well, it's a dream come true. More than I ever could have hoped for in my lifetime.'

I had no idea who he was talking to, but clearly what was being said wasn't for my ears and I turned away, thinking I'd silently backtrack to the kitchen door and then work in the office until Algy was free to talk.

'I'm only sorry it's taken me so long to make my way here this summer,' came the response to Algy's delight at welcoming this visitor. 'I can tell you – it really has taken me an age to find my courage and work my way up to doing it.'

I stopped again, only this time out of shock rather than discretion.

'Josh,' I mouthed.

His accent was unmistakeable. It was Josh who was sitting with Algy in the Wynbrook conservatory. But why? Suddenly, the flake in my cone I'd been wishing for just minutes before felt entirely unnecessary.

I rushed around to the kitchen door and clashed with Mum on the threshold.

'Daisy!' she gasped. 'What's got into you, flying in here like that?'

'Who is Algy talking to?' I asked, feeling a horrible combination of shock, nausea and upset. 'Who is Algy talking to in the conservatory?'

'I don't know.' Mum frowned. 'I didn't even know he had company. I'd better make some coffee if he's got visitors. Are you all right? You look awfully pale.'

'No,' I stammered, backing away. 'No, I'm not all right.'

A faint tinkling came from inside the house.

'That blasted bell,' Mum tutted. She had set Algy up with the tea bell his great-grandmother had used, after he'd had his tumble, to save him having to shout for her and clearly he hadn't kicked the habit of using it. 'I'm banishing that. He's more than capable of using his feet to come and find me now.'

'I'll come back later,' I said numbly, desperate to get away. 'I have to go.'

'I'd rather you didn't,' said Algy's voice, suddenly close behind me, making me jump. 'Because I'd just decided to use my feet to come and find you, Daisy.'

I sat in the conservatory opposite Algy, with my hands neatly folded in my lap and the world spinning around me, as Mum carried in a tray. Josh, smartly dressed in a navy polo shirt and with his hair tidier than I had ever seen it, jumped up to take it from her and with a slightly shaking hand, set it down on the table between us. I could see Mum was busting to ask a hundred questions, but Algy's solemn demeanour didn't suggest he was in the mood to chat and so she snatched up the offending bell and walked out again.

'Daisy,' Algy calmly said, 'would you mind being mother?'

I poured coffee into each of the cups, but left out the cream, not wanting to presume preferences, even though I knew what both the men would like. I could tell Josh was looking at me intently when I passed him his cup, but I refused to meet his eye for fear of what I'd see reflected back at me. I was still feeling so wobbly; I wouldn't trust myself not to cry or shout and those were the last reactions I wanted to display.

'And now,' Algy smiled at me, having added cream to his coffee and taken a sip, 'I'd like to introduce you to my grandson. My grandson, who was taken from here more than two decades ago and who I hadn't heard a word from since, until today.'

He sounded astounded rather than calm and my cup rattled so violently in its saucer that I put it down again, untouched. Josh didn't say anything.

'I know you know Josh already, because he's told me,' Algy carried on as if he wasn't telling me anything particularly shocking at all. 'I know now that you've known him since the day you came back to Wynbrook, Daisy, but what you haven't been aware of—'

'Is that he's lied the whole time about who he really is,' I snapped angrily.

No wonder Josh hadn't wanted to visit the estate every time I had suggested it. He'd doubtless wanted to cherry-pick his moment instead and the information I'd supplied him with about Algy not being himself had obviously been deemed the ideal moment to appear. But for what purpose?

'Not lying,' Josh said quietly. 'I've never lied. I just never—'

'Told the truth,' I cut in again, still furious.

Laurence's earlier message might have been unwelcome, but it was nothing compared to Josh's deception. I'd had him pinned quite simply as someone who was spending the summer in a quaint Norfolk village, enjoying the beach and having some fun, but I should have known there had to be more to his continued presence than that. It should have been glaringly obvious that there was some bigger reason than sunshine and a summer fling with a local to keep him here.

'Perhaps if we gave you a little context, Daisy?' Algy suggested.

'No,' I said, standing up abruptly. 'I don't want to hear it. I've already been made a fool of by one man this summer and I have absolutely no desire to allow it to happen again.'

As I walked out, I thought perhaps it was a little late for

that, but I was determined to do what I could to limit the damage to my heart that Algy's bombshell had just inflicted.

'What's on earth's going on?' Dad demanded. 'What's happened?'

On autopilot, I hadn't realised I'd walked back to the cottage, rather than to the summerhouse, but I found him and Mum in the kitchen and just after I walked in, Nick and Penny arrived as well.

'What's happened?' Nick asked Mum, who had clearly wasted no time in putting some feelers out. 'Your message sounded urgent, Janet. Is it Algy?'

'In a way,' I said, answering on Mum's behalf as I flopped down on a chair. Every last atom of energy felt as if it had floated out of me. 'His grandson has turned up.'

'What?' Mum gasped, her hands flying to her chest. 'Is that who that was?'

I had assumed she'd been listening at the door after delivering the coffee, but apparently not.

'They're sitting in the conservatory drinking your coffee as we speak,' I said, 'and Algy appears to have welcomed him with open arms and without question.'

'No way!' Penny said, adding her surprise to Mum's.

'When did this happen?' Dad commanded, sounding ready to rally the troops. 'Are they up there alone?'

I was intrigued to know what was behind his and Mum's reaction. I knew I had every right to be flabbergasted and upset as a result of Josh's duplicity, but why did they both appear less than thrilled? Was Algy in some danger from this returning relative? Was he going to need protecting from the handsome American interloper?

'Does he look like Algy?' Nick asked, then added, 'By which I mean, how can we be sure that this person really is who they say they are?'

'I couldn't see a family resemblance myself,' I told him, as I wondered why Sam hadn't questioned Josh's name when he booked his cottage. 'But you'll recognise him.'

'How?' Penny asked.

'Because you already know him – it's Josh. Algy Alford's grandson is Josh.' Penny's mouth fell open. 'That's the guy I've been seeing,' I added for Mum and Dad's benefit because I couldn't recall ever mentioning his name to them.

Mum turned to me.

'And he never mentioned—' she began and I quelled her with a look. 'Of course, he didn't. You would have said . . .'

'I had no idea,' I said, resting my head in my hands. 'No idea at all.'

I didn't mention the books full of Wynbrook photos or the fact that Josh had been unwilling to show his face on the estate but eager enough to listen to me tell him all about my childhood and Algy's recent low mood. All of that combined could have given me a clue, but I'd had no reason to put them together, had I?

'So,' I sighed, looking again at Mum and Dad, 'tell us why Algy doesn't have anything to do with his son? It might give us an inkling as to his grandson's motive for suddenly turning up unannounced.'

'Assuming he does have a motive,' Penny said.

'I know you like to see the good in everyone, Pen,' I huffed, 'but on this occasion, there might not be any to find. Go on, Dad.'

'Well,' Dad began to explain, 'Algy's only son, Thomas, wanted him to sell the entire estate well over twenty years ago.'

'Was that when most of the agricultural land was sold off?' Nick asked. 'Just before Algy set the fruit farm up?'

'That's right.' Mum nodded. 'Thomas wanted shot of the whole place. He reckoned there was no future in it and it would only sink into debt and decline with the loss of the arable land and farming income. He had no faith in his father's soft fruit venture.'

'But that wasn't the real truth behind his desire to sell, was it?' Dad said scathingly. 'What he really wanted was to take what he thought would be his share of the money and run. He wanted Algy to sell the entire Alford legacy to the highest bidder so he could invest his chunk in his American father-in-law's business, instead of waiting to inherit it in the usual way.'

'But Algy would never have agreed to that,' I said, shocked that he could be related to someone who was eager to part with his heritage for the sake of money.

My mind then conjured up an image of Laurence. He and Thomas sounded like they were both cut from the same cloth. My ex had become increasingly obsessed with wealth and status since I'd known him, which made me wonder why he was still interested in me. We were chalk and cheese when it came to what we thought was important in life.

'Of course Algy wouldn't,' Dad agreed vehemently, making me forget about Laurence again. Had he not telephoned earlier, I was certain I wouldn't have thought of him at all. 'And anyone with half a brain would have known that.'

I thought that said a lot about Josh's father.

'So, it was an argument about selling the estate that caused the rift in the family,' Penny surmised.

Dad nodded.

'Algy wouldn't entertain the idea of selling, and Thomas hated him for it, so he took his wife and son and told his father he'd never see him again. He cut all ties and left, everyone presumed, for America, and they haven't been heard of since.'

'Until now . . .' I unnecessarily pointed out.

'And now we know that Thomas did take the family to America,' said Nick, 'because Josh's accent is a dead giveaway.'

'I remember that little boy from when Thomas used to visit and argue with his father,' Mum said sadly. 'As I recall,' she then upsettingly added, 'he was packed off to boarding school when bartering with him didn't work.'

'That's terrible,' Penny sniffed.

'It was,' Mum agreed. 'He couldn't have been much more than seven. So I wonder why he's come back. What does he want?'

'Is he here to do his father's bidding?' Dad asked crossly.

'Is he here to worm his way into an old man's affections and succeed where his father failed?' Mum joined in. 'Is he going to convince Algy to sell up?'

I struggled to listen to their speculating. They were assuming the very worst of Josh, and even though I was devastated that he hadn't been upfront with me about who he really was, the initial shock of discovering his true identity had started to wear off, and I just couldn't see him as someone who would behave as badly as his father had done.

But then again, it wasn't all that long ago that I had assumed Laurence was faithful to me and had then caught him with his trousers around his ankles, so I was hardly an expert in seeing through people. Given my track record, I could hardly defend Josh's surprise appearance, could I?

'I think I should go up there,' said Dad, making for the door.

'Me too,' Mum joined in. 'I shouldn't have left really.'

'No,' I said emphatically. 'Don't go charging in. Give them some time. If Josh has got ideas above his station, then Algy is sharp enough to suss him out; he's bound to be wary given what his son did.'

Algy hadn't actually looked or sounded suspicious but I knew he wouldn't welcome our interference, no matter how kindly meant, and if he pushed us away that would make the situation even harder to monitor.

'If you go pushing in now,' I therefore warned, 'Algy will resent you for it, whatever the outcome with his grandson, and as a result, the damage to our relationship with him could be irreparable.'

'Daisy's right,' Nick agreed and I was relieved to see Mum and Dad stand down.

Penny was the quietest of all of us and she looked confused too. I knew she was recalibrating her feelings about Josh, and she wasn't the only one.

Chapter 23

I wondered if Josh might come to seek me out that day, but he didn't and I made no attempt to contact him either. Given the nature of our relationship, I felt like I was stuck between a rock and a hard place.

Just like Penny, I wanted to think the best of Josh – and not only because he was standout summer fling material – but my more than fond feelings for him kept muddying the water as I worked my way through every reason I could think of as to why he'd turned up at Wynbrook now and, on a more personal level, why he hadn't been upfront with me about who he was from the day we'd met.

I knew the best way to clear the air was to ask him outright, but my pride had taken a battering and I felt I needed to repair my armour a bit before I faced him. In the couple of days that followed his return to the family fold, I knew he'd been a constant presence in the manor because Mum had told me she'd heard him and Algy going over the entire place and that they'd also spent endless hours with their heads together in the conservatory.

Whatever Josh's reasons for turning up, he certainly seemed

to be making the most of catching up on lost time and I couldn't help wondering if he was being respectful in giving me some time to process it all or if I'd served my purpose now and was surplus to his requirements. Now I had been harvested of all the information he needed, was I just considered collateral damage and casually cast aside?

I knew it was the once bitten, twice shy adage that was making me feel that way and holding me back from calling in on him and Algy, but I'd been bitten twice in pretty quick succession and had no intention of either setting myself up as more of a snack or jumping to unworthy conclusions. Especially now I had so much more to lose – my dream job, my lovely home, ultimately my entire happiness. I hadn't talked to anyone else about how I felt either, because I had no desire to unwittingly feed into the local rumour mill, which was in full flow.

'You should know,' said Algy's voice behind me as I was tying in some sweet peas and completely lost in my thoughts, 'that I asked Josh to move into the manor with me before he went back to the village on Monday night.'

I straightened up and somehow stopped myself from saying that was fast work. I wasn't sure on whose part I would have meant and I didn't want Algy shutting down when this was the first time we'd spoken since I'd walked out on him and Josh.

'He'll get lost in all that space after staying in Sam's tiny cottage,' I said instead as I turned around. 'Which room will he be . . .'

My words trailed off as I took in the appearance of the transformed man in front of me. Algy's stick was gone and he was standing much taller. He looked years younger and the twinkle in his eye was back with more spark than I had seen since I'd returned. In the few days since he'd been reacquainted with his grandson, he'd miraculously turned back into the sprightly gent I remembered.

'No, he won't get lost,' Algy said, shaking his head and looking marginally duller again. 'Because he turned me down.'

'Oh.'

'He knows what everyone is saying about him,' Algy carried on, making me feel uncomfortable. 'That he's only come here to try where his father failed. I take it your parents have apprised you of the situation between me and my son, Thomas?'

I nodded and felt my face flush. Even though I hadn't personally fed into the thread of gossip about Josh, I had, of course, heard it. The general consensus was that he had arrived in Wynbrook to do his dad's bidding, but I just couldn't see that myself, even though I felt he had done wrong by me and it would have been less complicated and far easier for me to think the worst of him.

'Well, not telling everyone who he was from the get-go hasn't exactly helped quell the inevitable chinwagging, has it?' I pointed out. 'And I feel like he used me, Algy,' I added bitterly, airing my opinion for the first time and to the right person. Better to declare it to Algy than in front of a packed pub. 'I told him all sorts of things about this place and if he has come here with . . .'

I had been about to say nefarious intent, but remembering how Josh and I had jokingly used the word, I couldn't utter it again. I hated that our fun times were all now lost. So much for my reckoning that the most recent couple of weeks had turned what could have been a difficult time in my life into the best summer ever.

'He's come,' Algy evenly said, picking up where I left off, 'to get to know me and the estate. There are things you don't know about the situation, Daisy, so please try not to judge him too harshly. I can understand why you feel that he has treated you badly, but I promise he had more reasons than you can possibly imagine for holding back who he was.'

'And what were those reasons?'

'Not for me to say, my darling,' Algy sighed. 'But what I can tell you is that your parents' future is safe now, with Josh around. And yours too, if you decide to stay.'

I had known I wanted nothing more than to carry on living at Wynbrook until Josh was unmasked. Now, however, with things between us as they were, I wasn't so sure.

'What do you mean about the future being safe *now*?' I frowned as Algy's words sunk in. 'Was it not before?'

He moved out of the glare of the sun and I followed him.

'Well,' he said heavily, 'to tell you the truth, no, it wasn't. This whole selling blooms from Wynbrook idea wasn't set up with longevity in mind, you know.'

'It wasn't?' I swallowed, looking back at the flower beds.

'No,' he confessed, 'it was just something I had a fancy to try for a season before . . . before I put the estate up for sale, hopefully with the flower business, and the fruit farm of course, as added extras and profitable going concerns.'

I steadied myself by leaning on the top of a nearby spade.

'You're selling the estate!' I gasped, clutching at the handle.

'I had been *thinking* about selling the estate,' Algy quickly rephrased. 'And the thought of doing it was killing me. Why do you think I've been so glum these last few months?'

I didn't know about that far back because I hadn't been either at Wynbrook or in touch often enough, but out of every reason I could have listed to explain Algy's low mood, planning to part with the estate would never have featured.

'The last thing I wanted,' he then further said, 'was for the place to be sold by my son after my death, to someone who most likely wouldn't look after it as I would have wanted them to, so selling it while I was still alive would have ensured I could have picked the best buyer.'

If Wynbrook had been bequeathed to his son, then doubt-less it would have been handed on to the highest bidder with not a care for the consequences, but that or selling it himself hadn't been Algy's only option, had it?

'But you could have bypassed your son and left it to Josh, couldn't you?' I pointed out. 'You might not have previously had any contact with him, but you knew he was out in the world somewhere and you could have left it to him.'

Algy shook his head.

'I would never have done that,' he told me. 'Because Thomas had convinced me that Josh felt the same way about the place as he did and that he wouldn't want it either. Thomas told me that my grandson had absolutely no interest in either me or the Wynbrook Estate, and if it was left to him, he would sell up too. And without even coming to view it.'

Thomas sounded like a total toad, and that was putting it mildly.

'But Josh does want it?' I asked, feeling a flare of hope.

'I'm certain that he does.' Algy nodded, looking happy again. 'Obviously it's a lot for him to get his head around, so we're taking things slowly, but one thing I do know for sure is that

Thomas lied to me about how my grandson has always felt about this place. Among other things.'

'So, what's next for Josh?' I asked, wondering what those other things were, but feeling it wasn't my business to ask. 'How's he planning on getting to know the estate he might one day inherit and what running it entails?'

Algy looked at me and smiled.

'Oh, I know that look,' I said warily. 'You want something, Algy, don't you?'

'Well,' he said, 'the thing is, I'd really like Josh's introduction to the estate to be the same as mine was when I was a young man. Younger in fact than he is now.'

'And how were you introduced to it?' I frowned.

'My father encouraged me to work every part of it,' Algy told me, his eyes twinkling at the memory. 'I started with the housekeeping, then helped in the office, in the garden and out in the fields. I had a go at everyone's job and in doing so, earned the respect of all of the staff and got to know the place and what it took to run it from every possible angle.'

That sounded like a very sensible approach to me and no doubt accounted for what made Algy such a generous employer. If Josh went through the same apprenticeship, it could make him a competent potential estate owner too. That said, I couldn't see Mum and Dad welcoming him in to work with them. They were still wary and suspicious about his sudden arrival and the way he'd duped me for so long had done nothing to allay their fears about what he might secretly have up his sleeve for Algy.

'So, Josh will be doing the laundry for a while, will he?' I asked.

Algy grimaced.

'Your mum wasn't keen, I have to say,' he said. 'She said she's got so much to do and she doesn't need someone getting under her feet.'

'And Dad?'

'I didn't dare ask him,' Algy sighed. 'And I know Nick's too busy for Josh to start with him because he'll need supervising and training up. So, I was wondering . . .'

'What?' I frowned.

'I was wondering if perhaps Josh might be able to start here in the cutting garden with you, Daisy. Just doing some very simple tasks.'

My heart sank. I still hadn't had any contact with Josh since revelation day, so the thought of working next to him in my favourite place wasn't one I relished. I had quickly managed to quell my bad memories of the walled garden, grown to love it again and my work in it, and I didn't want anything to taint that.

Though, if in time Josh did become the owner of the estate, then I supposed I would have to get used to him being around. He would be my boss *and* my landlord if I carried on living in the summerhouse and running Wynbrook Blooms.

'You don't want to work with him either?' Algy said worriedly, when I didn't immediately answer.

I loved him for sounding concerned as opposed to cross. He might have recently transformed my life but clearly felt no desire to either pull rank or call in a favour.

'I know he didn't tell you what he should—'

'I'll work with him, Algy,' I interrupted. 'Of course I will. Tell him to be here for eight sharp, tomorrow.'

'That's very generous of you,' he said, smiling. 'Thank you. Your willingness might bring the others around. And one more thing: please don't tell anyone what I've just shared with you regarding my former thoughts about selling the place, will you? I have no plans to follow it through now and it will only make everyone feel insecure and unsettled and that's the last thing I want.'

'But if Josh ultimately decides he doesn't want to take Wynbrook on—'

Algy put up a hand to stop me.

'I'll cross that bridge if I come to it,' he said firmly, as a couple came into the garden looking to buy some blooms. 'Now let's say no more about it – agreed?'

'I won't tell anyone,' I promised. 'But why did you tell me, Algy?'

'Because,' he said, 'out of everyone here, you have the most cause to feel impacted by Josh's surprise arrival and subsequent behaviour, and I hoped that by giving you some context, it might make you feel a little better about his . . . former secrecy. Has it?'

'I think I probably need to talk to Josh before I can answer that.' I smiled. 'But I appreciate that you understand why I have been feeling so upset.'

'Of course,' said Algy, patting my hand, which was still holding the spade handle. 'Talk to him as soon as you can. It's imperative you clear the air.'

'I agree,' I sighed, but I wasn't looking forward to it.

With Josh due to arrive to help in the walled garden at eight that Wednesday, and the garden opening at ten, I decided to head to the beach in Wynmouth as soon as it was light. Thankfully, the tide was with me, and I strode into the chilly water and swam until my limbs started to ache, my nerves had disappeared and all thoughts of Josh were banished.

Oblivion had been what I had sought and found, but it didn't last long.

'Oh!' I gasped, as I opened the beach hut door and came face to face with the man himself, completely naked. 'Sorry, I didn't know you were in here.'

He held his towel in front of him and I realised the moment was an almost identical reenactment of when he'd walked in on me the day we met.

'I guess this makes us even,' Josh commented, colouring up. 'I've been for a swim.'

Given how focused I'd been when I was swimming, I hadn't spotted him. I didn't say anything or move and he gave me an unfathomable look in return.

'Hello,' he then said in a completely different tone. 'My name is Josh and I'm staying in the area. I'm also the long-lost grandson of Algy Alford, who owns Wynbrook Manor. When I feel brave enough, I'm hoping to introduce myself to him, but in the meantime, if you could keep that information to yourself, I'd really appreciate it.'

I don't know how he expected me to react to his belatedly more accurate introduction, but I wasn't about to congratulate him for getting it right second time around.

'If that was your attempt to turn back time and introduce yourself properly, you failed,' I told him bluntly and in spite of the fact that I knew we needed to talk. 'Time hasn't rewound as far as I can tell.'

'Actually . . .' he said, dropping the towel and reaching for his shorts. I looked away. 'I don't want to turn back time because

I wouldn't really want to change a thing. I had my reasons for not telling anyone who I was and I have no regrets about that.'

'Well, I—' I started to say, but he cut me off.

'Other than I wish I hadn't walked out in front of your car. Or walked in on you getting changed in here. Or walked into the pub when I did and had you bump into me, or—'

'I get it,' I said, through gritted teeth. 'You wish you hadn't met me.'

I turned around and walked out, letting the door swing shut behind me. I was already marching across the sand, still in my swimming costume and with my towel over my shoulder when he caught up with me.

'What I wish,' he said, lightly catching my hand which I quickly tugged free, 'is that I hadn't met you *before* I introduced myself to Algy. Then, when I'd had the chance to figure a few things out, I could have been honest with you about my identity from the start.'

'But then who would have supplied you with all the estate goss and childhood memories of the place before you turned up?' I said meanly, my tone letting him know how deeply I had felt his deception and how much I resented him for letting me rattle on while he absorbed everything I had shared without knowing who was really on the receiving end of it. 'Who would have let you know that Algy was at a low ebb . . .'

My words trailed off as a hard lump made its presence felt deep in my throat. I forcefully swallowed it down. I didn't mind showing Josh that I was angry, but I was not going to let him see that I was upset.

'I think it would be best if you didn't work with me today,' I said hoarsely and turned away.

'Do you know why I listened so keenly to you talking about growing up on the estate?' he called to my retreating back.

I kept walking.

'Because I was trying to imagine myself in your shoes,' he carried on loudly. 'I wanted to picture myself doing all of the things you got to do. I wanted to replace the visual I had of you as a child growing up at Wynbrook, with one of me. I wanted to see myself on the receiving end of the childhood I should have had, instead of the one that saw me dragged from boarding school and then around the US with no one place to call home and no continuity in either my education or my friendships . . .'

His words petered out and I stopped walking.

'I didn't plan for the summer to turn out this way,' he said more quietly. 'I didn't know how I was going to feel about you, Daisy.'

I turned back to face him, my traitorous heart beating wildly in my chest.

'I wasn't ready to turn up on the estate when I did either, but I got so scared when you said something was wrong with Algy that I knew I had to go because if something happened to him before I met him, then I never would have been able to live with the regret.'

'But why didn't you just tell me the truth?' I demanded, as I walked back towards him and tried to focus on the picture that was bigger than the feelings for me that he'd just alluded to. 'You could have trusted me.'

'Because to begin with, I barely knew you.' He shrugged. 'And by the time I felt like I did, I didn't know how to broach it. It felt like it was too late to come clean and I still had so much to work out.'

His words weren't the easiest to hear, but I knew there was truth in them.

'I've discovered recently that there's practically no one in my life who I can have faith in,' he continued, sounding bitter, 'so how could I immediately spill my best-kept secret to a woman I'd just met on a beach and embarked on a summer romance with?'

I preferred his definition of our relationship to Nick's – a romance sounded far lovelier than a fling – or I would have preferred it, if it was not now over. Because, given the complicated circumstances, and in spite of the fact that Josh had just said he had feelings for me, it had to be over, didn't it?

'But surely you can see how your behaviour has made everyone question their trust in you?' I said, firing a question back at him. 'Everyone around here really likes you, Josh, but we all *love* Algy and will do anything to protect him.'

Josh nodded.

'I know that,' he said, running a hand through his damp hair, 'but he doesn't need protecting, not from me, and I promise I had my reasons for not revealing my identity the second I showed up.'

'Will you tell me what those reasons are?' I asked him.

'I do want to, but I'm still untangling some of them and I'd rather not discuss any of it until I've got it all straight in my head. I started this summer with a bowl of very twisted spaghetti, but I'm slowly pulling it all out, strand by strand.'

I looked at him and sighed. That wasn't the answer I had been hoping for and the look on his face suggested he knew it.

'You do know that given my reason for coming back to Wynbrook, I'm not great with finding faith in people at the moment, don't you?' I reminded him. 'You're not the only one around here with trust issues.'

'I do know that,' he said, nodding. 'Your ex was an idiot to treat you the way he did. But I can promise you, Daisy, with my hand on my heart,' he pressed his open hand to his bare tanned chest, 'that there is absolutely nothing nefarious about my showing up here.'

I had no desire to smile and when I looked at Josh's face, I could see he wasn't trying to be funny or lighten the moment to get himself off the hook. He was in earnest and most likely hadn't even realised the significance of the word he'd used to express his sincerity.

'You promise?' I whispered.

'Cross my heart,' he vowed, looking deep into my eyes.

Hearing his heartfelt oath and thinking of what Algy had said, I allowed my own heart to open again, just the tiniest bit, and I promised myself I would do my best to believe him.

Chapter 24

Wynbrook Blooms was busy for the whole day, which was a blessing because it went some way to stopping me getting too distracted by the things Josh had said on the beach that related to me. True, there were a couple of times that I caught myself staring at him rather than focusing on the job in hand, because of course I'd taken back my statement on the beach that he shouldn't work with me and then given him a lift to Wynbrook, but for the most part, I managed to carry on unhindered.

The best part of the day was when Algy arrived with a lunchtime picnic basket for us all to share. It didn't take more than a minute to see him and Josh together to know the pair had bonded and I felt my heart further open when I thought about the more secure future of Wynbrook and the direction they might together decide to take the estate in.

I had even fallen to thinking about the future myself, in particular that of Wynbrook Blooms and how it could be turned into a much larger venture, assuming I could persuade the current and future owners to think beyond the parameters of the current set-up. Certainly, by the end of our day together in the garden, there was no doubt in my mind that Josh's future lay with the estate in some capacity or other.

Unfortunately, however, I didn't think that everyone in my life was yet as convinced about Josh as I was, and listening to the conversation at the impromptu barbecue gathering at Nick's place on Saturday night was further proof of that.

'He was all over the house when he helped me,' I heard Mum disapprovingly telling Penny. 'In and out of all the rooms as if he owned the place.'

Having spent such a successful day with me in the garden on Wednesday, Algy had then made a point of insisting that both Mum and Dad should give Josh taster hours over the next couple of days and that day, Saturday, he'd been with Nick on the fruit farm.

Nick hadn't needed anything like the coaxing my parents had had and he had also invited Josh to the barbecue. It transpired, however, that Josh had already arranged to spend the evening with Algy, talking and looking through some photos, so he wasn't available to quell the naysayers himself. Not that Mum would likely have been so forthright with her opinions had he been present, I was certain.

'Given that you'd asked him to do the vacuuming, Janet,' Penny mildly pointed out, 'it would have been impossible for him not to be all over the house, wouldn't it?'

Mum ignored that and Penny rolled her eyes at me. She was looking radiant, I noticed. Running the busy café and being engaged clearly suited her.

'And did you know that Algy offered him the use of one of his precious cars as well?' Mum then tutted. 'I heard him tell Josh he could have his pick of the lot.'

'And what did Josh choose from out of the garages, Mum?' I asked her, with far less grace than Penny had managed because I knew the answer.

'That tatty old bike,' said Nick in disbelief before Mum could respond. 'Out of the Bentley, the Spider and that gorgeous little Mini, he took that mangled, ancient bike!'

That was how Josh was currently getting between Wynbrook and Wynmouth every day. I didn't much like the thought of him negotiating the narrow lanes on two wobbly wheels, especially given the amount of tourist traffic but, having just listened to Mum, I could understand why he hadn't perhaps opted for four wheels. Turning up in the village driving any one of Algy's pristine and valuable cars would have caused further tongue-wagging and of course, I also knew that Josh was wary about driving on what he termed the wrong side of the road.

'How have you got on working with him today, Nick?' I asked, keen to find a true and trusted Josh ally among the gathering.

'Great,' he said, nodding, as he inexpertly flipped a burger. 'He was interested in everything and quick to catch on, even though Algy had initially thought he might need babysitting. He worked the entire day without so much as a grumble and I know that a few of the visitors were quite taken with his accent.' He laughed at some memory of the day. 'He's good for business. I'm hoping he'll be back with me again next week if he can spare the time.'

'Excellent,' I said, thinking that was more like it as I vigorously tossed the salad Penny had made and remembered how popular Josh had been during music night at the pub. 'And you got on well with him too, Dad, didn't you?'

'He certainly put in the hours.' Dad nodded and I began to feel even more hopeful. 'And he can work, I'll give him that. Didn't know much about gardening mind you, but was as keen to learn with me as he was with Nick. Though I can't help wondering . . .'

'You can't help wondering what?' I demanded, feeling deflated again.

'Oh, I don't know,' said Dad, handing out drinks, 'I know you're pretty struck on him, Daisy,' I felt my face flush, 'but I can't help wondering if his desire to pitch in might not be some sort of . . .'

'Some sort of what?' Penny frowned.

'Double bluff,' said Mum.

'What?' I squawked, letting the salad servers clatter in the bowl.

'Your father and I,' Mum carried on as Nick and I exchanged a look, 'think Josh might appear to be pitching in so eagerly to pull the wool over everyone's eyes. Sort of to lull us all into a false sense of security before he strikes.'

'That's ridiculous,' snapped Nick, sounding every bit as cross as I felt.

'We're just being cautious,' said Dad, giving Mum a look that suggested their conspiracy theory shouldn't have been made public.

I was pleased it had been though. At least I knew more of what Josh was still up against now.

'But why would you think that?' Penny asked, sounding appalled.

'Because we still don't know the whole story, do we?' said Dad.

'You yourself, Daisy, said that he told you that there's more to the situation than he's let on, but he's still not shared it, has he?' Mum then said accusingly to me.

'He's not let on or shared it because he's still sorting it all out,' I said angrily. 'Not because he's got something to hide or is planning how to steal the estate out from under Algy, like his father had wanted to do.'

Neither Mum nor Dad still looked convinced.

'I think his father, Thomas,' I therefore continued, 'has wronged both him *and* Algy in ways none of us knows, and until the pair of them have privately talked it all through and come to terms with it, they're not going to share the details with us or anyone else, are they?'

When I had found out who Josh really was, I had been furious with him, but now I had no suspicions about his motives and was keen to defend him. It had broken me a bit when he said he had tried to imagine himself in my place when I regaled him with tales about growing up on the estate, and having seen him work so hard and spend every spare minute with his grandfather, there was no doubt in my mind that he was the man both the estate and Algy needed.

I was also thinking that *I* needed him again too. Now the dust had settled, I was missing our intimacy. It was only the middle of August and I hoped my summer fling hadn't been entirely . . . flung.

'I suppose not,' Dad said reluctantly, huffing out a breath.

'I think we should talk about something else,' Penny suggested diplomatically.

'I agree,' said Nick, planting a kiss on her cheek. 'Tell us how the beach café has been this week. Are you still thinking that paninis rather than pupils are your future, Pen?'

I had been looking forward to us all spending the evening together, but Mum and Dad's continuing suspicions about Josh had put rather a dampener on the gathering. Thankfully, however, the man himself found a way to cheer me up again.

'Hey!' I waved as I approached the summerhouse and spotted him sitting on the veranda in one of the rocking chairs.

It was after dusk and the outside lights were all twinkling and I had left a lamp on inside too. My little bolthole looked cosy and inviting – even more so with the addition of Josh – and I tried not to think about how it might feel in the middle of winter without insulation to keep the chill out. There was a small woodburning stove installed, but would that really be enough to stave off the bitter January cold?

Josh put a finger to his lips and when I reached him, I realised why.

'How have you managed that?' I whispered, as I cooed over Luna, who was curled up and purring on his lap.

'Oh, it was all her,' Josh said quietly. 'She came to me, rather than the other way around.'

'I think that's how it works with cats, isn't it?'

'I guess so,' he said, as Luna stretched out, jumped down and rather than shooting off, looked pointedly at her empty food bowl.

Algy would be thrilled about this sudden progress. And thinking of Algy . . .

'How was your evening?' I asked, opening the door to let us in.

'Revelatory,' Josh sighed, following me inside and carrying in a rucksack I hadn't previously noticed he had with him.

'Oh?'

I filled the cat bowl, but couldn't tempt Luna to come in,

so closed the summerhouse door, leaving her to eat outside, before we were inundated with moths.

'How was your night?' Josh then asked me.

'Mine was pretty revealing too,' I sighed, biting my lip.

'Care to share?' he asked.

Given what I had discovered were my parent's real thoughts about him, I didn't think I did.

'Not really,' I said. 'Do you?'

'I think I should actually,' he said. 'I have a feeling there are a few people around here who are still doubting my motives for turning up and having now talked things through properly with Algy, I would like to paint you the full picture, Daisy, and then perhaps I'll consider filling them in too.'

'I would appreciate knowing more,' I said, hoping what he had to share would have enough detail to put an end to my parents' suspicions and maybe even shut down the entire rumour mill for good.

I opened the fridge and pulled out a bottle of white wine.

'Can I tempt you?' I offered.

'Yes, please,' Josh smiled, 'but only a small one. I need to be stable on my feet for the cycle ride back to the village.'

'Perhaps,' I said boldly, feeling encouraged by his smile as I filled two glasses, 'you might prefer to stay.'

The air between us, which was already warm, suddenly felt charged with electricity.

'Oh, well, in that case,' he smiled again, taking the glass from me and clinking it against mine as our eyes met, 'a large one it is.'

Feeling the familiar tug of attraction, I knew we were back on track to regaining what we had enjoyed before and I gave him a tour of the summerhouse as he hadn't previously visited, paying particular attention to the new mattress his grandfather had so kindly supplied. Josh sat and bounced on it approvingly with a wicked grin playing about his lips. I was hard pushed to resist the urge to join him.

'So,' I said, once we were safely back downstairs and sitting together on the sofa, 'you and Algy have finished talking then.'

'About my manipulative father, yes.'

'Oh, dear,' I said, taking a sip of my wine, 'that doesn't sound good.'

'It isn't,' Josh said wearily. 'I still haven't really got my head around the depths he sunk to, to interfere in and ruin my and Algy's relationship.'

He got up and retrieved a box and a bag he'd somehow squeezed into his rucksack and then sat next to me again.

'Letters,' I said with a frown, as he lifted the lid on the box and tipped out the bag. 'So many letters. And that's Algy's handwriting – I'd recognise it anywhere.'

Josh then proceeded to explain.

'It was the discovery of these letters,' he told me, 'that kicked off my decision to come here in the first place. My father had recently said a couple of things about Algy and Wynbrook that didn't tally with what he'd always maintained in the past so, when he was safely out of the way, I went in search of evidence.'

'And found . . .'

'Hidden in Dad's office, every birthday card, Christmas card and accompanying letter Algy had sent me via my mum's parents' address since we left here until the year I turned eighteen.'

'Oh, Josh!' I gasped.

'Obviously I'd had no idea Algy had tried to keep in touch with me because my father had always maintained that he had thrown us off the estate when Dad had tried to suggest ways the place could be more efficiently and profitably run.'

'But that's not what happened—' I rushed to say.

'Don't worry,' interjected Josh. 'I know that now. I know that it was my father who wanted to sell up and when Algy said no, Dad took us away and cut all ties.'

'I can't believe anyone could be so cruel,' I said, as tears sprung to my eyes, imagining the grief Algy must have felt as a result of the loss. 'Especially a parent.'

'And this is only my side of it,' Josh said, sounding choked himself. 'Algy has a letter too. Sent from my father the year I turned eighteen. He insisted Algy stop trying to maintain contact as I clearly wasn't interested in him. Dad told him that was why he'd never heard back from me. According to the vitriol my father wrote, I didn't care about some ancient estate in the middle of nowhere or an old man with no vision and I'd told my father to write all of that, and worse, on my behalf.'

'So, your dad had told you that Algy had abandoned you and wanted nothing more to do with you and then told Algy that you weren't interested in him . . .'

'That pretty much sums it up,' Josh said, looking at the letters and cards from his grandfather that he had so recently discovered.

'But why did your dad keep these?' I asked. 'Why not destroy the evidence?'

'I have no idea,' Josh sighed, 'but thank goodness he didn't, otherwise I would never have found out the truth. Do you understand now, Daisy, why I didn't want to announce myself as soon as I arrived?'

'But surely these letters and cards were proof enough that you were loved?'

'They were,' he said, 'they are, but I was scared. What if, during the years after I turned eighteen, Algy had tarred me with the same brush as Dad had disgraced himself with. His letters to me had stopped that year. There had to be a reason for that, didn't there? I didn't know when I arrived, that Dad had written to him, so I was spending my time in Wynmouth trying to fathom out how he might feel and react before I declared myself.'

'I see.'

'I was so angry with Dad, I turned up in Wynmouth on impulse, having booked Sam's cottage using Mum's maiden name so no one would make the connection,' he went on. 'And I thought I'd have time to do some digging while I decided what to do next, but then . . .'

'I nearly ran you over.'

Josh smiled at that.

'But then you landed in my life, Daisy,' he amended, 'with your connection to Wynbrook and even though everything you said about Algy made me desperately want to meet him, I still felt cautious and knew I had to work my way up to it.'

'Of course.' I nodded.

'But then when I realised, as a result of your concern for him, that Algy might be unwell and that I might not have the time I'd thought I had, I just booked a taxi and . . . turned up.'

'So, in the end, it was another impulse decision that got you here to Wynbrook,' I said, 'rather than the carefully thought-out plan you thought you'd have the time to put together when you first arrived in the village.'

'In the end,' he smiled, 'that's exactly what it was and given Algy's more than warm welcome and this joint purging of information Dad has poisoned us both with that we've gone through tonight, I can't help wishing I'd come straight here and bypassed the village altogether.'

'But then,' I said, putting down my wine and taking his hand, 'I never would have almost clipped you with my car . . .'

'That's true.' He smiled. 'And I wouldn't have walked in on you naked after your swim.'

'Or had me bump into you in the pub.'

'That's also true.' Josh grinned. 'All those precious moments would never have happened, would they?'

'Not a single one.'

We were quiet for a moment then.

'So,' I eventually said, once I'd temporarily tamped down the desire to jump on him again, 'you now finally know the truth behind your father leaving Wynbrook and taking you with him.'

'I do.' Josh nodded. 'Knowing Dad wanted to sell the estate, and snatch what he thought would be his share, sounds very much like him. The selfish idiot. And I also know that Algy has recently been seriously considering selling up so he could choose the most sympathetic buyer for the place himself. He said he'd told you that.'

'He did, though I wouldn't have mentioned it, not even to you, because he'd asked me not to tell anyone.'

'He trusts you without question, Daisy.' Josh smiled. 'And I can understand why.'

'And I feel honoured that he does,' I said. 'Algy is as dear to me as my own family. Can we be completely certain that selling the estate definitely isn't on the cards now?'

'Not even in the deck,' Josh said firmly. 'Wynbrook Manor Estate is staying in Alford family hands and being run as it has always been. By which I mean, with the welfare of its staff and the environment at its heart.'

'Algy's got you well trained already!' I laughed. 'That's his mantra.'

'That he has,' Josh happily agreed. 'Though I've had a couple of fresh ideas for the place myself that I might want to set in motion.'

'Such as?'

'All in good time.' He grinned again. 'They're both very good things, so there's no cause for alarm. They just need further thinking about before I share them, even with Algy.'

'Well, that's all right then,' I said, shifting closer. 'Might one of those ideas involve giving me the go-ahead to give the decor in here a bit of a spruce up?'

Josh looked around.

'I don't think it needs sprucing up,' he said, with a seductive smile. 'But I wouldn't mind taking a closer look at the paint-work up on the mezzanine, just to be sure . . .'

'I think that can be arranged,' I said, standing up and pulling him to his feet. 'In fact, I know it can.'

Chapter 25

As seemed to be my habit since moving into the summerhouse, I woke almost as soon as it was light the next morning and in spite of the fact that I hadn't had much sleep. Josh's inspection of the paintwork had lasted hours and been hugely satisfying.

'Good morning,' he said and smiled as I stretched out next to him in the bed.

'Good morning.' I smiled back as I turned to face him and pushed my messy hair out of my face. 'What time is it?'

'Still early,' he sighed, moving closer and kissing me. 'You've got hours before you need to open the garden.'

I pretended to pout.

'Don't go thinking that because you're now effectively my boss, you can bring work into every conversation,' I said, kissing him back.

'I wouldn't dream of it,' he laughed.

'Though actually this is one job I don't mind talking about all the time.'

What a novelty that was.

'That's further proof,' Josh smiled, 'not that I think you needed it, that you're in exactly the right place.'

'As are you,' I sighed contentedly.

'Do you mean in your bed or on the estate?'

'Both,' I giggled, pulling him on top of me. 'You're of value everywhere.'

A while later, we shared breakfast on the veranda, in the company of Luna, who seemed to be getting bolder by the day, and a thought occurred to me.

'Josh . . .'

'Um,' he said, looking up from the book he was reading.

Is there anything sexier than a man reading? Especially when it's one of your childhood favourites. It was my hardback copy of *Anne of Green Gables* that he'd chosen from the bookshelf and been immersed in.

'I was just wondering where your mum featured in your father's cruel plan to keep you and Algy apart?'

Josh put the book down on the table and sat back in the rocking chair. I noticed he'd neither cracked the spine nor turned down the page, which was another big tick in his box.

'I honestly don't know,' he said, with a small shrug. 'The letters Algy wrote were sent via Mum's parents' address, so I'm wondering if she had known something about them.'

'That's what I was thinking,' I mused.

'But I'm certain she would have passed them on to me if she had been aware of their significance,' he said, frowning. 'Because she's absolutely nothing like Dad. He's hard-nosed and materialistic, whereas she's a much gentler soul. I think Dad only married her because of her family's success and the helping hand my grandfather was willing to offer when Dad cut ties here. I'm certain that connection to the money is the only thing that's ensured Dad's never left Mum . . .'

'Perhaps you should call her,' I suggested, noting the conflict in Josh's expression that the not knowing had prompted. 'Or email.'

'And say what?' he sighed. 'How do I even begin to broach what I unearthed in Dad's office and as a result, where I am now? If it turns out that she had no prior knowledge of the letters, it's going to be quite a shock.'

'I agree,' I grimaced, thinking it wasn't a conversation I would want to have. It had the potential to change her entire opinion of the man she was married to. 'But if your father discovers you've taken the letters and then accuses her of being involved . . .'

Thomas Alford struck me as the kind of man who wouldn't think twice about throwing his weight around. He didn't sound like a good match for Josh's mum at all. I had a sudden vision of a woman who had never lived the life she had dreamed of. Rather she was someone who had bobbed along in her husband's wake. I hoped the image was wrong.

'You're right,' Josh said gloomily as he distractedly ran a hand through his hair. 'I know you are. I'll talk to Mum as soon as I can.'

'And can I talk to my parents too?' I asked. 'They're still,' I chose my next words with care, 'keen to protect Algy, but if they knew the reason why you hadn't come straight here when you arrived in Wynmouth, I'm sure they'd . . . stand down.'

Josh gave a wry smile and I guessed the subtlety I'd aimed for hadn't quite hit its mark.

'I agree that they, and everyone else who still thinks I'm on the make, should at least know that I'm planning to stay and work alongside Algy.' I winced at the way he'd described what the doubters were thinking, even though the definition was right. 'But I think it should come from me, rather than you.'

'If you're sure?'

'I am,' he said with a nod, sounding resolute. 'Let me talk to Algy and we'll come up with a plan for where and when.'

'Are you here to help?' I asked Dad when he appeared in the walled garden later that morning, as a queue of bloom seekers was beginning to form.

'I'm not actually,' he said. 'I'm here to issue an invitation.'

'Ooh, you sound like Alan Rickman playing Colonel Brandon,' gushed the woman at the front of the line as she fanned herself with her sunhat.

'Who?' Dad frowned.

'Never mind,' I laughed, knowing exactly the scene in *Sense and Sensibility* she was referring to.

While the woman and her friend discussed the merits of Alan Rickman versus David Morrissey in the role of Colonel Brandon on screen, I quickly carried on talking to Dad.

'To lunch or dinner?' I guessed.

'Dinner,' said Dad. 'You won't have time to stop for lunch today.'

'I might if you stay and help me,' I suggested, then a thought occurred. 'Please don't tell me Mum's cooking a roast today – it's sweltering.'

'No,' Dad said, with a wry smile. 'She's not.'

'Thank goodness for that.'

'Algy is.'

'What?' I squawked.

'He and Josh are cooking a Sunday roast together. Algy reckons it's high time his grandson was reacquainted with a proper Sunday dinner like he would have eaten here when he was little.'

I rather liked the thought of Josh and Algy cooking together, but not in the middle of a boiling August day.

'I'll have sweet peas in my posy, please,' said the Austen fan, who had now exhausted the Colonel Brandon topic. 'And some Alchemilla too.'

'I better get on,' I said to Dad. 'Otherwise my dinner will turn into supper.'

'And I will help,' said Dad, who always had his secateurs somewhere about him. 'Just until we've cleared this queue.'

I was exhausted by the end of the afternoon and especially relieved that Wynbrook Blooms was going to be closed for the next couple of days, because by the time I locked the garden gate, there was barely a flower left. Hopefully, between then and Wednesday, there would be enough coming through for me to crop again.

'All right?' said Dad, who had been inspecting the greenhouses and checking the watering system was correctly set up to cope with the extra hot weather.

'Knackered,' I declared, as I swigged down the last of the water from one of the bottles I'd filled earlier. 'And ready for my dinner, even though I said earlier it would be too hot to eat it. Who else has been invited?'

'Me and your mum, obviously,' said Dad. 'And Nick and Penny.'

'A select gathering,' I mused.

I realised then that the meal would doubtless be the moment that Algy and Josh told everyone else what Josh had told me.

'You're doing such a good job here, my love,' Dad then thrilled me by saying as he looked around.

'Do you really think so?' I swallowed.

'Yes,' he said with feeling. 'I really do.'

'Thank you.' I nodded, feeling choked. 'I can't tell you how much I'm loving it, Dad. I'd been looking for something to fulfil me for so long and I found it right on our doorstep.'

'Where it had always been,' said Dad, sounding upset. 'I never should have blocked your way before, Daisy. I'm so sorry.'

'All water under the bridge,' I insisted, because it was time for us to move on. 'All I'm interested in now is making this project a success.'

It was on the tip of my tongue to share the ideas I had come up with, but just like Josh had said about his, they needed further thought and running past Algy first.

'I think it already is a success,' said Dad, looking around again. 'But I hope there'll be more to offer your customers by Wednesday.'

'Me too,' I laughed.

'I should have known you were destined to have your hands in the soil when I picked your name, shouldn't I?' Dad carried on contentedly, as he led the way towards the path that would take me back to the summerhouse and a cool shower.

'You picked my name?'

'I did,' Dad chuckled. 'A portent if ever there was one.'

'A bit like yours,' I laughed. 'There's always a Robin some-where about the garden.'

'That there is,' Dad agreed, and I felt blessed to have our relationship so strongly repaired.

I didn't think there was going to be the same outcome for Josh and his dad, especially after his father found out he'd discovered Algy's correspondence and carried it back to Wynmouth. Which reminded me . . .

'Crikey, Dad!' I exclaimed, having checked the time on my

phone, which I kept buttoned up in my shorts pocket, and realised how late it was. 'We'd better stop dawdling and hurry up. Algy won't be impressed if his dinner burns.'

'And I won't be either,' said Dad, changing direction so he was heading towards the cottage. 'I'm ruddy starving.'

'No flowers,' tutted Algy, when I turned up feeling fresh after my shower, but empty-handed.

He was looking dapper in a striped shirt and cravat and absolutely nothing like the wizened and grumpy old man who had faced me the day I arrived back at Wynbrook.

'I'm afraid not,' I laughed. 'Though that's actually a good thing because it means we've sold them all. Well, all of the ones in the cutting beds anyway.'

'Oh, well done,' Algy applauded.

'I'm not entirely empty-handed though,' I said, as I looked behind me.

Sitting on the path and laboriously washing her paws was Luna.

'She followed me all the way from the summerhouse,' I said happily.

'Well now,' Algy beamed. 'Isn't that wonderful? And look how much better her condition is already as a result of all the extra attention she's been getting.'

She hadn't got close enough yet to receive much from me, but what she'd had in general was clearly making a difference. We'd never got to the bottom of what had been taking the food Algy had been putting out for her, but whatever it was, it wasn't stealing it from the summerhouse veranda and Luna was looking healthier as a result.

'She'll look even better after a slice of beef,' said Josh, who walked out of the kitchen to join us, wearing a stained apron as he attempted to fan himself with a tea towel.

'Hot in there, is it?' I teased.

'Hotter than the sun,' he puffed, his cheeks glowing.

'Which is why we're eating outside,' said Algy. 'Why don't you go round, my dear?'

'Is everyone else here already?' I asked.

'They are,' said Josh, looking a little nervous. 'Though not everyone is outside. Your mum's currently holding court in the kitchen and checking the veg.'

No wonder he looked jittery!

'I told her we didn't need any help . . .' Algy began, but he knew the sentence didn't need finishing.

'We'd better get back in there,' said Josh, fanning himself again. I knew now his escalated temperature wasn't only the result of the weather and the heat wafting off the Aga. 'See you in a minute.'

It felt wonderfully cool round the back of the manor and I sank gratefully, but less than gracefully, into a chair.

'You look nice,' said Penny, her eyes sparkling. 'That's a pretty dress.'

'Thanks,' I said, sitting up straighter and smoothing the front of it down.

'What's the occasion?' Nick teased.

'Dinner at the manor,' I said, in my poshest voice. 'I thought I should make an effort and as my work gear was grubby, sweaty and rather stinky, I could hardly wear that, could I?'

'Now, that's fine talk for a mealtime,' scolded Mum, who I hadn't realised was behind me.

She was talking slightly differently too and I wondered if

she was going to go full-on Hyacinth Bucket for Josh's benefit. The grin Penny and Nick then gave me suggested they were also weighing up that possibility.

'Would you do the honours please, Nick?' Algy asked as he joined us and indicated an ice bath, rather than ice bucket, where a few bottles of champagne were currently reclining. 'A little fizz will, I think, help lubricate proceedings.'

He'd obviously noticed Mum's modified tone as well.

'Especially on an empty stomach,' I mischievously added.

'Don't worry,' said Josh, who was now dithering on the granite paving and looking nervous, 'I'm about to start plating up.'

'I'll help,' said Mum.

'No need,' Penny jumped in, in a way that was ferociously firm for her. 'You sit down, Janet. I can help Josh.'

Josh looked as if he could have kissed her for coming to his rescue and within minutes, we were all tucking into succulent slices of beef, seasonal veg, crispy roast potatoes, lashing of flavoursome gravy and absolutely enormous Yorkshire puddings.

'These Yorkshires are miraculous,' Mum declared and I noticed her champagne flute had been drained a second time.

'They're Josh's doing,' Algy said with a hint of pride.

'Under your instruction, Algy.' Josh blushed. 'I've never had these back in the States.'

I wondered if he was ever going to call Algy 'Grandad', but I supposed it was still early days for the pair of them.

'Well, they're perfect,' said Dad. 'Best I've had in a long time.'

'Because Mum hasn't made any in a long time,' I said quickly, making sure I freed him from the hook he'd just swallowed.

'Beginner's luck,' Josh said modestly, but I could tell he was pleased the dinner had turned out so well. 'I haven't had a roast like this since I lived in the UK when I was little and I wish I could remember them from back then. This food alone is worth me staying on for.'

'So,' said Mum, suddenly completely sober, 'you are thinking of staying on then?'

'Let's clear these plates,' suggested Algy, 'and then we can have a little chat before we fill ourselves up even more with pudding.'

By the time the two men had between them first explained about the letters and cards Algy had sent but Josh had never received and then stated in no uncertain terms that Wynbrook Manor and the estate would be left to Josh, who very definitely *did* want to run it and intended to keep it in the Alford family, there wasn't a dry eye around the table.

'Your wretched father,' Mum said, her posh accent thankfully abandoned, as she leant over and sympathetically patted Josh's arm, 'has a lot to answer for.'

'Indeed, he does,' Algy readily agreed, 'but there's nothing to be gained by wasting further time in fretting about him, is there?'

'Hear, hear,' said Dad, raising his glass.

We all did the same.

'To the future,' said Josh.

'To the future!' everyone toasted in unison.

Algy looked at me and winked, and I knew that he definitely wasn't going to mention that he had been thinking about selling the estate. I was pleased about that.

'I do have a feeling there are going to be some changes happening round here in the future,' he did then say to everyone. 'These young people are going to keep us all on our toes, but the essence of Wynbrook and the things that really matter will be further enhanced, not lost.'

Given what I had in mind for Wynbrook Blooms and indeed, myself, I could heartily agree with that and the look on Josh's face told me that whatever his idea was, was going to be exciting too.

'And are we going to hear about those changes tonight?' Dad asked.

Algy shook his head.

'I think we've had enough excitement for one evening, don't you?' he laughed. 'And besides, I haven't even been apprised of them myself yet.'

'I promise my idea is nothing any of you will object to,' Josh was quick to clarify.

'And mine isn't either,' I added and reached for Josh's hand.

'Quite the double act, aren't they?' Penny giggled, then hiccupped.

'Indeed, they are.' Mum nodded, raising her glass to us both and I knew without a doubt that the ghost of Laurence, that had still occasionally been shadowing me since my return, was finally laid to rest.

Next there was pudding to celebrate with – shop-bought meringues with Wynbrook berries and cream – then dancing and a lot more champagne.

As I looked at Algy twirling Mum, Penny and Nick smooching with not a millimetre between them, Luna curled up on the chair Algy had been sitting on and Dad deep in conversation with Josh, I let out a breath and thanked my lucky stars. This, at last, was what I had been waiting for. This was my best summer ever and there couldn't possibly be anything left to happen that could ruin that now, could there?

Chapter 26

The ecstatic feeling lasted long into the following week. Early on Monday, after another wonderful night with Josh in the summerhouse, I drove us both into Wynmouth. Algy had been most insistent the previous evening, before everyone headed off, that Josh should move into the manor and used us, his dearest friends, to convince his grandson that he should.

'You absolutely must,' Mum had slightly slurred, and I had bitten my lip to stop myself from laughing. I'd never seen her tipsy before. 'It's your birthright and it's high time you claimed it.'

Josh had finally been persuaded that making the move was the right next step, but we had a couple of things we wanted to indulge in in the village before we packed up the cottage and he made a permanent move to the manor.

'Isn't this glorious?' I gasped, as I stopped mid-stroke in the sea and started to tread water.

The temperature had initially felt bracing, despite the rapidly rising temperature of the morning, but in that moment it was perfect. Plenty cold enough to cool me down, but not so chilly that I was dithering about going in.

'It is,' Josh agreed, as he reached me.

He pulled me into his arms and I found myself wishing there weren't so many families already set up on the sand and paddling, because I could have been quite tempted to take the moment further.

'Race you back!' Josh then shouted, completely breaking the spell and swimming speedily off with a splash and without giving me any opportunity to catch him.

We lay on our towels for a while in front of the beach hut to dry off, then went inside to get changed.

'You know the day I arrived,' Josh said as he peeled off his swim shorts, 'and walked in on you here . . .'

'I vaguely remember.' I grinned, thinking it felt like forever ago now, given how much had happened since, but it wasn't actually that long ago at all.

'I thought I remembered this place,' Josh said falteringly. 'Just a hazy memory of coming here, or somewhere very much like it.'

'Maybe you did. I'm sure your parents must have brought you to the beach at some point.'

'Mum might have done, I suppose,' Josh mused.

'You could always ask her,' I suggested. 'Did you contact her yesterday?'

He let out a breath.

'No,' he said. 'I bottled it.'

'I don't think you bottled anything,' I said sternly. 'Given that you faced everyone else last night and cleared the air about what had happened since you'd been taken from Wynbrook and why you've now come back, that was enough to contend with for one day, wasn't it?'

'I guess.' Josh smiled.

'Why are you smiling?'

'Because you sounded so cross with me.'

'Not cross *with* you,' I said, stepping closer to him. 'Cross *for* you. You're going through such a lot, so give yourself some credit. You can't do it all at once, can you? I think you need to be a bit kinder to yourself, don't you?'

'I suppose I could be,' he agreed, readily succumbing to the kiss I then bestowed upon him.

'Anyone home?' came a voice from outside.

It was Penny.

'Yes,' I shouted back. 'We are. Go away.'

She ignored my request and opened the door.

'I hope you're not up to no good in here,' said Nick, who was with her, as he looked between us. 'That's not what this place is for, you know.'

'We would have been if you pair hadn't barged in,' I pouted and Nick laughed.

Though really, I would never have done anything more than kiss in the hut. It would have been disrespectful.

'What are you doing here, Pen?' I asked. 'We were going to come down to the café for lunch later.'

She rolled her eyes at that.

'It's not open today, remember?'

'Oh, bugger,' I said. 'I completely forgot you decided to keep the place closed on Mondays after all.'

'Even I need a break sometimes,' she laughed and I was pleased that she was taking at least some of the time off that she was entitled to ahead of the start of term at the beginning of September. 'The twins are very good, but they're not up to running the place entirely on their own,' she added.

'It'll have to be the pub then. Are you up for that?' I asked Josh.

'I guess.' He shrugged, then pulled on his T-shirt. 'I have to face the rest of the village sometime, don't I? And maybe word will have got round about me being a good guy, rather than a bloke on the make, by now.'

I was about to say that it might take longer than just the few hours that had passed since he talked to everyone back at Wynbrook, but Penny spoke up before me.

'Well,' she said, looking pleased with herself, 'we've just had coffee in the pub and made a point of very loudly telling Sam some of what you told us last night, Josh, so rumours about you will still be circulating, but they'll be much more positive ones now.'

'We didn't share the personal stuff,' Nick added hastily, 'about the letters and so on, but we did confirm that you're here for good and that one day you'll be taking over the estate from Algy and keeping it in the Alford family.'

'Thank you for doing that, guys.' Josh smiled gratefully and I felt my heart flip at the thought of him being around forever, as opposed to just the summer. 'That's brilliant.'

'It was our pleasure,' Penny said, blushing.

Apparently, not even a recently engaged person was immune to my current beau's beautiful charms.

'And knowing that I'm in for a warmer welcome than I expected,' Josh then said to me, embracing the moment, 'let's head back to the cottage to wash the sea off us now and then go straight to the Smuggler's for something to eat afterwards.'

'All right,' I willingly agreed.

'Would you like us to come to the pub with you?' Nick asked.

'No,' said Josh, 'but thank you for offering. You two enjoy the beach hut, while you've got the chance.'

I scooped up my towel and bag.

'And don't do anything in here that we wouldn't do,' I called over my shoulder as I sashayed out.

If Josh wrung his hands once between leaving the cottage and walking into the pub, he did it a hundred times, and that was no mean feat given that the two buildings were next door to each other.

'Stop stressing,' I said as I caught his hand and kept hold of it. 'You know it's fine. Penny and Nick have already done the hard bit for you.'

'Oh, I know,' he said, 'and I'm ever so grateful to them both, but I'm still nervous about what people are going to say to my face.'

'Well, well,' announced Sam, who was coming out of the pub to add something to the chalkboard in the lane, 'if it isn't the lord of the manor.'

Josh's face dropped and I squeezed his hand.

'Are you going to grace us with your presence?' Sam carried on, not having noticed that Josh thought he was being serious. 'It would be wonderful if you came in and raised the tone. There's nothing but rum-swigging pirates and reprobates turned up so far this morning.'

I tutted and rolled my eyes and went to follow Sam inside, but Josh stayed rooted to the spot.

'He's kidding!' I said, giving his hand a tug. 'Come on.'

'You do know I was joking, mate?' Sam then said, rushing back to clarify, when he realised Josh hadn't budged. 'We're all absolutely over the moon for you. And Algy. Truly.'

'That we are,' said George, who had wandered down the lane with Skipper and was now standing behind Josh. 'I'm only a relative newbie in Wynmouth, but I've heard tales of your father, my boy, and I'm delighted that you're nothing like him.'

'I'm not,' Josh said in earnest. 'I'm nothing like him at all.'

'So come inside and tell us how you've ended up here then and why,' Sam said encouragingly. 'We heard some of it from Penny and Nick earlier, but the horse's mouth is bound to be better than second-hand.'

'Yes,' agreed George, 'and do get a move on, young man. I'm in need of another shot of caffeine and you're blocking my path to it.'

'Come on.' I smiled.

Josh crossed the threshold and rolled his eyes as Marguerite stepped out from behind the bar to curtsy while Tess tugged her forelock.

'You're all idiots.' Josh grinned, getting the joke, and everyone laughed.

Sam insisted that our drinks were on the house and once Josh had added the merest details to what Penny and Nick had already explained, interest in him died down and everyone went back to their own conversations. I had a feeling most of them were probably about Wynbrook, but I didn't point that out to Josh as his shoulders were finally looking less hunched and he was sounding more relaxed.

'My main reason for calling in,' he said to Sam, 'is to let you know that I'm going to be moving out of the cottage today. Algy has talked me into moving into the manor.'

'Quite right too,' said Tess, smiling. 'He must be absolutely thrilled that you've finally returned to the fold.'

Josh looked wide-eyed.

'I haven't thought about it like that before,' he said, his eyes tracking intently to mine. 'But it is a kind of return, isn't it?'

'Absolutely,' I agreed.

'I do have a home, after all,' he added with a gulp, and I blinked hard. 'There is somewhere in the world that I belong.'

'And it's the same place as me,' I said softly.

Josh reached for my hand and our eyes stayed locked. We had both come back to Wynbrook Manor this summer and neither of us had any intention of leaving it again. Would that mean our relationship also had the potential to last longer than the summer? So caught up with the monumental changes my life had been going through, I hadn't yet considered that!

'I won't have time to sort it today,' said Sam, as he cut through the moment and made Josh reluctantly tear his eyes away from mine. 'But if you leave it with me, I'll see if I can sort you a refund for the weeks you won't now be staying in the cottage.'

'No, don't do that,' Josh insisted. 'I booked it for the whole of the summer and I wasn't expecting to get any money back now I'm moving out early. I wouldn't expect you to leave it empty until my booking expired either. If you can let it again, then do.'

'Are you sure?' Tess asked.

'Absolutely,' said Josh. 'There's still plenty of summer left so you might as well.'

'Actually,' said Marguerite, 'I wouldn't mind moving in for a bit as I've decided to stay on in the area, if that would be okay with you, Sam? I still haven't found anywhere to rent and it's high time I got out of your hair and your spare room.'

'And my bathroom,' laughed Sam. 'This woman likes her products.'

'Hey!' she objected, with her hands planted on her slim hips. 'I travel light!'

'Yes,' said Sam, 'you travel light, but you have a hell of a lot of stuff delivered when you land!'

'I thought you were in an Airbnb somewhere, Marguerite?' I frowned, while Tess batted Sam with a tea towel.

'I was when I first arrived,' she told me, 'but I fancied a change and Tess offered.'

'Which was a *huge* mistake,' Sam said theatrically.

'No, it was not,' tutted Tess. 'But moving into Crow's Nest might not be a bad idea.'

With the cottage's next resident already decided, Josh and I headed back there to pack so he could quickly vacate and Marguerite could move in.

'You're another one who travels light,' I said, once his few things were stowed in my car and he'd returned the door key to the pub.

'But I did have all those letters and cards from Algy to carry with me originally, don't forget,' he said as he tried to open the passenger window, which had been jammed stubbornly shut since the temperature had soared. 'They're at Wynbrook already.'

'Having discovered them, I would have thought it would have made more sense to leave them back in the US. Just in case your dad, for some reason, decided to check on them and found they'd gone.'

'I have considered that myself since I got here,' said Josh. 'But so far, so good, in terms of him not finding out what I've done. And,' he added, 'I think there was a part of me that was scared Dad might take it upon himself to destroy them, even though it looked like they hadn't been disturbed for years. I couldn't risk them being lost, especially before I'd had the chance to read them all, so keeping them with me felt like the safest option.'

'You did the right thing then,' I said and nodded. His father was a vindictive man and he wouldn't have thought twice about destroying the evidence of his deception if the fancy took him. 'Now, let's get you back to Algy. I know he must be desperate to get you moved in.'

Having made sure early in the day that everything was well in the walled garden, Josh and I spent the rest of Tuesday together. He showed me the room he'd picked out in the manor, which overlooked the garden and then, with Algy's blessing, we headed off. He was preoccupied with further coaxing the cat into his kitchen, so wasn't going to miss us for a little while. Luna was making great strides in becoming tame. It was miraculous what the lure of cooked chicken could do.

Josh and I didn't travel all that far. The lack of aircon in my car made the thought of a long excursion more than unpleasant, and besides, having both so recently fallen in love with Wynbrook, neither of us felt inclined to leave it too far behind.

'This place is bliss, isn't it?' said Josh, looking across the sand to where the tide was just on the turn.

'Just a bit,' I willingly agreed and my heart leapt to hear him sound so happy. 'Hey look, a starfish.'

We had decided to spend a while exploring the rock pools slightly further along the coast than Wynmouth, which was currently enjoying an influx of summer visitors.

'That's so pretty,' said Josh.

'And look there,' I said, pointing. 'Did you see that crab just peeping out?'

By the time we looked up again, the tide had rapidly advanced so we beat a hasty retreat back to the dunes where we ate the picnic Josh had made in the manor kitchen.

'I feel a bit bad eating this shrimp roll,' I said, with a wistful look back to the where the pools were now filling with seawater.

'I'll take it off your hands,' Josh said, grinning.

'I don't feel that bad,' I laughed, taking another bite.

Once we'd finished, we packed the basket back up, making sure we didn't leave any litter behind, then found a more sheltered spot where we wiled away an hour reading. Josh was still enjoying the company of Anne Shirley, while I was perusing an online prospectus I'd earlier downloaded. Having inspired Dad to follow his academic dreams, there was something I was feeling inclined to look further into as well.

'What are you so engrossed in?' Josh asked, when he put the book down to take a drink.

'Oh,' I said, shielding my eyes from the glare of the sun as I looked across at him. 'It's something I'm considering doing later in the year.'

That said, I would need to talk to Algy about it first and then make up my mind soon after that as September was suddenly not that far off.

'I'm intrigued,' Josh further said. 'Tell me.'

'All in good time,' I said, putting my phone down. 'How are you finding Anne?'

Josh didn't push me to tell him and I was grateful for that. I knew there were things he was still ruminating over too, so it didn't feel like secret-keeping. Rather, information gathering so that when the time came to talk, we'd have all the information we needed.

'Delightful.' He smiled. 'Though it feels a little absurd that I came all the way to the UK to discover an American classic.'

'Well,' I said, moving closer to him, 'at least you've found her now.'

'And you, Daisy,' he said, planting a sweet kiss on my lips, 'thank goodness I found you too.'

'I agree,' I said, kissing him back. 'You've made this summer far more satisfying than I initially thought it was going to be.'

He looked at me seriously and I drew away a little.

'What?' I frowned.

'We are good together, aren't we?' He swallowed, his Adam's apple rising and falling in his throat.

'So good,' I agreed.

'And I'm not just talking about in bed,' he said and my heart stuttered. 'I think we make a pretty good team all round, don't you?'

He couldn't have given me any clearer an indication that his feelings for me stretched beyond the reaches of what you would expect from a fun summer fling and I was keen to let him know that I felt the same way too.

'Hey! Watch out!' someone shouted, just as a beach ball came flying across the dune, hit my head and toppled our open water bottle over.

Josh snatched up my book, saving it from a soaking and I grabbed my phone.

'I'm sorry,' said a young boy who came racing up, scattering sand to retrieve the ball. 'Dad kicked that, not me.'

'No worries,' I said, handing it back to him and feeling relieved that Josh and I hadn't been indulging in a moment of passion.

Josh set the now-empty bottle upright again on the sand.

'Shall we make a move?' he suggested, as the family game of football taking place just below us escalated in volume. 'I daresay you want to check you've got flowers to sell tomorrow, don't you?'

I did, but I would have much preferred to carry on our conversation.

'All right,' I said. 'Yes, everything was looking fine earlier, but it wouldn't hurt to have another look. Do you fancy staying with me tonight?'

'I'd love to,' he said and I hoped I'd be able to set the scene to tell him that I was in complete agreement about us being good together – in bed and beyond. 'But I promised Algy I'd watch some home videos he's found. He reckons I might be in a couple of them.'

'Oh, that's amazing. I hope you are on tape somewhere.'

I was disappointed that we wouldn't be spending the night under the same roof, but knew that continuing the process of piecing his past together was something that would make Josh happy. Anything Algy could offer him that would connect him to Wynbrook was always going to be welcome because his father's desire to move him about when he was growing up had ensured he had endured a very fractured childhood.

'I'd love to see you running about the place in a nappy,' I laughed, thinking how cute Josh must have been as a toddler.

'Are you teasing me?' he laughed back.

'Absolutely,' I said, standing up and brushing the sand off my shorts.

'Well, I wouldn't if I were you,' he said, grabbing my ankle and making me screech. 'Because I bet your parents have got far more embarrassing baby photos and videos of you than Algy has of me!'

'Oh, crikey,' I grimaced, remembering some less than flattering haircuts I'd been subjected to and the mortifying school photos that chronicled them. 'I didn't think of that!'

Chapter 27

The next day was cool and cloudy, perfect for a day working in the sheltered wall garden. There weren't that many customers, so I was able to get some further tying in and sorting out done, which gave me ample opportunity to mull over what Josh had said in the dunes and wonder how I could stop him from asking my parents to see the photos they had of me growing up, on the pretence of wanting to feel more a part of the Wynbrook family.

On the journey back to the estate, when I had said sulkily that this wasn't a fair tactic, he had grinned mischievously. 'Whatever works!' he said.

I had a feeling that taking a look further into my childhood was something he wasn't going to forget about and I eventually decided I would simply have to embrace the situation. So, at the end of the day, when a lingering customer had finally left – there was always one who turned up at the last gasp and then dithered over making a decision about their preferred colour palette – I locked the gate and headed to Mum and Dad's cottage.

Knowing now that even Mum had warmed to Josh, I thought

it would be nice for the four of us to spend a proper evening together. Dad was Wynbrook born and bred, so he would be able to fill Josh in further about the history of the estate and its running, and if I was present when the collection of photo albums came out, I would at least be able to have a chance at vetoing the very worst ones.

'Whatever works,' I laughed to myself, feeling pleased with my crafty plan.

There was a ridiculously sleek car parked outside the cottage that I didn't recognise, but I didn't let that temper the spring in my step and I bowled up the path feeling full of bonhomie and buoyed up by the good time I was currently having back at home.

That was, until I reached the door and recognised the voice that answered Mum's question about wanting another cup of tea.

'No, thank you, Janet,' it confidently said, though how its owner had the arrogance to sound confident was beyond me. 'Do you think Robin and Daisy will be much longer?'

'I wouldn't have thought so,' was Mum's terse response. 'Daisy will either still be in the walled garden or in the summerhouse, so it won't take long to track her down.'

'I really wouldn't mind going to find her myself,' came the voice again and my stomach twisted. 'It feels like forever since I had a look about the place.'

And hated it, I bitterly thought as I braced myself, then quickly parted the old-fashioned but still favoured vinyl fly curtain hanging over the doorway and stepped inside.

'Laurence,' I said crossly to the back of his head. 'What are you doing here?'

He twisted round to look at me and I felt not a single flicker of the attraction I had formerly felt for him. If anything, the sight of him sitting at the table in my family home made me detest him all the more. What right did he think he had to just turn up?

'He wanted to see you, Daisy,' said Mum, over the top of his head. I couldn't make out what she was thinking, but I hoped that manufacturing a reconciliation wasn't on her mind. 'Your dad's out looking for you as we speak.'

'And why on earth would you want to see me, Laurence?' I furiously frowned. 'I can't imagine we have a single thing to say to one another.'

He gave me a complacent smile that I found utterly irritating.

'Oh, but we do, Daisy,' he said, standing up and tucking in his chair. 'We really do.'

I walked back outside again, in the hope that he would follow me and he did. I didn't want to become embroiled in an exchange of words with Mum in earshot.

The sight of him looking so superior and self-assured had made me wish that I'd told everyone why I had left him when I arrived back and then Mum would have sent him away with a flea in his ear on sight, rather than treating him to tea and shortbread. And the best tea service, I had noticed with annoyance. Not even my homecoming had warranted that.

'Go on then,' I said bluntly. 'You can say what you think you need to say and then you can leave because I have to get back to work.'

'According to your beautiful Insta account,' Laurence then surprised me by saying, 'Wynbrook Blooms closes at four and it's a fair way after that now, isn't it?'

I opened my mouth to object, but no words came out.

'I have got that right, haven't I?' he asked, with an ostentatious glance at his Breitling watch. 'You close the garden gate at four o'clock?'

'Yes, that is right, but there's still plenty of work to do beyond selling the flowers. There's watering to get on with and the days takings to register.'

I didn't like the thought that he had been watching my life and change of circumstances online. It wasn't something I had considered he might do before and it made me even more annoyed with him.

'But surely you can spare me just five minutes?' he wheedled. 'Or would it be better if I came back later? Perhaps I could take you out for dinner somewhere, Daisy.'

The last thing I wanted was to have the threat of him reappearing hanging over me.

'Five minutes, then,' I said, as I buried my hands in my shorts pockets and arranged my features into the best bored witless expression I could muster. 'Get on and say what you think is so important, Laurence, because I can't bear the thought of you coming back here again. I thought I was completely rid of you.'

He looked both shocked and hurt, but I was the injured party in our former relationship, not him, and I was keen to remind him of that.

'Come and sit in my car,' he suggested. 'We won't be overheard in there.'

A brief glance over my shoulder confirmed that Mum was lingering just the other side of the door curtain, so I did as he had suggested, even though I didn't want to be in such close proximity to him. His aftershave might have been expensive, but it was cloying too and in the confined space of his sleek car it would doubtless be intense.

'What do you think of the new wheels?' he asked, once he was settled in the driving seat.

'You know very well that as far as I'm concerned, one car is much like another, so not much.'

Though of course, no other car on the planet was like my lovely, ancient jalopy with its unreliable passenger window and intermittent electrics.

'Why are you putting on your seatbelt?' I then asked, as I realised Laurence had pushed something and started the engine. 'I haven't got time to go anywhere with you and what's more, I don't want to.'

I went to open my door, but he was already moving off and I had no choice but to pull my belt on too.

'What the hell do you think you're doing?' I demanded, once I was buckled in. 'Let me out, this instant.'

His behaviour was akin to kidnap and I was trapped with no safe means of escape.

'Not until I've had my full five minutes,' he said, roaring up to and over the cattle grid and turning left towards Wynmouth.

I hoped his suspension was expensive to replace.

'Go on then,' I said angrily. 'Start talking. You've wasted at least a minute already.'

He leant over to reach for my hand, but I snatched it away.

'What the hell?' I growled.

'I thought I was going to have to apologise to your parents first and then woo you back,' he smiled, looking at me, rather than the narrow road and appearing completely unaware of how entirely inappropriate he was being, 'but having talked to your mum, I'm not so sure I have to do either of those things now . . .'

'What are you talking about?' I seethed, as he shot around a tight bend with just one hand on the wheel.

'Well,' he said confidently, 'I had already guessed that it really was you who had called the flat and that you were just saying it was your dad when you left that message.'

'No,' I said through gritted teeth. 'It was definitely Dad who called. Not me.'

'And now I know you haven't told your parents the reason why we've not been together these last few weeks,' he blithely carried on, 'I can only assume that's because you've been working your way up to getting in touch again. You've just been punishing me for my little . . . indiscretion, haven't you?'

I didn't think it was possible to feel any angrier, but his stupid speech took me to never before experienced heights of frustration and fury. Had he always been such a moron?

'So, let me get this straight,' I said, as a car blared its horn when Laurence raced by taking up far too much of the narrow road, 'you think that I haven't told Mum and Dad that I saw you screwing someone else because I actually intended to forgive you for doing it.'

Laurence winced. I wondered how he would have put it, but obviously didn't ask.

'Why else would you have kept quiet?'

'To avoid having to make the humiliating explanation,' I ground out, 'and to stop my father, Nick and Algy coming after you with pitchforks and gardening shears.'

I didn't add that I hadn't wanted to further upset my parents by having them think the worst of him because heaven only knows how he would have misconstrued that.

Laurence laughed in the face of my implication that life-changing injuries could have been incurred if I had spilled the beans.

'I know you wanted to make me suffer, Daisy,' he said. 'And rightly so. My behaviour was appalling and I'm very sorry for it.'

At last, he had taken ownership of what he'd done.

'It was a stupid one-off and I can promise you, it will *never* happen again.'

'Oh, that's all right then,' I snapped.

'Is it?'

'No!' I bawled.

He took a moment to process that, but didn't reach the conclusion that I had hoped he would, that is, that it was time for him to shut up.

'And I'm also sorry,' he carried on exasperatingly, 'that I spent the whole time we were together trying to turn you into someone you're not.'

'Are you?' I said sarcastically. 'Are you really?'

'Yes,' he said, as he pulled into the clifftop car park that overlooked the beach at Wynmouth and scattered the gravel. I couldn't believe we'd reached it already. 'I am, because this gardening lark clearly suits you.'

It was my turn to laugh then. I was pretty certain he couldn't think of anything worse than horticulture for a career, for me or him. I'd never once seen him with mucky hands.

'I'm being serious,' he said, as the car came to a sudden stop. 'You've never looked better.'

I took the opportunity to jump out and strode off towards

the steep path down to the sand. I didn't think he'd follow me because he wouldn't want to risk his designer leather shoes, but I was wrong.

'You've obviously found your place in the world, Daisy,' came his voice close behind me. 'And you're radiant as a result.'

Did he really think that some honeyed words were going to make up for his infidelity, and why was he suddenly so keen to tell me that he thought my new direction – or return to an old one – was a good thing?

'Well,' I said, stopping dead and turning to face him, 'I feel better now, knowing I've got your seal of approval.'

'Good,' he said. 'I hoped you would.'

It was all I could do to stop myself from pushing him off the path.

'And it's wonderful what you've done for Algy too,' he carried on as I turned back around and continued the precarious descent. 'Your mum said he's like a changed man since you arrived back.'

'Did she?' I would be having a word with Mum.

In the future, she would be banned from telling Laurence anything.

'Yes,' Laurence said as I jumped down the final couple of feet, 'she did. She also said he couldn't sing your praises highly enough and I can tell from the photos of the pair of you together that you've posted online, just how fond he is of you.'

'And I'm very fond of him too,' I answered.

Had Laurence ever listened to a word I'd said about Algy before, he would have already known that, but for some unfathomable reason, he was only interested in my relationship with my summer saviour now.

'He hasn't got any family of his own, has he?' Laurence then ventured and a part of the real motive behind his unexpected appearance and praise immediately slid into place.

Thanks to his fancy footwear, he was a little slower getting down than me and I turned round to look at him as he gingerly, and rather pathetically, hopped down on to the sand.

'So, what do you think?' he asked, once he'd caught his breath and I hadn't filled him in on Algy's family history.

'About what?'

'You,' he said, pointing at me. 'Me,' he said, pointing at himself. 'Us. You and me getting back together.'

I shook my head.

'You're actually being serious, aren't you?' I said numbly.

I turned away and walked quickly in the direction of the village.

'Of course, I'm being serious,' Laurence insisted as he rushed to catch me up. 'Why else would I be here? Who else in the world would I ruin these shoes for?'

I looked down at his feet.

'They're not ruined,' I said. 'They're just sandy.'

'Daisy!' he snapped, sounding frustrated.

I was pleased to finally get a rise out of him rather than the other way around.

'What?'

'That's not an answer.'

'Hey!' hollered a voice from further along the beach. 'Daisy! Hey!'

It was Josh. He was waving like a loon and I could tell from his tone that something was amiss. I jogged towards him, with Laurence muttering, hot on my heels.

'What's wrong?' I called, when I was close enough for him not to have to shout back.

'Who's that?' demanded Laurence, sounding put out.

'Who's that, Laurence?' I said, coming to a stop again. 'That's Josh Alford.' Laurence's eyes were on stalks when he registered the surname. 'Algy's grandson.'

'What?' Laurence spluttered. 'But I thought . . .'

'You thought,' I said, finishing what he had realised would not be a good thing to admit out loud, 'that in lieu of any family of his own, and given how close we've become again since my return to Wynbrook, that Algy might one day consider leaving Wynbrook to me. Didn't you? And if that happened and we'd got together again, then you'd be in line for a piece of the Alford estate too.'

Laurence didn't deny it and I felt further repulsed by him now that I had worked out and voiced what his real, and wholly unpalatable, reason for turning up and trying to win me back had been.

'Didn't you?' I repeated angrily.

'Your Insta posts said you were like family,' he spluttered pathetically.

'We are. Algy has always been like a grandfather to me, but in terms of blood, he's related to Josh who actually loves the estate and one day, it will be him who inherits it. So, I tell you what, why don't you put the moves on him?'

Laurence looked at Josh, who was now standing as close to me as it was possible to get, and then back to me.

'Total waste of time though,' Josh commented, as he looked Laurence up and down. 'You're really not my type.'

Laurence's face flushed the deepest red.

'I take it this is your ex, Daisy?' Josh asked. 'He fits the description your mum gave me to a T.' Perhaps she hadn't been duped into using the best cups and saucers after all. 'I went to the cottage to look for you and she was worried that you'd driven off with him.'

'I didn't have much choice about that,' I said, taking Josh's hand. 'He drove off the second I sat in his car on the pretence of us having a chat *and* without my consent.'

'Did he now?' Josh growled and I was pleased I'd got a tight hold on him.

'But he's leaving now,' I said, stepping slightly in front of Josh. 'Aren't you, Laurence?'

He looked at me and chewed his lip before his gaze dropped to his shoes.

'Yes,' he said. 'I'm leaving now. There's nothing here for me.'

'And there hasn't been for a long time,' I said vehemently.

He looked back towards the path to where his car was parked at the top of the cliff.

'Is that the only way back?' he muttered.

'Yep,' said Josh, sounding thrilled. 'It'll be a steep ascent in those slippery soles.'

'A slippery character like him should manage it, no problem though,' I remarked and Josh laughed. 'Though if I was him, I'd take the much longer way back. Walk right through the village and then along the road to the car park entrance.'

Laurence didn't say anything further and strode off as best he could, back towards the steep path, rather than the more sensible route I'd suggested.

'Hopefully,' I said, letting out the longest breath, 'that really will be the last I see of him.'

Josh gave my hand a squeeze, then kissed the back of it.

'Did you come charging to Wynmouth just to find me because Mum was worried?' I asked, gazing up at him.

'Sadly not,' he confessed, his brows knitted together. 'I came to ask for help with a crisis of my own. I didn't expect to find you in the midst of one of your own.'

'That doesn't sound good.' I frowned. 'Forget mine, it's sorted now. Tell me what's happened? And more to the point, how did you get here?'

Chapter 28

As we rushed back to the pub car park, which was where Dad was waiting for us, Josh explained what was behind his crisis and it turned out to be far more worrying than my reacquaintance with my materialistically obsessed ex.

'Mum called me,' Josh puffed, 'to warn me that Dad might turn up at the manor.' I stopped in my tracks and he reached for my T-shirt sleeve. He gave it a tug to get me moving again. 'Come on. She said he could literally arrive at any moment.'

'What?' I gasped, picking up the pace. 'As in right *now*? Your father might literally be about to turn up at Wynbrook now?'

'Yep.' Josh nodded. 'That's what Mom reckoned, once she'd worked out the timing of his flight.'

'I'm guessing he's realised the letters are missing then,' I tutted, after I'd taken a few more speedy but leg-deadening steps.

Why was walking across sand always such hard work when you were in a rush?

'Afraid so,' Josh said resignedly.

'Couldn't your mum have given you more of heads-up? This is pretty short notice.'

Josh shook his head.

'She didn't know,' he told me. 'Apparently, Dad emailed her about what he was doing just a couple of hours ago. He's away with work a lot, so she hadn't given his absence from home a thought – until he got in touch and said he was on his way to Norfolk having taken a particular flight to Heathrow.'

'I wonder why he told her at all,' I puffed. 'Surely, he must have known she'd tell you and that would ruin the . . . surprise?'

'His arrogance probably got the better of him,' Josh said darkly.

Thomas Alford and Laurence really were peas shelled from the same pod then.

'So I'm guessing your mum didn't know about the letters?'

'No,' Josh said, 'but she does now – she's literally packing a suitcase and leaving Dad as we speak. She said this was the final straw and that she's moving out to our house in California, which is the one she's always loved the most, and filing for divorce.'

I didn't know what to say to that. The world Josh's family – or at least one side of it – lived in, sounded absolutely nothing like mine. And actually, I was grateful for that.

'Oh, love,' said Dad, jumping out of the car the second he spotted us. 'Your mum was so worried that she sent me to find you as soon as Laurence showed up, to give you a minute to compose yourself, but obviously we missed each other some-where in the garden. Are you all right?'

'Apart from being in shock,' I told him, as I gave him a hug, 'I'm fine. Laurence has gone again now – this time for good.'

'Why are you in shock?' he asked, frowning, as he pulled away and looked at me intently.

'Well,' I said, as Josh climbed into the passenger seat, 'for a start, given what you've just said about Mum, you and her seem to have had quite a change of opinion about my ex. You both always thought Laurence—'

'Yes, well,' Dad interrupted gruffly, 'opinions change when the need arises, don't they? And your mum and I had already realised that it was him who had been in the wrong over something, not you, even before he turned up putting on airs and graces.'

'I see.' I nodded, feeling relieved they had truly got the message without me having to share all of the details.

'Come on,' he said, opening the back door for me. 'We need to hurry up because it's going to be out of the frying pan and into the fire, unless I'm very much mistaken. We need to be at the manor and on alert in case Thomas turns up. Has Josh filled you in?'

'He has,' I sighed. 'What a day.'

Josh looked ashen on the drive back to Wynbrook and I was just about to ask him if he was all right when my mobile started to ring.

'Hey Nick,' I said.

'Hey, Daisy. Is Josh with you? I've tried ringing his mobile but he's not picking up.'

'Hold on.'

I tapped Josh on the shoulder and passed the phone between the seats.

'It's for you,' I told him. 'It's Nick.'

'Hey Nick,' he said tentatively. 'What's up? I know, sorry, I left it at the manor.'

He was silent for a few seconds while Nick talked and then let out a ragged breath.

'Oh god, no,' he gasped, scaring me witless. 'We're almost there.'

'Two minutes,' said Dad, who put his foot down a little, even though he didn't know what Nick had said.

'We'll be two minutes,' Josh relayed to Nick. 'Okay, we'll meet you there.'

He passed the phone back between the seats.

'What is it?' I swallowed, taking it from his shaking hand. 'What's happened?'

'Penny has just arrived at Nick's place and said there's an ambulance parked up outside the manor.' Dad's foot pressed even harder on the accelerator. 'I think something must have happened to Algy.'

'Oh no,' I sobbed. 'Please no.'

'It's not even half an hour since you talked to your mum, Josh,' Dad tried to reassuringly say. 'I'm sure nothing serious could have happened in that time.'

'Well,' said Josh, 'we'll soon find out, won't we?'

Dad's gaze flicked to mine in the rear-view mirror and I bit my lip. I hoped he was right and nothing, serious or otherwise, had happened.

As we rounded the final bend to reach the turning for Wynbrook, it became apparent, however, that quite a lot could have happened because an ambulance turned right out of the end of the drive and shot off with its siren blaring and lights flashing just as we went to pull in from the left.

'What do you want me to do?' Dad asked Josh, as he stamped heavily on the brake, making my seatbelt lock up. 'Drive to the manor or follow the ambulance?'

'Drive to the manor, Dad,' I urged, when Josh looked torn and didn't answer. 'We don't know who's in the ambulance yet, so there's no point chasing after it.'

'Daisy's right,' Josh said. 'Let's get to the manor and find out what's happened.'

My phone began to ring again, just as the manor came into sight, but the panic and dread coursing through me quickly abated because Algy was standing on the drive, waving his stick to let us know that whoever had been carried off, it wasn't him.

'Oh, thank god,' said Josh, sounding shaken but relieved.

'We're here,' I said to Nick on the phone, even though he was standing there too and could see the car.

'What's happened?' Josh demanded, jumping out as soon as Dad stopped. 'Are you all right, Grandad?'

It wasn't the moment to flag that he had called Algy 'Grandad' for the first time, but my goodness, there was a huge lump in my throat and Dad looked misty-eyed too, as he opened the back door and helped me out.

'I'm fine,' said Algy, as his grandson towered protectively over him. 'I'm fine, but I'm sorry to say, your father isn't.'

'It was Dad in the ambulance?' Josh gasped, looking back along the drive.

'Afraid so,' said Algy. 'He turned up almost the second you and Robin had gone. He immediately started ranting and then keeled over. I called for an ambulance and thankfully one had been stood down after a hoax call nearby. Not that I'm pleased about the hoax, obviously, but your father was very lucky by all accounts.'

'He's had a heart condition for years,' Josh told us. 'But he's never been hospitalised as an emergency before, as far as I know. He's had enough warnings though . . .'

'He said he'd come to warn me about you,' Algy started to

say as Mum came dashing along the path, with a duster in her hand. 'He tried to tell me that he'd sent you here to do his dirty work for him and butter me up so I'd put the place on the market.'

'You didn't believe him, did you?' asked Josh.

'Of course, I didn't,' Algy said.

'What an idiot,' said Dad.

'Me or Dad?' Josh sniffed.

'Both of you,' Dad tutted, which made Josh smile. 'We all know you're here for the right reasons, my boy.'

'That we do,' Mum agreed, as she gave me a hug and a kiss on the cheek. She was clearly relieved to see me, but subsequent events had now overtaken what I'd just been through. 'I hope you gave him what for, Algernon,' she added as she flicked the duster about agitatedly. 'I hope you gave back as good as you got.'

'I started to,' he swallowed, but then his face began to crease, 'but then he . . .'

'Let's go inside,' Penny suggested soothingly in her best teacher voice as she quickly herded us all together.

'I'll make some tea,' said Mum. 'I'm sure we could all do with a cup and some extra sugar for the shock.'

'That we could,' I wholeheartedly agreed.

'We weren't even gone half an hour,' Dad said, sounding dazed as he shook his head. 'I can't believe all this has happened in such a short space of time.'

The situation made me feel even more furious about Laurence turning up. Had he stayed away, we would have all been on site and able to look out for Algy and possibly even stop Thomas from putting further stress on his heart and keeling over as a result. I hoped Algy wasn't going to start blaming himself for what had happened.

'I need to get to the hospital,' said Josh, who had a tight hold on Algy's hand, but relinquished it so Mum could walk Algy in.

'Not yet you don't,' Dad said firmly. 'The ambulance won't have reached the hospital yet and you won't be able to see your father until he's been assessed and properly admitted.'

'Dad's right,' I said, when Josh looked doubtful. 'Have a drink and maybe something to eat and then we'll go together.'

We stalled Josh for as long as possible, knowing that his father could be literally hours waiting to be assessed, but eventually I caved and drove him to the hospital the ambulance crew had told Algy they were heading for.

Josh had tried to telephone ahead, but it had been a long time before anyone picked up and then he was only given the scantest information – nothing more than confirmation that his dad was there.

'Are you okay?' I asked, as I slipped my hand into his when we arrived and headed towards the ward he'd been directed to via the main reception.

'Not really,' he said.

'Of course you're not,' I sighed. 'Sorry, that was a stupid question.'

'I'm so pleased you're here, Daisy,' he said, rather than confirm my foolishness.

'I'm pleased I'm here too,' I told him, squeezing his hand tighter.

I hated the thought of him having to make this trip on his

own, though I was relieved Algy had been talked out of coming with us.

'I think this is it,' Josh said, with a nod to a sign above some double doors.

Once we had buzzed and been admitted to the ward, we heard Josh's dad before we saw the room he was in. Josh knew who it was because he immediately recognised the angry raised voice and it didn't take a second for me to work out that there couldn't be that many American slash English accents shouting the odds at the overworked nursing staff.

'Is this really the best you can do?' came the voice in a tone of utter disgust. 'Well, I want moving first thing tomorrow.'

'We would be delighted to move you,' said a tired-sounding nurse as she backed out of the side room and closed the door.

Josh and I walked over to the nurse's station.

'I'm sorry to say, that's my dad in there,' Josh said apologetically to the nurse, who was now behind the desk. 'His name is Thomas Alford and I'm Josh Alford.'

The nurse, who looked exhausted, perked up when she saw who was talking to her.

'You're Mr Alford's son,' she commented, trying to sound professional, which I knew could be a stretch when faced with the blond and bronzed Adonis.

'I am,' Josh confirmed. 'But don't worry, I'm absolutely nothing like him.'

She gave me a fleeting glance and I returned her look of relief with a smile.

'I can't deny that I'm pleased to hear that,' she sighed. 'He's not a happy man, is he?'

'Nope,' said Josh. 'Never. And I apologise for that.'

'No need for you to apologise, my love.' She smiled.

'Well,' Josh carried on, 'I hope no one here is taking his foul outpouring personally.'

Clearly, this wasn't the first time Josh had had to deal with the fallout from his father's bad and rude moods. What a horrible father to have. I could imagine Josh apologising for him wherever they went: restaurants, shops – everywhere where they came into contact with hard-working people just trying to go about their business.

'Sadly, we're used to it,' said the nurse in a matter-of-fact tone, then added, 'but from what I've experienced of him so far, he's . . . next level.'

She then checked herself, which couldn't have been easy, given what she and the rest of the staff had been subjected to. I could still hear him sounding off and, as far as I knew, he was in the room on his own so no one was listening. His continued rage couldn't be doing his already strained and stressed heart much good.

'I'm going to page the consultant who has assessed Mr Alford, so he can talk to you himself,' the nurse said. 'And then perhaps I could ask you to fill in the forms your father has refused to look at?'

'Of course,' said Josh, sounding a little embarrassed.

'I'll go and find a seat,' I said to Josh. 'Just come and find me when you're sorted. There's no rush.'

'You don't want to meet Dad?' Josh asked, raising an eyebrow in faux surprise.

'Perhaps not tonight.' I smiled. 'Maybe when he's feeling in . . . a better frame of mind.'

'Never then,' said Josh, planting a soft kiss on my mouth.

'Quite possibly not,' I responded, quickly kissing him back.

While Josh was kept occupied with the consultant and then the nurses – did the form filling really require all three of them – and then his dad, I sat at the end of the corridor and mulled over the day's events. There was certainly plenty to think about.

I looked through the list of Wynbrook Bloom Instagram followers, but couldn't spot Laurence among them. He'd either created an account and set it to private so I couldn't identify him or was searching for the page every day rather than following it, not that it really mattered.

Now the materialistic moron knew I wasn't in line to inherit a rural fortune, I felt certain he'd stop keeping tabs and retreat for good, both online and in real life. And good riddance. Maybe he'd even unfollowed the account already.

Josh and Algy, on the other hand, were stuck with Thomas because he was family. Even if they didn't want to be tied to him, they were, by blood. Knowing Josh as well as I now did and having heard more than enough of his father in the brief time I'd been in earshot, I knew which branch of the family I preferred. I'd had my ups and downs with both my mum and my dad over the years, but as the nurse had said of Thomas Alford, dealings with him were next level.

I had just arrived back on the ward, having fulfilled the sudden urge to go outside and phone my parents to tell them we would never mention Laurence's name again, that I loved them and that I was very happy to be back living, and now also working, on the estate, as well as giving them a quick update about what was going on at the hospital, when Josh came to find me. His shoulders were hunched and he looked absolutely exhausted. I guessed there had been no kind words or make up moments between him and his dad. Perhaps they weren't going to be tied for life, after all . . .

'How'd it go?' I asked.

There was no point in asking him again if he was okay because he clearly wasn't.

'Not well,' he said grimly. 'Not well at all.'

'I'm so sorry,' I sympathised, as he sat on the seat next to me.

'It's fine,' he said, leaning forward and pushing his hands into his already messy hair. 'It was bound to happen sooner or later and it's not as if I've lost anything.'

'What was bound to happen?' I asked.

Josh sat back and rested his head against the wall and for a moment I thought Thomas Alford's temper had caused his heart to give up for good, but it wasn't that.

'My grandfather already was, but I'm now also officially estranged from my father,' Josh told me. 'And I always will be.'

'Oh, Josh,' I whispered.

'It was inevitable,' he said with a shrug.

'And are you sad about that?' I asked.

'No,' he said, shaking his head, 'I'm not. If anything, I'm relieved, to be honest. I've spent a lifetime trying to be good enough for him, but I was never going to meet his impossibly high expectations, was I?'

'Given what I've heard of him tonight,' I nudged, 'I don't think anyone could.'

'I think I always reminded him too much of Grandad,' Josh said and I smiled. 'I thought it would feel strange saying it,' he smiled too, 'but it doesn't.'

'Good,' I nudged again.

'I think Dad could see so much of his father in me that our relationship was never going to be a success.'

'I can't even begin to imagine what he's just said to you about those letters and you coming here and falling in love with Wynbrook,' I said with a shudder.

Josh gave a wry smile.

'And I'm certainly not going to tell you,' he laughed, sounding more like himself. 'That's not language I would ever wish to repeat.'

'So, what now?' I asked. 'For your dad, I mean. How long has he got to stay in here?'

'The consultant is willing to let him go as soon as possible, which I'm sure will come as no surprise.'

'Er, no.'

'He'll probably be discharged the day after tomorrow.'

'Those poor nurses until then, though,' I said. 'What will he do after that? Will he be able to fly straight back to the States?'

He certainly wouldn't be recuperating at Wynbrook. There wasn't going to be a kiss and make up happy-ever-after along this branch of the limited Alford line.

'I think he's planning to,' Josh told me. 'His assistant is already on a flight and he'll assess the situation when he gets here. He'll probably advise a rest in a five-star hotel somewhere for a few days first, but knowing Dad, he won't listen.'

'His assistant? I can't believe there's anyone in the world who would willingly take that job on.'

'Oh, believe me, Jerome is *very* well renumerated for putting up with Dad and his epic tantrums.'

'I had no idea there was that much money in the world,' I tutted.

If Thomas Alford was prepared to rant like I'd heard that

evening, with a heart condition flare-up hampering his flow, I dreaded to think what he was capable of when he was as fit as his condition allowed.

'So,' said Josh, reaching for my hand, 'Jerome will arrive tomorrow and I can leave here without a guilty conscience because I did try to patch things up with Dad.'

'You did?' I gasped.

'I did.' He nodded gravely. 'And Algy video-called, with Penny's help, and he tried to reconcile us too, but my father was having none of it, so now we're both done with him for good. I think Algy was feeling guilty about what happened this afternoon—'

'I was afraid he might be,' I interrupted.

'But having heard more of Dad's bitterness tonight, he's realised the outcome was inevitable.'

'Well, that's something. It's been quite a day for saying final goodbyes to destructive relationships.'

'Hasn't it just?' Josh agreed.

'Thank goodness you've fallen in love with Wynbrook.' I smiled. 'It would have been terrible if you'd travelled this far and gone through all of this for it not to work out.'

'That it would,' he sighed.

'You sound exhausted.'

'I am. I really am.'

'Come on, then,' I said, as I stood up. 'Let me drive you home. I bet you're going to sleep for a week.'

'I might just,' he said, taking my hand, but not standing up. 'You do know that Wynbrook isn't the only thing I've fallen in love with this summer, don't you, Daisy?' he said.

I looked down at him and felt my breath hitch.

'I think so,' I whispered.

He gently manoeuvred me, so I was standing right in front of him.

'I've fallen in love with you too,' he said softly as he gazed up at me.

I stared deep into his eyes and for a moment wished we weren't in a busy hospital corridor, but then realised, when love declares itself, the location doesn't matter. All that counts is the two people saying the words and I felt more than ready to say them back.

'And I love you too,' I told him. 'I love you, Josh Alford.'

Chapter 29

A few sunny days had flown by since Thomas Alford had turned up at Wynbrook Manor, cruelly attempted to cause a rift between his recently bonded father and son and then almost immediately left again, only in an ambulance rather than the taxi he'd arrived in. His assistant Jerome had informed Josh that the pair of them were now holed up in a Norwich hotel until such time as they could fly back to America and there were no plans for the Alford men to ever get together again.

I was feeling exhausted after an extremely busy, but brilliant, August bank holiday weekend for Wynbrook Blooms, which had seen me extend the opening hours to include the Monday because the weather had been kind, the plants had flourished and the customers had kept flocking in to buy our fabulous flowers after visiting the fruit farm.

It was now early Tuesday afternoon and having spent the morning unwinding and relaxing in the summerhouse and bonding further with Luna, who was becoming almost affectionate when the mood took her, I was on the hunt for my beau and heading dreamily through the gorgeous garden towards the manor.

The cutting garden was looking rather depleted again, but I had been making further notes, more detailed now, as to how I would extend it, both in terms of size and season, if Algy decided it was destined to become a permanent addition to the Wynbrook portfolio. In fact, all of my ideas had come together in the last few days and Josh had said his plans were shaping up nicely too. I put that down to us having declared our true feelings for one another and being both more relaxed and secure as a result.

I had already labelled parts of the last few weeks as the best summer ever, but the last few days had cemented the title firmly in place. We had been practically inseparable since our heart to heart in the hospital corridor . . . and very happily so.

However, the summer itself was moving on, wasn't it? Only that morning I had felt chilly enough to reach for a shirt to cover my camisole before eating breakfast on the veranda. How much longer would it be before I caught the scent of woodsmoke? Not that I minded, because I was already looking forward to autumn at Wynbrook.

'And then he said,' I heard someone shriek from the kitchen, as I imagined myself dressing the summerhouse with dried leaf garlands, more twinkling lights and drinking pumpkin-spiced everything on the veranda, 'perhaps Johnny would like a stiff one too!'

I covered my mouth with my hand to stifle the giggle that had leapt into my throat and I was back in August again, autumn suddenly forgotten.

'And did you give him one?' I heard Algy ask.

There was definitely more than a hint of mischief in his

tone and I thought I should leave my visit until later and was about to turn tail, but was spotted.

'I see you out there, Daisy!' came a singsong voice.

'And I hear you, George,' I said, stepping properly into view.

Algy and George had only been very recently introduced, but had got along like a house on fire, and both George and Skipper were now regular visitors to the manor.

'Are you going to answer Algy's question?' I grinned.

'Not in front of a child like you,' George said and smiled back, as he straightened his silk scarf and stood up. 'I'll tell you tomorrow, Algy,' he winked.

'Don't leave me in suspenders!' Algy objected, but George wouldn't say more.

'I better be heading back to Wynmouth,' he said instead.

'Have you called the taxi?' I asked him.

There was only one locally and it must have been doing a roaring trade in ferrying George to Wynbrook and back.

'Not yet,' he said, pulling out his phone.

'In that case,' I offered, 'let me take you. I'm heading to Wynmouth myself.'

'Are you sure?'

'Absolutely. Though I'm hoping to take Josh with me. Is he about?'

I yelped as Josh's arms suddenly wrapped around my waist from behind and he spun me around.

'I was just looking for you,' he said, when he put me down and the world was the right way up again, but only just. 'Fancy a swim?'

'I'd love one,' I said, giving him a kiss. 'My stuff's still in my car from last time.'

'I'll go and grab mine,' he said, rushing off.

'Ah, young love,' sighed George, as he looked between us.

'Young love indeed,' said Algy, smiling at me. 'Don't forget to be back here by six.'

'What for?' I asked. It was the first I'd heard of something happening this evening. 'And do I need to bring anything?'

'Your mother has seen to the eats,' Algy told me. 'Did Josh not mention it?'

I shook my head.

'Did Josh not mention what?' asked the man himself as he bounded back in record time with his swim shorts and towel thrown over his shoulder. 'Oh,' he then said to me, 'we're having a little get-together tonight, Daisy. You need to be here for six.'

Algy rolled his eyes.

'Right you are,' I laughed. 'Come on then troops, before the tide turns.'

Having dropped George off, then had our fill of swimming in the sea and dried off in front of the beach hut – which had been the backdrop to so many recent happy moments – Josh and I decided to head to the pub for lunch.

'Here they are,' said Sam, smiling, as we crossed the threshold, 'love's young dream.'

'Sam,' tutted Tess. 'Leave them alone.'

I wondered how word about us being together, together as opposed to summer together, had spread, but didn't bother to ask. We lived in a village with a competent gossip network, so the details of who had said what were irrelevant really.

'Yes, do pipe down, Sam,' said Marguerite, with a pretty pout. 'You know I had my heart set on picking up the pieces and being Daisy's rebound relationship when Josh headed back to the States.'

'Oh, really?' Josh laughed.

'That,' Marguerite grimaced, looking at me, 'sounded far less creepy in my head.'

'Good to know.' I nodded. 'How are you enjoying life in the cottage?'

'It's so good,' she sighed happily. 'I honestly don't think I'm ever going to want to move out or leave Wynmouth.'

It amazed me that the tiny Norfolk village could hold such appeal to seasoned world travellers such as her and Josh. I knew Josh had come to the coast for a very different reason to Marguerite of course, but nonetheless, they'd both fallen in love with the place I'd grown up in and I'd fallen back in love with it again – amongst other things – too.

'Unfortunately, she doesn't pay holidaymaker's rent,' Sam teased Marguerite, 'so I'll be turfing her out soon.'

'Hey,' she objected. 'Then where will I go?'

'I'm sure something will turn up,' I told her.

While Sam poured our drinks, Tess made us a local crab salad sandwich apiece and I looked around for a table and spotted Penny, poring over what looked like some paperwork, in the corner next to the window.

'Have you got enough light to read by in here?' I asked her as I walked over and she leapt sky high. 'Sorry,' I said, unable to stifle a laugh because she had looked so comical. 'I didn't mean to make you jump.'

'It's fine,' she flushed, gathering the pages together. 'I was just finished anyway.'

'Can we join you?' Josh asked.

'Of course,' Penny obliged, but I got the impression she hadn't really wanted to be disturbed.

'Is that café paperwork?' I asked, while she stuffed everything in her bag and Josh went to get her a drink and our food order.

'Um, not really,' she said rather elusively. 'But it is sort of related.'

It wasn't like her to be secretive, so I didn't ask further because it must have been something private for her not to elaborate.

'You're coming to the manor tonight, aren't you, Penny?' Josh asked, once we were all settled and well on our way to being fed and watered.

'Yes,' she said. 'Nick said to be there for six, but not why.'

'Well, at least you knew that much,' I tutted, giving Josh a nudge and almost dropping my sandwich as a result. 'I didn't even know a gathering was happening.'

'Well, you do now,' Josh countered, but didn't provide us with further details.

'A Wynbrook family gathering,' I grinned, 'I like the sound of that. It makes us all sound like one special clan, doesn't it?'

'That does sound good,' Penny agreed, 'though I'm not really a part of the family, am I? Does fiancée status count?'

Josh gave her a look I couldn't fathom.

'Of course it does,' he said earnestly. 'You're definitely part of the family, Penny.'

She flushed at that and when I winked at her, she blushed an even deeper shade.

'I don't suppose I could get a lift with you guys, could I?' she asked. 'It would save Nick having to drive out to pick me up.'

'Of course you can,' I nodded, 'but where's your car?'

'With Nick,' she told me. 'His is playing up again, so he's using mine.'

Nick's car was about as reliable and as old as mine.

'Grandad has said he wants to get me on the road soon,' said Josh, sounding terrified. 'I'm dreading it. He reckons the best thing to go out in is the Bentley because everyone gets out of the way for that, but I just know I'll put it in the verge or something.'

He looked scared but comically so, and I could see Penny was trying not to laugh at the thought of him and Algy heading out to conquer the tourist traffic together.

'I tell you what,' I said, 'why don't we get you going in my car before you tackle the Bentley? A few more scratches on mine won't matter and we'll wait until the holiday season is over too.'

Josh visibly relaxed.

'I would prefer that,' he said keenly. 'I've never really been a fan of driving, so that would make me far happier.'

'And as you know,' I said, leaning over and kissing him, 'your happiness is very important to me.'

'And your happiness is very important to me too,' he said, kissing me back.

'In that case,' I smiled, 'how about you treat me to a bag of Kettle Chips. A packet would be the perfect accompaniment to the other half of this sandwich.'

By six o'clock that evening, we were all gathered in the conservatory at the manor. Light rain was falling and, in the distance, towards the sea, there was an occasional rumble of thunder. It was blissfully cool but not everyone appreciated the change in the weather.

'Was that Luna?' Algy asked me, as a bundle of black fur rushed out from under one of the wicker chairs and through an open door into the manor.

'I think it was,' I said in surprise.

It wasn't like her to venture right inside, but the weather had rather forced her hand. Or forced her paws . . .

'She's finding her place at last,' said Dad, looking to see where she'd scuttled off to.

'That she is,' Algy agreed, as Mum and Josh arrived with trays of food from the kitchen and set them down on the table. 'And she's not the only one.' He winked at me. 'In fact, that's the perfect thought to start this meeting with, isn't it, Josh?'

Josh hadn't heard what Dad had said, but Nick spoke before he could point that out.

'Meeting?' Nick frowned, sounding concerned. 'I thought this was a social occasion. Is everything all right, Algy?'

We all looked at him expectantly.

'Perhaps meeting isn't quite the right word,' suggested Josh. 'We're hoping it will be more of an exchange of ideas and a sharing of plans rather than anything . . . formal.'

A hush fell over the group and we all took a seat at the table.

'Well,' said Mum, with a nod to the packed platters, 'whatever it is, let's eat first, shall we? I haven't been working in that kitchen all afternoon for everything to go to waste.'

'I'd better just check on Luna,' said Algy, standing up.

'She's curled up on your office chair and she's fine,' said Dad, who I hadn't realised had followed her inside to make sure she was all right. 'Let's eat.'

Everyone dug in heartily and, with the addition of some very lovely wine that Algy had brought up from the cellar, we all began to relax again.

'Now,' said Algy, once everyone's plates had been cleared and a few glasses of rosé, red or white had been enjoyed, 'let's get this . . . non-meeting . . . launched, shall we?'

We all looked at him expectantly and I thought what a relief it was to already know that Wynbrook was in safe hands, otherwise we would all have been on the edge of our seats with trepidation.

'Quite a few of us sitting around this table,' Algy continued, looking at each of us in turn, 'have gone through some pretty phenomenal changes this summer and I thought it would be lovely to get us all together to celebrate them—'

'Hear, hear,' Dad interrupted and Mum hiccupped.

Josh looked at me and grinned. Perhaps some of us had enjoyed more than a few glasses of the wine. That said, my parents weren't big drinkers, so even two for them would have been enough to warrant impromptu toasts and hiccups.

'And also, to share anything else that might be about to come to fruition as a result of those changes,' Algy continued and I noticed Penny's cheeks were crimson again. 'I know Josh has an inspired idea up his sleeve and I'm guessing Daisy has too.'

'Me?' I gasped, when I realised my name had been mentioned.

'Yes.' Algy smiled. 'Tell us, my dear, what you've got in mind for expanding Wynbrook Blooms next year. I know you will have given it some thought and I'm very much hoping that you'll take the role of manager on full-time and carry the venture even further.'

I looked at him and swallowed. It was going to be hard to talk over the lump in my throat, but I was excited to give it a go.

'Really?' I whispered.

'Really.' Algy nodded. 'You've already proved the idea has got legs and there's no one I'd like to run my passion project more than you, Daisy, Daisy.'

'In that case,' I said delightedly, 'I'd love to make it my passion project too. And expand it.'

'Go on,' Algy encouraged.

'Well, I have been thinking and I'm hoping there'll be somewhere on the estate that we can turn over to growing a lot more flowers, which will make it a far bigger venture.'

Algy nodded in approval.

'And,' I felt inspired to continue, 'following Dad's lead with his new-found love of learning,' he'd now told everyone about the access course to his degree that he was currently undertaking, 'I'd like to go to college. Perhaps study floristry or horticulture on a part-time basis, so I can fit it in with running Wynbrook Blooms.'

'I think that sounds like a wonderful idea,' Dad said tearfully.

'So do I,' Algy agreed.

'I've been thinking about running workshops too – eventually,' I laughed. 'I know I'm getting ahead of myself, but once I have the knowledge, that might be an interesting progression to the business. Oh, and dried flowers,' I blurted, getting further carried away on the wave of enthusiasm for my new life. 'I'm thinking about trialling dried flowers too.'

'The old barn would be ideal to hold workshops in and dry the flowers,' Nick said, nodding. 'And it shouldn't take too much work to convert it for that, should it?'

I was thrilled he sounded so keen, as utilising the barn would put us in much closer working proximity.

'I wouldn't have thought it would take much at all,' said Algy. 'Well done, Daisy. You've certainly grown my idea since I first mentioned it to your dad.'

'That she has,' Mum agreed, looking proud. 'We're so happy to have you back here with us, love, and the thought of you continuing your education now you've returned to your passion is wonderful.'

'Thank you, Mum,' I said, feeling choked.

'And what about you, Penny?' Algy asked and everyone's attention turned to her.

She looked at us all and drew in a long breath.

'Well,' she puffed, fidgeting in her seat and looking at Nick, who nodded reassuringly, 'just as you and Robin have decided to pick up education again, Daisy, I've had a good look through my contract,' that explained the paperwork in the pub, 'and decided to . . . I've decided to . . . leave it.'

'I had a feeling that you might, my dear,' Algy said gently.

'My time running the business for Sophie, after the few initial hiccups, has been so exciting. I don't want to launch anything like the beach café, but I'm all for giving something a shot in some capacity – after I've worked the required notice period at school, that is.'

'Well, that's a relief,' laughed Algy, as Josh did the rounds and topped everyone's glasses up again. 'Isn't it, Josh?'

'Just a bit,' he said and grinned, raising his glass to his grandfather and drinking deeply.

'Why?' I asked, looking between the two of them and

wondering what they'd cooked up, metaphorically speaking, because there was definitely something afoot.

'It's a relief,' said Josh, looking at Penny, 'because I've also been thinking about how to expand things here on the Wynbrook Estate and I was wondering about turning a part of the barn into a tearoom.'

Penny's eyes were suddenly on stalks.

'I think it would be just the thing to bring together the fruit farm and Wynbrook Blooms,' Josh elaborated. 'There's nothing like it anywhere for a few miles and there's plenty of room in the barn to accommodate your ideas, Daisy, and make the whole thing a sort of bakes and blooms combined business.'

'And obviously, we're going to ask you if you'll run the tearoom for us, Penny.' Algy grinned, rather stealing Josh's thunder, but he didn't seem to mind.

'You want me to run a tearoom here?' Penny asked, sounding flabbergasted.

'Yes,' said Josh, 'and we'd like to have you with us on board right from the get-go, to help with the planning and set-up.'

'The Wynbrook Blooms and Bakes Afternoon Tea Experience,' Penny said dreamily and it was obvious she was sold on the idea and could already imagine what it was going to look, smell and taste like.

As could I.

'So,' I said excitedly, looking at my friends, 'the three of us would be working together?'

I didn't think the evening could get any better.

'The four of us actually,' Josh smilingly corrected me. 'I'm hoping to split my time between working with Robin in the garden and Nick on the fruit farm. I've been bitten by the

outdoor bug since I worked with you all and I rather fancy a
life working out of doors.'

'Everyone says that until the winter, mate,' said Nick, jumping
up and pulling Josh in for a back-slapping hug, 'but you're in
it now, so welcome aboard, whatever the weather.'

Right on cue, a clap of thunder boomed and we all began
to laugh and cheer.

Our celebrations and further discussions went on long into
the evening. Penny and Nick had quickly decided that she
should move into his cottage on the estate and I suggested
that Marguerite might be interested in renting Penny's place
in the village while she decided what to do with it in the
long term.

'Isn't it thrilling to think,' I said, as Josh and I walked back
to the summerhouse once the rain had eventually stopped and
with Luna following on just a few paces behind us, 'that by
the time autumn really gets underway, all four of us will not
only be working, but also living, on the estate.'

'It really is exciting,' said Josh, picking me up and spinning
us both around on the wet brick path. 'What a summer we're
having, Daisy!'

'Best summer ever,' I laughed, when he put me back down
again.

'Best summer ever,' he echoed, linking his arm through mine.

'We both had something taken away from us here when
we were younger, didn't we?' I said thoughtfully, once we'd
walked a few more steps and my head had stopped spinning.
'You were taken from your family and I was denied my love
of gardening . . .'

'And we've made our way back to both,' Josh smiled, 'at exactly the same time.'

'It's fate,' I said, feeling incredibly grateful that we had ended up landing back at Wynbrook together. On exactly the same day, in fact. 'We're meant to be here.'

'And, what's more,' he said, as we stepped into the light of the summerhouse veranda and he pulled me into his arms and held me close, 'we're meant to be here together.'

'I love that,' I whispered, as he bent to kiss me softly on the lips. 'And I love you.'

'And I love you too,' he said, when he finally drew away. 'And I can't wait to discover what the autumn holds for us, can you?'

'I really can't,' I said, as I rested my head on his chest and noticed Luna was waiting by the door to be let inside, 'but for now, I'm very happy to keep enjoying the summer.'

'Me too,' he agreed. 'Me too.'

It was miraculous to think that two lives, three if you included the little cat, could be so completely and happily transformed in such a short space of time and I knew that no matter what the future held for us at Wynbrook, these last few weeks we'd shared together, finding our feet, would always be known as our best summer ever.

Acknowledgements

It feels truly extraordinary to be writing these acknowledgements for the twentieth time, but it's happening! I'm doing it. If you had told me ten years ago that I would be doing this today, I would have been astounded.

Ordinarily, I use this space to say thank you to so many people, but this time around – and even though I'm immensely grateful to EVERYONE who has helped me birth this book – I'm saving this spot primarily for just two.

This book is dedicated to two wonderful women – Clare Hey and Sara-Jade Virtue. Without them, there wouldn't be twenty books on my writing-room shelves with my name on the cover. There would be no *Sunday Times* Bestseller declaration gracing the cover of every title since *Sleigh Rides and Silver Bells*, no million sales and no RNA Award.

Clare and S-J are where this incredible journey started and it seems only fitting that this book, a decade after the first, should be dedicated to them. And of course, I'm going to throw in a mention for the rest of the incredible team. And my awesome agent, Amanda Preston because, although she joined the party ever so slightly later, she's played a rather large part in the adventure, too!

Thank you all so much for continuing to make my dream come true.

With all my love,
H x

P.S.
And huge thanks to Debz, Alison Williams and Cookie for picking the name, Luna. It suits the little black cat who features in this book perfectly.

About the Author

Heidi Swain lives in Norfolk. She is passionate about gardening and the countryside, and collects vintage paraphernalia. *Best Summer Ever* is her twentieth novel.

You can follow Heidi on X or Instagram @Heidi_Swain or visit her website: heidiswain.co.uk

All Wrapped Up

Clemmie Bennett has been renovating beautiful
Rowan Cottage on the outskirts of the small town of
Wynbridge following a very public heartbreak in her
childhood home town. The popular Instagram influencer
lost her husband, sold their home, and has been cosied
up the Fens and living a very private life, but now she
feels it's time for a change.

A chance encounter with co-owner of The Cherry Tree
Café, the bubbly Lizzie Dixon, pulls her into organizing
Wynbridge's first-ever Autumn Festival, and her once quiet
life is soon a distant memory. With the whole town rallying
behind the event, she discovers a new sense of purpose.

And when local vet Ash falls hard for Clemmie, she begins
to wonder if she's ready to move even further on from her
past and fall in love again . . .

AVAILABLE TO PRE-ORDER NOW

The Holiday Escape

Ally and her dad, Geoff, run a creative retreat
from their home, Hollyhock Cottage. They give
their guests their dream coastal break, but Ally
hankers after something different.

Ally's survival strategy is to escape out of season
and pretend to be the person she always imagined
she would be. She meets Logan while she's away in
Barcelona and he turns out to be *exactly* the kind of
distraction she's looking for.

With her spirits restored, Ally returns home, picks up
the reins again and sets her sights on another successful
season. But when Logan unexpectedly arrives on the
scene, she soon realises she's in for a summer that's
going to be far from straightforward . . .

TURN THE PAGE FOR AN EXCITING EXTRACT

Chapter 1

It wasn't so much that I was *ready* to take another trip, more that the scales had now tipped me into *over-ready*. I had reached home – or to be more precise, my parent's home – saturation point, and was craving the sanctuary of a few days escape before I said or did something I would doubtless end up regretting.

Thanks to a hectic winter and early spring schedule spent further updating Hollyhock Cottage, it had been months since my last getaway and now, right at the end of March I was poised to take some much-needed time out to refresh and reset before the start of yet another busy season living and working in Kittiwake Cove.

I was so desperate to leave the Dorset coast and all its associations behind that I would have happily settled for any destination, but as luck would have it, I was off to a city I loved, Barcelona, courtesy of a cheap flight and a cracking deal on accommodation due to a last-minute cancellation.

Just as it always did, my heart picked up the pace as I stepped into the airport and immediately headed for the restroom, where I would walk in dressed casually and for comfort, and come out transformed into the sleek, sophisticated European city-dweller I longingly wished I was.

My phone pinged with a WhatsApp notification just as I finished repacking my bags post-makeover and I pulled it out of my pocket. I knew who the message would be from and, down to the last letter, what they would have typed.

> Hey Ally! All absolutely fine here, so don't worry
> about a thing. Eat, drink, sleep – or not ;-) – repeat
> and we'll see you in a week! F x

Even though I had the message memorised from my previous trips, it still made me smile and I felt a huge rush of love and gratitude for my best friend, Flora. If it weren't for her stepping up and taking my place at home this week, I wouldn't be heading off to Spain on a sanity saver. I'd be back at the cottage with my dad, turning myself inside out and pretending that I was happy with the life I was living.

One that I had fully embraced and was immersed in, rather than one I still felt bound to go along with as a result of an emotional tangle of deep-seated obligation, anxiety and fear. I let out a long breath as my eyes began to prickle and my throat tightened.

'No,' I told myself, swallowing hard. 'You're not doing that, Ally. Not today.'

I gathered up my bags, pulled back my shoulders and stepped out onto the busy concourse. It was time to find my gate.

Having taken my fair share of cheap flights during the last few years, I knew the best strategy, for me at least, was to keep my head down, my earbuds in (even though there wasn't necessarily anything playing through them) and not become embroiled in tedious small talk.

It was a lesson I'd learned the hard way on a flight to Rome where I'd been stuck next to the ultimate manspreader – not ideal in the cheap seats – who insisted on loudly and inaccurately mansplaining every topic he thought he was an expert on and none of which I could have escaped being subjected to, as I was trapped in the seat next to the window.

The thought of attempting to squeeze past him had been enough to put me off trying and I'd been booking the aisle option ever since, even though I would have much preferred the seat with a view.

'Excuse me, young man,' said a voice beside me, 'would you mind putting my bag in the overhead locker? I can't quite reach it.'

'Of course, sister,' came the kind response, which was followed by some close proximity shuffling. 'No problem at all.'

My curiosity was piqued, not only by the deliciously deep voice of the man in question, but also by his use of the word, sister. My guess was they weren't related, so what was that about? I couldn't take a sly peek because the guy was now putting the bag in the locker directly above my head, potentially putting me in danger of a face to crotch situation, which I had no desire to risk.

After further shuffling, I felt a light tap on my shoulder and glanced up into the face of a serenely smiling elderly nun. That explained the sister reference. I pulled out my earbuds and smiled back.

'I'm just along here with you, dear,' she said, nodding at the window seat.

'And I'm in the middle,' added the nun's young man, who was tall enough to easily look over the top of her head.

In less than a second, I had taken in dark blonde hair, a smattering of stubble and beautiful beguiling green eyes, however, it was the stunning smile that caused the biggest flutter in my chest and the heat to spread up my neck and across my face.

'Of course.' I swallowed, rushing to stand up.

As I moved into the aisle, I could practically feel Flora's elbow nudging me in the ribs and see her wide-eyed expression and excitedly raised eyebrows. We'd been friends practically since birth, so she would know this guy was exactly my type, but it was far too early in the trip to be thinking about hookups and hot sex. I hadn't even decided what I was going to call myself yet, so unexpected in-flight entertainment would not be a sensible indulgence.

That was the other thing about my overseas adventures. I didn't just dress like someone else; I actually became someone else. Name, career, the whole shebang. I adopted a completely made-up persona. I was never Ally. I was never someone who lived by the seaside. And I certainly never shared a house with my dad.

Once the plane touched down and my passport had been checked and put away again, that was the moment I started to truly live my dream life. My quick change in the airport loos always got the ball rolling, my en-route planning supplied the finer details and by the time I reached my accommodation, I was immersed in my fantasy life. More often than not, I role-played the life I had thought would become my reality after I'd received my MA in Spanish and history. The life I would have embraced, had Mum's heart not prematurely given out.

I took a deep breath and banished further thoughts of Mum, as the guy with the seat next to mine inched into place. He smelt crisp, cool and citrus fresh. Definitely good enough to eat. Clearly, my head had got the memo that it was too early to be thinking about hook-ups and hot sex, but my previously dormant libido had eagerly turned a blind eye to it.

Having given him a few seconds to get comfy, or as comfy as he was going to be with his knees practically squished into the rear of the seat in front of him, I slipped back into place and surreptitiously glanced at his left hand. Not that the absence of a ring indicated someone wasn't already spoken for, but it was generally considered a starting point.

Perhaps I *should* throw caution to the wind and dive straight in. A little flight flirtation couldn't really hurt, could it? I wondered how Sister whatshername would react to that going on right next to her . . .

'Pear drop?' she asked, with uncanny timing, as her hand reached inside her capacious handbag and pulled out a rustling paper bag. 'If I'm focused on one of these, I find my ears don't pop half as much on take off.'

'Thanks,' said the guy, his fingers quickly dipping in to the bag and coming out with a whole handful. 'I'm a bit of a nervous flier, so any distraction is welcome.'

He didn't look nervous, but his smile had faltered and there was a slight tremble in his voice.

'Oh, don't you worry,' our travel companion said soothingly, 'we're in good hands.'

'Well, that's a relief.' He swallowed.

'I'm Sister Lucia, by the way,' she added.

'And I'm Logan.'

'Pleased to be travelling with you, Logan,' she said. She patted his arm and leant forward to look at me. 'And what about you, my dear?' she asked, offering me the bag of boiled sweets.

'Oh,' I said. 'No, thank you. My ears are usually fine.'

'And what's your name?' she further enquired.

I knew from past experience that I didn't have time to hesitate. It definitely looked suss if you had to stop and think what your name was.

'Flora,' I said, blurting out the first name I thought of. 'I'm Flora.'

I hoped I wasn't blotting my copybook by lying to a nun. Given that I was only going to be in her presence for the duration of my flight, I supposed I could just as easily have been Ally, but old habits die hard. No pun intended.

'Oh, how lovely,' Sister Lucia exclaimed. 'Perhaps after Flora, the patron saint of the abandoned, who teaches us how to forgive after betrayal?'

The real Flora, my best friend Flora that is, had only been betrayed once and she'd certainly never forgiven.

'I don't think so.' I smiled, sitting back in my seat.

'Perhaps after the Roman goddess of springtime and flowers?' Logan suggested, his smile growing wider again. 'That was her name, wasn't it?'

'Oh, yes,' I said, returning his smile with my own and despite the fact I had absolutely no idea, 'that sounds more like it.'

'Don't underestimate the value of forgiveness,' Sister Lucia was quick to sagely say. 'It can be as beautiful as any flower or sunny spring.'

Logan turned to look at me, his green eyes meeting mine. They locked for a moment. He was even better looking close up. I found his knowledge of Roman goddesses rather alluring, too. Logan had hit the jackpot. He had both brains and beauty. I knew, given the opportunity, I'd forgive him anything.

'And what about the origins of your name?' Sister Lucia asked, when neither of us responded. 'Do you know the meaning behind yours, Logan?'

He looked away again and the spell was broken.

'Little hollow,' he said. 'It's Scottish.'

'Is it a family name?' Sister Lucia asked. 'You don't sound Scottish.'

'No,' he shrugged. 'My mum just liked the sound of it.'

I was rather keen on the sound of it, too.